Search for the Truth

What people are saying about this novel:

I will read this book again. And maybe again.
Amy

I found it to be a captivating read and loved it!
Hilary

I really enjoyed this book, and found it quite impossible to put down – I was so involved in the story, and the romance at its heart was simply wonderful.
Anne

Wow! This was a brilliant book! Full of love, doubt, suspicion and quite a lot of humour!
Annie

I would recommend this novel for any reader who enjoys a good love story, wants a richly detailed story that draws you in and won't let you go until the final sentence.
Marsha

Search for the Truth

Kathryn Freeman

Where heroes are like chocolate – irresistible!

Published 2016 by Choc Lit Limited
Penrose House, Crawley Drive, Camberley, Surrey GU15 2AB, UK
www.choc-lit.com

A CIP catalogue record for this book is available
from the British Library

ISBN 978-1-78189-302-9

Printed and bound by Clays Ltd

To my boys (hubby and sons). It is a mother's duty to embarrass her children – and by writing love stories, I have certainly succeeded. I love you.

Acknowledgements

When I first wrote this book I was unpublished – the dream of publication felt a million miles away. Thanks to the incredible encouragement from family, friends and work colleagues who became friends, I ploughed on. My reward is my name on the front of this book. In comparison their reward – their name on the inside – seems meagre, but is extremely heart felt.

First thanks go to my greatest fan and my most hardworking sales person – my amazing mum.

Family are so special, they support you when you're down, rejoice when you're flying high. Thank you to my special family: David and Jayne, my other mum and dad and all the gang from Fleetwood. Yes, I'm going to name some of you this time, not just to embarrass the heck out of you, but to tell you how much your encouragement means to me: Aunties Audrey and Shirley, Uncles Harold and Bob, cousins Kim, Shelley, Kath, extended cousins Karley, Kirsty and Hayley.

An author can always tell a true friend – they ask about your books, even though they must be bored to death of them by now. So forgive this roll call, but it's my way of saying how really grateful I am for your continued enthusiastic support: Charlotte, Sonia, Gill, Neve, Jane, Tara, Anissa, Bee, Janet, Sue, Phil, Kaye, Mr H, Priti, Sheyline, Laura, Michele, Helen and Fiona.

Finally, there wouldn't be a book if it wasn't for Choc Lit and their tasting panel (Olivia F, Samantha S, Elke N, Janice B, Jade C, Betty S, Jane O and Maggie F). And this book would be only half the book it is now if it wasn't for my very wise editor. Thank you, thank you, thank you.

Prologue

Tess filled cups with steaming hot tea. She eased sandwiches onto plates and fussed around refilling bowls of crisps. Anything to keep busy. Anything so she didn't have to think about the fact that she'd just buried her mother.

Tears spilt from her eyes but she ruthlessly wiped them away. She'd done enough crying. For today at least, she had to be strong. Her gaze strayed towards her father, who stood talking to his brother. God, he looked old. When had that happened? When her mother had first been diagnosed with cancer? When she'd relapsed? Or as recently as last week, when she'd taken her final breath?

The hand on the bag of crisps shook violently, showering them over the table.

'Hey, sis, I think we've got enough now.' Her brother calmly took the bag away from her and scooped the scattered crisps into the bowl.

'Sorry.' She sobbed out a breath, then inhaled sharply and picked up a plate of sandwiches. 'Right. I'm going to offer these round.'

Mark prised the plate from her hands and put it back on the table. 'Come here. Have a hug with your big brother first. Then go to the loo, do whatever it is women do to repair their faces, and come back out looking less like an extra in a horror film.'

He wrapped his arms around her and for a few precious seconds they both took strength from each other. Then she pulled away and tried to smile. 'Thanks, I needed that.'

She was pretty certain his pale face, with its bloodshot blue eyes, didn't look any better than hers did. 'Shit day,' he stated, running a hand through his floppy hair.

'And it won't get any easier for a long, long time.' Again

1

her eyes sought out her father. 'Especially not for Dad. But we'll be there for him, and for each other. We may be down to three musketeers, but it's still—'

'All for one, and one for all,' they said in unison.

Knowing she was on the verge of further tears, Tess darted off to the toilet, grimacing at the face that stared back at her from the mirror over the sink. She'd always been pale, but right now she was almost translucent. Combine that with the bruises under her eyes thanks to a lack of sleep, and Mark's horror film retort wasn't far off the mark. Quickly she smoothed on concealer and added some blusher. After forcing a smile onto her face she went to join the assembled mourners.

Most she recognised. Friends of her parents, people she'd grown up with, relatives from both sides. But walking towards her was one she didn't. A dark-haired woman, slightly older than herself, who looked nervous and out of place.

'I'm not sure if you remember me?'

Tess frowned. Maybe the face looked familiar? 'Have I seen you at the hospital?'

'Yes. I'm Avril. Your mother was being treated by the same consultant as mine. I saw you a few times in the waiting room.' She bit her lip. 'I was so sorry to hear she'd passed away.'

'Thank you.'

'I hope you don't mind me coming here today. I know it seems like an intrusion, but … well, I heard you were a journalist?' Confused, Tess nodded. 'Your mum once mentioned it to mine, that's how I know. She was very proud of you.'

Emotion balled in her throat. 'That's kind of you to say.'

Avril ghosted her a smile. 'Sorry, I'm making a meal of this. And talking about it at your mother's wake must seem so insensitive, but I wasn't sure how else I would find you if I didn't come here today.'

'It's okay.' Tess bit back her irritation. The woman was

clearly a bag of nerves but she sensed Avril had something important to say. If she ever got round to spitting it out. 'I'm happy to talk now. Would you like a drink? To sit down?'

'No, no. I've taken up enough of your time. You need to go back to your family. I just wanted you to know that ...' She closed her eyes briefly. When she opened them again, they were filled with tears. 'My mother died two days ago. It was a heart attack, and all very sudden. The nurse at the hospital let slip that yours had died a few days earlier, also from a heart attack. It seemed a very strange coincidence, what with them both being on the new treatment. I mean, I don't know the circumstances of your mother's death, and maybe she had heart problems—'

'She didn't,' Tess interrupted, feeling suddenly terribly sick. 'Well, not that we knew of.'

'Mine had high blood pressure, but ... again, I'm sorry if this upsets you, I really am, but it struck me as very odd that they'd both died of the same thing. I tried to ask some questions but the hospital staff were very dismissive. I've found it difficult enough to extract information on my own mother; they certainly won't tell me anything about yours. But I thought, as you're a journalist, you might want to dig into this? If it's not too distressing, of course.' Her final words came out in a rush. 'I do hope I haven't made this awful time even worse for you.'

Tess put a hand to her stomach, trying to calm the lurching. 'No, it's kind of you to come here today, especially when you're grieving yourself.' She touched Avril's arm in sympathy. 'I'm so sorry to hear about your mother, too.'

For a moment she paused, trying to assemble her myriad thoughts. She'd had her own doubts about her mother's death, but tried to dismiss them as the wild accusations of a shell-shocked, grieving mind. What if they weren't? What if there was more to her mother's death than a simple heart attack?

Her heart pounding in her ears, Tess asked, 'Are you sure they were taking the same treatment? Zaplex?'

'Yes. I know because, again, your mum talked to mine about whether she should try it. It was new, so I guess she wanted to reassure herself it was okay. My mum had been taking it for two weeks before ... before she died.'

Tess's heart went out to the woman. She knew exactly how raw she felt. 'Look, why don't you leave me your contact details? I'll give you a call and we can talk about it a bit more.'

Avril delved into her handbag and pulled out a business card. 'Thank you. Both for that, and for hearing me out. Again, my condolences.'

As she turned to leave, Tess placed her hand on her arm. 'Avril, I promise I will look into this, for both our sakes.'

Chapter One

'I'm just phoning to wish you luck.' Her brother's voice echoed round her car, courtesy of the hands-free phone.

Tess concentrated on parking between two new BMWs. She tried not to glance at the large office building looming intimidatingly across the car park. Tried not to notice how her fingers trembled as she turned off the ignition. Or how her pulse had gone from calm to manic in the blink of an eye. Instead she focussed all her attention on her brother.

'Thanks,' she replied, her mouth feeling suddenly very dry. 'I think I'm going to need it.'

'So, remind me, what's your new job title?'

'Corporate communications manager.'

He whistled. 'Sounds pretty glamorous.'

'Maybe, but that's not how I'm feeling. Terrified. Yes, that would work, though heaven knows why, because I don't even want their blasted job.'

'Hey, come on, don't start getting the wobbles now,' he replied, demonstrating the sort of sympathy she expected from her cherished, slightly spoilt older brother. 'Remember the reason you're doing this.'

'I am, but I'm telling you this sounded a lot easier on paper than it does now.' Her eyes drifted over to the high tech office building and the giant knot in her stomach tightened.

'What's complicated about what you're about to do? Just stride in there and play a role. You were happy enough playing the gutsy heroine when we were kids.'

'Sure, *twenty years* ago.'

'Come on, loosen up. It'll be a walk in the park.'

'Easy for you to say. You're not the one who has to go into a big scary building and pretend to be really excited about working for a company you hate.'

She heard him chuckle softly over the phone. 'You know how last Christmas I bought you a jumper ...'

'The fluffy one that dropped white fibres on every surface I came into contact with?'

'That's the one. Well, I didn't know you hated it until I spotted it in the charity shop bag. If you can fool me, you can fool this industry lot. And it's only for a few weeks.'

'I know. All I have to do is keep my head down and avoid being fired before I have a chance to do what I'm really here for.' A deep sigh escaped her. 'Except now I'm actually here, the job feels so, well, real, I guess.'

'Come on, Tess, you know you can do this. It's our best shot at finding out the truth about Mum's death.' There was a pause. 'Of course, I can't force you. If you really don't want to go in there, you can leave now. Chicken out.'

For a fleeting moment, Tess considered doing just that. Forgetting the whole stupid charade and driving straight out again. Then she recalled the reasons why she was here. And her brother's cutting but accurate last two words.

'I'm going in,' she told him firmly. 'It's taken eighteen months for this opportunity to present itself. If I back out now my name will be mud and I'll never be able to come back.' And never find the answers.

'So stop wasting your time talking to me and get your dainty backside into the big scary building before you're fired for being late.'

Laughing her goodbye, Tess ended the call and acknowledged that her brother was right. It was now or never. Climbing out of her car, which looked small and old compared to most of the other cars around it, she walked determinedly towards the towering concrete and glass monstrosity.

Helix Pharmaceuticals, the sign proclaimed in bold purple letters.

She was entering *the dark side*.

Warily she slipped through the revolving glass door and

strode across the reception area, her heels clicking against the polished marble tiles. The trappings of drug company profits surrounded her, helping to push away the nerves and replace them with anger. Designer leather seats clustered around sleek low coffee tables. Dramatic, vivid, and no doubt hugely expensive works of art hung on crisp white walls. Ahead of her was a streamlined glass top reception desk, complete with the obligatory smart female receptionist. She could be walking into the sales and marketing offices of a luxury property developers, she thought with disgust. Not a pharmaceutical company. Where was the clinical professionalism? The sense of science, of treating patients and diseases? Indeed, any evidence at all that this company existed to help the sick get better, rather than earn itself and its shareholders a big fat profit.

She paused. So much for that stern talking to she'd given herself in the car. The one in which she'd chanted over and over again *the pharmaceutical industry isn't evil and I don't hate it*. She'd been here less than a minute and already she'd started to slip.

Taking a deep breath, she walked up to the desk. From now on she was going to *be* that communications manager. The one thrilled at the prospect of working for this company.

'Hello. Tessa Johnson. I'm here to see Georgina White.' She gave the young girl on the desk her biggest, *I'm so happy to be here*, smile. 'She's going to be my new boss. Today is my first day.'

The receptionist barely glanced at her. Clearly a new member of staff wasn't exciting enough to warrant her undivided attention. 'Welcome to Helix,' she recited in a robotic monotone. 'Do you know where you're going?'

Tess was sorely tempted to say *no, please could you show me*, just to see her reaction, but annoying the receptionist probably wasn't on her top ten list of things she had to do today. 'I do, thanks. I remember from the interview.'

Accepting the temporary security pass, Tess passed through the barrier and then up the stairs to where the corporate communications team were based. Walking past the rows of open plan desks she made a point of noticing that none of the employees currently hunched over their computers had horns, cloven hooves or forked tails. In fact they looked like perfectly ordinary, decent people. Working here simply to earn a living. Doing what they were told to do. If she was going to expend energy disliking people, and considering the reason she was here that was highly likely, then she needed to reserve it for those at the top of the organisation. The ones who actually gave the orders.

'Tessa, hi. It's good to finally have you on board.'

Georgina came out of her glass-fronted office to greet her. Relatively few employees actually had offices, and those exclusive few who did had to put up with at least two glass walls. It must be like working in a goldfish bowl.

'It's good to be here,' Tessa replied with a smile, trying her best to sound sincere. Officially she'd started with Helix last week, but she'd spent that on a different site, undertaking an induction course with a group of other new employees. Today she was going to actually start work.

Just thinking about it brought the butterflies out in her stomach. Her motivation for joining Helix might be deeply personal, but the professional in her was more than a little intrigued to see how she'd get on being on the other side of the fence for a change. Trying to influence the story, rather than write it.

'You've certainly arrived at an interesting time,' Georgina told her as she found her a seat in her office.

'Oh?'

She must have sounded as wary as she felt because her boss smiled. Probably pushing fifty, Georgina had the type of pretty, round face it was hard not to like. Tess had been expecting a dragon when she'd attended the interview.

Finding instead a smiling, middle-aged, mother-like figure had been a welcome surprise. Not that Georgina looked like a pushover. Her eyes might twinkle, but they were also very sharp.

'You're going to be working mainly for Jim Knight, the president of research and development. He only joined Helix a couple of months ago himself and I hear he's already got a number of new initiatives up his sleeve.' Georgina's smile turned into a grin. 'I doubt boredom will be a problem for you.'

'Well, there's nothing quite like jumping in at the deep end.' Tess plastered another smile on her face and hoped she sounded enthusiastic enough. So much for keeping her head down and easing her way in. This sounded like being pushed straight into the firing line.

'Don't worry, Tessa. If I hadn't thought you were capable of doing this job I wouldn't have recruited you. I know it's going to take a bit of time to get used to how we work, but your previous experience in journalism will give you a real insight into what the media need from us. To be honest, that's why I hired you. People who've only ever worked on the industry side tend to always look at things the same way. I'm hoping you'll give us some fresh ideas.'

'And I hope you'll still be saying that in a month's time when I continue to fire those new girl questions at you every five minutes.'

Georgina laughed. 'Trust me, you'll soon get the hang of it all.'

'So what's the new president like?' Tess tried not to laugh. *President?* How pretentious. 'I hope patience is one of his characteristics.'

'Ahh, well, patient isn't perhaps the first word that comes to mind when I think of Jim.' Georgina's lips twitched in a knowing smile and she sat back against her black leather chair. 'To those of us who've worked for Helix so long we feel like part of the furniture, it's fair to say he's not so new, either. He actually worked in the clinical team for several years before leaving to join a start-up company two years ago.'

Georgina looked like she was about to add to that, but then stopped. Interesting. Was there more to Jim's jumping ship than her boss was letting on?

'Professionally speaking,' Georgina continued, obviously deciding against gossiping with her new recruit, 'Jim's horrifyingly bright. Sharp as well as smart. He's also totally straightforward, speaking his mind often to the point of bluntness, and extremely hardworking. Qualities he expects in the people who work for him.' Georgina's eyes twinkled once more as she leaned towards her conspiratorially. 'Speaking as one woman to another,' she whispered, 'he's also been dubbed the pharmaceutical industry's answer to George Clooney. Think George but taller, broader and without the smile. We're all a little afraid of him, and a little in lust with him.'

Jim was having another of those mornings when he wondered if coming back to his old company really was a good idea. Once again he'd found himself in a heated discussion with his boss.

'It has to be next week, Geoff. We need to dig deep and get the hell on with it.'

Geoff Gardner, chief executive officer (CEO) of Helix Pharmaceuticals and one of an increasingly select group of people whose opinion Jim valued, glared back at him. 'I realise you want to make an impression, Jim. You've been back with us eight weeks and now it's time to make your mark. I understand that.'

Sighing, Jim pushed back on his chair. 'With respect, this isn't about me. It's about the fact that this company doesn't have a pipeline of potential drug candidates strong enough to sustain it when the key products go off patent. Put simply, in a few years there will be a bloody big gap in revenue unless we do something about it now, and fast.'

'And you think the answer is to totally restructure the way your department runs?'

'It's an answer, yes. It will cut costs, thus improve revenue, but more importantly it will help us to identify and develop new medicines faster.'

His CEO grimaced. Not a good sign. 'But you've only been back a short time. How can you be absolutely certain what you're proposing is the right course of action? We should think this through a little more. Maybe bring in some consultants to advise us, rather than going off half-cocked next week. Announcing massive redundancies and unsettling the very staff we need to keep motivated.'

Jim clamped down firmly on his jaw, fighting to control his frustration. Pissing off the CEO wasn't the wisest career move for a fledgling research and development (R&D) president. But give him strength, hadn't this already been dissected and discussed ad nauseam at last week's executive team meeting? And hadn't they already *agreed* with his plans at that very meeting, damn it?

'Again, with respect,' he replied, grinding his teeth in a bid to keep to the calm and unflappable image he was trying to cultivate, 'I'm not going off half-cocked. Don't forget I've worked in this organisation for most of my career. I might not have been here for the last two years, but trust me, little has changed. Which is the root of the problem. The whole industry has been moving forward while Helix seems to have been treading water.'

He watched as his CEO flinched. 'I guess I have to put my hands up to allowing that.'

For a brief moment Jim closed his eyes. Great. First a grimace from his CEO, now an all out flinch. 'Look, I'm sorry if I sounded harsh—'

Geoff put up his hand, effectively silencing him. 'No need to apologise. You've always called a spade a spade. And you're right. Helix is in a mess, which is exactly why I pushed Derek out and got the board to persuade you back.'

At the mention of his predecessor, it was Jim's turn to flinch. Derek Stanley. Previous Helix R&D president. Also his old boss and, in Jim's opinion at least, a bastard of the highest order. He'd known that returning to Helix to fill Derek's shoes would inevitably lead to reminders of the man. Equally inevitably, to reminders of why he'd had to leave. Not that he regretted the move. Just the reason behind it. Oh, and the heartache and humiliation that had accompanied it.

'Okay, Jim.' Geoff's voice interrupted the unpleasant flow of his thoughts. 'Let's do this your way. What you're hearing is the hesitation of a man who's been in this job too long.'

Jim frowned at his one-time mentor. 'That doesn't sound like you.'

'Don't look so worried. I'm not planning on sailing into the sunset just yet. At least not until I've groomed you to take over.'

'You ... what?'

Geoff laughed. 'Come on, don't be coy, you know damn well that's what the board and I have got in mind. Impress us over the next few years, and my job is as good as yours.'

Christ. Jim shook his head. Reminded himself to close the mouth that had gaped open in shock. Hell's teeth, he really hadn't expected that. Hoped for it in time, yes, but for Geoff to come right out and tell him he was being *groomed* for future CEO. Inside he performed a few cartwheels of joy. Outside he simply nodded and smiled. 'I'll do my damnedest to prove my worth, but I'm mighty glad you're not going anywhere fast. Age and wisdom are invaluable when it comes to counteracting the sometimes hasty mistakes of youth.'

The older man cracked a smile. 'Enough of the blarney. Your plan for a major reorganisation of the R&D side of the business is a bold, decisive move, but also carries significant risk. Let's hope, for both our sakes, I won't have to put that wisdom to the test in the next few months.'

That sobering thought stayed with Jim as he walked slowly back to his office. Were the changes he was considering a gross misjudgement? Was his planned reorganisation not about increased efficiency but rather his own arrogance? His determination to clean away all the reminders of Derek's organisation and put his own stamp on it instead? Shaking his head, Jim resolutely pushed open the glass door to his office. He wasn't a man prone to self-doubt or recriminations. For whatever reasons, and yes, perhaps not all of them were purely business, he'd made his decision. Now he'd stick to it. The worst thing a company could do, was do nothing. He wasn't going to let that happen to Helix any longer.

His mind set, he sat down at his sleek modern desk and flicked through his appointment diary. Ah, next up was a meeting with the new communications manager, Tessa Johnson. She'd better be good. They'd be working together closely over the next few months and he didn't have the time to spoon feed some dizzy, wet behind the ears, comms woman.

Pausing outside Jim's office, Tess stifled a smile. The George Clooney description Georgina had given her wasn't far off the mark. Not far at all. From what she'd glimpsed, Jim also had an impossibly handsome face, deep, dark eyes, and black hair peppered with grey, though in Jim's case there was only a dusting. Hardly surprising, as she'd heard the Helix R&D president was a relative spring chicken. At just shy of thirty-six he was one of the youngest at his level within the industry. He also had to be one of the best looking, surely.

Obviously aware of her hovering outside his office, Jim glanced up. She was pinned back by a pair of eyes so dark they looked black. For a heart-stopping moment she found it impossible to glance away. Impossible to do anything other than stand rooted to the spot and stare back. Then he stood and moved towards her. Tall. He was definitely tall. And broad. Together with his darkly handsome good looks, he radiated an impression of strength and power.

Straightening her spine, she held out her hand to him. 'Hello. I'm Tessa from corporate comms.'

His hand enveloped hers in a firm grip. 'James Knight. Call me Jim.'

His face remained unsmiling and his eyes raked hers, assessing her. She'd always imagined brown eyes to be warm. His were like lumps of coal. Despite the warmth of the office, she shivered slightly.

'So, have you had much experience of working in the pharmaceutical industry?' he asked, motioning for her to sit down opposite him.

Tess manoeuvred her legs so she could perch on the edge of the chair. 'No. My previous roles have been mainly in journalism.' His mouth tightened and she didn't need to be an expert on mind reading to see how well that fact had gone down. Sitting straighter, she raised her chin. 'I've spent the last week on the Helix induction programme, learning how a pharmaceutical company works. The last six years I've spent understanding how the media works, mainly in journalism but I also had a short stint working for a local television network. I'm more than qualified to do this job, Mr Knight.'

His eyes warmed fractionally. 'Point taken. And it's Jim. In this company we go by first names.' Relaxing back on his leather chair he considered her carefully. 'What are your first impressions of Helix, Tessa?'

Though she had a strong suspicion the question had been asked to test her, she figured she had nothing to lose by taking the bait. Georgina had said Jim valued openness and she'd never been afraid to open her big mouth. 'If you want my honest opinion, my first impression of the company sucks.'

She waited for a reaction, and was slightly disappointed to find there wasn't one. He didn't bluster, didn't raise his eyebrows in horror. In fact he didn't move a muscle. 'I don't mean the people,' she added hastily, anxious not to come across as a total cow. 'I actually meant the inside of the building. The reception area, to be specific. If someone came in off the streets and wandered into Helix, they'd be hard-pressed to guess what the company did until they actually spoke to the staff.'

Jim narrowed his eyes. 'What do you suggest?'

'Get rid of the splashy works of art. Replace them with pictures that have some relevance to what you do. Reminders of what you should all be working towards. Curing disease, prolonging lives, helping patients.'

The dark eyes narrowed further. 'Thank you for your frank opinion,' he replied in a deceptively mild tone. 'And to a degree, I think you're right.' Nonchalantly picking up a pen, he drilled her with his gaze. 'But just to ensure there isn't any doubt, *none* of the people who work for Helix need reminding why they're here.'

The stare, clearly designed to intimidate, worked. No longer George Clooney, he'd morphed into Clooney's stern, cold brother. She was made to feel very aware that she'd overstepped whatever mark he considered as acceptably blunt, and jumped straight into being plain rude.

Before she could apologise, he was speaking again. 'I expect Georgina has filled you in on the fact that we're about to start making some sweeping changes in the R&D side of the business, so if you were hoping to ease gently into the role—'

'I'm not afraid of hard work,' she interrupted.

He regarded her steadily. 'Good.' Then his lips twitched and he almost seemed to smile. Almost. 'I get the feeling there's very little you're afraid of, Tessa.'

Before she had a chance to wonder what he meant by that,

he was standing up and shaking her hand, signalling the end of their meeting.

Tess said a quick goodbye and legged it out of his office, unable to work out if it had gone well or not. She was inclined to think not. Certainly telling him his company sucked hadn't been a stroke of genius on her part. If this had been a real job she'd have still given her honest opinion, but hopefully used a less inflammatory word than *sucks*.

And that was the nub of it. If she was going to go through with this, to actually work for this company, then she had to do the job properly. Someone like Jim Knight wouldn't suffer fools gladly, nor would he tolerate the type of sloppy behaviour she'd just displayed. She needed to pull herself together and start acting like a professional: get to grips with her new role, learn how the organisation worked. Make a far better impression on the R&D president next time she met him.

With a resigned sigh she returned to her desk and turned on her shiny new computer. While waiting for it to boot up she began to read the information Georgina had left in her in tray. Hopefully somewhere in there was a manual on how to be a communications manager. In five easy steps.

Chapter Two

The following afternoon Tess was surprised to find herself invited to the weekly meeting Jim held with his heads of department. They'd helpfully introduced themselves the moment she'd walked in, but already their names had leaked from her mind. Sitting and listening to the banter that flowed easily across the table she felt very much like the new girl at school, struggling to keep up with a never-ending sea of fresh faces and 'in' jokes.

'How are you finding Helix so far?' The man on her left finally spoke to her.

'A bit intimidating, if I'm honest.' She grimaced. 'Sorry, I can't even remember your name.'

'It's Frank. I'm the CMO.' At her blank look, he grinned. 'Chief medical officer. I'm afraid we use a lot of acronyms and abbreviations within pharma.' He chuckled. 'Within the pharmaceutical industry. Perhaps someone should put a list of them together for new starters. We've got AEs, CTAs, CTXs, DSURs, EMA, FDA, GCP—'

'Stop!' She put her hands over her ears and he laughed again.

'Seriously, if there's anything you need help understanding, give me a call.'

'Thanks. I might well do that.'

'What are you trying to do to the poor girl, Frank? Scare her off in her first week?'

Tess swung her head towards the voice and found the only other female in the room staring back at her, a small smile playing around her blood red lips. Hers was the one name she could remember. Barbara, head of the clinical trial department. She was attractive, Tess guessed, with her dark hair and olive skin tone. She was also downright rude. How could a fellow woman call her a *girl*? A *poor girl*, at that.

It was not only unprofessional, it was demeaning. But just as Tess was about to deliver the words *thank you, older lady, but I don't scare easily*, which would have been highly satisfying but probably not wise, Jim walked in.

Immediately conversations stopped and heads turned his way. It was a pretty impressive entrance. She guessed the combination of his devastating good looks and aura of power made it hard to ignore the R&D president.

He made no small talk. After a brief nod of acknowledgement he strode to the computer, inserted his memory stick and waited for his presentation to load. The room was silent. A few moments ago the atmosphere had been warm and jovial, now it was stark and businesslike. A tone set by the man at the head of the table.

As the screen behind him lit up, Jim finally spoke. 'Thanks for coming.' His rich, deep voice was grave, matching the expression on his face. 'Before I begin, I want to stress that everything you are about to hear has to remain totally confidential until next week.'

His stern face scanned the room, making her wonder if he had bad news to deliver. Then again, maybe he always looked like that because he hadn't exactly been Mr Warm and Fuzzy the last time she'd seen him. The body language at play around the table intrigued her. Most were nodding, slightly in awe of their leader. One or two had their arms folded, clearly champing at the bit, wanting to find out what all this was about. Barbara eased back against her chair, cool as you like, a slight smile on her painted lips.

Jim's eyes flickered over each of them in turn, as if taking a mental register, and for the briefest of moments his mouth tightened when he reached Barbara. It was enough for Tess to wonder what the story was there, but not enough for her to draw any conclusions.

* * *

As his eyes landed on Barbara, Jim forced himself to give her the same dispassionate look he'd given everyone else. He'd seen her a few times since he'd been back, but he wasn't quite where he wanted to be yet – detached, unaffected, indifferent. Once, two years ago, she'd torn his heart from his chest and he was finding her betrayal tougher to forget than he'd bargained for. She looked harder than she had then, older. Obviously being a two timing bitch wasn't good for the complexion. Or perhaps all wasn't well in the soft little love nest she'd created with Derek, after turning his world upside down. Not that he gave a damn any more, he reminded himself. He might have to endure some awkward meetings now she was reporting to him, but by God he was going to enjoy her being on the back foot for a change.

Shrugging off his thoughts, Jim clicked onto his first slide. 'This is a graphic representation of the number of new drugs coming through the Helix pipeline over the next ten years. In contrast to previous versions you might have seen, I've removed the tricks we use to portray a thriving pipeline to the outside world.' Which meant he'd removed each mention of a different formulation of the same drug. The sprays, the capsules, the creams, the slow release tablets. He'd also taken out the combination therapies. The ones where two drugs were put together in the same tablet, ostensibly to help compliance, but often to extend the patent life and revenue stream of the products.

What remained was a simple graphic of anticipated novel new therapies. The breakthrough innovations that a cutting edge pharmaceutical company should be all about. It was a frighteningly bleak picture. A fact confirmed by the collective gasp around the room as they slowly took in the implications of the slide.

'You don't need me to tell you the major revenue streams from our key brands will start to trail off in the next few years.' He rummaged around in his pocket for a laser pointer, then gave up and used his fingers. Damn lasers were useless anyway. 'You also don't need me to tell you we don't have sufficient new development coming in to make up that shortfall.'

They stared back at him, their expressions very different from when he'd first entered the room. Then they'd been relaxed, no doubt miffed at being in another ruddy meeting, but untroubled. Now their faces were tense, their eyes uncertain, worried. All bright people, they probably had a good idea what he was about to say next.

'Dramatic changes are needed,' he told them quietly, 'and needed now. We have to find ways of discovering more novel medicines but with reduced costs and increased efficiencies.'

He moved to the next slide. His new R&D organisation. 'I believe the only way to achieve this is by reorganising the way we discover and trial new therapies.' He pointed to the blue boxes on the slide. 'That means our research teams are going to be working in smaller, more focussed units which concentrate on specific target areas. These will be mainly anti-infectives and anti-cancer therapies.'

He clicked to the final slide. The one he knew would lead to a burst of questions. 'Reforming the current teams into smaller units, cutting out middle management and no longer working in non-target therapy areas will inevitably lead to considerable job losses. A fact we'll have to live with, in order to give this company a fighting chance of survival in the future.'

His harsh words were met with a stunned silence. It went on so long he started to consider if he'd been too blunt, but quickly dismissed the thought. No. This was business. And sometimes business was bloody tough.

'How on earth are we going to motivate our teams with the threat of all this going on?' asked Frank.

A valid question and one he'd expected. 'We'll complete this process as quickly as possible, but motivation will come from a desire to keep their job,' he replied flatly. 'Nobody is safe. Everybody will have to reapply for their position.'

Barbara gaped at him. 'That sounds downright cruel to me.'

He worked hard to suppress a grim smile. If anyone knew the meaning of the word, she did. 'You call it cruel, I call it necessary. The skills needed in the new organisation will be different from those in the past. Scientists will need to demonstrate they have the capabilities to work in it.'

'Some motivation,' she muttered under her breath.

Jim looked at her sharply. 'This organisation is currently carrying a lot of scientists. People who are simply biding their time, working towards retirement. We can't afford to keep allowing this. We need to stir things up, get some fresh blood leading the teams. Create a much needed sense of urgency.'

'That's a bit harsh on a lot of good employees. People who ...' The head of pre-clinical trailed off as Jim caught his eye.

'Reality is often harsh.'

'What about the people you get rid of?' Tessa asked quietly. 'Scientists who've given the best parts of their lives to making this company what it is today.'

Jim flicked a gaze over the woman he'd met yesterday. Tall, very slim, bordering on skinny. Her red hair, no doubt called something fanciful like auburn or chestnut, was tied in a prim knot on her head, giving her the impression, at least, of efficiency. Deep blue eyes stood out vividly above sharp cheekbones. Freckles ran across the bridge of her nose and cheeks, standing out against her pale skin. It was a striking, yet at the same time wholesome looking face. Milkmaid meets catwalk model.

Not that you're interested in what she looks like.

'The term is displaced, Tessa,' he reminded her, 'not got rid of, and this is a business, not a charity. Yes, it's rough on those who'll lose their jobs, and yes, we'll look after them as best we can, but at the end of the day we're here to make a profit.'

'I thought we were here to develop new medicines to help fight disease and improve patients' lives.' Tessa stared back at him, those bright blue eyes full of challenge.

'If we don't make a profit we can't develop new medicines. End of story.' A fact that often escaped journalists who wrote scathing accounts of massive drug company profits and the extortionate price of breakthrough medicines.

The room was now about as lively as a morgue – boy did he know how to kill a mood. He turned off the computer. 'Are there any further questions?'

Almost as one they shook their heads, no doubt too terrified to speak. He was clearly so good at playing the unfeeling bastard he'd convinced them all he was one. Great, if he wanted to rule by fear, but he didn't. He was rather hoping for respect.

Letting out a silent sigh, he drew the meeting to a close. 'Okay. Naturally you'll receive more information about the practicalities and logistics as we go through the week, but remember, this was a heads up for your ears only. Don't speak a word of this to anyone outside this team.'

As the group moved out, Jim walked towards Tessa. 'Can you stay behind for a minute?'

She gave him a *who me?* look. For a fleeting moment he pictured her in a school uniform and bouncy red pigtails, glaring at the teacher who'd unfairly picked on her.

'If this is about what I said in the meeting—'

'It isn't,' he cut in quickly. Hell, did she really think he was that small-minded?

'Oh, okay.'

She stood defiantly before him, totally unfazed by his seniority. Ordinarily he would have appreciated such confidence, but there was something about Tessa's attitude. He couldn't put his finger on it, but it made him want to unsettle her. Make her show him some respect.

'I'm going to need a communications plan from you for

this reorganisation. Have it ready to go through with me tomorrow afternoon,' he told her brusquely. 'I'll clear my diary.'

She didn't bat an eyelid. 'Fine.'

As she went to walk out of the door, he called her back. 'Oh, and Tessa?' She turned, arching an eyebrow, her willowy body poised. 'I'm not afraid of being challenged. It creates a healthy, open, environment. Just make sure it doesn't turn into a rant.'

With a brief nod she sauntered off. He couldn't help but notice she was wearing a pair of outrageously high shoes. And had seemingly endless legs.

Tess had never been so relieved to open the door of her apartment. Home, at last. Without bothering to shrug off her jacket she walked straight through to the sitting room and slumped onto the sofa. What a day. At least after Jim's request that afternoon ... she grimaced. *Request*, sure, make that his *order*. At least after his order she'd been so petrified at the prospect of putting together his flipping communications plan she hadn't had a chance to think about anything else. Her confident *I'm more than qualified to do this job, Mr Knight* bravado was fast collapsing around her ears. Right now she was teetering out of her depth.

Huffing out a breath, she began unravelling her hair from its very business like knot. Teetering? She was, in fact, *totally* out of her depth. As a journalist she'd seen press releases from corporate companies like Helix, and attended media briefings. She'd also happily picked them both apart. But faced with setting those very things in motion for an organisation she didn't fully understand and definitely didn't like, she had no clue where to start. And that was before she considered the internal stuff. Communicating to the staff ...

With a sigh she carefully eased off her favourite Manolo Blahnik's. Shoes. Her passion and her downfall. She lived like a relative pauper, but her feet were always encased in the best her money could buy. In order to feed that addiction though, she needed an income. And for an income, she needed to keep this job.

So who did she know who'd worked in a big corporation and might have put together something like this? Picking up her phone she began a trawl of the contact list. When she reached C, her face split into a smile. Hugh Coleman, editor at the *Daily News*. He'd been her boss up until she'd left to join Helix. He was more than that though. He was a former lover and, thank God, still a good friend. She pressed dial.

'Well, if it isn't Miss Communications Manager,' he drawled, answering on the first ring. 'Don't tell me you've had enough of the corporate world *already*?'

'Yes, I think I have.' A sudden rush of despair hit her full on. What on earth was she doing, working for a company she didn't respect, all for a mission she probably didn't have a cat in hell's chance of achieving?

'Hey, come on, Tess, this isn't like you. You never give up, especially not at the first hurdle.'

She attempted to swallow down the self-pity. 'This first hurdle seems pretty enormous.'

'But just think, when you've jumped it, you don't have to keep on jumping, so to speak. In fact, if we're carrying on with the hurdling metaphor, you only have to leap enough hurdles to give you time to find out if the company has anything to hide. After that you can scarper off the track and straight into the changing rooms. Then, following a quick shower, obviously, it's back to the *Daily News*.'

Her lips twitched in the beginnings of a smile. 'I know. It's just ...,' She let out a deep sigh. '... I underestimated how difficult it was going to be, you know, pretending.'

'You don't have to pretend to be anyone but yourself, Tess. Treat it as the new job it is. The rest will come, in time.'

'I guess.' But if it did, would it bring her the peace of mind she longed for? God, she hoped so. 'You're just trying to cheer me up so you can get your story.'

He laughed. 'Too right. What editor wouldn't want a feature exposing more of the dark evils of the pharmaceutical industry?'

'Jeez, Hugh, you don't change.' Though she shook her head, she was soon laughing with him. 'Okay then buster, if you want the story, you need to help me. As things stand, if I don't put together a genius communications plan by tomorrow afternoon, I've got a feeling I'll be out on my ear. Pushed out by the ruthless but broodingly handsome R&D president. No more job, no more story.'

'Broodingly handsome, eh? I take it things aren't all doom and gloom then?'

His words forced another chuckle out of her. 'No, I suppose not. At least I can ogle him while he's giving me my marching orders.'

'There'll be no sacking,' Hugh replied firmly. 'Not while there's a possibility of a story for me. So it looks like we've got a busy evening ahead of us. You order the pizza, I'll bring my brains.'

Smiling, Tess put down the phone. At least now she felt more in control. With Hugh's help there was every chance she could put together a plan that even Mr Cold-Hearted couldn't disagree with. Even if did take her all night. And prevented her from catching up on her favourite soaps.

Chapter Three

Jim looked up from his desk to find Barbara loitering outside his office. Automatically his body let slip a sigh. A deep expiration that seemed to come from his soul. So far he'd only seen her in team meetings. Their scheduled one-to-one had been rearranged so often he'd started to think she was avoiding him.

Surreptitiously he studied her, noticing how unusually nervous she looked, and wondered if she was as wary of him as he was of her. To him, she represented his greatest humiliation. To her, he was probably a minor embarrassment. A fling she'd forgotten to end when a man with more power and clout had come along. The fact that she'd continued to sleep with him, while also banging Derek had been a bitter pill to swallow. Sometimes he wondered if the deception had hurt more than the ending of the relationship. Either way, he'd been left reeling. He hadn't bloodied Derek's nose, despite being sorely tempted, but his own blood had run cold ever since. Women still caught his eye now and again – he'd not lost all of his manhood. Just the important part. His heart. He had no interest in leaving himself so painfully vulnerable ever again.

Putting down the report he'd been reading he carefully set his expression to neutral and motioned for her to come in. He noticed she made sure the door shut firmly behind her.

'Hello, Barbara. Finally, a meeting you haven't rescheduled.'

She had the grace to look slightly uncomfortable. 'Sorry about that. I've been travelling a lot, visiting the key clinical research sites.'

'I'd started to think you were avoiding me.'

Her lips parted and she slowly, he'd bet on deliberately, licked her lips. 'You know I would never do that.'

Now it was he who was feeling uncomfortable. He decided to plough straight in. 'I scheduled these one-to-ones to get to know my team better. Given our ... history that isn't necessary, so let's get down to business. What are your key areas of focus for the next two months?'

'Seriously?' Her dark eyes bored into his. 'We're going to talk work?'

'There isn't anything else I need from you.'

Her body stiffened as his arrow found its mark. 'Fine.'

For the next fifteen minutes she clearly and concisely outlined the priorities and issues for her clinical department. He asked questions, she answered them. By the end he almost believed she was his clinical research head. Not his cheating ex.

'Okay, thank you,' he said when she'd come to a halt. He nodded at the door, indicating the end of their meeting.

She remained seated. 'Isn't it time we cleared the air?'

'Cleared the air?' He almost laughed. 'Didn't we do that two years ago?'

'We need to talk about what happened between us, Jim.'

His jaw tightened. 'If I recall, it went something like this. I came back from my meeting earlier than I'd expected, popped round to your office to surprise you, only to have the surprise turned right back on me when I found you draped over your desk, naked and sweaty underneath Derek. I shouted, you shouted. Derek tried to disappear behind the filing cabinet. What other air is there to clear?' His voice had risen and his fists were now clenched at his side. So much for appearing indifferent.

Annoyed at his loss of calm, he rose to his feet and moved to the front of his desk, making sure there was still plenty of space between them. The desire to throttle her had probably dimmed by now, but it wasn't worth the risk.

'I finished with Derek four months ago,' she told him softly.

He waited to feel something at her announcement. Pleasure, satisfaction, maybe even a dart of anticipation that she was free once again. Thank God all he felt was apathy. 'And that's relevant to me because ...?'

She frowned, deepening the lines on her still very attractive face. There was something earthy about her, sensual, sinful almost. It had been that edge that had lured him in the first place. That and her voluptuous curves. They'd mesmerised him so much he hadn't noticed the hard, calculating woman beneath them. Not until it was too late.

'Jim, please, stop being so cold.' Gracefully she stood, easing herself into his personal space. 'What happened to the passionate man I fell in love with?'

'You fell in *love* with?' He gave a hollow laugh. 'Give me a break. I was just a stepping stone, a plaything until a more powerful man came along.'

'That's not true. Derek was ...' She turned away and went to pull down the blinds on the glass office doors. The hairs on the back of his neck began to prick. 'Derek was an aberration. A foolish mistake.' Having made his office space more private, she moved back towards him, standing even closer than before, deliberately skimming her soft curves against him. 'You were the one I always loved, Jim.' Her voice was low and throaty, her eyes wide and pleading. 'Please, you have to believe me.' Her hand reached out to touch him. To grasp hold of his ...

Thank God, only his hand. Instinctively he steeled himself against her touch. Once she'd been able to arouse him by just a look, a tilt of her lips. Now he wasn't sure what he'd feel and wasn't in the mood to find out. He was starting to peel himself away when there was a knock on the door and Tessa strode in.

'Oops, sorry.' Her eyes widened as they flicked over the pair of them: Barbara clutching his hand, her body almost plastered against his chest. 'I'll come back later.'

'No need,' he replied tightly. 'Barbara was just leaving.' Vibrating with anger – at himself, the situation, Barbara, hell, the world – he stalked back to his desk.

'This conversation isn't finished, Jim,' Barbara told him quietly. Then, after giving Tessa a cursory nod, she strode out of his office, her hips swaying provocatively beneath her tight skirt.

'Well, that was, umm ...' Tessa tailed off and lifted her shoulders in an embarrassed shrug.

'Unprofessional?' He supplied. Christ, he could kick himself. The moment the blinds had gone down he'd sensed trouble but done bugger all about it.

'I was going to say awkward.'

'Yes, I guess awkward covers it, too.' With a deep sigh he went to sit down at the table he used for informal meetings.

'I should have waited for you to answer before I barged in.'

'Yes.' But if she had, he dreaded to think what might have happened. 'Look, Barbara and I ...' He tailed off when he caught sight of her face. 'Are you smirking?'

Jim looked so off balance, a cross between irritation and mortification, that Tess felt the urge to grin, okay, yes, smirk. Perhaps even giggle. A sure way to get fired. 'No, I'm not, not really. And please, you don't have to explain anything to me.'

'No, I don't, do I?' He drummed his fingers on the tabletop, then seemed to catch himself and force them still. 'But then you'd have to work with a man you believed to be an office letch. One who liked to abuse his position and force more junior female staff into having sex with him.'

She stopped smiling. 'I wasn't thinking that.'

'No?'

She shook her head. She'd been thinking a lot of things. Such as *Was Barbara the reason he'd left the company a couple of years ago?* And then there was the much more worrying *What would it be like to have an affair with this man? To have him hold you against his powerful body, stare at you with his dark, dark eyes and kiss you?* Unbelievably inappropriate, but a million miles away from the ones he'd believed her to be having.

He spoke into the now uncomfortable silence. 'Barbara and I used to date, but it was several years ago now and I have no plans to start it up again. What you saw then was ...' He expelled a breath, cleared his throat. 'Look, I just wanted to make it clear that I'm not the type of man who sleeps with women who work for him. It's a personal rule of mine.'

Wow, was he trying to warn her off? How arrogant. She might fancy him, but she was a long way from liking him. 'Well, I'm glad we cleared that up.'

His almost black eyes narrowed but he chose not to comment on her slightly sarcastic response. Instead he motioned for her to sit down. 'So, I take it you've come here to go through the communications plan?'

'Yes.' It was a relief to talk about work again, even if it was the comms plan she was now terrified about showing him. Thanks to Barbara, she doubted he was in a warm, receptive mood at the moment. Taking a deep breath, she held out a copy to him. 'Here's the draft plan. If you'd like some time to read through what I've suggested—'

'Talk me through the main points,' he interrupted. 'I can read the details later.'

'Right, okay. You're the boss.' Oops. He didn't return her smile. Simply flicked her a cool, enigmatic glance. 'Obviously the critical point is that the employees hear about the reorganisation before we inform the press,' she continued with fake confidence. 'But we don't want to leave too long a gap between the two announcements or the information will leak out in a manner we'll have no control over. I've consulted with the human resources team and the line managers will speak to their teams early Monday afternoon. Following that I'll submit the press release and then arrange for any media interviews. I've pencilled in a major broadcast to the whole organisation Tuesday morning.'

A quick glance in his direction found him flicking through her document, his face expressionless. It was the first time she'd sat this close to him, so close she could smell the expensive musk of his aftershave. Almost touch his tanned skin. He really was almost brutally handsome. Quickly she dropped her eyes back to her report, before he caught her staring.

'That seems to cover everything,' he finally remarked, placing the copy on the table.

His hands looked strong and capable, she noticed, then rolled her eyes at the fact that she *had* noticed. 'How comfortable are you with dealing with the media?' She scribbled an irrelevant note in the margin of her report. Anything to avoid gawping at him.

'I'm used to it, if that's what you mean.'

She risked another glance. 'I'm sure you are, but when was the last time you had any training?'

Twin brown pools locked onto her. 'Why, do you think I need some?'

'I think it would be wise to spend some time considering how you want to come across,' she ventured as tactfully as she could. 'I mean I haven't seen you in front of the press, so maybe you'll take a different stance with them than you did in the meeting yesterday.' She halted as he raised a dark eyebrow.

'And if I don't?'

'Umm?'

'If I don't change my stance with the media?' he prompted darkly.

Bugger. So much for tact. She considered her next words more carefully. 'When it comes to announcing large-scale

31

job losses, sensitivity is the key. The pharmaceutical industry already has a pretty poor reputation with the media, so discussing mass redundancies with all the warmth of a polar ice cap isn't exactly going to enhance it.'

And yes, speaking of sensitivity, perhaps that last remark could have done with some, though to be fair he didn't look any more pissed off now than he had when she'd started.

'Is that what you think I did yesterday? Talk with the warmth of a polar bear?' He sounded calm, a bit too calm.

'Well, actually I said polar ice cap, but really, I guess the point is the same—'

'I'm not going to pussyfoot around this issue, Tessa,' he interrupted coldly. 'I won't spin it, pretend it's something it isn't.'

'No.' She could admire him for that, at least. 'And I wouldn't want you to. But you could be more *caring*,' she responded, emphasising the last word.

Jim glared back at her. 'You think I *don't* care that these people will be losing their jobs because of me?'

It seemed that hole she was digging herself was getting deeper. 'Well, that's the impression you give.'

'It's a false one.' A muscle twitched in his jaw and his eyes blazed.

'I'm sure it is false,' she agreed, though privately she had her doubts. 'Which is exactly why you need to make sure people know you *do* care. And we're not just talking about the media here, but the employees, too. They all need to see that while you're not afraid to make tough decisions, you are human. You do understand how they're feeling.'

'And how do you propose I go about doing that? Turn up wearing a jumper with a big red heart, and the words *I care* blazoned across it in neon lights?'

His guarded expression made it impossible to work out whether he was secretly amused, or being damningly sarcastic. 'You know, that's not a bad idea.' Though she found it hard to picture him in a casual pair of jeans, never mind a crazy jumper.

To her surprise, his lips twitched. 'Okay, message received. When I make the announcements, I'll try to come across as a human being.'

'And the jumper?'

'I think we'll pass on that for now,' he replied gruffly, though a hint of amusement warmed the depths of his eyes.

Determinedly Tess dragged her focus back to her notes. Bloody hell. Up to now she'd found it easy to remain largely unaffected by his brooding good looks. However, when his eyes twinkled. Wow. If he ever smiled, he'd be dynamite.

'I've also suggested we hold some sort of event in a few weeks' time,' she continued, bringing herself back to the day job. 'Perhaps a party that acts as both a farewell to those who are leaving, and a celebration of the achievements of the last ten years.'

He glanced up in surprise. 'Do you really think people who are being, what was your phrase, *got rid of*, will want to come to something like that?'

Which was exactly her worry. 'I'm not sure. Maybe it will be a huge gamble but I can't help thinking that employees who've given a lot to the organisation shouldn't be shuffled out without some sort of send-off. An event like this would send a strong message that Helix is proud of what its people have achieved. It will also draw the line in the sand under the old R&D organisation, creating a platform for the new one.'

Jim considered the woman in front of him. Young and naive in the ways of the industry she might be, but already he sensed she was pretty smart. The party was definitely a gamble, but it was also fresh, different. He enjoyed having a punt now and again, if the odds were right.

'An unusual idea, but I like it. Let's push ahead, but don't announce anything until you gauge how much interest there is. If it's planned sensibly, we shouldn't incur too many costs if we decide to cancel.'

'So says a man who likes to hedge his bets.' Her eyes were laughing, just as they had when she'd burst into his office and found him with Barbara. He couldn't tell whether the laughter was with him, or at him. 'I don't think that's what we should be doing here though,' she added. 'I see it as part of a schedule of events during the reorganisation phase. Perhaps even part of the announcement. If we hurriedly suggest a party a few weeks down the line, it will look like an afterthought. Putting it out there now gives you that human side. As part of your speech you can stress how important everyone's contribution has been over the years, which is why Helix has planned an event to celebrate their achievements. Of course, sadly, the R&D organisation can't carry on in the same way. Times change, companies have to change with them.' She stopped and smiled awkwardly. 'Sorry, I think I was getting a bit carried away.'

'I see I don't have to worry about writing a speech,' he remarked wryly.

Surprisingly she blushed, looking so uncomfortable he felt the need to put her at ease.

'Sorry. That was a lame attempt at humour. It's good to see enthusiasm, Tessa.' The bugger of it was that with her face flushed, and looking slightly wrong-footed, he found her quite startlingly attractive. Before he'd had her down as pushy but interesting. Now she looked positively sexy. And he was losing his marbles if he was considering, no matter how hypothetically, the feminine attributes of a young woman who reported to him.

He ran a hand through his hair and settled his thoughts. 'Okay. We'll keep the plan as it is. Event and all. But if we're left with a huge ballroom and only five attendees …'

'Then to those five employees, it will be worth it,' she added earnestly.

'Perhaps,' he acknowledged, 'but I'm going to have a hard time convincing the board of that.' Closing her report, he stood up. 'We'll have to leave it there as I'm late for my next appointment.'

Welcoming the distraction, he took out his phone and quickly checked where he was needed next. From beginning to end, this meeting had been unnerving, to say the least. He'd begun it fending off Barbara, and ended wanting to launch himself at Tessa. Christ, he'd obviously gone far too long without a woman. Perhaps it was time to hit the singles scene again.

By the time he looked up from his phone, Tessa was edging out of the office. A slender lady with deep red hair, a face that was too pale and crazy high shoes. Today it was bright pink stilettos, the same colour as her shirt. Daring with her hair colour, but it worked.

'Tessa.' She paused in the doorway. 'Good work. I think we're going to get along just fine.'

As he watched her disappear he reflected how strange it was that the dark haired voluptuous woman he'd used to love had left him cold, yet this younger, skinnier red headed woman had sparked his interest.

Chapter Four

Settling down on her comfy red sofa, Tess picked up the TV remote control and began to scan the evening line-up. Usually it was something she did with great anticipation, but this evening her mind was on other things. Bizarrely, it kept skipping back to her meeting with Jim and specifically to his completely unexpected praise. At his two paltry words, *good work*, her lips had instantly curved into a totally goofy grin. Unbelievable. Not only had she constructed a plan to improve the image of the very company she wanted to bring down, but then she'd burst with pride when its R&D president had told her it was good.

She was living in a crazy world right now – and she was probably the craziest thing in it.

Time for a dose of reality. And it came to something when that reality was American soaps, she thought with a laugh. She was just getting into an episode of *Friends* she'd only seen five times, when the phone rang. With a small hiss of frustration, she went to answer it.

'Hey, little sis.'

Frustration turned to pleasure. 'Hey, big brother.' She glanced down at her watch in surprise. 'After nine o'clock at night. Why aren't you at some wild party rather than checking up on me?'

'Because, sister dear, I'm too old for wild parties. You're the one who's still in her twenties. Just. What are you doing in?'

'Recovering from a hard day at work,' she replied dryly. 'And I'm still two years away from thirty so you can stop the sarcastic age comments.'

'I can't. It's my duty as a brother to be rude and annoying to my sister. So how is the new job? I take it you did finally step inside the scary building?'

'Ha ha.'

'And? Have you found out anything yet?'

She looked up at the ceiling. 'Blimey, Mark, give me a break. I've only been there a few days.'

'Sorry.' There was a deep sigh on the other end of the line. 'I just want to find out the truth.'

'So do I.' For a moment there was silence on the phone and she knew they were both remembering the same thing. 'But even if we do, it won't bring Mum back.' Tears stung at the back of her eyes.

'I know.' His voice was as scratchy as her own. 'But what if someone in Helix was responsible for her death? We can't let them get away with it. Hell, I can't even close my eyes without seeing her on that damn hospital bed, the life drained out of her.'

Her tears surfaced, falling from her eyes in a steady stream. Tess swiped at them with the back of her hand. 'Me, too. Heaven knows, she wasn't meant to die like that. Not when she was fighting the cancer so well.'

'That damn cancer drug must have caused the heart problem. I still can't see any other explanation.'

'Neither can I.' She was a journalist, trained to look at all angles, but each road she'd travelled so far had led her to the same place. 'If we add up the fact that the hospital staff admitted they were aware of several heart attacks in cancer patients given the same treatment. Then the Internet search on chat rooms and cancer websites showing dozens more cases, with some families even saying they're planning lawsuits. Heck, even the coroner said he couldn't rule out that the new treatment had caused her death.'

'He just didn't have enough evidence to prove it,' Mark muttered.

'And I'll find that evidence,' she promised. 'We know pharmaceutical companies have been accused of hiding data on their products to stop bad publicity. To stop doctors from seeing the full risk potential. If Helix are guilty of doing that, I'm going to prove it.'

'I know you will.' He paused. 'I'm only going to say this once, so listen hard. I really admire you for doing this, Tess.'

Emotion clogged her throat and she tried to cover it with a laugh.

'But promise me you'll be careful,' Mark continued, oblivious to her meltdown. 'Mum would hate to be the cause of you getting into trouble. Please don't get caught delving into confidential files without permission.'

'Just because I'm your younger sister, it doesn't make me stupid,' Tess cut in. 'I won't do anything underhand. I'll find a legitimate reason to look into this.'

'Good, because your family's relying on you. Other families, too, because we certainly don't want anyone else to have to go through this hell.'

She squeezed her eyes shut. 'I won't let anyone down.'

Long after they'd said their goodbyes Tess remained on the sofa, her eyes closed. The burden of responsibility weighed heavily on her shoulders, but bizarrely it didn't feel as if it was crushing her. In fact she felt energised, because at last she was doing something positive. For months she'd been almost comatose, shock and grief leaving her numb. There'd not just been the pain of losing her mother, but effectively her father, too. He'd suffered stroke after stroke following her mother's death and was now in a care home. All that was left was the empty shell of a once vibrant man.

Her loving, tightknit family – decimated – less than a day after her mother had started a new cancer therapy.

A year and a half later, and her death still left a gaping hole. One made deeper by the nagging belief that it could have been prevented. That someone in Helix Pharmaceuticals had known that the new drug, Zaplex, carried a risk of heart problems in susceptible patients, but had covered it up. Determined, no doubt, not to limit the use of their potential blockbuster. Putting sales before the lives of patients. Her mother, and others like her.

Tess felt her muscles tighten, her jaw clench. Restlessly she jumped up from the sofa and stalked through to the bathroom. What she needed now was a long, hot soak. Something to ease the tension. God knows, she didn't want to think of her mother with such pain and anger. She wanted to grieve properly, to heal, but she couldn't. Not with all this uncertainty surrounding her death.

Now she had the chance to remove that uncertainty. To dig into the secret files on Zaplex and find out the truth about the drug. She might not be exactly sure what she was looking for, but she was pretty certain she'd know when she saw it. And then?

Tess shrugged off her clothes and, with a groan of pleasure, relaxed into the steaming hot bubbles, her mind picturing the look on the faces of the Helix top brass when they realised that their fledgling communications manager knew exactly how to work the media. To her personal advantage.

Jim gritted his teeth and crunched out another twenty lengths of the pool. He'd made the effort to leave work on time, driven to the bloody place, bothered to change into his trunks. He might as well make the effort worthwhile. In his twenties, pounding out a mile in the pool after five on the treadmill had been a doddle. In his thirties, he was finding it harder work. Not that it was going to stop him. He could be a pugnacious son of a bitch when he wanted to be.

Heaving his shattered body out of the pool, he almost collided with another swimmer walking back from the other side of the pool. 'Sorry. Damn.' He glanced up at the swimmer's face. 'Bloody hell, it's you.'

He and Rick, who worked in the Helix IT department, went back many years, having bonded over beer and exercise. He'd been trying to catch up with the guy ever since re-joining Helix but so far it hadn't happened. Until now.

They shook hands and the taller, younger man grinned. 'Good to see you, too. Still pushing that old body of yours, I see.'

'Still wishing you could keep up with me, eh?' Laughing, Jim reached for his towel and threw it round his shoulders.

'Touché.' They walked side by side back towards the changing rooms. 'I hear you've entered the Surrey triathlon. Is that wise do you think, considering your age?'

Jim tried not to wince. His body was only too aware of the physical demands of the sport. 'You know, despite all thoughts to the contrary, life doesn't end in your middle thirties.'

'What group are you in now, veterans?'

They reached the changing rooms and as Jim pushed open the door he briefly considered letting it go in Rick's face. 'I'm a few years off that yet.' There had been talk of male veterans starting at thirty-five, like the females, but at the moment it was still forty. Not that the label bothered him too much. As long as he was finishing near the front, they could call him what they liked.

'Well, man, it's good to have you back.' Rick reached out and gave his back a friendly slap.

As Rick had a few more inches on his own six foot two and was built like a navvy, Jim had to brace himself to avoid toppling over. 'It's good to be back. I think.'

They showered quickly then headed for the bar to catch up on each other's news over a quick drink. Being men, that part of the conversation didn't take long. Or it wouldn't have done, if Rick hadn't caught him off guard with a serious question. 'Have you come across Barbara yet?'

He exhaled slowly. 'Yes.'

'And?'

'We're both still standing, if that's what you mean.'

'Come on, give me the truth, not the platitudes.' Rick looked him in the eye. 'How did you feel?'

Laughter burst out of him. 'How did I *feel*? Hell, you've turned into a pussy since I've been gone. I guess that's what marriage does to you.'

'Don't knock it till you've tried it,' Rick countered, a bit too smugly for Jim's liking. 'And don't evade. I meant, do you still have feelings for her? Or, to put it the way you'd understand, did you want to kiss her, or slap her?'

Jim ran a hand down his face, wanting to lie. Knowing he couldn't. 'A little of both.'

'Ouch.' Rick screwed up his face in sympathy. 'Still hurts then?'

'Hurt, past tense. I've wasted enough energy moping over that particular humiliation. And if I ever get involved with the opposite sex again, it'll be with someone with no ties to my working life whatsoever.'

'Well, it's good to see you're thinking ahead. And I've got to say, I admire your balls in coming back here.'

Jim let out another short laugh. 'The rumour mill still going strong then?'

Rick grinned. 'Don't be so sensitive. There's a lot of people who don't remember what happened.' Jim stared at him. 'Okay, some people.' Jim still stared. 'Hell, you're right. People have long memories, but being ditched helps to make you more human.'

'Thanks.' Given a choice, he'd have preferred the flashing heart jumper approach he'd mentioned to Tessa earlier. It would have been less embarrassing. And even in scratchy wool, a damn sight less painful. 'You want another?' he asked, pointing to Rick's drink.

'Yeah.' His phone started to ring and he glanced at the screen, then shook his head. 'On second thoughts, better make that a no.' Wincing, he answered the phone. 'Hello, sweetie. Yes, of course. I'm on my way now.'

Jim was still chuckling over Rick's desperate attempts to placate his wife when they walked out of the health club and into the car park.

'You're not still driving that heap of junk, are you?' Rick exclaimed, his eyes resting on the green E-type Jaguar.

Jim snorted. 'Leave her alone. She's a classic. Not only that, she'll beat your modern box off the lights.' For a nanosecond, until her old engine started to splutter. He chose not to mention that.

'Well, it's good to see you've still got a woman in your life. Even if it is of the metal variety.' Letting out a huge belly laugh at his own joke, Rick threw out a 'catch you later' and trotted off towards his own boring, predictable, German machine. And to his wife.

With a sigh, Jim wedged himself into the Jaguar's snug leather interior, running his hands lovingly over the walnut and mahogany steering wheel. Rick was right. The beautiful E-type *was* the only woman in his life. The only one he was prepared to commit to, at least, because he knew she wouldn't cheat on him. Wouldn't let him down. Well, the first part anyway. Being a vintage car, she did have reliability problems, but he could overlook those for the sheer joy he got out of driving her.

When he at last opened the door to his apartment, the top floor of a converted warehouse, he was ravenous. So it was a killer to look in his fridge and find so little in the blasted thing. There were two eggs and some cheese which, if he'd been the man on the adverts, he could have whisked into some fancy soufflé. He wasn't and he couldn't. It was a miracle he'd managed to survive as long as he had on his own. His mother had tried to impart a little culinary knowledge on him, and so had his school, but he hadn't taken much notice. Probably because he'd been far too focussed on the subjects he hadn't considered girlie, like sport and science, to worry about how to feed himself. Meals arrived on a plate when you were hungry, didn't they?

Twenty years later, he knew that wasn't the case – unless he phoned for a pizza. He was eating a lot of pizza.

As he shuffled despairingly through his ice choked freezer there was a ring on his doorbell. Maybe there was some telepathy thing going on with the pizza place. He could only hope.

He pressed the button on his intercom, his stomach rumbling in synch with the pepperoni images his mind was conjuring. 'Hello?'

'Jim, it's Barbara.'

Crap. He hesitated, taking a moment to regret his decision not to move apartments when he'd first left Helix. He'd loved this place too much. Where else could he wake up to a magnificent view across London from giant floor to ceiling windows? Well, now it was time to deal with a consequence of that decision. His ex knew exactly where to find him.

Resigned to his fate, he buzzed her up. Having it out with her now was probably for the best. He certainly couldn't afford any further encounters like the one in his office this morning. God knows what Tessa must have thought when she'd seen the blinds down and walked in to find Barbara plastered against him. In fact he doubted he needed to be God to know *exactly* what she'd thought. No wonder she'd had to stifle a laugh.

His stomach rumbled again, reminding him he needed sustenance. Especially if he had to deal with Barbara. Quickly he pressed speed dial on his phone and ordered a large pepperoni with extra jalapeño. Tomorrow he'd eat something that didn't come out of a box.

'I'm not disturbing you, am I?' she asked as she glided into the room.

He couldn't deny the woman still had a way of walking. Something to do with a slide of her hips. Whatever it was, it was downright provocative.

'I'm waiting for a pizza to be delivered,' he announced baldly.

She pouted. Just a little. 'What a shame, I should have

phoned. We could have gone out for a meal. You used to like that little Italian.'

'I don't think so,' he cut in quickly. 'Our days of having dinner out are over. We split up, remember? What do you want?'

She let out a small sigh and went to sit on his black leather sofa. The one they'd spent many nights cuddling up on. Some nights … he shook himself. Forget it. Not only did he not fancy this woman any more, she was a glaring reminder of how stupid he'd been.

'I want us to be friends again.' She patted her hand on the seat next to her. 'Come and join me.'

'I'll stick to standing.' He wasn't sure how distant he could remain if he did venture closer. His mind might have finished with her but his body wasn't always in agreement with it.

'Why?' she asked huskily, her lips now set in full sensual pout. 'Don't you think it's a shame, when we once had something so good between us, that now we can't even sit next to each other without hostility?'

He watched as she slowly crossed her legs, allowing him ample opportunity to follow their path all the way to the hem of her skirt, which had come to rest around her thighs. If that wasn't a strong enough signal she was here to reel him back in, the way she sat with her chest arched forward, displaying the curve of her full bosom, surely clinched it.

He guessed he should be flattered. Certainly a few years ago, he had been. Now he knew exactly what she saw in him, and it wasn't his looks, his personality or even his body. It was his newly achieved power.

'Perhaps you should have thought about what we had between us before you started shagging Derek,' he replied bluntly, looking down at his watch. Pizza was due in three minutes, though if she stayed much longer he'd lose his appetite. 'Look, I appreciate the overture, and that you bothered to come and deliver it in person. I can assure you that I'm perfectly capable of having a civilised, professional relationship with you at work without being told.'

'At work?' She swivelled her body round to face him. 'Is that really all you're interested in?'

He heard the quick swish of her silk undergarments as she moved and was disconcerted to realise he had a pretty good idea what she was wearing under her suit. 'Yes, Barbara. Work is all I'm interested in. Now, if you don't mind, I need to eat.'

With that he went to the door and stood, holding it open. He expected her to walk straight through it, perhaps sticking a finger up at him as she did so, but as she reached him she halted and looked up. 'I was a fool.' She stretched up to kiss him full on the lips. 'Good night, Jim.'

Silently he closed the door and leant back on it, wiping at the lipstick he knew was on his mouth. Jesus. Perhaps he shouldn't be so surprised he'd once fallen for her hook, line and sinker. Aside from being a cold, conniving, untrustworthy bitch, she was one heck of a woman.

With a sigh he shrugged off his jacket, yanked off his tie and was about to flop onto the sofa to wait for the pizza delivery when his phone rang. Glancing at the caller ID he raised his eyes heavenward. Another woman interrupting his pizza anticipation, though this was one he always had time for.

'Mum.'

'I'm surprised you can still remember the sound of my voice.'

'Subtlety was never a strong point for you, was it?' he muttered, knowing exactly where he got his bluntness from. 'And I phoned you last week.'

'But when you'd phoned you still hadn't met up with that floozy. You must have done by now.'

'You mean Barbara.'

'I mean that floozy,' she replied firmly. 'When she dared

to break my son's heart she lost the right to be called by her name. So, have you seen her?'

'I've just closed the door behind her,' he returned, smiling slightly at the conclusion he knew his mother would immediately jump to.

'James Knight, I hope you have more sense than to tangle in the sheets with that one again.'

'I do,' he reassured her. 'In fact I have so much sense I don't plan on tangling in any sheets for the foreseeable future.'

'It's not your sheets I'm interested in, it's your heart.' She paused. 'How did you feel, seeing her? Are you okay?'

First Rick, now his mother. He hadn't realised how much he'd worried those close to him. 'I'm fine, so you can stop worrying. She can't hurt me any more.' And though he crossed his fingers as he said it, he did believe what he was saying. 'Anyway, how are you and Dad?'

She was still talking when the pizza delivery came. And she was still talking when he polished off the final slice.

Chapter Five

It was Monday. Redundancy ... no. Tess shook her head and steered her mind into Helix company talk ... *restructuring* announcement day. Before she was needed in the lecture theatre for Jim's big speech though, Tess figured she just had time to kick-start what she came here to do, by a quick visit to the marketing department.

Marketing to her meant colour and craziness but the Helix marketing department wasn't as she'd imagined. No citrus coloured leather couches, or funky drinks machines. Other than a few large pharmaceutical adverts on the wall, it looked like every other department she'd seen in the building. Rows of open plan desks, with the occasional glass office.

Recognising the name of the brand manager on one of the desks, she coughed to make him aware of her presence.

'Hi, I'm Tessa, the new communications manager? We spoke on the phone the other day about me having a look at some of your marketing material for Zaplex?'

He was a young guy, couldn't have been more than twenty-five, and he had a fresh, open face. 'Sure, yes, take a seat. I've got a stack of stuff in my filing cabinet somewhere.' He opened the drawer and started to rummage through it. 'Why was it you wanted to see them again?'

Because I want to see whether you now admit it causes heart attacks, Tess thought grimly to herself. 'I'm new here and Zaplex seems to be the product everyone is talking about, so I thought I'd better check it out.' She smiled sweetly at him. 'You know, see what all the fuss is about.'

He laughed and spread the materials out in front of her. 'Well, here's a good selection. You've got the detail aid and the leave piece.'

'Whoa. I mentioned I was new, but I should say new to the industry and not just Helix. What is a detail aid exactly?'

'Sure, sorry. The detail aid is the material the representative is supposed to use when they discuss the drug with the doctor. I say supposed to, because most of the time we work our butt off producing these things only for them to remain in the rep's bag while they have a chat about the weather and dump a few pens on the doctor's desk as they leave.' He grinned. 'I should know. I was a rep myself until recently.'

'And the leave piece?'

'Literally the piece they leave with the doctor. A reminder of the conversation they've just had. Or should have had.' Again he smiled. 'Not a very original name, but then again, what do you expect from marketing.'

Tess picked up the glossy brochures. She'd expected something really gaudy, but actually the sales aid wasn't that bad. It was pink, a pretty shocking pink at that, but at least there were some scientific looking graphs in it. 'So, if I were a doctor, how would you persuade me to prescribe Zaplex?' she asked.

'You mean without giving you a pen?'

Tess smiled, surprised to find she liked the guy. He was refreshingly candid, so much so she found it hard to hold it against him that he was trying to sell a drug she still believed had killed her mother. After all, he could only work with information he'd been given.

'Well, I'd tell you that in clinical studies involving thousands of patients, Zaplex has been shown to improve survival rates of patients with late stage breast cancer compared to other more traditional treatments.'

'And the risks?' she asked, her voice suddenly croaky, probably because her heart was lodged in her mouth.

He leaned forward and took the detail aid from her, pointing to a page on side effects. 'That's the great thing about Zaplex. Sure patients still get side effects like nausea, tiredness and muscle pain, but when it comes to the more serious stuff, it's a lot less risky than the older treatments.'

'What about problems with the heart?' She knew she was pushing it, but she couldn't stop asking.

He shook his head, apparently unconcerned by her question. 'The trials didn't show any problems with heart or liver toxicity. It really is amazingly safe.' Then he put his hand over his mouth and laughed. 'Shit, I'm not allowed to say that.'

Immediately Tess froze, her heart banging violently against her ribs. 'What do you mean? Do you know something different?'

'No, no, nothing like that. It's just totally taboo to say your drug is safe in the pharmaceutical industry. It gets rammed home to us on a daily basis. You see we can't ever prove a drug is safe, so we're not allowed to say it. We can say it's well tolerated, but never safe.'

'Oh, okay.' God, surely he could hear her heart beating, it was so loud. 'Well, thanks so much for your help. It's been really interesting.'

It was a long walk back to the communications department, but Tess was still shaking when she made it back to her desk. For one heart-stopping minute she thought she'd had her answer. Of course it was never going to be that easy. If there was a cover-up, it would only be known by those much higher up in the company. Perhaps those who reported to the R&D president – or perhaps the R&D president himself.

Speaking of which … she looked at her watch and realised she had just five minutes to get over to the lecture theatre.

Four and a half minutes later, and panting from her sprint in killer heels, she cast her eyes around the packed theatre. Typical. The only seats left were on the first row. Obviously industry employees were as cowardly as students, preferring the anonymity of the back of a lecture theatre to the uncomfortable glare of the front row. Slipping quickly onto one of the spare seats, she watched as Jim strode easily up to the lectern. His manner was that of a man who felt no fear at facing a room full of intelligent, expectant employees, all eyes focussed on him. And that was despite knowing what he was about to say would hit most of his audience really, really hard.

The moment he settled his hands on the podium, the huge auditorium fell silent. Idly Tess wondered how it must feel to command that sort of authority. Something that came from far more than his job title. He had an air about him. Power, sex appeal, magnetism. Whatever it was, he seemed to have a hold over each and every one of them in the room. Herself included.

'Ladies and gentlemen.' His deep voice echoed around the theatre. It matched his looks to the letter. Rich, dark, slightly gruff. It wasn't too much of a stretch to imagine that voice rumbling in a woman's ear as he pulled her close.

Tess sat up with a jerk and determinedly tuned her mind into what he was saying.

It didn't take her long to realise he was a good orator, pacing his words, speaking slowly and clearly with a great deal of intonation. Not once did he refer to notes or read off his slides. Though he lacked the humour and charm she'd usually associated with eloquent speakers, his unique brand of energy, power and straightforward bluntness was equally as compelling. It didn't hurt that he was also devastating to look at.

'I want to take this opportunity to stress to each and every one of you how much the company values what you do and what you've achieved,' Jim concluded. 'Know that lives have been saved and quality of lives improved because of you. Because of the time, effort, expertise and passion each of you have put into the work that you do.'

Tess was astonished to find her throat tighten at his final

words. Blimey. He'd definitely taken on board her comment about talking with feeling. He hadn't needed the neon heart jumper after all.

As he finished speaking, Jim allowed his gaze to slip over the people sitting in front of him. Had they been convinced of what he was saying? Did they believe he was sympathetic to the impact the R&D reorganisation would have and understand it was the only way to secure the future for the company? Or were they thinking *what a bastard. He wants to make a name for himself and he's doing it by playing with our lives?* The faces staring back at him were grim. Whatever they were thinking, it sure as hell wasn't *he's a jolly good fellow.*

'Good job, Jim.' The head of human resources shook his hand as everybody slowly piled out. 'I think it went down okay. Put it this way, you're still alive. You haven't been lynched. You should take that as a positive.'

'Thanks for the vote of confidence.' He felt a sudden wave of tiredness. Most of the time he loved his job. Loved making big decisions, pushing back boundaries, being part of an industry that helped millions of people every year. On days like today though, when he felt like the bad guy, it was hard to remember the good stuff.

'Jim?'

Speaking of good stuff. He turned to find Tessa Johnson standing patiently by his side. Automatically his eyes dropped down to her feet. It was almost as if he couldn't wait to see what she was wearing today, though he suspected that had less to do with a fetish for ladies' shoes and more to do with the fact that looking at her feet allowed him to glance at her legs. On the other hand ... his mouth twitched in humour for the first time that day.

'Polka dots? And is that a pompom?' The black and white spotty high shoes had what he could only describe as a fluffy ball stuck on top of them. On most people they would look utterly ridiculous. On Tessa, with the long legs, trim black suit, and slender body, they were pretty damn perfect.

A faint flush spread across her cheeks. 'I thought the day was sombre enough already.'

Yeah, wasn't that the truth. 'Have you come to round me up for the press briefing?'

She nodded, perhaps a little too forcefully as a wisp of silky red hair escaped from the bun on top of her head. Without thinking he reached forward to touch it, surprised by how soft it felt. But now he was holding it, he didn't have a clue what to do with it. It felt far too personal standing there, touching her hair, so hastily he let go. 'You've lost a bit.' He pointed to the errant lock. 'I'd put it back, but I'm pretty useless when it comes to sorting out hair.'

She reached for the wayward strand and quickly and efficiently tucked it back in. 'I'm pretty useless when it comes to running research departments,' she replied with a smile.

He laughed, something he couldn't have imagined doing when he'd woken up that morning, and some of his tension eased away. 'Hell, I might be pretty useless, too,' he admitted, then realised that was the last thing he should be saying to his new communications manager. 'How do you think it went down?' he asked with a quick change of subject. 'Human enough for you?'

Tess was staring at him, her mouth slightly agape, as if he'd suddenly sprouted horns. Feeling distinctly uneasy, he coughed. 'Is that a yes or a no?' When there was still no answer he tried again. 'To me being human,' he qualified. 'Yes or no?'

'Errm.' She swallowed, hard. 'Sorry, yes, you came across very human. Not a glimpse of robot.'

'Reassuring to hear, I think.' She was still looking at him oddly when someone else came to claim his attention.

'The press call is at four p.m.,' she reminded him as he

52

started to move away. 'Can we meet ten minutes before that, in your office?'

He gave her a quick wave of his hand, indicating he'd heard her, before he was pulled into a side room.

Tess glanced again at the ticking clock, feeling more than a little apprehensive. She'd asked Jim to come early so she could take him through her briefing before they dialled in to the waiting media. It was now 3.54 p.m. Not that she was obsessing or anything, but in another minute it was officially only five minutes before the call.

'Sorry I'm late.' He eased into the room, rolling up his shirtsleeves as he sat down beside her. 'Anything you need me to be aware of?'

'Only three pages of briefing covering who's on the call and what they're likely to ask,' she snapped, totally unable to keep the edge of irritation out of her voice. Thrusting a copy of her briefing towards him, she reminded herself it didn't matter whether he mucked up the call or not. She'd done her part.

His dark eyes settled on her and she swore there was a glint of amusement in them again. What was it, *show Tess I'm actually human after all day*? Earlier he'd actually laughed. An honest to God, eyes crinkling at the corners, white teeth on full display, laugh. It had transformed him from coolly handsome to devastatingly sexy and for a few cringe worthy minutes she'd been rendered utterly speechless.

'Is this the same briefing you emailed me Friday evening?' he asked, glancing down at the neatly stapled document.

'Yes. I know it was late, and you must have a million other things to read, which is why I wanted to catch up with you now.'

'Then relax, Tessa. I've read it.'

'Oh.' That certainly took the wind out of her sails. 'Anything you need to clarify?' She looked over at the clock. 'We've got a whole three minutes.'

53

'Well, maybe I should use some of that time to tell you what a good brief it was. Succinct, yet very informative.'

She willed herself not to blush. And failed. 'I hope you're still thinking that after the call,' she mumbled awkwardly.

Once again he caught her off guard by grinning. His teeth were straight and white, his dark eyes looked browner, warmer. She was forced to remind herself that just because he could smile and look gorgeous, it didn't mean he was honest. Didn't mean he wouldn't do whatever he felt necessary to further his career. Because one thing was for certain. Jim Knight was a driven, highly ambitious man.

'Err, don't you think we should be dialling in now?'

He gave her another amused glance and Tess forced herself to stop thinking about Jim Knight and start getting on with her job.

Jim returned to his office an hour later and was just booting up his computer when Rick popped his face round the door. They hadn't had a chance to catch up since that evening at the pool.

'Can I come in, Mr President?'

'Only if you stop taking the piss out of my title.' God he hated it. What was wrong with Head, anyway?

'So, you survived.'

Jim raised an eyebrow. 'You're the second person to say that to me today. Makes me wonder if you all knew something I didn't.'

Rick moved languidly into his office and relaxed his large form against the door. 'Jim Knight, you're the only man I know who can announce large scale redundancies – good job, by the way – and still walk away with the prettiest lady in the room.'

'I ... you what?'

Laughing Rick stood up straight. 'Sexy redhead.'

'Ahh.'

54

Rick raised an eyebrow back at him.

'Sexy redhead who works for me and is therefore strictly off limits.'

'Says who?'

'Says me.' He gave his friend a steady look. 'I would have thought my track record in office romances would speak for itself.'

'Okay, I admit you had a bad experience with Barbara the Bitch, but that woman was an anomaly, not the norm.'

'I remain to be convinced.'

'Well, don't take too long over it. You're not getting any younger, you know.'

The phone on his desk buzzed. Jim was so relieved at the interruption he could have kissed the caller. 'Much as I'd love to sit here and talk to you about my love life, duty calls.'

Rick let out a laugh and backed out of the door, though not before murmuring, 'Coward.'

Jim started to smile, but a glance at the caller ID screen soon wiped it off. It was Pamela, his sweet but pretty clueless secretary. She'd come with the job. A hand me down from Derek. It had taken Jim two days of finding himself at the wrong place at the wrong time to realise he was better off doing most of his admin himself. Clearly it wasn't only in ethics and morals that Derek had lower standards than he did.

'Jim.' Her slightly breathy voice came through the speaker. 'I've got Geoff Gardner on the line. Is it okay to put him through? I don't know what he wants. Maybe I should have asked, but he is the CEO and I wasn't sure if it was right to ask the CEO—'

'Just put him through, thanks,' Jim cut in, grimacing. It was pretty damn ironic that, having just announced a slew of job losses, he couldn't magic away his secretary and replace her with a competent model. At least not without investing a great deal of time and energy, two things he didn't have much of at the moment. Still, her total incompetence aside, she did make him smile. Sometimes.

'Who is that?'

He sighed. 'Pamela, it's still me. Jim.'

'Oops. Sorry, I pressed the wrong button. I'll try again.'

'Jim.' Finally Geoff's voice came through. 'I was just calling to say congratulations. Your talk to the organisation and the media went down very well.'

He felt his shoulders relax. Funny, he hadn't realised how tense he'd been up till then.

'I've just spoken to a few members of the board,' Geoff added. 'They said you struck exactly the right balance between being business tough and people friendly. Good job.'

'Thanks, though I can't claim all the credit,' he admitted. 'We've had a new hire in corporate comms. She's the one who advised I should act more human.'

His CEO laughed. 'Is that what she told you?'

'Yep, to the letter.'

'Well, good on her. Sounds like a woman who's not afraid to speak her mind. You could do with a few people like that around you, advising you. Keeps a man from getting too full of himself.'

Didn't it just. Jim couldn't imagine the fiery communications lady ever being afraid to say what she thought. And if today was anything to go by, he was going to have to make sure he listened. Listened and maybe looked from time to time, but didn't touch. That was the key.

Chapter Six

Glancing across the crowded canteen, Tess caught sight of her new friend waving frantically from a seat in front of one of the floor to ceiling windows that made up the building. Outside, rows of regimented trees, part of the landscaped business park, swayed gently in the wind. It sure beat the sight of overflowing bins she'd had from the *Daily News* kitchenette where they'd had to make their own lunch.

After self-consciously waving back, Tess turned her attention to the contents of the well-stocked chill cabinet, picking out an egg and bacon sandwich on granary. A little bit of bad, a little bit of good. Okay the granary bread was slightly stretching the good part, but she'd join a gym next week. Clutching hold of a banana and bag of crisps as well, she wandered over to join the research scientist she'd met on the induction programme. Jeez, was it only three weeks ago now? Didn't time fly when you were knee deep in duplicity.

'Hey, great to see you.' She took a seat opposite and gave Roberta a wide smile. They'd connected on the programme, both sharing a love of chocolate and shoes.

Roberta angled her neck and took a look under the table. 'Christian Louboutin?'

Tess laughed and shot her own look under the table, catching a glimpse of the familiar red soles on her friend's feet. 'Snap.'

'I wore them especially for our lunch date,' Roberta replied on a giggle. 'It's all right for you office based people, but the labs frown on high pointy shoes.'

'So how is it in the bowels of the research department at the moment? People still reeling from the announcement?'

Roberta shrugged. 'Pretty much every person I've spoken to is resigned to going through the process. There was a lot of anger at the beginning, but it's hard to deny what's staring us in the face. We can vent all we like, but there isn't much of an alternative, I guess.' She took a sip of her coke. 'Bit of a bummer to find I have to face another job interview only a few months after the last one. Mind you, I had thought it might be last in, first out, so actually I'm quite relieved.'

'I think Jim's more interested in keeping fresh new talent,' Tess replied sympathetically.

'Jim, eh?' Her friend eyed her quizzically. 'To us in the labs he's God, or at least sir.'

Tess rolled her eyes. 'Well, he told me to call him Jim, so I do.'

'And what's *Jim* like? As sexy close up as he looks from afar?'

'Two very different questions. The answer to the first is ...' she trailed off. What was he like, exactly? If she'd had to answer that question last week she'd have said he was cold and arrogant, but now? 'He's tough, but fair, I think. Direct, certainly. Happy to praise. Listens.' She remembered him at the press briefing. How quickly he'd reacted on his feet to the questions. The way he'd obviously read the detail of her brief before the meeting. 'Plus he's incredibly sharp,' she added finally.

'And the answer to the second question?' Roberta prompted, her big hazel eyes watching with undisguised interest.

Tess had to laugh. Women might knock men for their obsession with bikini-clad babes, but they were quick to appreciate the attributes of a handsome, well-built male. And, she thought ruefully, she was no exception. 'The answer is yes, he is just as sexy close up.'

Roberta grinned. 'I bet beneath those sharp suits he has a pretty impressive body, too. Rumour has it he's into triathlons. I'm thinking you can't do one of those unless you're pretty fit.'

The news didn't surprise Tess. She, too, had gained an impression of thick, hard muscle lying under the R&D president's tailored shirts. 'I wonder if he goes to a gym,' she thought out loud.

'Why, planning on attacking him in the showers?'

Tess looked askance at her new friend. 'Not quite my style. But I am planning on joining a gym. I wondered where the nearest one was around here.'

'You just want to catch sight of him in his swimming trunks,' Roberta insisted.

Laughing, Tess shook her head. 'While that thought certainly has its merits, the reverse, *him* seeing *me* in my costume, absolutely terrifies me.'

'Why's that? You're long and slender.' Roberta looked down at her own, slightly overweight body. 'It's people like me who need to worry.'

Sleeping with you is like sleeping with a bag of bones. Even now Tess could remember word for word the insult hurled at her by her first boyfriend. 'Having curves is a good thing, trust me,' she replied quietly. Shaking off the memories, she reached for her bag of crisps. 'Anyway, speaking of bodies, have any caught your eye in the labs?'

It was Roberta's turn to roll her eyes. 'You know that image of the mad scientist? Crazy hair, crumpled lab coat, wild eyes? It's totally true.'

The rest of the lunch break passed away in laughter and giggles. Some good, honest people work here, Tess thought with a sizeable amount of guilt as she waved Roberta goodbye. People she was beginning to like, which was a dangerous way to think because she wasn't actually here to be the communications manager. The Helix employee. She was here to find out if the company had conspired to kill patients with advanced breast cancer. Like her mother.

A fleeting vision of her darling mum, smiling over at her, swum before Tess's eyes. After hastily blinking the image away, she made a snap decision and walked purposefully towards the office of Frank, the chief medical officer she'd met last week.

'Tessa.' Frank looked up as he saw her standing outside his door. 'Come on in. How can I help?'

She drew in a deep breath. 'I was wondering if you have a moment to clarify something with me. I'm having a bit of difficulty getting my head around the whole research and development process. You know, after a molecule is identified, how does the company decide which trials to undertake? And what happens to all that data?'

He laughed and pushed back from his desk. 'How many hours have you got?'

Okay, he was right. Her question was far too broad. She gave herself a moment to regroup. 'Sorry, that was a bit like asking for a quick answer to how the universe was created, wasn't it?' She let out a small laugh. 'And actually the basics of the drug development process were covered in the induction programme. I know there are different phases. Phase one is in volunteers, not patients. Phase two, in patients, is often used to define the dose. Phase three is the largest and after that, if it goes well, the company can apply for a license. Then I think there's a phase four, which is when a drug is on the market but you want to gain more evidence of its efficacy, or expand its license. It's just, I was thinking ...' She gave herself a mental kick. *Come on Tess, spit it out.* 'I was thinking that if I could look at the route that one of Helix's drugs had taken through this process, you know, as an example, then maybe it would come to life more.'

'Well, yes, sure.' Frank scratched his head and Tess prayed it wasn't a *what the hell is this woman really after* scratch and more of a *how do I quickly get her out of my office* scratch. 'I guess the easiest way is to look through a product monograph. That is basically a summary of all the information on a product, including details of the entire development process from the identification of the target molecule, to the ADME toxicology tests, sorry that's absorption, distribution …'

Frank continued to drone on, but Tess tuned out. The pharmaceutical industry might well be the scandalous den of iniquity the media made out, but it also involved lots of boring long words she didn't understand, or even want to understand.

'That sounds great,' she interrupted, smiling to take the edge off her rudeness. 'Do you have a copy of the monograph for Zaplex?'

He frowned. 'I'm not sure. The marketing team will be able to get you a copy, but I might have one around here somewhere.'

His office space was a disaster area. Folders and papers on every available surface. She didn't reckon much to his chances of finding one.

'Ah, here you go.' Like a proud father, he handed her a glossy looking brochure he'd pulled from under a now teetering pile of folders.

Tess took one look at the cover and her heart sank. This was just a marketing brochure. There was no way she was going to find anything in that. 'Right, thanks.' She tried to look suitably pleased. 'It looks like a great summary, but what if I wanted to see all the studies, and not just a selection?'

He looked bemused. 'Why on earth would you want to do that? I mean, I admire your keenness, but really, the monograph is pretty comprehensive. It lists out all the main trials.'

'Yes, I'm sure it does, but what about the other trials that aren't in here? Where would I find those?' Immediately she'd said the words she wanted to retract them. What had started out as a general question had now become far too specific. Bugger.

Frank narrowed his eyes. 'Well, the clinical team use a database to keep track of all the Helix studies, but you can't really want to look through that, can you?'

Yes, she screamed, but thankfully only to herself. To Frank, she gave the reply she knew he was looking for. 'Good heavens, no. That sounds far too comprehensive for what I need.' She waved the monograph at him. 'I'm sure this will be just the ticket.'

Thanking him for his time, she made a hasty exit. Maybe her spur of the moment decision to question Frank hadn't been such a good idea, after all. She'd come perilously close to making him suspicious. From now on, she'd have to tread a lot more thoughtfully and far less aggressively.

It was just after seven p.m. when Jim decided to call it a day. It had been a long, crappy slog of a day, one that at times had looked like it would never end. He'd started with a two-hour strategy meeting, filled with the obligatory hot air and little substance, and ended with an even more tedious session on budgets and finance. It was hard to know which was worse, but he was certain he'd rather have his molars extracted without anaesthesia to either of them.

Turning off his computer he stuffed it into his rucksack and trudged wearily down to the lockers to change. Today he was cycling home, something he tried to do three times a week, weather and meetings permitting. The fifteen-mile ride in the morning cleared the cobwebs, allowing him space to think. Plus it clocked up some much-needed training. The fifteen-mile cycle back home, however, that was something else. Often it was dark, usually it was late and unfailingly all he actually wanted to do was climb into a warm car and relax.

He was rounding the corner of the outside of the building,

heading towards the bike rack, when he collided with someone also leaving the building, only walking a lot slower. Probably on account of the incredibly high shoes she was wearing.

'Oh, bugger, I'm sorry.'

Tessa. She'd come out of nowhere and was now stumbling back on those crazy shoes. Turquoise today, without a pompom but with a neat little bow. Jesus, he *was* getting a shoe fetish. Quickly he reached out to steady her.

'Hey.' He held onto her forearm, very aware of how slim it felt under his large hand. If he wasn't careful he'd snap her in two. She was an intriguing mixture of fragility, steel and fire. Not a combination he'd come across before. Barbara had fire and steely determination but she'd never been fragile. Never stirred in him a desire to protect or nourish. Not like Tessa did, standing there with her hair coming out of her bun and her Bambi legs slightly akimbo. But though on paper she reported to Georgina, practically she worked *for* him. Imagine the rumours when that one turned sour. *My lecherous boss ...*

He shuddered and let go of her arm, though he remained very aware of how close he was still standing. Close enough that he could see the smattering of freckles across her nose, the slightly flushed cheeks, the bright sparkly eyes. He'd also inhaled an appreciative lungful of her scent. Not being much of a perfume man he couldn't put a name to it, but whatever it was, he had this bizarre desire to undo her prim knot and bury his nose in the fiery red hair to see if that smelt of her, too.

Abruptly he reeled back his thoughts. Not how he should be thinking of an employee. Especially when standing next to her in tight cycling shorts.

'Are you off home?' she asked, then bit her lip and shook her head. 'Sorry, dumb question. I mean, you're not exactly dressed for another meeting, are you?' She let out a soft, self-mocking laugh.

'Well, not the type I usually attend.'

She held his gaze. As the corners of her sexy mouth twitched upwards, Jim found himself catching his breath. God, he wanted to kiss her.

Snapping his head away he exhaled slowly and nodded over to the bikes. 'Well, I'd better get on my way.' He started to move then turned back and frowned. 'What are you still doing here anyway? Are we working you too hard?'

'Uh, no. I've already been home,' she admitted, avoiding his eyes. 'Then I realised I'd left my computer at work and there was something I hadn't finished, so I had to come back and get it.'

He noticed her clutching the laptop under her arm, along with ... really? 'Is that the Zaplex clinical monograph?'

Immediately she flushed. 'Err, yes. I, umm, well, I thought I'd read up a bit on one of the products.'

He laughed. 'Wow, you must be keen if you're prepared to wade through that.' She smiled, though once again she avoided his gaze, which unnerved him because she usually had no problem looking him straight in the eye, even when she was cross with him. Which meant – hell, maybe she knew he was attracted to her? Maybe his face had telegraphed the fact that he'd nearly kissed her? It was no bloody wonder she was looking like she wanted to run as far as she could in the opposite direction. 'Right then.' Jim hitched the rucksack onto his back. 'If you're okay, I'd better be off. Otherwise it'll be time for me to head back again. Don't work too late.'

He marched over to the bike stand and, after wrestling with the lock, jerked his thousand pound bike far too forcefully out of the rack. It was going to be a long, long ride home.

Chapter Seven

When Tess arrived at her desk the following morning she found a curt note stuck to her monitor. *Meet me in my office, Jim.* Clearly R&D presidents didn't need to use the word *please*.

The note didn't help her already frazzled temper. Not that it was Jim's fault she'd had to go back to work last night to pick up the Zaplex monograph she'd stupidly left on her desk, along with her computer. Or that, after the embarrassment of Jim seeing her with it, she'd then spent the evening wading through the damn thing, horrified by how many studies there were. And none titled *The Study that Shows Zaplex Causes Heart Attacks*. If she had to go through each one in turn in order to see if there was anything that signalled heart issues, it was going to take her forever. Again, not Jim's fault.

But helping to cover up issues with Helix's major new cancer treatment? *That* could still be his fault. He might have only been R&D president for two months, but he'd been around when Helix had been developing Zaplex.

With a heavy sigh, she swung back round and walked up the spiral staircase to the top floor. It was only as she climbed the stairs that she started to feel a twinge of anxiety. What if Jim wanted to see her because he'd somehow discovered why she'd joined Helix? Maybe Frank had realised that her request had been a little odd yesterday. Maybe he'd spoken to Jim about it?

By the time she reached Jim's floor, her heart was beating like the clappers, her stomach churning and her hands starting to sweat. She felt like she was walking to the gallows. It was hard to know which was most upsetting. The thought of being kicked out before she'd achieved what she came for, or the thought of achieving that aim and having employees who'd been kind to her, who'd trusted her, finding out she was a double crossing liar.

Clutching at the railing that overlooked the atrium, Tess took in a deep breath. No. She wasn't going to feel guilty, not when all she wanted was to find out the truth. She had a moral right to find out how her mother had died. If anyone should be feeling guilty, it was the Helix employees who'd knowingly hidden damaging trial results.

Feeling slightly better, and ignoring the fact that her legs were shaking like those of a newborn foal, she made her way towards Jim's office. As she neared it she heard him on the phone, his voice crackling with barely controlled anger. Heart in her mouth, she listened in.

Relief crashed through her when she realised whatever it was that had rattled his cage, it definitely wasn't her.

With a final grunt of exasperation he flung down the phone and beckoned her in.

'We've got a situation,' he ground out, firmly back into cold and authoritative mode. He nodded at her to shut the door. 'I've briefed Georgina on the phone. She's coming in but she'll be late. I thought I'd give you a heads up.' He thrust a newspaper article at her.

Scanning the press was usually her first job of the day, but obviously someone else had beaten her to it this morning. Reaching for the paper she looked at the circled article. *Drug costs spiral – is this why?* Whoops. One glance at the reporter's name and she had to suppress a smile. She knew the guy well enough to know he absolutely had it in for the pharmaceutical industry. In fact she remembered sharing grudges together once over a few drinks.

Raising her eyes she found Jim's dark angry ones staring back at her. A sharp reminder of whose side she was supposed to be on. 'Is the article as damning as it looks?'

'Read it, then you tell me.'

She took a moment to skim the first few lines. 'Well, the

first paragraph is pretty standard for an industry slur piece.'
The reporter had gone into detail of how the pharmaceutical
industry continues to bribe doctors by taking them abroad,
under the guise of a scientific conference, and plying them
with fine wine and food. 'Ouch, but that photograph isn't
helpful.'

'They aren't Helix reps.'

'Good, but even so, a picture of a crowd of doctors
lurching out of a nightclub, congress badges still round
their necks, being helped into a waiting minibus by what
are clearly company representatives.' She made a passable
attempt at a wince. 'It doesn't do much for the reputation of
the industry as a whole.'

'It gets better,' he said, heavy with sarcasm. 'Read the third
paragraph.'

'*This paper has even heard rumours that one
pharmaceutical company, Helix Pharmaceuticals, thinks
nothing of entertaining doctors in lap dancing clubs. Using
sex to sell drugs. Is this the action of a responsible company?*'
She winced for real at that one. 'Umm, I suppose you ...
sorry, I mean Helix, we, should be grateful the editor didn't
use that second sentence as a headline.'

'I don't think grateful describes how I'm feeling right now.'
His eyes blazed and his body almost vibrated with anger.

'No.' Quickly she scanned the final paragraph, which
went on to state that whilst the pharmaceutical industry
claimed it ploughed its profits back into research for the care
of patients, evidence suggested much of it actually went into
softening up doctors so they would prescribe their medicines.

'I'm going to need a briefing document and Q&A,' Jim
told her grimly. 'I have no doubt we'll be contacted for
comment, but I want to know exactly what *does* go on in
this company before I speak to anyone from the press.'

'Do you think Helix is entertaining doctors like this then?'
she asked, surprised by how ragged he looked. As if this was

more than just another issue to be dealt with. As if the article had really hurt him.

He stared at her with those dark, almost bottomless eyes. 'I hope not.'

She stood to go, but found she was unable to move. As if her legs were glued to the floor and her eyes transfixed on him. In a flash she recalled the sight of him yesterday, his muscular body in those tight, tight cycling shorts. He was the tall, dark, handsome female fantasy. Powerful, athletic, magnetic. Her eyes dropped to the sensual curve of his mouth, and involuntarily she ran her tongue over her lips, as if she could taste that mouth on hers. Taste his kiss.

Then she realised he was still looking at her. Watching her lick her lips. Suddenly his eyes weren't so dark. They glowed, like molten lava, as the air around them crackled with a sexual energy. Awkwardly she cleared her throat. 'Right, sorry. You need a Q&A. I'm on it.'

Jim watched as Tessa darted off. God, had he done it again? Following last night's debacle, when he'd been moments away from actually kissing her – just perfect coming from the bloody R&D president – he'd been hyper aware of remaining detached. Distant. But then she'd licked her extremely soft looking lips. After that he'd not had a chance in hell of keeping his thoughts to himself. Resulting in her scampering out of his office like a scared rabbit in stilettos.

He sighed and dragged a hand down his face. No doubt her lip licking had been in anticipation of a sticky doughnut on her desk. Not his tongue jammed down her throat.

Well, he'd just have to add that to his nightmare list this morning. The one entitled *I should have stayed in bed*. Top of the list was the continuing trauma of making hundreds of employees redundant. He'd been privy, thanks to the open plan, to several conversations that had included his name next to the words: *heartless, ruthless, cold and/or git.*

Next up was the newspaper article, which was crappy enough even if it was just speculation, but he had this terrible sense of foreboding that Helix hadn't moved beyond the shoddy sales gimmicks the reporter had taken great delight in describing. The pharmaceutical industry in general had changed a lot over the last few years. Dynamic, forward thinking companies, like the one he'd spent the last two years working in, no longer took the view that they should sell *to* a doctor. They wanted to work *with* a doctor. From what he'd seen, Helix reps weren't even trying to sell to the doctors. Indirectly, they were trying to bribe them.

He thrust the article onto his in tray. How long would it take him to drag Helix kicking and screaming into the future? And would he keep his job long enough to make that happen?

With a resigned sigh he picked up his phone. 'Pamela. Find out when Georgina's due to arrive and set up a meeting with her, Frank …' he hesitated. No, he didn't need Tessa. Not if Georgina was coming. 'And myself as soon as you can.'

'Tea and biscuits?'

What?

Obviously he'd said that out loud because when she spoke again, her voice was slightly defiant. 'Would you like tea and biscuits with your meeting? I can arrange with catering to send up some drinks. Probably you want coffee, as well as tea. Usually I order biscuits, too, but if you prefer I can ask them to do sandwiches, or cakes …'

His heavy breathing over the phone finally silenced her. Gathering all his control, he didn't yell the words *I'm not having a bloody tea party*. 'No. Thanks.' He wondered if she could hear him grinding his teeth. 'I just need Frank and Georgina. We can meet in my office.' And get our own flaming drinks.

Later that day Georgina and Frank arrived in Jim's office to discuss the press briefing, set up for an hour's time. Oh, and

Tessa was there, too. Apparently she wanted to listen in so she had the background to help with the call. Very diligent of her, but it now meant Jim had to sit through another meeting while trying not to look at her lips. Or her gorgeous blue eyes, or her long, graceful neck. Thank goodness the subject of the meeting was serious enough to retain most of his attention.

'I'm happy to do the press call,' Frank was saying. 'It's my responsibility.'

'No, I'll do it.' Jim quickly scanned through Tessa's brief. 'It will show the press how seriously we're taking this. To be honest, it isn't the call that bothers me. It's how to cut this type of behaviour out from the roots of this organisation.'

'Well, the UK team say they haven't actually taken any doctors to a lap dancing club.'

Jim raised his eyes and drilled them into Frank. 'Umm, funny how they worded that. Not "we don't entertain doctors in any way that's inappropriate", but "we haven't taken any doctors to a lap dancing club". Tell me, Frank, can you can sit there with your hand on your heart and tell me Helix representatives have never taken doctors out to restaurants or clubs they shouldn't? Never given them a gift they know is outside the industry code?'

Frank shifted uncomfortably in his chair. 'Well, no.'

'I thought not.' Jim sat back and clasped his hands behind his head. 'This company needs a shake-up regarding what's acceptable practice and what isn't. I'm putting it down as an agenda item for the executive team meeting tomorrow. For now, let's deal with this issue.'

'Okay then.' Georgina picked up the brief. 'The reporter states in his article that it was *rumoured* Helix have taken doctors to lap dancing clubs. If he actually had any evidence to back that claim up, he'd have used it. So I suggest we deny the allegation and keep any comment to a minimum.'

'If you think I'm going to sit on that call and deny this company ever entertains doctors in this way, when we all know damn well it probably does, you've got another thing coming, Georgina.' His jaw was clenched so tight he nearly couldn't get the words out. And why was Tessa looking so damn surprised? Had she expected him to deny everything, too?

'Jesus, Jim, if you don't quash the rumours it'll be tantamount to admitting we did it.' Frank was getting flustered now. 'We'll have the industry watchdog down on us like a tonne of bricks.'

'Relax, Frank. I'm not going to drop us in it, but I'm not going to lie either.' Jim stood up. 'I'm off to stretch my legs and get some caffeine.' He looked over to Georgina and then shifted his gaze to Tessa. 'I'll see you back here for the call.'

'He's not a happy bunny,' Georgina remarked as she watched Jim's retreating back.

Tess gave Georgina a sideways glance. Describing Jim as a bunny was a bit like calling a panther a pussycat. 'I guess this sort of thing is embarrassing for him.'

All the way through the meeting she'd sensed his rage. He'd been like a tightly coiled spring, ready to go off at a moment's notice. It was part of his attraction, that energy, that drive. Part of the Jim Knight magnetism she was becoming all too conscious of.

Georgina nodded. 'Jim's embarrassed, certainly. No one wants to face the press when they've been caught with their pants down, so to speak. But I think it's more than that. I think he's finally realising Helix isn't in the shape he thought it was.'

'What was the last R&D president like? Derek, wasn't it?'

'Smooth is the word that comes instantly to mind. Quite the charmer. One of those people who are a triumph of looks over substance.'

'Did they get on?' And, yes, Tess was definitely on a fishing expedition now. It seemed her fascination with Jim Knight knew no bounds. 'I mean, I know Jim used to work here until he left two years ago. Presumably he reported to Derek then, but I sense they're two very different people.'

They'd started wandering back towards Georgina's office. As her boss strode briskly on ahead and opened her office door, Tess wondered, for a frantic moment, if she'd pushed too far. But instead of closing the door in her face, Georgina beckoned her in and shut it behind them. 'No, Derek and Jim didn't get on,' she replied quietly. 'Not in the end.' Georgina walked to her desk and perched on top of it. 'I'm only telling you this because I don't want you to put your foot in it. Jim used to go out with Barbara.'

Tess watched her expectantly, nodding. She knew that bit already. It was the rest she was interested in.

'There are rumours about how it ended, though they're not always reliable. Suffice to say that one minute they were in a steady relationship, the next Jim had resigned and Barbara had taken up with Derek.'

'Ouch.'

'Exactly. Jim didn't say anything at the time – he's always been intensely private – but it wasn't hard to work out who had dumped whom. Not when you added together the rumours and the grim scowl on Jim's face when he was forced to come across her. Not surprisingly, he didn't hang around for long.'

'But now he's back,' Tess supplied, finding herself more interested than she wanted to be. 'It must be hard, with Barbara still working here.'

'Jim's not the type to let his emotions interfere with his work. I expect it's all water under the bridge now. Besides, he's got his eyes on a more important target.'

'Who's that?'

Georgina smiled. 'What, not who. It's common knowledge Jim and Geoff have a good rapport. As long as Jim doesn't do anything stupid, it's a pretty good bet Geoff will recommend

Jim as the next CEO when he decides to call it a day.' She looked up at the clock on the wall. 'Enough of this gossiping. If you're not careful you'll be late for the press briefing. The mood he's in at the moment, Jim will skin you alive.'

Tess didn't doubt it, so she set off back to his office as fast as her Jimmy Choos would allow her. Why had she chosen today to wear these gorgeous babies? As she scurried, rather ungainly, along the corridor, she mused on Georgina's last comment. Jim for CEO. It certainly made sense.

A small sigh of disappointment escaped her as it all came clear. First the reorganisation. Then the determination to clean up the public image of the company. It was to further his career. To prove he was capable of making big, bold decisions. Not because it was the right thing to do.

What a shame.

But what a good job she realised it now, before she started to like him.

When she arrived back at his office he was already sitting at his table, a steaming cup of coffee in front of him. His attention was focussed on the briefing document, his face unusually pensive. Sombre almost. As if all the vitality he'd carried earlier had drained from him.

'Do you need a moment? You look like you've had the stuffing taken out of you.'

His head snapped up in surprise, making her realise how personal her remark might have appeared. 'Sorry, maybe that was a bit too—'

'Honest? No, I've told you before, I appreciate candour.' He started to shake his head and laugh at the same time. 'Even if it does mean someone telling me I look like shit.'

She started to protest. After all, *shit* was a long, long way from how he was looking. 'I didn't say that.' Then she caught his eyes, his thoroughly amused brown eyes, and realised that when it came down to the wire, it was exactly what she'd said.

They shared a smile and unbidden, a warm glow shot through her. Help, she really must stop making him laugh, because when he did, heaven help her, when he laughed, her heart nearly stopped beating.

'Come in and take a seat,' he said, motioning to the chair opposite him. 'I was just contemplating the call. What's your take on this, Tessa? How do you think I should approach it?'

At last, a question she didn't need to think about. 'Honestly. The worst thing you can do to a reporter is avoid answering the question. They're trained to sniff out a fudged answer a mile away. The pharmaceutical industry has a pretty bad image with the press, so already they're expecting you to be evasive. Show them you're different.'

'Umm.' He gave her a long, level look. 'Tell me, why did you join this big, bad industry? You were a reporter before, weren't you?'

Gulp. The bottom fell out of her stomach and for a split second, Tess couldn't hold his gaze. But then the journalist in her leapt into action. The one who'd learnt how to bluster her way through hundreds of difficult situations over the years. She raised her chin, looked him in the eye and spoke as close to the truth as she dared. 'I wanted the challenge of something new. Plus I was interested to see if the pharmaceutical industry really is as bad as it's made out to be.'

He nodded, seemingly satisfied with her answer. 'And what is your impression so far?'

'I'm not sure,' she replied, which, oddly, was the truth. 'I haven't been here long enough to judge, though I can see you're determined to address some of the issues.'

His expression hardened. 'Not some, Tessa, all. This should be an industry people are proud to work for. When I think of everything a company like Helix achieves ...' He shook his head. 'That's what the papers should be discussing. Not shoddy behaviour that belongs in the Dark Ages.'

His eyes flicked over his watch, a sporty, masculine

timepiece that looked just about perfect on his wrist, set against tanned skin and a dusting of short, dark hairs. Because he had his shirtsleeves rolled up, she could see the hairs continued up his muscular forearm …

'Right, shall we dial in?'

Tess jumped. Oh boy, the press call. Hastily she opened up the line.

Jim dealt confidently with each of the questions fired at him. He was assertive without appearing cocky. Straight talking and honest rather than smooth and slick.

'I'm not saying this company has never undertaken such activities,' he told them candidly. 'We certainly need to put up our hands and admit that mistakes have been made in the past, but we're fighting to put things right. I ask you, please, to judge us not on what you might have seen before, but on what you'll see over the next few years.'

It was a rare touch of humility from a man in his position and Tess could easily imagine the reporters on the other end raising their eyebrows in surprise. Perhaps even re-considering the hatchet job they'd been planning. But was what she was seeing and hearing real? Was Jim a genuinely decent person, trying to do a difficult job? Or did he simply have an innate skill when it came to conveying sincerity? A skill that hid a different truth.

When the final question had been asked and firmly answered, Jim ended the call and pushed back on his chair, stretching his arms behind his head as she'd seen him do previously at the end of a meeting. She watched as his muscles bunched and relaxed underneath his crisp white shirt and experienced a sudden flush of raw, sexual heat.

Jeez, he might be an operator, clever enough to tell the press exactly what they wanted to hear, but right now it was hard to see anything other than a supremely attractive male. One who unsettled her more than any other man she'd ever met.

'Tessa?'

His deep voice brought her back to planet earth. To her mortification she realised she'd been staring at him. Flushing, she dropped her eyes. 'Well, that went well,' she mumbled, shuffling up her papers.

'We'll find out tomorrow, when we read what they write,' he countered dryly. 'Are you all right? You seem a bit distracted.'

That was one word to describe it. 'Sorry, I'm just a bit tired, I guess.' Even as she said the words, she cringed because he'd been the one with the tough day. 'I'm betting you know how I feel.'

'Because when you came in you thought I looked like—'

'Can we not mention that again?' she interrupted hastily. 'Please? And anyway you can still have the stuffing knocked out of you and look good.' Really, why couldn't she just shut up?

This time he looked more bemused than amused, so she decided to get out before she said anything more incriminating. 'Well, I'll leave you in peace.'

Jim found he couldn't take his eyes off Tess as she turned and walked out of his office. From the top of her glorious red hair, to her surprisingly understated but still amazingly high shoes, he watched until she was out of sight. She was a mass of contradictions and he was, alarmingly, totally fascinated by her. Cool and professional at work, yet she wore fun, sexy shoes. Forthright and outspoken, yet at times, like just now, she flushed like a schoolgirl. He found his interest in her stretching beyond the simple wonder of how she would feel, naked, pressed against him. Now he was musing about her as a person. What made her tick? He found it incredible to think she'd joined the industry just because she was curious. Who changed their career direction on a whim like that? It was mind-boggling.

'Fancy a beer?' Rick's tall frame wandered into his office.

Grateful for the interruption, and the offer, Jim powered down his computer. 'Are we working out first?'

'Sure.'

He quickly packed up and they walked to the car park together.

'Seen much of that sexy redhead today?' Rick asked as they neared their cars, wiggling his eyebrows in a suggestive fashion.

'If you mean Tessa, my communications manager, then yes.' While Jim fumbled with putting his key into the lock of his E-type, Rick casually aimed his fob at his BMW and pressed.

'Care to elaborate?' Rick asked, smiling smugly as Jim continued to struggle.

'We've been *working* together.' At last the blasted door opened. 'Some bullshit newspaper article about the sins of the pharmaceutical industry.'

'Ah, yes, even in the IT department we've heard about that. Sounds like trouble.'

'It is,' Jim grunted, chucking his briefcase onto the passenger seat. 'Especially as I'm pretty certain the content of the article wasn't all bullshit.'

'Bugger. So who are you planning on giving hell this time?'

'I'm going to start with the executive team tomorrow and then work my way down.'

Rick whistled. 'I'm sure glad IT don't fall under your leadership.' As he turned to walk towards his car, he glanced back over his shoulder. 'And don't think you've managed to distract me from the latest on the communications lady.'

Climbing into the driver's seat, Jim let out a deep sigh. Partly because he didn't want to talk about something that wasn't going to happen. Mostly because he *wanted* something to happen.

Chapter Eight

Jim chose to cycle to work the following morning. Exercise fired him up, which was exactly the frame of mind he needed to approach the executive team meeting. The so-called leaders had let Helix wallow for far too long. It was time to shake things up. Even if that meant pissing them all off, his CEO included.

Sitting at the head of the long boardroom table, Geoff Gardner looked down at his meeting agenda before nodding over at Jim. 'The first item is yours, I believe.'

Slowly Jim got to his feet. Inside he was pumped up, ready for a fight, but shouting and yelling weren't going to get him what he wanted. Not in the boardroom. It was a lesson he'd learnt the hard way. Now he tended to go with logical, reasoned argument. At least until his patience ran out.

'Yesterday Helix was in the newspapers for all the wrong reasons,' he began, easing one hand casually into his trouser pocket and resting the other on the back of his chair. 'Instead of writing about our latest innovations, the press were wasting column inches describing how we, in common with other pharma companies, still continue to bribe doctors to prescribe our medicines.'

'It must have been a slow news day.'

The words came from Jack Webber, head of the commercial side of the organisation and a royal pain in the arse. Jim glowered at him. 'The reputation of this company is trashed in the press and that's all you have to say?'

'Oh, come on, Jim.' Jack shrugged his shoulders and turned to the rest of the leadership team. 'This sort of thing happens all the time. Not much going on in the world so a reporter unearths a previous story about the evil pharmaceutical industry and embellishes it with a new photograph. As

I understood it, the article was a general one, not aimed specifically at Helix.'

'And that makes it right, does it?' Already Jim felt his stomach knotting with anger, and they were only on round one. When he'd made the decision to go with reasoned logic, he hadn't factored in dealing with Jack the Prick.

'Well, of course I'd rather they were talking about how many patients Zaplex saved last year, but hey, this is the real world. You don't always get what you want.'

'Maybe not, but you tend to get what you deserve.' Jim could feel his voice getting lower. If he wasn't careful it would soon be a growl. Moving to the front of the room, he drew in a deep breath and dug deep for his inner calm.

'We all saw the article, Jim,' cut in Geoff. 'Presumably you had a reason for bringing it to this meeting. Now would be a good time to get to that.'

'Okay.' Feeling the weight of his CEO's simmering impatience, Jim got straight to the point. 'The reason I raised it today is that we can't allow this type of behaviour to tarnish the reputation of Helix any longer. This report didn't carry a photograph of Helix representatives at the club, but it could have. Next time it might, because we all know activities like this still go on in this organisation, despite industry regulations clearly stipulating they shouldn't. We also know such behaviour is morally and ethically wrong.'

'Look, Jim.' Jack spread out his hands, as if trying to placate an unruly child. Automatically, Jim's spine stiffened. 'We hear what you're saying, and of course in an ideal world we wouldn't have to advertise our medicines at all. Doctors would simply prescribe them because they knew they were the best. Sadly we don't exist in that idealised nirvana. We have to promote our medicines to make money so we can invest in finding more. You should know. It's your guys who spend the money.'

'Yeah, we spend the money.' Alarmed to find his hands

itching to settle round Jack Webber's throat, Jim moved back, leaning against the wall in an effort to look nonchalant. 'But it comes to something when the commercial president practically admits he can't sell our medicines without resorting to bribery.'

Jack slammed his hand down on the table. 'Now wait a minute, I didn't say that.'

'Jim.' Again it was Geoff who interjected, sending Jim an icy glare with a clear warning to back off.

Jim nodded, accepting the rebuke. 'You're right, Jack. You didn't say that, and I know you realise it's wrong to bribe doctors.' *Well, you do now, you slimeball,* Jim thought to himself as his eyes swept round the room. 'So actually we're all on the same page. What I'm proposing is we make our stance on this much, much clearer by stamping out any activity that could possibly constitute a bribe. In other words we change our policy so we no longer offer so-called educational items to doctors, like pens and stress balls. Nor do we fund jollies to scientific conferences where we know damn well the doctors will spend more of their time in bars and on golf courses than in the scientific sessions.'

His statement was met with a deathly silence. Never mind hearing a pin drop, he probably could have heard a feather land on a mattress a mile away. Still, perhaps they were marvelling at how absolutely right he was. And perhaps there really were aliens on Mars.

'The industry code allows the provision of goods or services relevant to the practice of medicine.' Geoff finally spoke into the silence.

'I know, but I'm proposing we go beyond what the industry code states is acceptable behaviour. That way there is no opportunity for misunderstandings.'

'Are you out of your tiny mind?'

Jim had been wondering how long it would take Jack to find his voice. As predicted, the commercial president was almost apoplectic with anger, his too smooth cheeks flushed, his eyes spitting fire.

'Can you imagine what that would do to our sales?' Jack hissed. 'For God's sake man, you're acting as if we're the only pharmaceutical company offering such items. We're not. All the others are doing it too because, guess what, in most countries, it's within the regulations. The UK has moved to being a bit stricter, but then the ABPI have always been a po-faced bunch.' Jack shook his head and glared back at him. 'What you're proposing will leave the Helix sales force at a huge disadvantage.' He let rip a hollow laugh. 'Hell, we might as well simply get rid of them, too. Follow on from the hatchet job you're doing on your own part of the organisation.'

Hatchet job? Jim had to hand it to the bastard, he knew exactly where to aim his shot. 'Perhaps it is time the commercial side of the business was looked at,' he replied tersely. 'I'm sure it would also benefit from restructuring.'

'Gentlemen.' The authoritative, and clearly annoyed, voice of the CEO cut across their arguments. 'Let us not forget, we're all on the same side.'

Moving away from the wall, Jim forced his shoulders to relax and focussed his gaze back on the room. 'Yes, we are all on the same side. So I'm sure you, too, can see why we need to stamp out any activities not directly in the interests of science or patients.' He deliberately turned to Jack. 'Just because other companies do this too, doesn't make it right. The so-called entertainment we've just witnessed splashed across the tabloids, and the associated vitriolic press that goes with it, undermines the hard work this company does. When we give journalists the chance to knock us with cheap gimmicks like this, we're also helping them forget we bring new medicines to patients. That we actually save lives.' He let out a long, deep breath. 'Surely we can sell our products on the quality of the medicines themselves, and not the tacky extras that accompany them.'

'Tacky extras?' Jack was almost foaming at the bit. 'You arrogant bastard. We offer some doctors the opportunity to attend a scientific congress to further their understanding of the disease. We also provide items that support health professionals in their business, like a stethoscope or a notepad.'

Jim raised his eyebrow, itching to call the man a liar, but knowing his career would be down the toilet if he did. He'd seen with his own eyes how few doctors actually attended the scientific sessions at a conference. He also had a drawer full of flashy paperweights, stress balls and other desk toys designed not to support the doctor in his work, but to remind him to prescribe Helix's drug next time he got out his prescription pad. Good business, maybe, but pretty poor taste.

Geoff put up his hand, signalling the end of the discussion. 'Jim, you've made a bold proposal, but we can't decide on the right or wrongs without a proper analysis. Have you looked into how much this could cost the company in terms of sales?'

Jim walked back to his seat, mentally kicking himself. He'd gone about this half-cocked. He should have anticipated that one. 'No, Geoff, I haven't,' he admitted. Raising his head, he looked his CEO directly in the eye. 'Then again, sometimes we have to make decisions that aren't based on money. Sometimes it's about doing the right thing.'

Geoff's eyes hardened. 'I'm not sure the shareholders will agree with you on that one.'

'With respect, it's as hard to quantify the revenue impact of these sales gimmicks as it is to quantify the revenue impact of an improved company reputation.'

Geoff nodded, once. 'Point taken. And I'm not averse to doing things differently, as long it's right for everyone. By that I mean doctors, patients and the company.' His eyes shifted between Jim and Jack. 'I want you to work together on this and agree a revised company policy. If the board are in agreement, we'll put it into action.'

Jim felt a flare of triumph which remained even after Geoff tagged on the words *work together*. In fact his internal celebration remained during most of the next agenda item, right up to the moment he started to doodle out a list of all the things he had to do over the next two months. Still, what did he need with a life outside work, anyway? The buzz he got from his job was enough.

The meeting stretched out for several more hours. After finally calling it closed, Geoff motioned for Jim to remain behind. When the last person had left, Geoff firmly shut the door behind them, giving Jim his first twinge of anxiety.

'Jim, I backed you because I believe in you. You're ambitious and want to make a difference, which is good.' Geoff spoke quietly, his expression stern. 'But you have to watch your step. In order to make changes you need to take people with you, not ride roughshod over them as you did today.'

Jim grimaced. This felt a lot like being hauled in front of the headmaster.

'You've been here two months and already you've reorganised your entire department. Now you're proposing changes that go beyond your own empire and will fundamentally alter the way the commercial teams are allowed to operate.'

His grimace morphed into a shudder. Huge changes in a small time frame. Was his arrogance overpowering his common sense?

Geoff continued. 'Take my advice. Don't rock the boat so much you end up sinking it.' Slowly he walked towards the door but as he reached it, he turned back to give Jim a final warning look. 'If you do, you'll be the first to go down with it.'

Left alone in the boardroom, Jim's victory suddenly felt very hollow. Had he just performed the equivalent of career suicide? Shaking his head, he thrust his hands in his pockets and followed his CEO out. If he had, it was too late to change now.

Tess listened in astonishment as Georgina took her through the executive team meeting she'd just escaped from. 'Sorry, what did Jim say again?'

'Words to the effect that the commercial president was admitting his group weren't able to sell medicines without resorting to bribery.'

'Phew.' Tess let a whistle escape her lips. 'I bet that went down well.'

'About as well as a downpour at a wedding. I tell you, I thought there was going to be fisticuffs.' Georgina let out a peal of laughter. 'You know, there's nothing like a bit of old-fashioned male aggression in the boardroom. Bubbling testosterone, men squaring up to each other. It's been years since I've seen anything other than nauseating politeness. Trust Jim to shake it up a bit.'

Tess wished she'd been there. She'd only seen Jack Webber from a distance, but already she had the impression of a man who fancied himself. It would have been fun to witness Jim take him down a peg or two.

'The upshot of this meeting is that pending board approval, Jim's been given the okay to move forward with his proposed changes,' Georgina continued. 'As his communications liaison, you'll be working on it too, so consider this fair warning. Jim's got the bit between the teeth and I can't imagine he'll hang around once the board give their go ahead. Think charging bull, though perhaps with a little more thought about the direction he's heading.'

Later that week Jim summoned a meeting with the group he'd selected to work on the policy. He was, as Tess had been warned, in a formidable mood.

'We need a revised company policy on the provision of

educational goods and services by the end of the week,' he told them. 'Jack needs to approve it, but there will be no long-winded consultation with other stakeholders. Geoff has already agreed to the principles I've outlined, so it's a done deal. We're doing it this way, end of story.' His fierce gaze swept the room. 'Questions?'

There was a stony silence, leaving Tess with the distinct impression they weren't happy with being told what to do. She sympathised. She hated being talked at, too.

'There will be a lot of push back from the markets.' This from Frank. There was something about the chief medical officer, perhaps his puppy dog eyes or his eagerness to please, that made her think *bless him*. 'They aren't going to like you taking away some of their key selling tools. How are you planning to get their buy in on this?'

'Probably railroad over them, as he's doing with the rest of us,' muttered one of the other guys under his breath.

Tess tensed, because if she'd heard what had been said, so had Jim. But there was no vitriolic comeback. Instead Jim smiled, giving every impression of a relaxed, easy-going guy. Sure, and she was a double D cup.

'Frank,' Jim replied evenly, totally ignoring the jibe. 'Stop thinking as a Helix employee for a moment and start to think back to those days when you were a busy doctor. Which representatives did you admire most? Those who could get you to Florida on a conference, or those who could explain clearly and concisely how their medicines worked and why they would help your patients?'

'Okay, yes, of course it was the latter, but—'

'For far too long, the sales force have been using these gifts as a crutch,' Jim cut in, having got the answer he wanted. 'No longer are they using them to support their sales messages. The gifts have *become* the messages; the only thing the rep discusses. I know because I've spent the last two days out on the road, listening to them in action.'

Tess bit the inside of her cheek, fighting the urge not to giggle at the thought of the poor rep's face on being told Jim would be joining them for the day.

'Surely these highly qualified, intelligent people should be talking to doctors about our medicines, and not about the freebies they can give them?' Jim finished.

'I know that, and you know that, but telling *them* that will be far more difficult.' Frank, *bless him*, was still trying to get his point across.

'I've considered that, which is why I'll be the one delivering the message.'

All eyes in the room turned to Jim. 'What?'

'You heard me. I'm clearing my diary for the week after next. During that time I aim to speak to each of the key markets. Those I can't physically get to, we'll do as a videoconference with their closest neighbours.'

For a moment there was a stunned silence. Tess included. Was the man crazy? Did he not need to sleep? Then, without warning, her mind started to click into the PR possibilities.

'We need to package this up,' she announced, taking both the room and herself by surprise. 'You know, give the initiative a media friendly title. Revision of the policy on educational doodahs and thingimijigs, or whatever it was you called it, isn't exactly memorable.'

Out of the corner of her eye, she saw Jim start to smile.

Feeling bolder, she continued. 'Considering the damning newspaper report earlier this week, an initiative like this could be just the response the press are looking for. Going back to the grass roots, stamping out all the old behaviours, turning a new leaf. However we phrase it, if this is handled correctly, Helix could be seen as a company striving to bring more integrity to the pharmaceutical industry.' Oh boy, she couldn't believe she was saying this. Why was she suggesting a way to clean up the reputation of the very industry she hated?

Involuntarily her gaze drifted over to Jim's matinee idol handsome face. Their eyes clashed, blue meeting dark chocolate brown. To her astonishment, Jim looked more than simply pleased. He looked as if he wanted to hug her.

'Thanks, Tessa,' he said, his eyes still locked on hers. 'It's great to finally hear something positive. Is two days long enough to come up with a suggestion of how we can package this to both the internal staff and the press?'

Tess had no idea if it was, but she gave the only answer she knew was acceptable in Jim's world. The only answer a woman could give a man who was looking at her like he was now. Sexy, vital, utterly compelling.

'Sure, I can do that in two days,' she said as the air left her lungs and her mouth turned to dust.

Chapter Nine

'*Sure, I can do that in two days.*' The words haunted Tess the following day as she lived and breathed the campaign to clean up the sales and marketing side of the Helix business. In her saner moments, when she wasn't in a meeting with the agency or poring over a power point template on the computer, she paused to ask herself what on earth she thought she was doing. It was a question her brother also asked when he phoned that evening.

'Let me get this straight,' Mark said, his voice dripping with incredulity. 'You can't come to the Robbie Williams concert with me tomorrow night, a concert incidentally where tickets are like gold dust and I've only got a spare one because someone pulled out, because you're *working*?'

'Umm ...'

He didn't give her the chance to reply. 'And this is for the same company we agree is evil and you're only with so you can determine the exact level of evil.'

'I know it sounds stupid, but yes.'

'You've gone bat crazy.'

'If you'll just let me finish,' she interjected crossly. 'This new initiative I'm working on is actually a good thing. Whether or not it's being implemented to further a certain R&D president's career, or because he really believes in it, I'm not sure. But whatever the reasons, it's the right thing to do.'

'Because?'

'Think about it. Having doctors prescribe a product because they believe it to be the best, and not just because they're being taken to Florida by the sales rep, has to be better for patients, doesn't it?'

'I guess.'

'Plus, the more firmly I embed myself within Helix, the more I gain Jim's trust, the better position I'll be in to follow up on Mum's cancer drug.'

He sighed. 'I see you have it all worked out. In your own mind at least. Still, there aren't many men who entertain as well as Robbie.'

On that they could agree. Then again, there weren't many men as powerfully persuasive as Jim, either. It scared her to think she might not be doing all this solely to earn his trust. That a part of her – a small and distinctly feminine part – was doing it to impress him.

Two days later, utterly exhausted and with her brain feeling as if it had been sliced open and its contents drained, Tess was at her desk, ready to present her communications package to Jim. The appointment had been set for four p.m. but already his secretary had called to say he'd be late. Apparently he was still driving back from an offsite meeting. Great.

Feeling her shoulders droop, Tess slumped back against her chair. How she longed for a deep, hot bath. A glass of wine. A bar of thick chunky chocolate. One at a time or all at once, she didn't care. Heaving out a deep sigh she started to go through the presentation she'd put together. Again. Tonight she'd be dreaming of the blasted thing.

By the time her phone finally rang it was nearly half past five and she was starting to feel absurdly nervous.

'Tessa, it's Pamela again, Jim's secretary. I'm sorry but he's only just made it in. Do you still want to go ahead with the meeting? I can always tell him you got tired of waiting and went home, as any sensible person would at this hour.'

Tess tried to imagine the look on Jim's face if that happened. 'No, it's okay, I'll come right up.' As if her system could cope with going home and doing all this again tomorrow.

When she reached his office she found him at his desk, his eyes fixed firmly on the computer screen. So firmly she wasn't sure he'd even noticed her arrival. It gave her a moment to stare at the powerful shoulders straining against his shirt. A moment for the woman in her to appreciate the view.

Jim was reading the latest email from Jack Webber, aka pain in the backside. The commercial president had prevaricated over the policy wording so many times that Jim had taken the precaution of doing everything by email, so he wouldn't be caught pummelling the man to the ground. They had, finally, come to an agreement Jim felt he could work with, particularly as he knew he'd be the one explaining the new policy to the organisation. Funny how there wasn't room in his presentation for those vague, ambiguous words Jack had insisted on adding.

Now it looked like the outwardly smooth, inwardly devious Webber was all for delaying the roll out of the revised policy, claiming the sales force needed more time for training. Yes, they probably did need training, but in how to discuss the relative merits of the Helix brands over their competitors. Not in the difference between right and wrong.

As Jim saw it, Helix had operated in the grey area for too long, pushing at the boundaries of decency and common sense. All he was doing was taking them back to the simplicity of black and white.

'Err, Jim?'

Distracted, he looked up to see Tessa. Bugger. He'd forgotten all about his meeting with her. He looked at his watch. Damn, his very late meeting with her. 'Can you give me five minutes? And a coffee, black, no sugar.' He focussed back on the monitor.

Tess cleared her throat. 'I will wait five more minutes for a meeting that's already an hour and a half late, but you can get your own coffee.'

With that she turned on her heel, all four slender inches of it, and stalked out of his office.

Stunned, Jim watched her exit. It simply dripped with attitude. Then, with a shake of his head, he started to chuckle. Hell, it wasn't often someone said no to him, but on this particular occasion he'd probably deserved it. Deciding a reply to Jack Webber could wait, he stood and walked over to the coffee machine.

There he found Tessa, clutching two cups.

'Look, I'm sorry—'

'Here.' She thrust the cup into his hand.

Her vivid blue eyes burnt with a good degree of, if not anger, then strong irritation. It sat well on her, all that fiery temper. Made her look unbelievably hot. It wasn't too much of a stretch to imagine her fired up by something more sensual than a cup of coffee. Or to picture the release of all that pent up passion in a steamy session between the sheets.

Restlessly he thrust his free hand through his hair, pushing the erotic thoughts out of his mind. 'I don't expect you to fetch my coffee. You caught me at a bad moment. I was angry and tired. Not a good combination. I repeat. I'm sorry.'

'Apology accepted.' The anger left her eyes but the vivid blue remained. 'For the record, I don't mind getting you a drink, as long as you'd also ask the same of a male colleague. And adding please usually helps.'

'Understood.'

Their eyes met and awareness shimmered between them. Was it just his imagination or did she feel it too? This ache, this pulse of desire.

Breaking the gaze, he took a sip of coffee and tried to clear his head. 'Have you time to go through where you're up to with this initiative,' he ventured when he found his voice. 'Or do you need to get home?'

'I'm fine to stay.'

'Good.' Walking back to his office he caught her glancing sideways at him. No doubt checking whether his claim of being tired was, in fact, backed up by his appearance. He was pretty certain it was, because he felt ready to drop. If someone gave him a bed, now, he'd crash out on it. Then again ... he turned to look at Tessa. Maybe he wasn't so tired after all. Not if he was still capable of thinking of what he'd like to do on that bed. And it didn't involve any sleep.

'What was making you angry?' she asked as they sat down at the table in his office.

He let out a deep huff. 'Who, rather than what.'

'Let me guess. Jack Webber?'

A slow grin slid across his face. 'You catch on fast.'

'It makes sense that he doesn't like what you're doing. It's his part of the business most affected by the changes.'

'True, but I'd rather hoped he'd see this as a challenge instead of a threat.'

She stared at him, as if trying to figure him out. Then her lips twitched.

'Go on, say what you're thinking,' he told her when it was apparent she was just going to sit there with a secret smile on her face.

'You're someone who needs to take the bull by the horns, aren't you? I was just wondering if words like *no,* or *can't* were in your vocabulary.'

He laughed, enjoying her. She was direct, confident, totally unafraid of what he might think. 'You're right, they aren't. Neither is the phrase *but that's the way we've always done it.*'

'Yes, I can see you like to put your stamp on things. To make your mark.'

Whoa. 'This isn't about my ego, Tessa,' he corrected firmly. 'To my way of thinking, if we don't make an effort to do things differently, we'll never actually make a difference. Every time we make a change, we learn something new. Hopefully improve things. At least that's the plan.'

Her big blue eyes widened, but he couldn't tell whether it was in surprise or disbelief.

92

'Well, speaking of plans, let me go through what I've put together.' She opened up her computer and turned the screen towards him. 'We thought a suitable name for this initiative could be "Leading with Science".'

'We?'

'Myself, Georgina and the agency we involved. It combines the two features we really want to emphasise. The fact that Helix is leading the way in this area, and that it is all about science, not gimmicks.'

He nodded thoughtfully. 'I like it.'

'Good.' She brought up her overview slide. 'Your briefing of the markets next week will just be the start. If you're in agreement, we can use the "Leading with Science" banner to address many other aspects of the business.'

As she began to take him through the rest of her presentation, he tried to concentrate. He really did. At least as much as any man could concentrate after putting in a twelve-hour day. What she was presenting was well thought through, simple and clear. Impressive, particularly from someone with so little industry experience. But by the end his wayward mind began to focus on her, rather than what she was saying. The creamy soft skin. The long, slender fingers as they tapped out the last two slides on the computer keyboard. He went as far as wondering what those fingers would look like trailing over his rough, darker body.

'Jim?'

He gave a guilty start and found Tessa glaring at him, her face tight with annoyance. Damn. Reaching for his cup he swallowed down the rest of his coffee. 'That was a very comprehensive presentation, Tess.' She continued to stare stonily at him. 'Sorry, do you prefer Tessa?'

'Either is fine,' she replied coolly.

So it wasn't the name that had riled her. 'I can see you've put a lot of effort into this, Tess,' he tried again, preferring the shortened name. It made her seem more approachable, though God knows, he shouldn't be encouraging that. 'I particularly liked the analysis of what other companies are doing in comparison. Good thinking.' Surprise flickered across her face and he fought to hide his grin. She clearly thought he hadn't been listening at all. 'I really appreciate what you've done and the hard work you've put in,' he added. 'I have to be honest, there have been times during these last few days when I've thought everyone was against me. Except you.'

He watched her blink and look away. 'What you're doing is right.'

'I'm glad you think so.' His voice sounded suddenly rough and he found he had to cough to clear his throat.

Her eyes returned to his and this time he wasn't imagining it. A frisson of sexual tension zinged between them. He only had to look at her face to know she felt it, too. Her blue eyes were brighter than usual, her cheeks tinged with pink. If he moved just a few inches, his mouth could be on hers, tasting those plump, luscious lips.

Jesus.

His answering throb of arousal was totally inappropriate, but vividly real.

Pushing back his chair, he widened the gap between them and crossed his legs. Several years ago, he wouldn't have pulled away, wouldn't have hesitated. Decisive and instinctive by nature, he was used to going flat out for what or who he wanted. But then Barbara had come along. Once bitten, twice determined not to be bitten again, ever.

'About next week.' He dragged his thoughts back to safer ground. 'I've asked Pamela to draw up a schedule for the meetings with the main markets and to organise the flights. A week of planes and presentations.' He smiled wryly, already dreading it. In his mind he'd nicknamed it Hell Week.

'Will she be travelling with you?'

Jim tried not to look too horrified. 'No.' Bad enough

putting up with the dozy woman here in the office. He couldn't imagine actually travelling with her. He'd probably end up in Timbuktu.

'But won't you need someone to go with you? To help you with the logistics?'

'Ideally, yes.' But if that someone was Pamela, then no.

'I don't have any commitments next week. I can come with you, if you like.'

If he liked? He froze, momentarily stunned by her offer. But the very fact that his heart, and other body parts, leapt at the thought was enough to convince him that no matter how incredibly appealing spending a week with Tess sounded, it wasn't a good idea.

'Thanks but I couldn't ask that. To say it won't be fun would be an understatement. Think of stabbing needles into your eyeballs. Trust me, by day three that will seem preferable.'

She laughed, a lovely soft sound that flowed over him like a silk sheet. 'You're not asking, I'm offering.'

Tess wondered if what she'd just said made her certifiably nuts. Travelling the globe in a week sounded daunting enough, never mind doing it with Jim. Outrageously handsome, Helix R&D president, Jim. Who right now was looking at her as if he wanted to … kiss her? It had to be because he didn't want to do this trip alone. Who would?

But, she reasoned with herself, how could she help with the communications piece if she wasn't actually there to see this phase happen? And what better chance would she ever have to get close to Jim, to gain his confidence and thus move her own plans forward?

'Are you sure?'

She stared into his fathomless dark eyes and her pulse began to race. 'Yes, I'm sure,' she found herself saying. 'It will be a great learning experience.'

'It will also be bloody hard work.'

Annoyance rippled through her and she clung to it gratefully. 'You don't think I'm capable of hard work?'

'I didn't say that,' he placated. 'I just want to make sure you know what you're letting yourself in for. There'll be no time for sightseeing, or shopping.'

Of all the chauvinistic, pompous, belittling remarks. 'I presume you'd have said the same to a male colleague?'

His eyes hardened. 'To a male I'd have said there'd be no time for bar hopping.' Pushing a hand through his hair again, he exhaled heavily. 'Look, I don't have an issue with women in the workplace, Tess. If you do your job, I don't care what sex you are.'

Not entirely mollified, she rose to her feet. 'You don't need to worry. I'll do my job and keep out of the shops.'

'Good, then we should get along just fine.' She was almost out of the door when his voice called her back. 'And Tess? Thank you for offering. I hope you don't live to regret it.'

His eyes were so dark, his face, currently serious, so utterly good-looking. Why did he have to be so damned attractive?

Nodding once, she walked away. She hoped she wouldn't live to regret the trip, too. More, she hoped she wouldn't regret her whole journey into the murky world of Helix Pharmaceuticals.

Chapter Ten

Europe first, then onto Asia and finally the United States. That was the mind-boggling order of the week. The markets they couldn't visit in person would catch Jim's presentation by videoconference. It had all seemed so simple when Tess had helped Pamela plan it out in the office. Simpler still when she'd started to sort it out herself, having determined that Jim's secretary was the most disorganised person she'd ever met. If she'd been a leggy blonde, Tess might have understood why Jim kept her on. She wasn't. Maybe Pamela had some sort of hold over him. Perhaps she'd caught him in his office with the blinds down, trousers round his ankles ...

Feeling suddenly extremely hot, Tess loosened the button on her jacket. She didn't need that image of Jim in her mind right now. Not when she was waiting for him at the UK operating company office – just down the road from the global headquarters – where they'd already hit a snag. One she couldn't even blame on the useless Pamela. And they'd yet to board a plane.

'We weren't expecting you for another hour,' the office manager insisted as they clashed in the glass-fronted lobby.

What was it about pharmaceutical companies and their practical but soulless modern buildings?

Tess sucked in a deep breath and tried to keep patient. Not her usual style. 'As you can see from the schedule, Jim is down to visit at nine a.m.'

The older lady clucked and shook her head. 'It might say that on your piece of paper, dearie, but it doesn't on mine.'

Tess bit back the urge to ask to see her blasted piece of paper. 'Whatever it might say in your diary, the fact is the Helix R&D president will be arriving in this lobby in ...' She checked her watch. '... Half an hour, expecting to speak to all of your staff. What do you suggest we do?'

She could tell the moment it hit home to the office manager that it wasn't just Tess she was dealing with. Any minute now, it would be Jim Knight. A man squillions of rungs higher up the pay grade than she was.

Sheer, raw panic settled across her wrinkled features. 'Oh, yes, well.' To her credit she straightened her shoulders and nodded. 'I'll warn them upstairs. Send the coach company to pick up the sales force from the hotel. They can grab a drink and a bun for breakfast when they come in.' Grabbing at Tess's schedule she started marching up the stairs. 'We'll be ready for him, mark my words.' Then she turned and frowned. 'Though really, if he wants *everybody,* we're going to have to start a tiny bit later.'

'Problem?'

They both snapped their heads round at the sound of the deep voice behind them.

'Oh, Mr Knight.' The office manager, having been distinctly cool with her, positively gushed at the darkly handsome research president as he stepped out from the revolving door. 'It's so good to meet you. I'm Julie Pickford, office manager.'

Jim shook her hand, but his eyes zeroed in on Tess, with a look that clearly said *what the hell is going on here?*

'There's been a bit of a mix-up.' She dearly wanted to lay the blame at Julie's feet. Wanted to absolve herself of any involvement in this blunder, but in all honesty she couldn't. 'The UK team weren't expecting us for another hour.' She readied herself for the explosion.

It didn't arrive. Instead Jim simply nodded. 'Can we round the troops up any earlier?'

'Yes, I'm on that, Mr Knight. Right away,' Julie piped up, storming back up the stairs before coming to a sudden halt halfway up. 'Goodness, where are my manners. Would you like a drink? Somewhere to work while you wait?' She flushed and flapped her hands. 'Oh, I'm so sorry, you've got me all in a dither.'

Tess guessed Jim often experienced that sort of reaction. From his female staff, at least.

'Don't worry, Julie,' he replied smoothly. If he was angry, he was hiding it well. 'Mistakes happen. But let's rectify this one as quickly as possible. We'll wait for you in the lecture theatre.'

As Julie scampered upwards Tess turned to Jim and rolled her eyes. 'She wasn't that pleasant to me.'

'No?'

'No. It must be that Clooney thing you've got going on.'

He frowned, dark eyebrows lowering over puzzled brown eyes. Then he seemed to register who Clooney was and frowned even more. 'Hell,' he muttered under his breath. 'Where did that come from?'

The shocked look on his face told her he hadn't heard that reference before, and the way he was shaking his head and looking away made her pretty certain his question had been strictly rhetorical. Which only made the devil in her more determined to make him squirm. 'I thought you knew. You're known as the pharmaceutical industry's answer to George Clooney.'

Jim died on the spot. He felt a sting of warmth as his face flushed; something that hadn't happened since he'd turned teenager. Sure he knew he was attractive. He'd been blessed with the height and broad shoulders women seemed to like and he'd used both to his advantage when seeking out female company socially. But at work ... hell, he wanted to be known by what he did, not what he looked like. He cast a glance at Tess who was watching him with evident amusement. Okay, maybe there was a small, shallow part of him that hoped he *was* as handsome as Clooney. At least in Tess's eyes.

'Sorry, have I embarrassed you?' she asked, looking a little worried now.

'That's one word you could use. Flattered and irritated are

99

two more.' He considered her, taking in the gorgeous hair, the long body, the clear blue eyes. 'How would you feel if the office compared you to that supermodel. You know, the tall redhead?' He narrowed his eyes, trying to remember. 'Lily someone or other. Except of course you're much ...' Bugger. Where was he going with this?

'Scrawnier?'

'Hell, no. I was about to say ...' Sexier. That had been the word on the tip of his tongue. At the forefront of his brain. 'I think it's better you don't know what I was about to say.'

'Because you don't want to upset me.' She quickly averted her eyes.

He touched her arm, forcing her to look at him. 'Whatever you're thinking, if it is in anyway on the negative side rather than the positive, you're totally wrong. I don't happen to like catwalk models much. They look so untouchable. I prefer my women to look ... and okay, it really is time to move on.'

Tess looked as if she wanted to argue the point, but he turned away, opening the door for her, effectively ending the conversation.

'You realise this delay means we're probably going to be late for the plane,' she told him as they arrived at the lecture theatre. 'You're due to talk to the French operating company in Paris at one p.m. and then the Germans in Berlin after that.' Her mouth twisted and she let out a deep sigh. 'We've only just started and already the schedule is falling apart. I can't even say for certain it wasn't my fault. I'd love to blame Pamela, but truly she didn't have much to do with the logistics after ... well ...'

'After you found out that if you asked her to organise a piss up in a brewery, she'd give out the wrong address, wrong time and order tea and biscuits.'

She gave a laugh of surprise. 'Yes, exactly. So it was probably me who gave Julie the wrong time. Maybe I sent her an earlier draft.'

Once more he touched her arm with his hand. His need to touch her was becoming a habit. 'Tess, it's fine. Forget it. The day will work out.'

Her big eyes stared at him. 'Are you really always this calm when things go wrong, or is it an act?'

Jim stifled a laugh. Calm was the last thing he was feeling, and it had damn all to do with the schedule cockup. Missing planes didn't worry him. He went by the motto that it was crazy to expend energy worrying about things he couldn't change. If they missed a connection, they'd get another one. If they had to push the next meeting back an hour, they would. No, it wasn't this morning's delay that was eating him up. It was Tess. Did she know how much she was driving him crazy, standing next to him in that tight purple suit? He shouldn't have accepted her offer to come with him on this roadshow. Being with her all day was going to be a heck of a lot more stressful than any of the presentations he'd be giving.

She was still looking at him, waiting for an answer. 'Mostly I'm calm,' he hedged.

'You might need every inch of that calm travelling with me.'

He eyed her thoughtfully. 'Don't tell me you're one of those people who has to get to the gate the moment they call the flight?'

'Umm, yes, I'm afraid so.'

He let out a low laugh. 'Well, this should be an interesting trip.'

While Jim delivered his presentation, only half an hour later than planned, Tess tried to analyse her feelings for the man. There was no doubt that physically he'd tied her up in knots from day one. But she wasn't the type to act on pure attraction; her mind had always been stronger than her hormones. So now she had to rely on that mind to keep reminding her why she couldn't, shouldn't, *didn't* like him. Because if she added *like* to the lust, then the situation became a lot more dangerous.

Especially as none of this was real.

She wasn't really the communications manager, working with Jim to improve the reputation of Helix. She wasn't the woman she suspected he was actually starting to warm to. No, she was the cow who was going to be working against him. The thought sent a chill through her system. *Remember why you're here*, she told herself. *Remember your mother.*

Forget how one look from Jim's dark eyes can cut you off at the knees.

Feeling like Jim's stooge, Tess trailed him for the rest of the day. From taxi to airport lounge, to plane, taxi again, then on to another lecture theatre. They had brief moments apart, like the fifteen or so minutes following the call for both the Paris and Berlin flights, when Tess immediately dashed off to the gate. Jim of course remained in the business lounge, reading his emails. He turned up just as they were boarding, a wide *I told you so* smirk on his face.

At last they checked in to their hotel in Berlin. Finally, thank goodness, a building with character. Ornate columns and a sweeping marble staircase. Carved wooden furniture and plush velvet sofas instead of everything made of steel or leather.

Jim glanced across the hotel lobby towards the bar. 'I'm too wired to call it a night. Are you ready to crash, or do you fancy joining me for a quick drink?'

Tess's feet were screaming out for her to sit down. Airports and stilettos really didn't go together. 'I could go for a glass of Merlot.' She looked down at her feet. 'And taking my shoes off.'

She noticed Jim's eyes automatically drift down to her feet, then sharply back up again, as if he was afraid to be caught staring at that part of her anatomy. It made her want to laugh. Her feet were hardly worthy of a second look, though her shoes definitely were. Patent red Salvatore Ferragamos. Beautiful.

'Right, a glass of red and a sit down.' Jim grabbed the cases and carried them both purposefully over to the bar.

Tess followed him, hobbling slightly, wondering if she'd packed any lower heels in the suitcase Jim was now carrying. The vivid pink flowery one that looked about twice the size of his black Samsonite.

'You know we could have asked the hotel porter to take the cases to our rooms,' she told him as she sank down onto a blissfully comfortable sofa in the corner of the bar.

He gave her a rueful smile. 'True. I wasn't thinking.' Then his eyes travelled over her case. 'What *have* you got in there?'

'You mean aside from a dozen pairs of shoes?'

He let out a low chuckle and as she watched his face light up and his eyes crinkle, her breath caught in her throat. When he smiled, he almost redefined the word sexy. 'You know, there isn't a day goes by when I don't thank God I'm not a man,' she told him, trying to keep her face deadpan.

Amusement glittered in his eyes as he cocked his head, clearly trying to figure out where she was going with this one.

She looked pointedly down at his very expensive looking, but very dull flat, black leather shoes.

'Ah, but you don't see what I wear in private,' he replied, also trying to keep his face serious, but totally failing.

For a moment they both sat there, grinning like idiots at each other. She felt that pull again, that desire to reach out and touch him. It was so strong she had to clench her hands by her sides to make sure she didn't. His smile slowly left his face and his eyes darkened to almost black, and she knew he'd felt it, too.

'I'll go and order those drinks,' he croaked, abruptly standing up and making his way to the bar.

I can do this, Jim told himself as he clutched at the wine glass and whiskey tumbler. I can have a quiet, winding down drink with a work colleague. Without it leading to anything else.

Then he watched Tess discard her heels under the table and wriggle her toes on the thick pile carpet. God help him. Who knew a woman's feet could be so erotic? Tearing his eyes away from them, he plonked himself down on the seat opposite.

'Cheers,' he said gruffly, grabbing at his drink and taking a large swig.

She held up her glass and, with a lot more finesse than he'd managed, saluted him back. 'Here's to no more muck ups like this morning.'

'It didn't matter in the end, did it?' He tried not to look too smug, but clearly failed.

'You've got an *I told you so* expression on your face.'

'Sorry.' But he wasn't. Especially as her eyes were smiling back at him. Feeling that rush of desire again he reached for his whiskey, needing the sharp burn.

'How do you think today went?' she asked as she settled back against the soft velvet sofa.

'Good.' He swirled the whiskey in the glass, giving himself a moment to get back to the only relationship he could have with this lady sitting opposite him. Work. 'The UK team were okay because their regulations are so tight now, this won't be such a huge change. As for the French and Germans, I think they understand it's the way the regulations are moving, so they might as well bite the bullet now.' He smiled over at her. 'If they weren't convinced by what I was saying, those headlines you'd prepared, showing them what they could be faced with if they carried on the way they were, certainly drilled the point home. That was a stroke of genius.'

A delicate flush stole across her cheeks. 'Genius might be overstating it a bit, but I'm glad I could use my background to some advantage.'

'Yes, I have to confess I was a bit sceptical about how a journalist with no previous industry experience was going to manage in the role.'

'Really?'

He glanced at her sharply and saw she was teasing. 'I was that obvious, huh?' Shaking his head, he held her gaze. 'Well, I was wrong,' he admitted. 'You've more than managed. You've excelled.'

Her eyes darted towards the drink she was clutching and another blush coloured her cheeks. It intrigued him that a woman who had no problem standing up to him became flustered at a compliment. 'Do you miss it?,' he asked. 'Being a reporter?'

Tess shifted, crossing one long leg over another. 'Well, I wouldn't be circumnavigating the globe in a week if I'd stayed at the *Daily News*, that's for certain.' Downing the rest of her drink in one long swallow she stood and picked up her shoes. 'I think it's time I headed off. It's an early start tomorrow.'

Surprised at the abrupt change of subject, Jim quickly knocked back the last of his whiskey. She obviously wasn't a girl who liked to talk about herself very much. A fact that made her highly unusual, in his experience. 'I'll walk you up.'

It seemed like the right, gentlemanly thing to do. Especially as they still had their damn cases. But when he stood with Tess in the crowded lift, her body almost wedged against his, his thoughts became anything but gentlemanly. He'd wondered for days what she'd feel like pressed up against him. Heaven help him, now he knew. She was standing with her back against him, her neat round buttocks nestled perfectly against his crotch. Slim, firm, warm. Jesus.

Gritting his teeth, he inhaled sharply, catching a lungful of her scent. Intensely feminine but with a hint of wild sexy. Double Jesus. Desperately he pushed his body back against the lift, trying to create some much needed space between them. If the doors didn't open in the next few seconds, this powerful attraction he felt towards her was going to become blatantly obvious.

Finally the lift stopped at their floor, but it was too late. Those lovely soft buttocks were now pressing against a very hard part of him.

Pushing his way out he followed Tess down the corridor, clutching at their cases for dear life. What the blazes did a man say to a female work colleague who he'd just – he couldn't articulate the words, not even to himself. He wanted the ground to open up and swallow him, but here he was, still walking next to her. Unsurprisingly, Tess was picking up the pace, almost running, clearly anxious to get away from him and retreat to the sanctuary of her hotel room. Bugger, bugger, bugger.

Should he say something? *Sorry I became aroused? Sorry you were forced to feel my throbbing member against your perfectly rounded backside?* He exhaled a sharp breath. Better to leave it alone. Say nothing. Maybe she hadn't noticed.

When she reached her room, she turned but kept her eyes fixed firmly on the floor. 'Good night, Jim.'

Of course she'd bloody well noticed. And now, if he didn't say *something*, there was going to be this awkwardness between them, with her no doubt terrified that at any moment he was going to jump her. 'Look, about what happened in the lift.' Great start. Now what? He jammed his hands in his trouser pockets and swore softly. 'I'm sorry.'

'There's no need.' She looked down at the keycard in her hand, still avoiding his eyes. 'I understand you weren't coming on to me.'

'No, I wasn't. I wouldn't.' He let out a deep sigh. 'That isn't to say you're not attractive. Just that ... hell, I'm your boss, for God's sake, or as near as damn it. What I said a few days ago, about having a personal rule not to date anyone who works for me. I meant it.' He broke off and raised his eyes to the ceiling. 'And that made it sound like you'd want to date me, which of course you'd be crazy if you did.' Again he paused, dragging a hand through his hair, trying to find his equilibrium. 'Really, I just wanted to reassure you that you're safe from any unwanted advances. I promise, I won't, you know, come on to you.' He cursed. 'Maybe this is a good time for me to shut up.'

Finally, she looked him in the eye. 'Jim, it's all fine. Let's forget this moment ever happened. It's better all round.'

'Thanks.' He tried to smile, but found he was too mortified to conjure one up. Instead he bid her goodnight and walked hastily away to his room.

Behind her door, Tess closed her eyes and leant against it. Her legs were trembling, her mind a swirl of opposing emotions. She should hate this man. As a daughter, for what he may have been complicit in. As a woman, for what had just happened in the lift. But he hadn't tried to push it under the carpet. He'd been up front, dealing with his very human reaction honestly. And if she was to use that same honesty, she'd have to admit that when he'd pressed against her, the feeling he'd engendered in her hadn't been fear, or disgust, but desire.

Chapter Eleven

Spain passed in a blur and once again Tess was in an airport business lounge, this time waiting for a flight to Rome. Idly she scanned the faces of the other travellers. Most of them were men in dark suits, carrying briefcases or flicking through emails on their mobile phones. How can people do this every day, she wondered. It was only day two, but already she was dreading another flight. Another hotel room.

She snuck a glance at Jim, wondering if he hated travelling, too. It was hard to tell, because after the *Lift Incident* last night, as she'd started to refer to it in her mind, he'd been determinedly distant. Yesterday in the lounge they'd talked. Now all his attention was focussed on his computer screen. All day he'd been like this, going out of his way not to touch her, avoiding all but the barest minimum of eye contact.

She hated it. She found she missed his conversation. His occasional dry humour and accompanying sexy smile.

Taking another sip of tea from the standard business lounge white cup and saucer, she stole another glance at the magnetic man sitting next to her. This time he wasn't absorbed in his laptop. He was looking across the lounge, frowning. Turning her head, she tried to see what was troubling him. 'Jim? What's wrong?'

Suddenly he lurched to his feet and strode briskly towards the window. That's when she saw what the problem was. A man was slumped awkwardly across the sofa, holding his chest. As she watched, Jim flung off his jacket and helped him carefully to the floor. Then, after instructing those around him to call the medical services, he calmly began doing CPR. Instinctively Tess stood up, but then halted. What could she possibly do, other than get in the way? She didn't know any first aid, and besides, Jim looked to have it all under control, working on the patient like a true professional.

That's when it hit her. He was.

Funny, she'd not thought of him that way, not as a doctor. Sure she'd seen the title on his auto signature, but she hadn't made the connection until now. It made it even harder to understand how someone like him could deliberately hide information from fellow doctors. Information that could help them in the treatment of their patients. Didn't doctors take a Hippocratic oath? Swear to do no harm?

The medical crew arrived a short while later and Jim made his way back towards her. Out of the corner of her eye Tess saw several pairs of female eyes following him, knowing they could see what she did. A tall, strikingly handsome man in a white shirt and bold tie, his jacket slung carelessly over his shoulder.

'Well spotted,' she murmured as he sat down, torn between admiration for what he'd just done, and anger that this gorgeous man could be one of the bad guys.

'Just lucky. I happened to be glancing across the lounge when I saw him collapse.' He leant forward, arms resting on his knees. It was only then that she saw his hands were shaking slightly.

'I'd forgotten you're a doctor.'

He gave her a small smile. 'Most of the time, so do I.'

'But not today.'

Taking in a deep breath, he glanced back at her. 'No. I guess CPR isn't something you ever forget.'

'Do you think he'll be okay?'

Jim nodded. 'He had a pulse when the medics arrived.'

She couldn't help herself. She reached over to squeeze his hand. 'Then you probably saved his life.'

He stared down at their hands, hers pale, his tanned. 'I hope so.'

For a few long seconds she kept her hand there, not wanting to move it. His was long fingered and strong.

Capable. Warm too, and now she was starting to enjoy holding it far too much. Quickly she removed her hand.

'Why did you join the industry, Jim?' she asked after a few moments.

He raised a dark eyebrow. 'You ask that in a tone that implies you don't approve.'

Careful. Hastily she shook her head. 'No, it's not that. Obviously the pharmaceutical industry needs doctors. I guess I was just thinking that it seems like a soft option, you know one with better pay and more regular hours. But you don't strike me as a man attracted towards the easy or the comfortable.'

'All true.' He gave her a slight smile. 'After I qualified, I specialised in oncology.'

'Proving my point. A tough option.'

'Yes. My mum's sister, a real character, you know, the classic lovable but crazy aunt. She was diagnosed with cancer while I was studying medicine. It became a long standing joke between us that I was going to become an oncologist and then cure her.' Exhaling slowly he leant back and stretched out his long legs. 'She died a few months before I qualified.'

'I'm sorry.'

He acknowledged her words with a slight nod of his head. 'The idea of being able to help others like her stuck with me, so that's the direction I took. As time went on though, I became increasingly frustrated and disillusioned by the lack of effective medicines at my disposal to treat the patients coming through the door. That's when I decided to jump ship, so to speak.'

'Did you start in the labs?'

'No. I'm not a scientist. I joined the clinical research team, where the focus is on patients. Designing and running studies to determine if the drugs that work in a lab are actually safe and effective in patients.' He turned and fixed her with his shrewd dark stare. 'Why do you ask?'

Yes, Tess, why on earth did you ask? She tried not to look away. Tried to be as honest as she could without letting slip her opinion on the industry he'd joined. 'I was just trying to understand your motivation. When you have the power to save a life, like you just have, it's hard to see how you could walk away from that into something more ...' She struggled for a word that wasn't derogatory. 'Remote.'

'You don't think what we do in industry helps save lives, too?' he asked quietly, his eyes searching out hers, forcing her to keep contact.

'Well, yes, I guess it does, in a way.' She couldn't hold that intense look, not whilst knowing she was lying. Pretending to feel her phone vibrate, she stood up. 'Sorry. I need to take this.'

She was aware of him continuing to watch her as she walked away, his face quizzical, his eyes full of questions.

The Italian operating company gave him a tough time, but nothing Jim hadn't expected. The Italians liked to think they were unique, so being told they had to toe the line with everyone else was never going to be an easy ride.

What he *hadn't* expected was his conversation with the Italian HR director afterwards, when she'd asked for a moment alone in her office.

'So, that is the situation we are faced with, I'm afraid. Your arrival is ... perfect timing, I think you say?'

Jim swallowed back a sigh. He was damned if he could see anything perfect about what she'd just told him. 'You say you've conducted all the necessary investigations?'

'Why, yes. This is not the first time we 'ave had a complaint of sexual 'arassment against Doctor Mario Lombardi. The management team 'ere are all in agreement that 'e should go. We are 'appy to do this ourselves, but with you coming today, and because Doctor Lombardi is such a prominent figure, maybe it will be better coming from the R&D president?'

'Okay. But let me see the paperwork first.' It felt hugely uncomfortable firing a man without at least seeing the evidence.

'Why sure.' She turned to a large grey filing cabinet and plucked out a thick file. 'You can use my office, I 'ave a meeting now, but please phone when you're ready.' Her mouth curved in a small smile. 'You, or should I say *this matter*, is more important.'

As he took the heavy file from her Jim's heart sank. Not a quick read then. After she'd closed the door behind her, he pulled out his mobile and called Tess. 'Sorry, I'm in the office of Gabriella Medici, the HR director. I've got an ... issue to deal with.'

'Anything I can do to help?'

He was about to say no, because after all this was confidential and she was his communications manager, not an expert in HR. But hell, he valued her judgement. 'Sure, if you can find your way here.'

By the time he'd taken off his jacket and scanned through what he felt was important, Tess was popping her head round the door. 'What's the problem?'

Without warning an image of him standing behind her in the lift flew into his mind. 'Sexual harassment claim,' he replied bluntly, determinedly pushing the picture aside. He hadn't harassed her, at least not intentionally. And he wouldn't.

'I see.' She eased into the office and closed the door. 'Against whom?'

His eyes flew to hers. 'Not against me,' he returned sharply, feeling immediately queasy. Bloody hell, had she thought—

'I didn't think that,' she interrupted evenly. 'You're not the type.'

'I'm not?'

'No. I can't imagine you'd have to harass a woman for sex. It's more likely the other way round.'

112

Deciding it would be arrogant in the extreme to admit he'd had his moments, Jim kept quiet.

'So, am I allowed to ask what's happened in this case?'

He pushed the file towards her. 'One of the clinical research scientists has claimed her department head made improper advances towards her at an offsite meeting, making suggestive remarks about them saving the company money by sharing a room. She claims it isn't the first time he's made inappropriate comments.'

'That's twice you've said the word *claims*. Don't you believe her?'

For a woman with a fiery temper, he thought, Tess could be pretty cold when she wanted to be. 'I know the man. He's a brilliant scientist and comes across as a decent guy.'

She gave him a small, cool smile. 'Just because he comes across as decent and smart doesn't mean he's not capable of doing something nasty or underhand.'

Was it his imagination, or were her eyes slightly accusing? 'I realise that, but it's easy to knock a man for his poor judgement from a distance,' he countered flatly. 'Far less easy when you have to stare him in the eyes and sack him for it.'

She swallowed visibly. 'Oh, is that what they want you to do?'

'Yes.' He ran a hand down his face. What a bloody day. He'd begun it breathing life into a stranger in the airport lounge. It looked like he was going to end it finishing the career of a man he liked and admired.

As Jim rubbed a weary hand over his face, Tess couldn't help but feel sympathy for him. He wasn't a man who wore his heart on his sleeve, but she could tell he was upset. Motioning to the file he'd shoved towards her, she asked, 'Would you like me to take an unbiased look at this then?'

He nodded once. 'Please.' Then he looked at his watch. 'And I'm afraid after this I'm going to have to ask you to change our flight for a later one.' He pushed back his chair. 'But meanwhile I can just about manage to get you a drink.'

By the time he'd returned, and surely it had taken him so long because he'd been accosted at the drinks machine, not because he didn't know how to use it, Tess had finished reading the report.

He handed her the paper cup and sighed. 'I don't need to ask your verdict. It's written all over your face.'

'You didn't need me to read the file, either. You knew as soon as you'd read it yourself.'

'Yeah. Didn't mean I wasn't hoping I'd missed something, though.' He shrugged on his jacket and yanked up the tie he'd loosened. 'Okay then. I'll give you a call when the dirty deed is done.'

'Fine.' She watched him walk to the door, shoulders straight, his expression grim. 'And Jim, remember it's Mario Lombardi who's done the dirty deed, not you.'

He gave her a glimmer of a smile before marching off down the corridor.

For a long while after Tess remained in the office, quietly drinking the tea he'd brought her.

Was Jim another outwardly decent man capable of something nasty? Or was he really the person she was seeing?

The one who, despite her best endeavours, she was starting to like.

Chapter Twelve

The flight change meant they had four hours to kill in Rome. Tess tried not to get too excited as she waited for Jim in the reception area of the Italian office. She knew he'd probably want to spend it working in the business lounge, but surely that didn't mean she had to as well? Seeing the Spanish Steps, or the Vatican, was infinitely more appealing.

The moment he strode past the security gates and into the reception area though, the thought of doing anything so frivolous seemed somehow disloyal. He looked utterly drained.

'Dare I ask how it went?'

'It went,' he replied tersely, his eyes scanning the front of the building. 'Is that our cab to the airport?'

'Yes. Sort of.'

His dark eyes snapped back at her. 'I'm not in the mood for guessing games, Tess,' he warned.

Okay then. 'It's *your* cab back to the airport. I know you said there would be no time for sightseeing or shopping, but our re-arranged flight to Singapore doesn't leave until this evening, so I'm going into Rome for a few hours.'

'I see.' He rubbed at the back of his neck. 'So I sit at the airport while you swan around Rome?'

She baulked. '*Swan*? I'm stretching my legs for a few hours before I have to wedge them into another flipping plane.'

His eyes flared. 'I warned you this would be a tough trip.'

'I know you did, and I'm not complaining. Just making the most of a few precious hours of down time.' She took in his rigid shoulders, his tense jaw line, and sighed. 'You look like you could do with a few yourself.'

He grunted, rolled his shoulders, then let out a long, deep exhale. 'You're not wrong. What's the first place on your sightseeing list?'

'Tea and cake by the Spanish Steps, followed by an ice cream next to the Trevi Fountain.'

'I'm starting to see a pattern.' Slowly his lips curved upwards. 'And I like it. Do you mind if I tag along?'

Her heart performed a little flutter. 'Of course not.' But as they walked towards the cab, she felt it her duty to point out all her plans. 'If there's time I wouldn't mind a quick look at the Vatican though. Only from the outside, I know the queues are always enormous. And of course there's that amazing street with all the shops.'

'The Corso?'

She almost stumbled. 'Wow, you know it.'

'I know about lots of things I don't necessarily enjoy visiting. Like the dentist and the supermarket.'

'Please tell me you didn't just compare shopping in Rome with going to the dentist?'

For the first time in what seemed like hours, his face relaxed into a full smile. 'Come on then, Audrey, let's take a little *Roman Holiday*.' As her mouth opened to reply with something along the lines of Audrey Hepburn had dark hair, not ginger, and was a zillion times better looking, he added, 'And just because I know a few old movies, it doesn't mean I like to watch them either.'

It was busy on the Spanish Steps, but they found a café at the top and enjoyed a drink looking down on the mass of tourists as they crowded on the steps. Gradually Jim started to unwind. Whether it was the change of scenery, or the company, he didn't want to speculate.

'You're looking slightly less grim now,' Tess commented as she put down her drink. 'Was it really bad, having to sack him?'

He was a man who valued honesty over anything else. 'Yes.' For a few seconds he toyed with his cup, debating whether he should step into slightly murky waters. 'I'm aware it was the right thing to do, that what he did was unprofessional and just plain wrong, but equally I can't help but feel what a waste of a talent. Here's a man whose skills have helped us develop several life saving therapies, yet he's unlikely to work in the industry again now he has this on his record. And all because of a woman.'

'All because he wanted something he couldn't have,' she corrected. 'It wasn't the woman's fault what he wanted was her.'

'No.' And he could see that, he really could. 'But sometimes the lines between work and outside work become blurred. It's late at night, you're away from the office, you've had a few drinks. Sometimes you forget to act like the boss. Sometimes you act like a man.'

Slowly she shook her head. 'You're forgetting the point. He wasn't sacked because he had a relationship in the workplace. He was sacked because he repeatedly harassed a woman who wasn't interested. The fact that he was her boss only made it that much harder for her to tell him no.' Her eyes met his. 'Which is why sacking him was so important. It sends a message that Helix will support others if they ever get caught in a similar situation.'

Jim knew all that, too. He just wished to God he wasn't quite so attracted to the woman who was telling him this. A woman who worked for him.

'Right, I think it's time for the Trevi Fountain and an ice cream,' she announced, pushing back her chair.

He glanced at the crumbs on her plate – the remnants of a sfogliatella, an odd-looking Italian pastry filled with some sort of cream. 'Why are you not fifteen stone?'

She laughed. 'Metabolism. Plus I don't eat like this all the time. But when in Rome ...'

They walked to the Trevi Fountain, and Jim was impressed that she was able to stride out at a reasonable pace, considering she still wore crazy high shoes. So far she'd worn a different pair each day. It seems she hadn't been kidding about the dozen pairs in her case.

'Are you sure you still want an ice cream?' he asked as she eyed up the amazing array of flavours in the large geletaria.

'Of course. Who goes to Rome and doesn't sample the gelato?'

'People who don't like ice cream?' he hazarded.

Immediately she swung round to face him. 'Oh my God, you're one of them, aren't you? An ice cream-o-phobe?'

She was looking at him as if he was an alien life form. 'What's to like?' he countered. 'It's cold and totally lacking any substance. Hell, you don't even eat it, you have to lick it. And how can it be called a food substance when it disappears in the heat?'

Her eyes filled with a disconcerting mixture of sympathy and disbelief. 'Have you even tried gelato?'

'I've tried ice cream.'

'That's like saying you don't like champagne when you've only tried Asti Spumante. Or you hate cruises when you've only been on a cross channel ferry. Or you—'

'I think I get the message,' he cut in dryly. 'And if it'll shut you up, I'll try one. What do you recommend?'

She eyed him quizzically, her nose wrinkling, her eyes dancing. *You're her boss*. He repeated the words over and over again in his mind. 'I think you're a mint choc chip,' she stated finally. 'Cool, but with a bit of bite.'

He decided he quite liked that. 'Okay then, if we're choosing flavours for each other, do they have chilli and macadamia for you?'

Her jaw dropped. 'A what?'

'Fiery and a bit nuts?'

She let out a strangled laugh. 'Oh boy, that was really bad. I mean, really bad. But I'll keep with your nut idea and go for pistachio.'

They took their ice creams and walked towards the

famous fountain. It wasn't the first time he'd seen it, but it was the first time he'd seen it whilst licking an ice cream. Sorry, *gelato*.

'What do you think then?' she asked with a playful smile.

'I think …' He became distracted by the sight of her tongue peeping out to lick at her lips. 'I think you've got a bit of gelato on your chin,' he murmured. Instinctively he raised his hand to wipe it off, but the moment his thumb touched her skin he felt the throb of it shoot through his arm and straight to his groin.

'Oops.' She made a husky noise, part cough, part laugh, and her cheeks flushed. For several long, pulsing moments he stared into her eyes. He wanted to kiss her so much it hurt. 'Jim?'

His name, whispered from those enticing lips, sounded scratchy, making him hopeful she felt the same way. *But you're still her boss.*

He snatched his hand away, turning his attention to the near naked men wrestling with the horses at the foot of the fountain. 'Why don't we throw a coin into the fountain to make sure we visit again?' Hell, his voice didn't sound a lot better. He cleared his throat. 'Maybe have some more gelato.'

She grinned. 'So you do like it, after all?'

He wasn't convinced it was the gelato that was causing his heart to thump.

As she turned away from the fountain, throwing a coin with her right hand over her left shoulder as tradition dictated, he realised he'd never seen her so bubbly, her face lit up with laughter. This was the real Tess, he imagined. Not the wary, slightly formal version he saw in the office, but this easy going, fun-loving person.

And heaven help him, she was even more captivating.

They were finally boarding their flight to Singapore, site of the Asia Pacific office. It was a great place to go for a holiday, but one heck of a long way to go for a meeting. As they walked through business class he glanced towards Tess, who still looked as fresh as a daisy in her sleek dark green trouser suit.

'This is where jet lag really comes into play,' he warned her as they settled into the bucket shaped seats. Their seats faced each other, with only a thin plastic barrier dividing them. At the moment it was down so they could talk. He made a mental note to make sure he pulled it up when they tried to sleep. The idea of sleeping right next to Tess made him incredibly uncomfortable. What if he murmured her name in his sleep? He wouldn't put it past himself because he'd been having some pretty erotic dreams about leggy redheads recently.

He yanked his computer out of its case and powered it on. In reality he'd be lucky to catch even five minutes' shut-eye with the amount of work he had to trawl through during the flight. Served him right for choosing sightseeing over a stint in the business lounge, he thought gloomily. But he could still taste the mint choc chip gelato.

'Umm, I think I'm going to watch a film and then try and grab some sleep.' Tess eyed up his computer. 'But if you're working, it'll make me feel really guilty.'

'Don't. This trip is going to be exhausting enough as it is. Rest while you can. I will, as soon as I clear a few items off my list.'

She sighed. 'I'll try, but I'm not too good in planes. I tend to need a big, soft bed before I can get to sleep.'

Jim steeled himself not to go there. Not to start to picture her in that king size bed, her lithe body stretched out across the silk sheets, her stunning red hair trailing over the plump feather pillows. He swallowed, hard. 'I recommend a few glasses of wine and a film that's long and tedious.'

She laughed softly. 'A suggestion I can certainly go with. Any recommendations for a soporific film?'

'Anything with Hugh Grant in it, for starters.'

'Let me guess, you're more of a Jason Statham fan.'

'At least in his films something blows up every ten minutes.'

'Which wouldn't help me sleep. Right, looks like I'm going to bed with Hugh Grant then.' She giggled slightly at her own joke before lowering her eyes to the in-flight entertainment magazine.

As the flight wore on, Jim found he couldn't help himself. He kept glancing over at her. It had seemed rude to pull up the barrier while she'd been awake, so instead he'd ploughed through his work, making a real effort not to watch her. Then her eyes had drifted shut. No doubt Hugh had done his job. After that, he spent a disproportionate amount of time looking at Tess, rather than his computer. And he had no inclination to pull up the barrier.

Was he becoming a little too obsessed with her? Having a gorgeous female to admire from afar was one thing, but since his cock-up, literally and figuratively, in the lift, his thoughts had strayed beyond the *afar*. Right now, they were in vivid close up. He dragged his eyes away, acutely aware that only a few hours ago he'd fired a man for something not dissimilar.

Determinedly he opened up another document on his computer. All he had to do was get through the next few days. Once he was back in the more secure surroundings of the office environment, his awkward attraction would hopefully disappear. At the very least, he would be able to manage it better.

Thanks to having to take a later plane out of Rome, they were forced to go straight from the airport to the office. It wasn't just that which made the presentation to the Asia Pacific management team hard going though. The culture in the region was very different to that of Europe or North America. Giving gifts was commonplace. A matter of simple courtesy, the group told Jim vehemently, time and time again.

'By not giving a gift, Helix would be considered extremely rude,' the regional director insisted. 'It would lead to us losing all the business we currently have.'

'I understand it will be tough, but as a company we need to take the same stance across the globe,' Jim stated firmly. 'We can't make exceptions. Your challenge will be to look for other ways to extend that courtesy. Options that have more scientific or educational value than rice cakes.'

He reiterated the point time and time again but Tess noted that even his strong shoulders started to droop by the end of the session.

As they headed towards the hotel in a taxi, Tess snuck another furtive glance at him. Lines of weariness were etched across his face, giving it a tired, craggy look. Why did it make him look even sexier, when the same exhaustion on her face made her look scarily anaemic?

'How much sleep did you actually get on the flight?' she asked.

He rubbed briefly at his eyes before replying. 'Is that you saying I look like shit again?'

'Tired,' she countered, her heart fluttering at his crooked smile. 'You look tired.'

'To be honest,' he told her as they headed into the tall tower block of a hotel, 'right now I *feel* tired. They didn't understand what I was saying. It's too big a culture shock for them.'

'Probably, but it doesn't mean they won't come round to your way of thinking eventually. Just give them time. Perhaps another visit in a few months.'

He gave her another rueful smile. 'Are you volunteering for that one, too?'

The twinkle in the depths of his eyes told her he was expecting her to groan with horror, so it was incredibly humiliating to admit that the thought was far from unappealing. Having spent the last few days with him, it was becoming harder and harder to see him as the big, bad pharmaceutical company chief. Far easier to see him as a dynamic, powerfully attractive, surprisingly approachable man.

He was still waiting for an answer.

'I think you can manage without me.'

'Perhaps, but I'd rather be *with* you.' He looked as shocked as she at his statement and hurriedly added, 'I don't know about you, but I need to shower, eat and then crash.'

It must have been a slip of his tongue, Tess told herself, trying to calm her suddenly racing heart. God knows, exhaustion could do that. She was pretty punch drunk with tiredness herself. 'I'm not sure what my body is telling me it wants. I don't even know what time it is.'

'You have to ignore the time on trips like this and just go with your instincts. I've had a curry for breakfast before now, just because that's what my stomach was telling me it wanted at the time.'

Tess laughed. 'That's one thing I know I *won't* want for breakfast. Mind you, right now ...' Her stomach gave a little rumble. '... food sounds like a good option.'

'Do you fancy meeting up in half an hour and grabbing something to eat?' He picked up his case. 'We could even go wild and venture outside the hotel. The locals conjure up some amazing food.'

'What, you mean another chance to see some of the country we're visiting, rather than just an office or a hotel room?' She grinned. 'Sure, why not?'

And just like that, she didn't feel quite so tired any more.

Chapter Thirteen

The fascinating sights, sounds and smells of a night out in Singapore left Tess awestruck. They combined to create an air of exotic intimacy further enhanced by the man at her side. Tonight she was seeing another side of Jim. The formal suit had been discarded in favour of a snug white T-shirt and low-slung faded jeans that moulded to his supreme male physique. In business attire he was suavely handsome. In casual gear, he was mouth-watering.

With the confidence of a man who knew his way around, Jim had whisked her off to what he'd blithely claimed was *the* place to eat in Singapore. She'd been worried it might be stuffy or fancy, but the bustling, vibrant Hawker centre was neither. Locals sat on casual tables and chairs, surrounded by a bewildering array of food and drink stalls all contained under a single roof. So far she'd eaten chicken satay, fried black noodles and a gorgeous tasting rice dish. Pleasantly full, she was ready to head back when Jim insisted on bringing her one final Singapore delicacy.

'Here you go.' He thrust a large glass towards her, full with pink foaming liquid and topped with a bright yellow umbrella. 'When in Singapore.'

'What on earth is that?' She eyed the frothy creation warily.

'Don't look so alarmed. It's a Singapore Sling. Originally developed for the Raffles Hotel. It's the Singapore equivalent of gelato. You can't leave the country without sampling it.'

'Okay.' She took a cautious a sip. 'Umm. Dare I ask what's in it?'

'Pineapple juice mainly.' Then he laughed when she narrowed her eyes at him. 'Okay, and a smattering of gin, cherry brandy and Benedictine.'

She almost choked. 'If I drink this, I'll be under the table.'

'I'll make sure you get safely back to your room. And into bed.'

Startled, she looked across at him but he avoided her eyes, playing instead with the pink paper umbrella from his drink, which looked absurd in his very masculine hands. Perhaps she was the only one reading erotic messages into everything he said.

By the time she'd finished the drink she was almost ready to keel over. Noticing her capitulation, Jim draped a supportive arm around her shoulders and helped her towards a waiting taxi.

'Sorry,' she mumbled, resting her head against the back seat. 'I think the alcohol has gone straight to my head.'

Gently he pushed her eyelids shut. 'Doze for a while. I'll wake you when we get to the hotel.'

She tried, but was too aware of his body sitting next to her, all hard angles and pulsing heat. The taxi turned a sharp corner and she was catapulted against a solid shoulder. 'Sorry.' Struggling to sit up, she gave him a lopsided smile.

'Don't be.'

His voice sounded gruff and when she looked into his dark eyes her breath caught in her throat. Tonight his eyes were on fire. A rush of pure hot desire raced through her system, pooling between her legs.

'Tess.' At the husky tone, she shivered. Then those hot eyes dropped to her mouth. 'God help me, I really want to kiss you.' He reached up and traced her lips with his thumb. 'I need to kiss you.'

His head edged closer to hers. She could see the fine lines around his eyes. The absurdly long dark lashes that swept over his lids. 'If you don't want this to happen you need to move away now, because once I claim your mouth, there'll be no escape.'

Of its own volition her body swayed towards him, rather than away, craving his touch. Everything that had happened up to this point suddenly didn't matter. She was a single

125

woman. He was a single, powerfully sexy, man. She wanted this, too.

His lips found hers, confidently nudging them apart, and Tess groaned out her pleasure. There was no hesitancy, no gentle probing. With a mouth that was both hot and hungry Jim took control, taking them from nothing to a flat out tonsil tangling snog in a matter of seconds. He didn't caress with his hands, or move his mouth from hers. He simply decimated her with the touch of his lips and the daring sweep and thrust of his tongue. She swore her bones actually started to dissolve.

'You at hotel.'

The stilted English words of the taxi driver crashed into the moment and Tess jerked her head away. Confused, her body on fire, breasts aching beneath her soft cotton shirt, she gulped in some much needed air.

Gently Jim touched her face with his hand, a wry smile crossing his handsome features. 'Wow,' was all he said. Then he climbed from the taxi and helped her out.

They were both silent as Jim settled the fare. Jeez, when was the last time she'd made out in the back of a cab? Try never. But what would happen now? Please God he wouldn't apologise, like he had after the *Lift Incident*. Or worse, remind her, as if she needed reminding, that it wasn't a good idea for them to be acting on this incredible chemistry they had.

Right now she didn't want to be sensible. She wanted to be wild.

As the taxi disappeared off down the road, Jim reached out and pulled her hard against him. 'Where were we,' he muttered thickly before settling his hands on her hips and once more plundering her mouth. Thank you, God.

Jim knew he'd lost control of his mind. He'd been hyper aware of her all evening but the moment she'd brushed against him in the cab, all resolve had flown out of the window and his libido had taken over. Drawing back slightly

126

he ran his eyes over her beautiful, flushed face, then down to the top of her delicate breasts, just visible through the low neck of her blouse. How could she go braless and expect him not to notice? And, once he'd noticed, how the hell was he supposed to be able to push the vision out of his mind?

Damn it. He lowered his head to feast once more on her mouth, his hands snaking under her blouse and across her long, smooth back. She felt unbelievable. So soft and warm. As his hands wound their way to the front of her blouse, towards her breasts, he suddenly realised what he was doing. Pawing at her in front of the hotel entrance, in full view of the hotel staff and guests.

Exhaling hard, he pulled away. 'Shit. Sorry.'

She looked up at him with those amazing blue eyes and he read both desire and … anger?

'You don't need to apologise,' she told him stiffly, trying to turn.

He drew her back, trailing kisses over her face. 'Hey, I'm not sorry for kissing you. Just for doing it so publically. There's a time and a place for this type of behaviour.' He reached for her hand. 'So help me, this is most definitely the time, but not the place.'

Her eyes sparkled back at him and he almost dragged her through the lobby, for once not appreciating the delicate heels she wore. He was happy to have those heels wrapped around his hips in a few minutes but right now they were delaying his progress. 'Corny but …' He pressed for the lift. '… your room or mine?'

The lift doors opened and before she had a chance to reply he was pushing her back against the wall, his mouth devouring hers. He couldn't get enough of the taste of her. Essence of Tess, with a sprinkle of Singapore Sling.

'Don't you have a rule?' Tess whispered, but even as she said the words, she arched her hips towards him, making him groan.

'What?' he asked distractedly, planting burning kisses all over her flushed skin. He wasn't interested in talking.

The lift doors opened and he dug into his pocket, searching for the damn keycard. She opened her handbag and handed him hers. 'Use mine. It's closer.'

'Hallelujah.'

He half pulled her to the room and within seconds he was pushing open the door and taking her in his arms again. 'This blouse has been driving me crazy all evening,' he told her as he ran his hands over the light cotton, rubbing his hand gently over the tight, bud like nipples underneath.

He heard her suck in a breath. 'That feels so good.'

The fingers of his other hand slipped under her waistband and his mouth slid down her throat and into the neck of her blouse.

'Oh God, Jim.' She broke off momentarily as his fingers found what they were looking for. 'You told me you had a rule,' she panted as his tongue made circles on the flesh above her breasts, dipping tantalisingly down towards her nipples. 'You don't sleep with people who work for you.'

'Sod the bloody rule,' he replied gruffly, reaching for the buttons on her blouse and grappling them with little finesse. 'Besides, I'm not planning on doing any sleeping.'

She moaned as his fingers brushed her heated flesh. 'But will you still think that tomorrow morning?'

'Tomorrow can take care of itself.' But then unbidden and unwanted snippets of an earlier conversation reared their way through his lust. Sexual harassment, pushing himself onto a woman who wasn't interested. He froze. 'This is what you want too, isn't it Tess?'

'Yes.'

'Thank heavens for that. Can we finish talking now?'

She laughed and made a gesture as if she was zipping her mouth closed.

* * *

Suddenly Tess found herself lifted up into Jim's strong arms and carried to the bed. It wasn't quite the sweet, tender stuff of fairy tales. In fact Tess thought it had more to do with Jim getting what he wanted, i.e. her on the bed, as quickly as possible. Nor was there anything sweet about the look in his eyes as he stared hungrily down at her. He was definitely more Big Bad Wolf than Prince Charming, but she couldn't wait for him to gobble her up. She'd done with trying to do the right thing. Maybe she should have reminded herself of the reasons *she* shouldn't be doing this, rather than focussing on his rule. Maybe they'd both regret this in the morning. But for now, she didn't care.

Her skin shivered in anticipation as he slowly peeled off her skirt, his gaze almost reverent as it glided over her legs. Tess knew she had reasonable legs; they were something she was proud of. Unlike other parts of her body.

Her eyes swung automatically towards the ceiling as Jim began undoing her blouse. She didn't dare look at the expression on his face now. As he undid the final button and drew the blouse apart, his movements stilled. 'Jesus.'

At his rough exclamation the desire drained out of her. Replaced by a crushing disappointment. How had she let herself believe a man like Jim could possibly find a stick like her attractive? It was different when she had her clothes on. Then men waxed lyrical about her willowy frame. But once her true figure was revealed ... hell, she'd been a bloody fool to believe Jim's eyes would continue to blaze with the same intensity. She knew his type. Barbara. Sexy curves. Large breasts. About as far removed from her scrawny, man-like body as it was possible to get.

Squeezing her eyes tightly shut, damned if she was going to cry, she angled her head away from what she knew was a look of disguised disappointment in his eyes. She couldn't do this any more. When she'd thought he'd been as carried away as her, it had been different. Now if they continued, he'd be doing it out of pity. Her heart heavy in her chest, she reached for her blouse.

His hand shot out, gripping her arm. 'Hey, what's wrong? What are you doing?'

Tess found she couldn't look at him. 'It's okay. I understand.' She tried to shrug off his grip, desperately wanting to hide herself.

'What do you understand?'

'You're not interested any more,' she replied tightly, her humiliation now layered with a touch of anger. Wrenching his hand away she immediately covered her breasts with her arms.

'What?' His exclamation was loud enough that she was finally forced to look at him. 'You've got to be out of your mind.'

Feeling vulnerable and totally exposed she shook her head, continuing to grip her arm around her body as if her life depended on it.

His face gentled and he lightly touched her face with his fingers. 'Look at me,' he whispered, forcing her eyes to look into his. 'Why wouldn't I be interested?'

Tess bit her lip, shaking her head. She just wanted to be left alone.

'Tess?' When she refused to look at him he let out a deep sigh of frustration and moved off the bed. 'Don't you want to do this any more?'

She blinked. 'It's not that I don't want to.'

'You think *I* don't?' He stared at her incredulously. 'Tess, do I look like a man who doesn't want to make love to you?' Carefully he took her hand, easing it away from her body and laying it on the huge bulge that strained against the zip of his jeans. 'Do I *feel* like a man who doesn't think you're the most beautiful woman he's ever set eyes on?'

'When you took off my blouse,' she whispered, 'and saw my breasts, you froze. You swore.'

'Because you've got the most incredible body I've ever seen,' he told her, shaking his head in disbelief. 'How could you possibly think anything different?'

'You're not the first man to be disappointed in me.'

'Disappointed? Bloody hell woman, just look at yourself,' he told her roughly, capturing her hands and revealing her breasts once more. 'Your legs are endless, your skin so smooth and pale and unbelievably sexy. Your breasts are small, but that's what makes them so exquisite. They're like perfect rosebuds.' He gave her a smile full of self-mockery. 'Heck, they're so gorgeous they've even got a philistine like me waxing poetic about them. Tess, you're so beautiful it almost hurts to look at you.'

It sounded like a cliché until she looked into his eyes. They blazed with a desire that was surely impossible to fake. He really does find me attractive, she thought with utter amazement. Tiny breasts and all.

He dropped a tender kiss on her mouth. 'Please don't tell me you're going to put that shirt back on.'

As his lips nuzzled hers and his warm, slightly rough hands moved once more over her body, Tess knew she had no intention of putting her clothes back on. 'No, not as long as you take yours off.'

With a laugh that sounded a lot like relief, Jim dispensed with his clothes and slipped on a condom. Clearly he wasn't taking any chances that she'd back out again. She only had a brief moment to take in the beauty of his muscular chest before he moved back over her, settling the hard lines of his body against hers.

'Damn,' he croaked as skin met skin. 'You feel—'

'Like a bag of bones?' God, why couldn't she keep her big mouth shut, and her stupid insecurities to herself?

He snapped his head back. 'Whoever told you that?' Then he shook his head and rained tantalising kisses across her face. 'Forget it, I don't want to know. Whoever it was, they were a bloody idiot.' Shifting slightly, he nestled between her legs, his arousal thick and heavy against her stomach. It left her reassuringly in no doubt what *he* thought of how she felt. 'I was going to say, you feel amazing. And that if I don't get inside you soon, I think I'm going to die.'

Funny, that was just what she was thinking. Tess clasped his powerful body closer, running a hand over the corded muscles of his back while she spread her legs to encourage him in. She gasped as he slid into her, feeling a thrill all the way from her toes to her breasts. With a tilt of his hips he thrust deeper, building on the pleasure. As if that wasn't enough to torture her senses, he also lowered his head and began to flick a lazy tongue across her hardened nipples. It felt astoundingly sexy. Astounding because her breasts had never felt like that. Ever. With a moan of pleasure she arched her back to provide him better access.

He picked up the rhythm, his hips straining, thrusting more powerfully into hers.

'God this feels good,' he groaned, his face a mixture of tension and pleasure. 'So good I can't hold off much longer.' He planted a searing kiss against her lips. 'Come for me, Tess.'

His words catapulted her right over the edge. As she drifted back to earth he growled out her name, jerked his hips one more time and found his own release. Collapsing on top of her with a satisfying thump.

When he finally levered himself off her and onto his back, drawing her close, Tess was struck by the thought that never in her life had anything felt as right as it did to be in this man's arms.

Which was madness, because it should have felt so very wrong.

Chapter Fourteen

What the hell had he been thinking? Jim thought angrily as he thrashed up and down in what the hotel laughingly called their large leisure pool. He snorted, at the same time executing an indelicate tumble turn. The result had him inhaling a mouthful of chlorine. After a few coughs and a fair bit of spluttering he continued his furious progress through the water, all the while remembering that thinking hadn't been high on his priorities last night. He'd been focussed purely on feeling. Alas, as indescribably good as that had been, it was now the cold light of day.

And he'd woken to find himself naked in bed with his communications manager. His arms wrapped so tightly around her he'd had one hell of a job extracting himself.

Way to go, Jim. Exactly what a man in his position should be doing.

Halfway through a roadshow aimed at cleaning up the company's act and he'd been stupid enough to participate in the most seedy act of all. Taking advantage of a younger, junior member of the company. Sleeping with her when exhaustion, not to mention the influence of a strong alcoholic cocktail – one *he'd* bought her – had combined to bring her defences crashing down.

For the last two days he'd preached about the Red Face test, imagining the headlines if the press decided to splash what you were doing over their front page. The aim being, if the imagined headline didn't make you cringe with mortal embarrassment, what you were doing was probably okay. He didn't need to picture the headline to know that what he'd done was just plain wrong. Never mind his frigging personal rule about not sleeping with women who worked for him. Or the fact that he'd just spent the last few years recovering from a work-based relationship that had blown up in his face.

Forty minutes later he dragged his body out of the pool and into the shower. With the hot spray beating against his skin he tried to work out what on earth he was going to say to Tess.

Ten minutes later, his heart thumping more than it had during the entire time he'd been in the pool, he knocked on the door of her room.

She opened it dressed in the hotel robe, wet hair tumbling in curls over her shoulders. Her face was devoid of make-up, her eyes a startling blue against her alabaster skin.

He inhaled sharply. Right now he found it hard to blame himself for what he'd done. In fact he just wanted to do it all again. And again.

'Hi,' he finally croaked. Not the most enterprising of starts. 'Can I come in?'

She nodded and stood aside.

'I wanted to apologise for last night,' he began, moving into the room and towards the bed.

The very place where, a few hours earlier, she'd wrapped her incredible legs around him. He forced his eyes away from the bed and towards her.

'I shouldn't have let last night happen,' he told her softly. 'It was wrong.' Slowly he dragged a hand down his face, trying to gather his wits. 'God knows, I don't need the Red Face test to know that.'

At first she looked a little startled at his words, but then she gave him a small, understanding smile. 'How would your headline go? Singapore Fling?'

He tried to smile back, though it was damn hard to, when he felt like such a shit. 'Something like that. But it's the opening sentence. *He bought me this giant cocktail and then, when I was on my knees with tiredness, followed me into my hotel room.*' He shook his head and swore softly under

134

his breath, hating how bad that sounded. Hating even more how close it was to the truth. 'Hell, Tess, it's that part which makes me sick with shame.'

Tess sunk down onto the bed. 'Whoever wrote those words, couldn't have been there,' she told him quietly. 'As I recall, it was a mutual decision. You didn't force yourself into my room. I willingly gave you my key.'

Jim moved further into the room and stood over by the large window, desperate to put some distance between them. Otherwise he'd do something stupid. Like take her in his arms.

'I appreciate your version, but the fact is I took advantage of you when you weren't able to think straight,' he told her gravely. 'I'll understand if you want to file a complaint.'

'A what?' Tess gaped at him.

'I abused my position.' He tugged a hand through his hair, his body language betraying his self-directed anger. 'Christ, I've just sacked a man for less. At least Lombardi didn't go as far as sleeping with anyone.'

Tess wasn't having this. Yes what they'd done had been wrong, incredible, but wrong, though not for the reasons he was thinking. It had been wrong of *her* to sleep with a man she was investigating. A man she might end up betraying. 'You didn't abuse anything,' she told him heatedly.

He shook his head slightly and the shame she read in his dark eyes made her chest tighten painfully.

'How can you say I didn't use my position to my advantage?' he asked, his tone less controlled now, harsher. 'Technically I might not be your line manager, but I am senior to you. A fact that didn't exactly make it easy for you to say no to me.'

Despite the circumstances, she found herself laughing. 'I know we discussed this back in Rome, but seriously, do I strike you as a woman who would feel pressured into doing

135

something she didn't want to?' she asked dryly. 'I didn't want to say no,' she continued, looking him straight in the eye. 'So I didn't. You gave me every opportunity to, but I still didn't. I gave you my key. I chose to invite you in. I wanted you in my bed.'

'Still, I'm sorry.'

And now his insistence that last night was one giant mistake on his behalf was starting to hurt. Just like it had hurt to find herself alone in the bed when she'd woken up. Neither should matter, but they did. 'I tried to warn you that you'd regret it in the morning,' she told him, turning slightly so he couldn't read her eyes.

A bit of grim left his face and a wry smile tugged at his mouth. 'Yeah, you did. And if I recall correctly, I wasn't in the mood for listening.'

He surprised her then by moving towards her, closing the gap he'd previously left. Lifting his hand, he gently touched her cheek. 'Just to be clear, I don't regret making love to you.' The eyes that she'd once described as like coal were a rich, molten amber. 'That was a privilege. An honour. What I regret is that we work for the same company. That I'm senior to you, so whatever you might say, it smacks of misuse of power.' He dropped his hand to his side and moved away, towards the door.

'So what happens now?' Her voice came out in a whisper and she tried to blink away the tears that threatened to fall. Dressed in jeans and a dark polo shirt, his handsome face earnest, he was a powerfully visible reminder of why she'd let her hormones rule her head last night.

'What happens now,' he repeated, his voice so deep it made her toes curl, 'is that I promise to keep my trousers firmly zipped and we continue our professional relationship as if last night never happened.' He turned and placed a hand on the door but before opening it, he glanced back over his shoulder. 'Oh and I advise you to keep as far away from me as you can, because, God help me, when I look at you, I still want you.' His dark eyes glittered. 'My willpower is only so strong, as you've already witnessed.'

The moment he closed the door behind him, Tess collapsed onto the bed and shut her eyes, unsure what to feel. It should be relief, because he'd put an end to their affair before she'd had to. But my God, the words he'd uttered, the expression in his eyes when he'd said them. She'd found herself melting. Worse, she'd felt her heart slowly opening up to him. Was she so starved of male attention that she was letting a few well-chosen words turn her to mush? She had to believe that was the case, because the alternative, that she was actually falling for him, was too terrifying to contemplate.

Within hours they were walking into the business class section of another plane, for yet another flight – to North America. This time Jim made sure he kept the divide between Tess and himself firmly up.

Not that it seemed to matter. He was aware of her presence all the way to San Diego.

Chapter Fifteen

There was time for a quick shower at the airport before a waiting car whisked them off to the Western USA office. Then it was a brief round of introductions and onto the lecture theatre. From her seat on the front row – a position she'd been forced into because she was due to present – Tess glanced back at the cavernous theatre and gulped. How many eyes would be watching?

She huffed out a breath. She only had a few slides to deliver. Slides she'd presented several times already on this trip. It wasn't worth getting her knickers in a twist over. Today was no different than Singapore, or Rome, or the UK. Except it was. Today she'd be presenting to an audience three times larger than before. And in front of a man she'd slept with.

Once more she fidgeted on her seat, turning away from the hundreds of people packed behind her. Trying not to look at the man sitting next to her. As her heart bounced beneath her ribs, Jim put a warm, steadying hand over hers.

'Are you okay?' he asked very quietly, his eyes focussed on the general manager of the Western office who was currently on stage making the introductions.

'No,' she admitted. 'There are too many eyes watching.'

The general manager finished his introduction and Jim stood up, but not before turning to whisper into her ear. 'Pretend they're all naked. It's what I do.'

A grin started to slide across her face until she realised all she wanted to do now was picture *him* naked.

As she mentally grappled with that erotic image, Jim began his talk, presenting in a confident, powerful style that appeared so effortless. People like him had the skill, charisma, whatever it was, to command a room. Others didn't. No matter how many people they imagined naked.

When it came to her turn Tess accepted she wasn't going to be great and settled instead for being as good as she could be. She spoke slowly, remembering someone once telling her that if she thought she was speaking too slowly, it was probably coming across about right. The moment her slides were over she dashed back to her seat, feeling like a wrung out dishcloth. No doubt looking like one, too. In direct contrast Jim, immaculately handsome, finished off the session in his energetic, punchy, no nonsense manner.

The floor opened up to questions.

'This honesty and integrity is all very good,' came a voice from behind her, 'but is it going to apply to *everything* we do, or just to the promotional side of things?'

Her first thought was, wow, what a dynamite question. So far on this trip there had been a lot of grumbling from the markets about how much the revised policy put them at a competitive disadvantage in terms of selling. This was the first time she'd heard other parts of the business mentioned. Intrigued, Tess turned to look at the questioner. Young, smartly dressed in a charcoal grey suit and pale blue shirt, his hair neatly combed, he had the words *marketing* written all over him.

At the lectern, Jim narrowed his eyes, his expression slightly puzzled. 'Would you like to explain exactly what you mean by that?'

'Well, what about the studies we do that don't have the results we want so don't always get published. Do they also come under this new initiative?'

A hush came over the room and Tess held her breath, the hand at her side forming an automatic fist in an expression of solidarity. She couldn't have planted a better question if she'd tried. She'd been so caught up in the Jim Knight whirlwind she'd almost lost sight of why she was here. Now the very issue she'd joined the company to investigate was out in the open. Requiring an answer.

She swung her eyes back to Jim. His body language hadn't changed. One hand was still nonchalantly in his pocket, the other relaxed on the lectern. But she could sense, even if she couldn't actually *see*, that he was wrong-footed.

'At the moment the focus is on the commercial side of the business,' Jim told the questioner, straightening up and putting both hands on the lectern. 'But the principles of honesty and integrity should run through everything we do. I'll follow up on the publication policy as soon as I get back to the office.'

And so will I, Tess thought to herself. *So will I.*

Quickly answering the remaining questions, Jim uttered a silent prayer of thanks that none were as controversial as the first. He should have seen that coming – but he hadn't. In his determination to bulldoze through these changes he'd managed to miss out a big chunk of what 'Leading with Science' should be about. Transparency in publishing clinical trial results. The issue had been in the press enough over the years. How on earth had he managed to overlook it?

Following the end of the session he was dragged into a few management meetings and it wasn't until he was finally in a cab on the way back to the hotel that he was able to take a mental breath. Thankfully Tess had already left. No doubt she was now checked into her room, catching up on the sleep he hadn't allowed her to have the night before.

No. He wasn't going to think about that. Today was a sharp reminder that he couldn't afford any distractions. *Especially* those that came in the form of gorgeous, leggy redheads. Was she the reason he'd taken his eye off the ball regarding the publication policy? God only knew. But he'd already let one woman interfere with his life at work, with calamitous results. He'd be a fool to go down that road again.

He checked into his room, raided his suitcase for a pair of trunks and headed straight for the pool. Sure it was going to be the size of a postage stamp, but it was either swim or run and he really didn't have the energy to run.

Striding out from the changing room, he came to an abrupt halt. Just what he needed. Tess. Fluidly slipping through the water in a sleek black swimsuit. As she reached his end she turned and caught sight of him.

'Hi.' She rested her arms on the side of the pool, strands of her hair streaming across her shoulders like deep red ribbons.

He swallowed, aware his trunks were tight and streamlined. Not that she hadn't seen it all already. 'I thought you'd be catching up on some sleep,' he replied, quickly slipping into the pool. Grateful for the cold.

'I slept a little but my body clock is in another time zone entirely. I'm done here though,' she told him as she moved towards the steps. 'The pool's all yours. Can we catch up in the bar later?'

'Sure. Give me an hour.'

With that he ducked under the water and began striking out across the pool, his powerful stroke making waves through the calm surface.

Tess had swum like a dolphin. He was more killer whale.

Tess was already sitting in the bar when Jim arrived, exactly an hour later. The swim had helped to revive him. The sight of Tess, casually but tastefully dressed in loose silky trousers and a wrap around blouse, invigorated him a lot more.

Taking a deep breath, he walked towards her, all the while trying not to think about how incredible he knew she looked *under* those clothes. By the time he reached her, it was all he could think of. Bloody perfect.

He swallowed hard. 'Would you like another?' He nodded at her half drunk glass of wine.

She shook her head, soft red hair shimmering in the subdued lighting. 'No, thanks. I think we've seen enough of what drinking and tiredness can do to me.'

He met her gaze and knew that they were both remembering Singapore. Though he tried to look away, the blue of her eyes was too tempting. He'd give anything right now to reach out and take her hand. To lead her back to his room and take her to bed.

'I rather liked what drinking and tiredness did to you,' he told her softly. Immediately her eyes dropped to her glass and he kicked himself. He was supposed to be stepping away, not going full throttle ahead. He caught the attention of a passing bartender and ordered himself a beer.

'How are you holding up?' he asked, steering the conversation back to safer ground.

'Good thanks.' Then she let out a half laugh. 'Who am I kidding? I'm shattered. Never mind not knowing what time it is, I don't even know which day of the week we're on.'

'Only one more to go, Tess.' He studied his hands, trying to work out how to say the next words without it sounding like another come on. 'You know I really appreciate you helping out like this. I was planning on doing this alone, fully understanding that it would be hell on earth, but it was only me I was putting through it. Then you offered to come along. Any decent guy would have politely turned you down, but I decided to be selfish.' He looked straight into her eyes. 'Still I can't regret my decision. What I started out calling Hell Week has, in fact, been anything but hell. Thanks to you.'

And yes, he'd said too much, because now he knew they were both thinking back to the part that had been far closer to heaven. At least it had for him.

Tess dragged her eyes away from Jim's soulful deep brown eyes and his blindingly handsome features. She couldn't afford to be unravelled by him, his words or his looks, again.

'Thank you,' she replied, her voice sounding soft and husky. Come on, she willed herself. Stop being dazzled.

Forget how amazing this man made you feel. Remember Mum. Reaching out, she snatched at her glass and gulped at her wine. 'Well, what did you think of today's session? That question about publishing studies was a bit of a surprise, wasn't it?' Feigning casualness, she leant back against the soft chair and watched for his reaction.

'You can say that again.' He ran a hand distractedly through his springy, dark hair. 'I should have seen it coming, but I didn't.'

Tess crossed her legs, trying to divert attention from her heart, thumping away so hard he could surely see it. 'So what is the Helix stance on publishing results from clinical trials?'

The bartender arrived with Jim's beer, obscuring her view of his face for a few moments. By the time the waiter had moved away, Jim's eyes were on his beer and not on her.

'To be honest, I don't know,' he admitted, bringing the glass to his lips and draining a large mouthful.

Unconsciously she sat forward, clasping her hands in front of her. 'How can you not know? You worked for the company for years. I understand you headed up clinical trial programmes. Surely you had to know what you were doing with the results?'

'My focus was on getting the studies done,' he replied evenly, 'not publishing the results.'

'But what was the point of doing the studies if you weren't going to tell everyone what the results were?'

'I didn't say we didn't publish the results.' Now his voice held a trace of irritation. 'Just that it wasn't my focus.'

'Well, it should have been,' she retorted, far too sharply. Biting down on her temper, she continued in a more placatory tone. 'Sorry, it's just that I can't see how you can put patients through your clinical trials and not automatically make sure the information gained was made public. Surely that's why you do the studies – to improve the knowledge on your products so you can enhance the care of future patients?'

His dark eyes grew cold. 'Do you really think I need you to tell me that?'

'I don't know, do you?' The words flew out of her mouth, driven by the image of her mother, lying dead on a hospital bed. Abruptly she rose to her feet. 'I'm going to call it a night.'

'Wait.'

It was a single word, but spoken with such authority she automatically halted.

'Are you really going to hurl accusations at me and then not give me the right to reply?'

He was angry. Not shouting, red in the face angry but cold, rigidly in control angry. It was even more effective. Awkwardly she sat back down.

Jim settled his glass back down on the low table. 'Of course I should know the publication policy,' he told her with his trademark blunt honesty. 'The fact that I don't makes me look and feel sloppy. And of course results from clinical trials should automatically be made public. The truth is, I can't, hand on my heart, tell you that has always happened.' Tiredly he rubbed at his face and she caught a glimpse of the exhaustion she knew he must be feeling. 'Hell, Tess, I can't even guarantee all the studies I was involved with were published. I'm not sure what that makes me, but I do know the first opportunity I get when I'm back in the office, I'm going to sort this out. Whatever has, or hasn't been happening in the past, we will be a company that publishes the results of every single clinical study we undertake.'

'Good.' He looked so sincere, Tess found herself believing him. There was something about the way he spoke, the almost brutally frank way he said what he was thinking, that hacked away at her defences. He could have told her to butt out, mind her own business. Disciplined her, even, for her rudeness, because she had been. Instead he'd openly admitted he'd been wrong. Unsure what to say next, she reached for her glass, only to find there was nothing in it.

'Do you want to grab something to eat?'

His question took her totally off guard and she gawked at him. 'I'd have thought, after my last outburst, you'd have had enough of my company for today.'

He quirked a dark eyebrow. 'I've told you before. I don't mind people speaking their mind. I prefer that to letting the thoughts fester.'

'Even when it leads to rudeness?' She couldn't help herself. She started to smile.

His lips twitched in response. 'It keeps me on my toes. So, shall we eat?'

Over dinner Jim was funny, knowledgeable and compelling to listen to. She found herself hanging on his every word, enjoying his anecdotes. Enjoying his company.

By the time they rode back in the lift together, she was once again only too aware of the man behind the R&D president title. The one who smelt of fresh hotel shower gel, with undertones of dark testosterone. Who wore faded denim jeans and an aura of rugged power.

She was smitten. So much so, it was terrifying. Did he feel the same way? As if he could read her mind, his deep brown eyes suddenly pierced hers, heat flaring in their depths.

She had her answer.

Wordlessly they exited the lift and came to a halt outside her room. Her hands trembled slightly as she reached inside her handbag for the key. Sexual tension hung heavily in the air.

'I, err ...' She didn't know what to say. Every cell in her body wanted to invite him in, except those in her brain, which told her she mustn't. Today had shown her that Helix didn't always publish the results of their studies. In which case there was a chance they hadn't published some results on Zaplex. So getting any closer to Jim would be stupidity of the highest order.

'I think this is where I need to say goodnight.' His eyes belied his words. They made it clear saying goodnight was the last thing he wanted to do.

Unconsciously she licked at her lips, imagining him kissing her there.

'Tess,' he groaned, reaching out to lay a warm hand on her cheek. 'I want to kiss you so much it hurts.' He bent towards her, his lips a tantalising breath away from hers. Desire swirled fiercely in his eyes.

Suddenly he drew back. 'I'll see you tomorrow morning.'

She nodded, then pushed her way into her room, letting the door fall back with a bang. So close. She'd been so close to asking him in. If he hadn't pulled back …

What a mess. She was here to avenge her mother's death. Not to help improve Helix's reputation, as Jim believed, but perhaps to irrefutably damage it.

Perhaps, in the process, to irrefutably damage him.

With a sob of despair she flung herself onto the bed.

Chapter Sixteen

Another day, another part of the globe, though at last they'd landed in their final destination, New York. Tess stared out of the taxi window, awed by the sight of Manhattan; the skyscrapers that towered above the horizon, seemingly coming out of nowhere. It had been a dream of hers to visit the Big Apple, though in that dream she'd been wandering down Fifth Avenue, weaving in and out of the shops, clutching an array of designer bags. Not sitting in a stuffy office building.

She looked across at Jim, who had his nose buried in a report.

'I don't suppose we could squeeze any shopping time into today's agenda?' she asked wistfully as the yellow taxi threaded its way towards the heart of Manhattan.

'Is this the shopping I warned you we'd have no time for?'

She huffed out a sigh. 'Okay. Stupid idea. Much better to spend the next few hours in the hotel than in the shopping mecca of the world.'

He chuckled, the grooves at the side of his mouth deepening. 'Well, you put the schedule together.' He studied his watch. 'By my reckoning, we've got to be in the office in two hours. Going straight to the hotel gives us time to refresh, grab a bite to eat and go through the afternoon's itinerary.'

'I suppose.' She stared longingly at the skyline.

'On the other hand—'

'We could forget about showering and dash crazily round the shops instead, grabbing a hot dog from a stand along the way,' she finished for him.

'And the itinerary?' His eyes twinkled.

He was teasing her, this man she'd once believed to be cold and unfeeling. 'We go over that on the journey to the office.'

'It seems you have an answer to everything.' His eyes fell to her feet. 'Don't tell me, you're heading for the shoe shops.'

She grinned. 'Whatever gives you that idea?'

He shrugged. 'Beats me.'

She couldn't resist waggling her shoes at him. Today it was her Salvatore Ferragamos. Possessing a relatively small heel, a concession to the ridiculous amount of walking an airline passenger was subjected to, they were in bright cerise suede with a silver buckle. 'What do you think?'

'I think they make me want to reach out and touch.' He sighed, shaking his head. 'Sorry.' Then he sighed again, deeper this time. 'In case you haven't realised, I'm finding this whole purely professional thing pretty damn hard.' He crooked a slight smile. 'And sharing that piece of information with you isn't going to make it any easier. So, I'll start again.' Taking in a breath, he nodded down at the shoes. 'I think they're very you. I also think you must be a magician to fit so many of them into your suitcase.'

She wanted to tell him that she, too, was finding this more than hard, but that wasn't going to help the situation either. 'You should see me when I go on holiday. It's a good job I'm not quite as obsessed with clothes as I am with shoes.'

Jim smiled back, but it was a tired, strained smile, as if he'd rather be anywhere than in this taxi, with her. Or maybe he was simply struggling with what to say next. After all, she *was* talking about shoes and shopping.

'Look, I know you don't want to hit the shops, but if you could just drop me off somewhere near a large store, I'll zip round and be back at the hotel in time to leave for the office.'

'No, I'll come with you.' As the words left his mouth he grimaced, as if he was hardly able to believe what he'd said.

Tess looked at him uncertainly. 'You want to come shopping?'

For a brief moment he seemed about to rescind his offer. Then he laughed softly. 'No, I don't want to go shopping. I can think of many things I want to do in the next two hours,' he gave her a heat filled look. 'Shopping is definitely not on that list. However making sure you arrive safe and sound at the office is, so I'll come.'

Tess bit her lip and tried to ignore the rush of desire his hot eyes instilled in her. Instead she imagined his impatient, glowering presence as he followed her round the shops. He was hardly the type to bestow insightful advice on style and colour.

'It's okay,' he told her dryly after he'd given instructions to the driver to drop their cases off at the hotel. 'I won't cramp your style. Just point you in the right direction, and corral you when it's time to leave.'

True to his word, he left her to dash up Fifth Avenue while he strolled off to grab a couple of hot dogs.

Half an hour later, armed with two Saks carrier bags, she scanned the sidewalk for a tall, dark, handsome man. Laughing at the corny image she snuck another look inside her bags. A pair of sublime Diane von Furstenberg leopard print wedges and some neat Dolce & Gabbana silver sling backs that would surely go with *anything*.

When she glanced up again her tall, dark handsome man was striding towards her. She began to wave and point at her bags but then caught sight of his face. He looked harassed. No, more than that. His calm had vanished. When she was close enough to see into his eyes, she knew something was really wrong.

'Are you okay?'

Tensely he nodded, thrusting a hot dog at her. 'I'm fine, but we need to be getting back to the hotel.' He appeared anything but fine as he bundled her unceremoniously into a yellow cab.

'What's happened? You look …' Upset was the word she wanted to use, but whilst true, she wasn't sure it was an appropriate description for a man like him. 'You look out of sorts.'

A muscle twitched in his jaw. 'I've had some bad news from home,' he answered in a tight voice. 'My father's had a heart attack.'

'Oh, Jim, I'm so sorry.' Tess reached to touch his arm, aware of how futile the gesture was but wanting, no needing, to try and comfort.

'He's still hanging on, thank God. Mum's with him.'

'Good. That will surely help.'

As Tess's big blue eyes drowned him with their sympathy, Jim shut his. He knew she was only being kind but he couldn't talk about this now. Not while his emotions were still so close to the surface. Once he'd got back to the hotel and taken a shower, collected his thoughts, phoned home again. Then, maybe, he'd be able talk.

Thankfully she seemed to understand and for the rest of the journey she quietly ate her hot dog, though she continued to rest her hand on his arm, occasionally rubbing it in a soothing gesture. Something he was very much aware of.

After checking in, Jim glanced at his watch. 'Can you meet me down here in twenty minutes?'

'Sure, but we can go straight to the airport if you like. I don't need to freshen up.'

He exhaled sharply. 'I mean, can you be ready to go to the office in twenty minutes.'

She gaped at him. 'What?'

'Tess, we need to leave in twenty minutes,' he bit out, struggling to hide his frustration. 'If you'd wanted longer you should have thought of that before heading off on your shopping spree.'

'Crikey, Jim, I'm not talking about the difference between twenty minutes or sixty minutes. I'm talking about the fact that your dad's just had a heart attack yet you're still planning on going into the *office*?'

'What do you suggest I do?' he snapped. 'He's lying in a

hospital bed thousands of miles away.' Christ, just the thought was enough to make his eyes fill. 'I can't help him right now.'

'I see, so it's out of sight, out of mind? You're going to neatly push his health into the back of your mind and carry on as normal?'

Wow. 'Yeah, sure I am. I mean, that should be easy enough to do for a cold-hearted son of a bitch like me, eh?'

'No. That's not what I said. I know you're not like that.'

'Forget it.' He was far too emotional for this conversation. That had to be why her words hurt so damn much. 'Look, there's no point in me sitting stewing while I could be doing something useful.' He rubbed at his eyes, knowing he was seconds away from breaking down totally, which would embarrass the hell out of both of them.

'You don't know how lucky you are he's still there,' she told him quietly, then turned to stride away, but not before he'd seen the tears running down her cheeks.

Confused, he held on to her arm, dragging her round to face him. 'Tess, what's wrong?'

She shook her head, trying to pull away from him, but he held her firmly. 'Tell me,' he whispered. 'Please.'

Her eyes stared, unblinkingly, at the floor and for several long seconds he thought she wasn't going to say anything. Then she looked up and swallowed. 'My mother died of a heart attack.' Her voice caught and the tears continued to flow, despite her efforts to wipe them away.

'Hell, I'm sorry. I didn't know,' he replied softly, his heart going out to her. 'How long ago was it?'

'Eighteen months.' He could see from the pain in her eyes that it still felt like yesterday. 'I wasn't there at the time. I was out with friends, at a party. My brother phoned with the news. By the time I arrived at the hospital, she'd gone.' Her words trailed off as her voice broke. 'It hurts that I wasn't there to hold her hand,' she whispered finally. 'It hurts that I couldn't tell her I loved her one more time.'

At the raw agony on her face his heart squeezed tightly in his chest. He didn't know what to say, how he could possibly help, so he simply took her in his arms and held her as she cried.

For a few minutes they stayed like that. Jim knew he should be thinking about his own parents, or about finding the right words to help console Tess, but the thought that dominated his mind at that moment was how perfectly she fitted into his arms. Which no doubt made him a selfish git.

Gradually her sobs faded and as she drew back he gently wiped away the wet stains on her cheeks.

'Sorry,' she hiccupped. 'You're the one who's just had the bad news. I should be comforting you, not the other way round.'

'No,' he replied firmly, easing further away. 'Your mother died. My father's still hanging in there.'

She nodded but averted her eyes, clearly embarrassed to have broken down so totally in front of him. Or maybe she still had him pegged as a heartless bastard who cared more about his work than his family.

Deliberately he tucked his hand under her chin and raised her eyes to look into his. 'I know I've got a reputation for being cold and unfeeling, some of it perhaps deserved, but I love my parents. Despite what you might think, this *has* shaken me up. I've checked to see if I can get another flight, but those leaving now aren't direct, so I wouldn't be landing in the UK any earlier. I figured I might as well finish what I came here to do rather than pace around an airport lounge, waiting for a connection.'

'Please, you don't have to explain yourself to me.' Her mouth curved in a slight, self-mocking smile. 'And I definitely shouldn't have said what I did. Keeping my thoughts to myself has never been a strength of mine. The moment you said the word heart attack, I shot straight back in time. All I could think was how much I'd wanted to be there for Mum, but I wasn't.'

'Hey, it's okay. I understand.' He sucked in a slightly shaky breath. 'If it helps any, I'm feeling totally useless right now.'

He could have added more. He was frustrated beyond belief that he couldn't do anything, guilty as hell that he wasn't there when his parents needed him, and terrified that by the time he did get home, it would be too late. But he couldn't voice those thoughts. There had been a time when he would have. A time when he'd trusted a woman enough to tell her everything he was feeling. No more. He wasn't going to open himself up to being hurt ever again.

Tess took hold of his hand in her long, slender fingers and squeezed. 'Keep thinking positively.'

'Yeah.' He tugged his hand away, thrusting it into his trouser pocket. God knows, it was hard enough to keep away from her when he was in control. Right now, he was feeling pretty damn vulnerable. 'I think a quick shower will help.' He looked again at his watch. 'Quick being the operative word.'

Several weary hours later they were finally on the plane home. Jim lay back in his seat, this time unable to work, unable to focus on anything but what he would be facing when he got home. Stupidly, he'd begun to think of his parents as immortal. They'd always been there in his life, for the good times and the bad, so he hadn't contemplated a time when they might not be.

When at last they landed, he was so mentally and physically exhausted he almost had to peel himself off the plane.

'This is where we part ways.' He turned to Tess as they walked out through customs. 'Have you got a car picking you up?'

'Yes, thanks.' She nodded over to where a smartly dressed old man was waiting with her name on his board.

'Good.' Jim found he was unable to move. It was crazy, but

he didn't want to say goodbye. Maybe it was the knowledge of what was waiting for him. Certainly that was easier to contemplate than the alternative. That he'd enjoyed this last week with Tess so much the thought of spending the next two days without her seemed impossibly bleak.

'What about you?' she asked. 'How will you get home?'

'I've got my car in the car park. Just as well, as I won't be going home for a while yet.'

The understanding and concern in her eyes nearly brought him to his knees. 'Will you be okay, driving? You look really tired. In fact, I could almost say you look like shit.'

He let out a weak laugh and she smiled back at him.

The desire to touch her became overwhelming, so he bent to kiss her. Just on her cheek – he wasn't a total moron. But at the last moment he caught himself, knowing even that was too intimate for a business relationship. Instead he picked up his case, his heart feeling heavy in his chest. An ache he didn't want, but couldn't get rid of. 'Thanks for all the effort you put in this week,' he told her gruffly. 'I couldn't have done it without you.'

She smiled slightly. 'Yes, you could.'

'Okay, maybe I could. But it wouldn't have been nearly as pleasurable.' Unable to stop himself, he gazed into her eyes, knowing she'd see from his expression exactly what type of pleasure he was remembering.

For a brief moment she held his look, but then she discovered a sudden fascination with the floor. He swore, knowing he'd made her uncomfortable again. Slowly he put down his case, about to, God, he didn't know. Hold her? Sure, that would really help clear things up.

Sighing, he jerked the case back up. 'Please pretend I meant the term *pleasurable* in a strictly professional way. You know, as in the trip was enjoyable. Better with a colleague than on my own.'

Tess was silent for a few moments, leaving him to wonder

if he should have let the comment slide. Not everyone appreciated his brand of directness.

'I enjoyed it too,' she finally replied, though she glanced over at the waiting chauffeur rather than looking at him. 'I hope your father is okay.'

'Thanks.' A sharp reminder that it was time for him to be thinking about someone else entirely. 'I'll see you next week.'

With that he strode off out of the airport and towards the car park. As he hauled his case into the boot of his car and slipped in behind the wheel, he took out his phone and dialled.

'Mum? I've just landed. I'll be there in a few hours. How is he?'

As he listened to his mother's words, reassuring him his father was stable, Jim's body sagged with relief. The weekend was going to be tough, but it could have been so much worse. Sure, instead of driving home and hitting the sheets for the solid twelve hours' sleep he so badly needed, he had a three-hour drive up the motorway to visit his father in hospital. But at least he had a father to visit. And anyway, maybe this was what he deserved. His penance for what he'd allowed to happen in Singapore. Taking advantage of a junior employee. Getting too close to a woman who worked for him.

God he was a fool. Driven by his hormones, rather than his brain.

He could only hope next week his brain would be back in the driving seat.

Chapter Seventeen

As Tess settled into the leather seat of the snazzy chauffeur driven Mercedes, she gave a silent prayer of thanks to Georgina for insisting she arrange for a car to pick her up from the airport. She felt utterly exhausted, far too tired to drive herself home. Instinctively her mind turned to Jim, wondering how he was going to manage to drive up the motorway. Knowing him, he'd be fine. In fact he was probably contemplating running the last ten miles, just for the hell of it.

She'd started the week believing him to be cold and unfeeling. She'd ended it pretty sure he was neither. Driven and determined, yes, but when he wasn't working, he was also warm, fun and surprisingly kind. In fact if she closed her eyes, she could still see the compassion in his eyes when she'd sobbed all over him. He'd taken a heavy emotional hit with the news of his father, yet he'd still had the humanity to console her.

'Did you have a good trip, ma'am?'

The chauffeur caught her eye in his mirror and Tess nodded.

'Go anywhere interesting?'

Only round the world. 'To Singapore and then the States,' she replied, keeping her answer short, hoping he'd get the message.

'Did you get to have any fun?'

Without you the week wouldn't have been nearly as pleasurable. She instantly recalled Jim's expression as he'd said those words. As he'd tried, and failed, to hide his hunger for her. 'Yes, I managed to find some time to enjoy myself.'

'How was Singapore? I've always fancied going there myself.'

Oh God. She shut her eyes as a wave of longing washed through her. Singapore. The place where she'd spent the most magical night of her life, but one she could never dare to repeat. 'Singapore was incredible,' she replied honestly, wiping away the tears that spilt down her cheeks. She had to stop this madness. This pining for something she couldn't have.

Obviously terrified his passenger was having an emotional breakdown, the chauffeur didn't pursue the conversation. It gave Tess the rest of the journey to remind herself the only relationship she could have with Jim from now on was one that enabled her to follow up on the publication issue raised in the US. One that allowed her to investigate Zaplex.

The car pulled up outside her home and Tess pushed all thoughts of work to one side and focussed instead on the simple pleasure of finally being in her own place. The bed wasn't made as immaculately as the hotel beds had been, the space wasn't nearly as tidy, but it was hers. Her photographs, her pictures, her furniture. A week of travelling with Jim might have turned her emotions upside down and inside out, but at least it had made her appreciate her home comforts.

After showering and unpacking, Tess called her brother and arranged to meet him where they always did on a Saturday afternoon. At her father's care home.

She was five minutes late as she pulled into the car park, not bad considering she'd only woken up twenty minutes ago.

'Hey, sis.'

She spotted him, waving from the seat outside the entrance. It was a tradition that they went in to see Dad together, both needing the moral support.

'Mark.' As he walked to greet her she hugged him close, pulling her arms around his tall wiry frame. They had their father's genes when it came to body shape, but their mother's when it came to hair and eye colour.

'How was the globetrotting?'

Blue eyes similar to hers twinkled down at her. Tess started to give him a flippant reply, but found she couldn't. The apprehension about seeing her dad, mixed with jet lag and the confusion over Jim was all too much. She burst into tears.

'Hey, what is it?'

Annoyed, she took out a tissue and wiped her eyes. 'Sorry, I'm being foolish. I'm tired from the travelling, and, well, you know how I don't like this bit.'

Ever since they'd had to transfer Dad here, coming to visit had become something to be endured, rather than looked forward to. Poor Dad. He really didn't know who they were any more. At least she didn't think he did. Sometimes when he looked at her, she thought she saw a spark of the man he'd once been. But then it disappeared and she was left wondering if it was just her wishful thinking.

Mark took her hand and squeezed it. 'Come on, let's go and say hello to him and then I'll buy you a pot of tea and a giant chocolate éclair.' He pulled at the hair she'd tied back in a ponytail. 'Where would you get a better offer than that?'

Tess made herself smile. Whatever life had thrown at her parents, at least she still had her brother. They were half the unit they had been, but they were still a unit.

Two hours later she had her lips firmly clamped around a chocolate éclair.

'He seemed better today, don't you think?' Perhaps it was the chocolate adrenaline rush talking, but the world seemed a bit brighter now.

'Ummm.' Mark had a mouthful of sugary jam doughnut. 'I agree.' He licked his lips, collecting most of the sugar but leaving some around the corners of his mouth. 'Less confused. I think towards the end he really did know who we were.' As he wiped his mouth with a serviette he studied her. 'Now, are you going to tell me what caused the meltdown earlier?'

Tess hesitated, buying time by sipping at her drink. Where to start? Should she start at all? But if she didn't talk to *somebody* about this, she was going to go slowly mad. And nobody knew her better than her brother.

'I slept with my new boss.' The moment she said the words, Tess sunk her head in her hands. God, that sounded terrible. And that was without the cloak and dagger stuff she was doing behind that same boss's back.

'You slept with *Georgina*?'

His expression was so thunderstruck she actually found herself starting to laugh. 'No, you twit, not that boss. The big boss. The president of research and development. Jim Knight.'

'Oh, right.' He ran a hand over his face, still clearly in shock. 'In some ways that's better. Not that I have anything against lesbians. I mean, they actually have some appeal, if you know what I'm saying.'

'Mark—'

He waved away her interruption. 'Shit, Tess, but in so many other ways, this is *so much* worse. You're telling me you slept with the main man? The one responsible for what goes on in the research department? What on earth were you thinking?'

Her laughter had dried up a few seconds ago. Right when his expression told her he'd worked out what she'd actually been telling him. 'I don't think I was,' she replied quietly. 'Thinking, I mean. I was just—'

Once again he halted her. 'No, thanks. I don't want to hear what you were just doing.'

She sighed. 'Mark, I'm so confused.'

With a grunt he crumpled up the serviette he'd been holding. 'I don't understand what there is to be confused about. You joined Helix to find out if there was any malpractice going on. To expose the company and people who decided not to publish critical evidence on the safety of

159

their drugs. In particular the drug Mum took.' He stared at her. 'Maybe people like Jim.'

'We don't know for certain Helix did hide data,' she retorted, annoyed to find her own words being thrown back at her. 'And even if they did, it wouldn't have anything do with Jim. He's only been R&D president for two months.' *But before that he worked in the research department for years.* She ignored the voice in her head. 'Besides, I've seen him at work. He cares not only about what he's doing, but also about how things are being done. I can't believe he'd do anything dishonest.'

Mark shook his head. 'Wow, he's really done a job on you, hasn't he?' He rocked back on his chair, hands in pockets, a scowl on his face. 'How can you be sure he isn't all smoke and mirrors and spin? A man doesn't make it to his position without having some secrets. I bet he hasn't always played it by the book.'

'I know. He's already admitted that when he worked for the clinical department he didn't always follow through on making sure the studies he ran were published.'

Mark thumped the table. 'There you go then. He's admitted to hiding results.'

'No.' Her voice was so loud several of the other customers looked over at them. 'There's a difference between being sloppy, as Jim called it, and setting out to deliberately mislead,' she elaborated in a loud whisper. 'I can't believe he's capable of the latter.'

Mark let out a deep sigh and reached across the table to place his hand over hers. 'Look, I know what you're doing is hard. It's much easier being on the outside, having that objectivity. Once you start working in these organisations, it's more complicated. They're run by real people, and when you get close to real people you start to form relationships. But you've got to be so damn careful. Especially if you're still planning to do what you set out to do.'

'Of course I am.' Tess snatched her hand away. 'I'm not about to let Mum, Dad or you down. I will find out whether Helix has anything to hide. And if they do, I will make them pay.'

'Okay. Then you have to take note of what I'm saying, or you'll get hurt in the blast Tess.'

He was right. Of course he was. It was exactly what she kept telling herself. In between fantasising about kissing Jim again. 'I will. No more getting close to the boss.'

'Promise?'

'Promise.'

Seemingly satisfied, he settled back on the chair. 'You know it would help if you found out who worked on the clinical trial programme for the drug Mum took. If it wasn't Jim, it would seem to put him in the clear, though he could still have been party to discussions on other clinical programmes.'

'I can't see Jim agreeing to hide results, Mark. I just can't.'

'Don't allow yourself to be hoodwinked. I don't care if he looks like George bloody Clooney.' She must have flinched because Mark's eyes zeroed in on her. 'No, he doesn't, does he?'

She allowed herself the small luxury of recalling Jim's face. 'There is more than a passing likeness, yes.'

'Isn't Clooney pretty old now?'

Relieved to have the conversation change direction, Tess smiled. 'You're a man. You fancy plastic young girls, usually the younger the better. You can't understand that women actually like a more mature man.'

'Are we talking about Clooney or this research guy now?' Mark interjected, clearly confused.

'Actually I was talking about Clooney. Jim is only thirty-six.'

He snorted. 'Old enough to have conducted a lot of clinical trials and buried a lot of data.'

There was nothing she could say to that. It was in her

hands to prove Mark wrong. She'd use Jim's promise to revise the publication policy as an excuse to find out exactly what they were currently doing regarding publishing results. And what they had been doing, and who had been doing it.

At the thought of how much she was betraying Jim's trust she shuddered and reached for her tea, hoping the warmth would erase the chill.

'You know that saying, being between a rock and a hard place? Right now I understand how that feels,' she said finally. She couldn't be honest with Jim and tell him why she'd joined the company, because then he'd fire her. If she didn't work at Helix, she'd never be able to find out whether Zaplex killed her mother.

'You have to put family first, Tess. Doesn't Mum deserve more loyalty than a man you've slept with, what is it? Once? Twice?'

Ouch. It didn't help to know Mark was right. She had to put all her muddled feelings for Jim aside and focus on finishing what she'd started.

Easier said, than done.

Chapter Eighteen

Jim was sitting in his mother's kitchen, trying to avoid any conversation that might lead to Tess.

'Who did you say you were away with all last week?' she asked as she walked to the sink to fill the kettle. It was a habit he always remembered as a child. No conversation of any importance had ever taken place without a mug of tea. He didn't have the heart to tell her he was more of a coffee man these days.

As her words slowly sunk into his sleep deprived brain he fought the urge to sigh, or swear, or both. It was the third time she'd asked that question since he'd arrived on her doorstep. The first had been polite interest. The second could probably be put down to the fact that her mind wasn't really focussed right now. But the *third* time? No, that had to be her incredible *Mum always knows everything* intuition kicking in.

'I told you, it was a new employee. The corporate communications manager.'

'And did you tell me this new employee was young, attractive and single?'

He shook his head in disbelief. 'No, Mum. I told you she was called Tessa. You made the rest up.'

'Oh, did I?'

She busied about filling the teapot with hot water from the kettle. Jim knew she felt better doing something, which apparently included grilling him, rather than being left alone with her thoughts. For the last two hours they'd been sitting by his father's bed at the hospital. He was off the critical list, thank God, but it was clear it would be a while before he was well enough to come home.

'Make mine a small one, please,' he told her as she poured

163

the hot tea into two large mugs. 'I need to hit a bed soon or I'll crash out on the kitchen table.'

'You won't be going anywhere until you tell me what happened between you and this Tessa last week,' she replied firmly, clattering the mugs on the table before sitting down opposite him.

He took a moment to study her, feeling a rush of tenderness towards the still attractive lady in front of him. Age might have increased the wrinkles and dimmed the hazel eyes, but the classic beauty remained. It was a face he loved, even when it was fixed on his with a steely determination.

'Why on earth do you think something happened?' he replied slowly, sipping his tea, keeping his body language deliberately casual.

'Because I've known you for thirty-six years,' she retorted smartly. 'If nothing had happened, you would have talked a lot more about the trip. But you've hardly said two words about it, so something must have done.' She cocked her head to one side and narrowed her eyes. 'Did you sleep with her?'

Jim gulped, glad the last slug of tea had already slipped down his oesophagus. Otherwise he might have choked on it. 'Since when did we discuss my sex life?' he asked in a strangled voice.

'Since that floozy—'

'Barbara,' he supplied.

'Umph. Since that floozy left you licking your wounds.' She reached a hand out to touch his arm. 'I've been worried about you. Now I'm wondering if I still have to.'

'Jesus, Mum.'

'Don't swear.'

He raised his eyes up to the ceiling. 'Give me strength. Suffice to say, you don't have to worry about me.'

'You're my son, I'll always worry about you.'

'But you just said—'

'Never mind what I just said.' She waved her hand at him, stopping his flow. 'Now, tell me about this Tessa.'

Slowly he took a sip of the hot tea, trying to work out how little he could get away with admitting. Then he let out a long, deep sigh. 'Mum, if you're going to insist on having this conversation, I need something stronger than tea.'

She clucked her tongue at him. 'Well, you've always been your father's son. Of course if he'd been here instead of in hospital ...'

Jim stood up and walked round the table, crouching down to put his arms around her shoulders. All of a sudden she felt older, frailer. 'He would have poured the whiskies out long before you filled up that kettle,' he finished off for her. 'He's going to be okay, you know.'

She nodded, tears slipping out from under her lashes.

'Obviously it'll take him a little while to get back to strength, but he will get there.' He'd spent a good part of his time at the hospital talking to the staff, reassuring himself that his father was in good hands.

'Yes, I know.' She squeezed his arm. 'And if you think for one minute giving me a cuddle will distract me from asking about this new woman of yours, you've got another thing coming.'

Shaking his head, Jim went to where his father kept the whiskey. 'You're a hard woman.'

'Nonsense. I'm a soft touch, which is why you always got away with murder as a child. Now pour out a healthy measure and tell me everything.'

He brought the whiskey back to the table and, after taking a deep, reassuring swig, shook his head and laughed. 'You know, there really isn't much to tell. We spent most of the time either in an airport or on a plane.'

'What about the time you spent in the hotels?'

A twinkle slid into her eyes for the first time since he'd arrived. He reckoned she'd missed her vocation in life.

Instead of a nurse, she should have been a police interrogator. 'We ate, sometimes we drank, then we crashed out with exhaustion.'

'Are you really going to tell me you spent a week with a gorgeous single woman and *didn't* sleep with her?'

'How do you know she was gorgeous?' he parried, playing for time.

'Because if she hadn't been—'

'I'd have said something by now,' he cut in, laughing at the triumphant look on her face. 'Okay, you win. Yes, she's stunning. Late twenties, tall, very slim, endless legs, long red hair, deep blue eyes, freckles on her nose, a real thing for crazy high shoes.' He halted, keenly aware he'd said way too much already.

'Not a bad description from a man who's trying to convince me nothing happened.'

'Jes—' He noted her beady stare and reworded. 'Come on, Mum. What do you want from me? It surely isn't the no holes barred gritty detail.'

'Tell me when I'm going to meet her.'

He took another gulp of whiskey. A couple more and he'd be sliding off his chair and sinking onto the floor in a drunken slumber. 'We're not at that stage, Mum. In fact I'm not sure we ever will be at that stage.'

'What do you mean by *that stage*?'

'I mean I'm not ready to bring her home to meet my parents.' It was easier than the messy truth. *I only slept with her once, when I got her drunk.*

'It strikes me you've never been ready to bring a girl home to meet us. With that floozy we had to come and gatecrash some event of yours in order to get an introduction to the woman you told us you were going to marry.'

And that should have been a clear signal to him, Jim thought bitterly. 'Look, I'm sorry about Barbara. Probably the fact that I didn't rush her up here to meet you was a sign that I wasn't absolutely one hundred per cent certain about her. I should have listened to my instincts.'

'And what are those instincts telling you about Tessa?' she asked quietly.

It was the million dollar question. Trust his mum to voice it. 'They're telling me she's special,' he answered, equally quietly. 'But that doesn't mean I'm going to do anything about it. She's a work colleague, junior to me. And don't forget the last time I dated someone from the office, it went disastrously wrong. I don't want this to flare up in my face, too.'

'Equally you don't want to be too afraid to risk your heart again.' She reached across the table and took hold of his hands. 'Don't let one bad experience sour you. The Jim I know is brave and bold, daring to push forwards. To take life by the scruff of the neck and drag it where he wants it to go.'

He smiled, wanting more than anything to believe that was still true. Certainly in work he felt it was. But in his personal life? He wasn't sure he had it in him any more.

It was late the following afternoon by the time Jim pulled up outside his apartment. He'd slept for twelve solid hours at his parents' house and yet he still felt tired. As he yanked his case out of the boot, he contemplated going for a run. It would probably do him good. He'd spent most of the day either sitting next to his father at the hospital or driving back down.

He was tossing up which route to run when he became aware of someone walking up behind him.

'Just come back from your trip?'

Slowly he turned. There had been a time when that soft, husky voice had lifted his heart. Now it sunk to his boots. 'Ten out of ten for observation,' he replied coolly, halting on the pavement outside his building. The last thing he wanted was for Barbara to follow him inside. 'What are you doing here?'

'So curt.' She shook her head, the shiny brown hair he'd once loved to run his fingers through dancing over her shoulders. 'Can't we at least be civil to one another?'

'I'll be civil in the office,' he replied bluntly. 'Out here I can do as I like. So, what do you want?'

She pursed her lips. 'Okay, we'll play it your way. I was sorting out my house and I found some of your things.' She looked down at the brown carrier bag she was holding.

'My *things*?' He stared at her, stunned. 'God, Barbara, it's been two years. Why are you only bringing them round now?'

'Yes, well, I don't clear out very often. Here, take them.'

He took hold of the bag and looked inside. A shaver, spare pair of jeans, T-shirt and a few boxers. Things he'd left at hers for those occasions he'd found himself staying over without planning to. It seemed like a lifetime ago. Wearily he shoved the bag back at her. 'I don't want them. Keep them for the next man who decides to stay over. He might be grateful for them.'

Reluctantly she took the bag, but her eyes didn't leave his face. 'I was rather hoping the next man would be you,' she told him in the voice she used to seduce, to get her own way.

Frustrated, tired, anxious to get rid of her, he cursed. 'Didn't you get the message last time? It will never be me. I've never been one for repeats. Once was quite enough.'

'I bet I can make you change your mind,' she whispered throatily, moving towards him.

'And how do you think you can manage that?'

'Like this.' She reached up, draping an arm around his neck and pulled his head towards her.

Jim could have resisted but a small part of him wanted to know how he'd react, so he didn't move away. Her lips brushed his cautiously at first, then more daringly, nibbling on his bottom lip. Something she knew he liked. With her mouth teasing his, her voluptuous breasts crushed against his chest and her hands curled into the hair at the back of his neck, he should have been toast. At the very least, he should be feeling something. But he felt absolutely nothing. When she broke away, he found he couldn't stop smiling.

'What's so funny?'

He shook his head and went to pick up his case once more. 'I've just realised I'm not into curvy brunettes any more.'

He'd turned his back on her and was walking into his building when he heard her bitter laugh. 'What are you into then? Stick thin redheads?'

He paused and for a fraction of a second – a fraction of a fraction – considered retorting that Tess wasn't stick thin. That she was slim and soft and toned. 'It's none of your business,' he replied tersely, opening the door and firmly shutting it behind him.

A long run and a hot shower later, Jim reflected that Barbara's visit had at least confirmed he was well and truly over her. Sadly it had also confirmed she knew him a little too well. Because the entire time her lips had been wrapped around his, he *had* been wishing she was a slender redhead.

He might well have finally climbed out of the frying pan, but damn if he wasn't now well and truly storming into the fire.

Chapter Nineteen

On Monday morning Tess was back at her desk, trawling through the ridiculous number of emails that had landed in her inbox during the last week. She was new – how could so many people be sending her emails? No wonder Jim spent so much of his time with his nose buried in his laptop.

And why was she thinking about him?

Determinedly she focussed back on her inbox, flagging emails she knew were urgent, though the first she actually opened was from Roberta. *If you're not too important to dine with a lowly researcher, how about lunch tomorrow?*

Tess contemplated hitting reply, but reached for her phone instead.

'Hey, it's Tess. How are you?'

'Is that Tessa Johnson, globetrotter and glamorous travelling companion to our research president?'

'Very funny. You can save the sarcasm for lunch tomorrow. I was calling to find out if you'd heard about your job yet?'

Tess held her breath as the phone echoed with the sound of a deep sigh.

'I'm in,' Roberta replied, 'but so many aren't. I have to admit, this isn't a great place to work right now. Those who haven't got a job are worried and resentful. Those who have are feeling guilty. I can't wait for it all to be over. It might have helped if there'd been more warning, but the suddenness of it all took everyone by surprise.'

Tess's heart tugged in sympathy, a feeling magnified by her shame. Good people were losing jobs they valued. Jobs they wanted to keep. Yet here was she, taking up a role she was going to happily toss aside once she'd done what she came to do.

Her heart heavy with guilt, she agreed a time to meet Roberta for lunch and tried to focus back on her emails.

'Tessa, have you got a minute?'

Grateful for the distraction, she turned to find Georgina standing behind her, waving some leaflets at her. 'Sure, yes.'

'There's a run in aid of a few cancer charities this Saturday. As cancer is one of Helix's key areas of focus, we're helping to support the charities by promoting the run. I'm also hoping some of our employees will do their bit by taking part. I still have a few places left.' She tilted her head and smiled. 'You look like someone who keeps herself fit.'

Tess folded her arms. 'Something tells me I know how this conversation is going to end.'

'Hey, come on, help me out here. You can do 5K or 10K, it's up to you. And it's all for a good cause.'

Tess didn't need to be reminded about the importance of cancer charities. They had often helped her mum through the painful journey after her diagnosis. 'Fine, I'm convinced. I'll be there.'

Georgina grinned with smug satisfaction. 'Well, that was easier than I thought. I didn't even need the thumb screws.' She started to turn, but then paused. 'Actually, there is something else you can help with.'

'Okay, you're my boss. Tell me what you want me to do.'

'It would be fantastic PR for Helix if we could get Jim to do the run, too. You know, the R&D president comes out of his ivory tower to get sweaty with the real people. I asked him a few weeks back and he said he'd see if he was free, but he hasn't got back to me. Could you check with him? I don't want to look like the pushy media lady.'

'Which, of course, is exactly what you are.' Tess smiled to take the edge off her words.

'Correct, but I work in very subtle ways.' Georgina cocked her head to one side and studied her newest recruit. 'Besides, I thought as you'd spent the whole of last week with him, you might have formed some sort of, I don't know, bond?'

Tess willed herself not to blush under her manager's obvious scrutiny. Not an easy task given her pale skin and red hair. 'We got on fine,' she replied simply, turning away just in case Georgina could read the truth in her eyes. 'I've a meeting scheduled with him this afternoon. I'll ask him then.'

The closer it came to the time of the meeting, the more Tess found herself twitching. She was suddenly absurdly nervous. Last week hadn't felt like real life. It had been as if her and Jim had spent five days travelling the globe in a little bubble, isolated from outside influences. Now the bubble had burst, and her life was back to being very real.

Had she *really* slept with him?

Her stomach churned as she walked towards his office. Anticipation, fear, desire. Shame. She was experiencing them all. Every single one.

He glanced up as soon as she reached the doorway, his expression not helping to calm her jittery nervous system one little bit. Sexy lips curved and a pair of deep brown eyes smouldered as he smiled at her.

'Come on in, Tess.' Slowly he stood and walked round his desk towards the table where he sat for informal meetings.

She cleared her throat, horribly aware of how much her hands were trembling. Unable to look him in the eye, she sat down on the nearest chair.

'Tess?'

She could feel the warmth of his body as he sat down next to her. Smell his tangy aftershave. If she reached out her hand, she'd be able to touch the soft cotton of his shirt. Feel the hard muscle of his bicep. Wringing her hands together, she placed them firmly in her lap.

'Are you okay?'

There was concern in his voice, but it wasn't that which made her heart flutter. It was the warmth and tenderness she heard, too. Easy to tell herself to keep her distance when she

172

wasn't sitting in the same room as him, but now ... Heaven help her, now all she wanted to do was touch him. Be held by him.

'Thank you, yes. I'm fine.' There, she'd managed to get some words out. Her voice sounded a bit rough, but at least it was a start.

'Did you catch up on some sleep over the weekend?'

She nodded. This was going to be fine. She could do small talk. He was being kind, leading the conversation, trying to diffuse the awkwardness. 'Yes I did. How about you?' And then she suddenly remembered. 'Oh, what am I thinking? How is your dad?'

Jim relaxed slightly at Tess's question. When she'd first walked in with her face tense and her body rigid, he'd been afraid he'd never see the real Tess again. That, he thought bitterly, was the trouble with sleeping with someone who worked for you. His office was a million miles away from the relaxed atmosphere of a night out in Singapore, drunk on cocktails, extreme fatigue and lust.

Though apparently lust wasn't a million miles away. 'Dad's doing well, thanks.' God he sounded hoarse. 'He'll be in hospital a while yet, but everything is moving in the right direction.'

'Good. That's really ... good.' With a small sigh she glanced down at her notepad. 'Well, I put this time in to discuss the ball next week.' Her eyes flickered round the room, looking everywhere but at his. 'You know, the one that will celebrate the achievements of the Helix research teams and say goodbye to those employees forced out through redundancy.'

'I know exactly why we're having the ball,' he countered dryly. 'I didn't need the reminder about forcing these people out.'

'Sorry,' she said with a blush. 'I wasn't thinking what I was saying.'

'Or perhaps you knew precisely what you were saying,' he replied, studying her. 'You don't agree with what I'm doing here, do you?'

'I didn't say that.'

'Then what are you saying?'

She hesitated and he realised he wasn't going to get her real thoughts, but a watered-down version. 'I think there were kinder ways of going about this process.'

'Like what?' He tried to keep his voice neutral, but it hurt that despite spending a week with him, she still thought he was callous.

'The announcement came out of the blue. These people had no time to understand what was about to happen. One minute everything was fine, the next they were applying for their own job. In my opinion, it was too fast.'

'So you think it would have been kinder to have a long drawn out affair? Leave people dangling, unsure of their future for several months before we actually acted?'

'It might have helped soften the blow. Given people time to plan for the worst case scenario.' Her temper was starting to spike. Even though it was directed at him, he preferred it to the quiet shadow who'd first walked in.

'Do you know what would have happened if I'd allowed more time?' He gave her no chance to answer. 'The talented scientists, the ones we desperately need to keep, would have quickly found themselves another job. We couldn't afford to let that happen.'

'*You* couldn't afford to let it happen,' she countered.

'No, you're right,' he replied flatly. 'I couldn't afford for them to go. Not when the future of the company depends on those very people finding and developing more products.' He let out a hollow laugh. 'But you don't think this is about the company, do you? You think it's all about me wanting to make a name for myself.'

When she didn't reply, he jumped to his feet, needing the

distance. 'Wow, you must be really regretting what happened between us.'

'What do you mean?'

'I mean sleeping with your boss is one thing. Sleeping with a man you don't respect, maybe don't even like, is something else.'

Her eyes darted towards his and he didn't try to hide the hurt he was feeling.

'I do like you,' she replied softly. 'That's ...' She shut her eyes momentarily. 'That's part of the problem.'

Inside his chest, his heart did a bungee jump. 'Good. Because I like you too, Tess. A lot.'

Their eyes met and he felt sure he could hear the crack of electricity as something fizzed between them. *Like* was far too weak a word for what he felt towards this woman, but he knew damn well he couldn't say any more. Certainly not here, in his office. Perhaps not at all. Still he felt compelled to touch her so he reached out his hand and clasped hers, needing the contact.

For a brief second her fingers tightened on his. Then she quickly withdrew her hand.

He sighed. 'I know. Here isn't the right place. Sorry.' He walked round to sit at his desk, giving them both some much needed space. 'Where were we? The ball, I believe.'

Tess gave him a quick, gratitude-laden look before launching into details of how the planning was progressing.

'Oh and there is one more thing,' she said finally. 'Georgina wants to know if you can make the charity run on Saturday.'

'Bugger.' He began to delve through his in tray. 'She did tell me about that, but it went right out of my mind. I'm sure she left me some information.'

'Don't worry, it's all in here.' Tess unwound her long, long legs and stood to hand him a leaflet. 'The time, the venue.'

'Thanks. Are you going?'

'It looks like it,' she replied in a resigned voice. 'I was kind of roped in.'

'Ah, the Georgina effect,' he told her with a grin. 'You're all ready to mouth the word *no*, but find *yes* coming out instead.'

Her eyes lit up as she let out a soft laugh and he found himself wanting to say *to hell with it*. He could work with this gorgeous woman *and* pursue a relationship with her.

Sure, as long as he lived in cloud cuckoo land, where all relationships ended in happy ever after.

'So, are you running?'

Her eyes were still smiling and because he wanted so badly to kiss her, he pulled his phone out of his pocket and tried to distract himself by scanning the messages. 'Looks like I am. Put me down for the 10K. Can't have them thinking I'm a lightweight.'

This time when she smiled he gave in to the luxury of drowning in her eyes for several heart pounding moments. Gazed at her until she flushed scarlet and fled from his office like a frightened deer.

Jim shoved his head in his hands and swore. God this was difficult. In fact it was starting to seem bloody impossible.

'Having a good day?'

He looked up to find Rick stood in the doorway, grinning.

'Something like that.' He waved his friend in.

'How did your little jaunt go?'

'My *business trip*,' he replied with emphasis, 'went well. Thanks.'

'And how was the lovely Tessa?'

Jim knew better than to hesitate, but by the time he'd formulated a reply in his head, it was too late.

'Ahh.' Rick nodded. 'I think I'm beginning to get the picture.'

Warily Jim glanced at his very open office door and then back at Rick. 'I'd deny it, but knowing you it would be a waste of my breath.'

'Exactly.' Rick went to close the door. 'And why waste

your breath on denial when you can use it to tell me everything instead.'

Jim grunted. 'There isn't much to tell. We had a one night stand. End of story.'

'You did?'

At the stunned expression on Rick's face, Jim's frame of mind took a further nosedive. 'Hell, if even you're shocked, it must sound bad.'

'No, I'm not shocked, not in that sense. There's no company rule on stuff like that, and you're two single – she is single, isn't she?' Jim inclined his head in confirmation. 'Okay then, you're two consenting adults, so hey, go for it I say. I just didn't actually expect you to.'

'Neither did I,' Jim admitted. 'But in a moment of weakness I did. And that's the end of it.'

'Sure, if you say so,' Rick replied agreeably. 'Then again, if that really was how you felt, I wouldn't have found you with your head in your hands, looking as if the world had just caved in on you.'

Jim's sigh was deep and heartfelt. 'For a geek you seem to think you know a lot about human beings.' When the geek didn't reply, just continued to look at him knowingly, Jim gave up and blurted out the truth. 'Okay, fact is, I'm crazy about her. I wouldn't mind so much if I thought it was all about sex, but it isn't. Just now she effectively accused me of being callous.'

Rick raised an eyebrow.

'The redundancies and the way I went about it,' he explained, shoving a hand restlessly through his hair. 'That's how I know I'm in trouble. Other people tell me that and it's water off a duck's back. The same words from her mouth and it's more a dagger to the heart. It hurts to know she thinks I'm really like that.'

'What, you mean to tell me you're *not* a ruthless bastard?'

He caught the gleam in Rick's eye and had to laugh.

'Okay, you've got me. Let's head off to the gym. I can sweat out some of this frustration and you can buy me a drink and remind me why we're friends.'

'Sure.' But Rick didn't move. 'So what are you going to do about the delectable Tessa?'

Jim shut his eyes, hoping for some sort of revelation. When he opened them again, he was still clueless. 'I'm not sure,' he admitted. 'I guess the prudent course of action is to stay well away.'

'And you've learnt how to be *prudent*, have you? Because the Jim Knight I knew two years ago didn't know the meaning of the word.'

Jim ghosted a smile. 'I suspect he still doesn't.'

Chapter Twenty

Jim sat in his fish tank of an office, elbows on his desk, reading through the Helix policy on publishing study results with a mounting sense of despair. It was littered with more weasel words and get out clauses than an escape artist's handbook. *Helix will seek to publish the results from the clinical trial programme.* Seek to publish? What on earth did that mean? Didn't seek mean to try? And how was that defined, exactly? Send the results to a totally unsuitable medical journal, wait for the rejection letter and then shrug your shoulders and say at least I tried? He scanned further down the policy and groaned out loud. *Helix will publish all results that are scientifically or medically meaningful.* After rubbing a hand over his eyes he looked back at the page. The words were still there. Meaningful? To who, exactly? To the clinician, the patient, or the company?

He let out a deep, ill-tempered sigh and clasped his hands behind his head, stretching out the knotted muscles in his shoulders. It didn't help that he was as much to blame as everyone else. He'd worked for this company for how long? And he'd never actually read this policy. Sure he'd been employed to obtain the results, not to publish them, but that didn't excuse him. He'd had a responsibility to the patients he'd enrolled in his trials, and to future patients, to make sure all the results were made available. Only that way could understanding of the disease and treatment be advanced. He'd failed to do that. For all he knew, results from some of his studies might never have made it out of the clinical study report.

He picked up the phone and stabbed out the number of his chief medical officer. One of the perks of his job, he thought grimly. If he was having a bad day, he could at least transfer some of that temper to someone else.

A few minutes later Frank sat down warily on the chair opposite him.

Jim almost smiled. The guy had clearly already sensed his day was about to go downhill. 'Tell me Frank, when was this publication policy last updated?'

Frank shifted uneasily in his seat. 'Well, as you know, in Helix we make it a rule to review our policies every two years.'

'That wasn't what I asked,' Jim cut in. 'What I want to know is when was the last time someone actually went through the detail of this policy, line by line, to ensure it fitted with the external view on publishing scientific data?'

'It was checked last year,' Frank replied defensively. 'It covers the current industry standards set by the IFPMA. You know, the International Federation of Pharmaceutical Manufacturers and—'

'I'm perfectly aware of who the IFPMA are,' Jim interrupted again, his voice icy calm. 'And of their standards. Tell me, are you happy to be part of a company that just does the minimum? The least it can get away with?'

He watched his CMO flinch and felt a flicker of sympathy. But not enough to let the man off the hook.

'Well, if you put it like that, no.'

Jim nodded. 'Good, because I'm not either. Helix should be leading the way, not dragging its heels. I want you to pull a team together and take a thorough look at what Helix should be doing regarding publishing its data. That means thinking about the standards we as a company want to set, not just checking whether we comply with what's already out there. Talk to other companies, hold discussions with key customers, including the journal editors. I want the first draft of a revised publication policy on my desk in two weeks. And I'm talking about a policy that fits with where we are now, and where we're going. Not one that harps back to the last decade. Have I made myself clear?'

From the look of fear on Frank's face, Jim guessed he

probably had made himself very clear. He wasn't averse to ruffling a few feathers in order to push people towards his way of thinking. Sometimes the end did justify the means.

'Oh, and Frank.' About to make his escape, Frank's shoulders dropped as he turned to face him. 'No bland, vague or ambiguous weasel words. Okay?'

Tess sat opposite Roberta in the canteen, eyeing up the large chocolate muffin next to her. Sadly before she could get her mouth round that, she had to brave the salad. And before she did that, she had to get down to business.

'Roberta, can I pick your brains? As part of this new "Leading with Science" initiative I'm working on, we're looking into the publication policy. I need to find out which studies have been published and when. Have you any idea how I can do that?'

Roberta chewed thoughtfully on her panini. 'Your best bet is probably the clinical study database. It lists all the trials and I think there's a link to the publication once it's been accepted. I'm not sure how thoroughly it's kept up to date, but it's a good place to start.'

'That sounds perfect. Do you know how I get access?'

'You'll need to get the system owner to agree it. I believe that's Barbara.' Tess couldn't stop the groan that spilled out from her lips. 'Not a huge fan of our Barbara, I take it?'

'Well, I can't say I know her – I've only met her a couple of times. But I had the distinct impression I didn't warrant her interest because I didn't have a penis.'

Roberta giggled. 'That's what I've heard, too. You know she and Jim used to be an item, don't you?'

At the mention of his name her pulse shot up a few beats. It unnerved her, though not half as much as the blush she felt creeping up her neck. She lowered her eyes to her salad and began to eat. 'Yes, I heard,' she replied carefully. 'Though I'm not sure what he saw in her.'

Roberta threw her head back and laughed. 'Other than the enormous boobs and flashing eyes, you mean?'

Tess clamped down on another mouthful of lettuce. She wasn't going to think about Jim running his fingers over Barbara's very full breasts. Determinedly she swallowed the salad down and reached for the chocolate muffin. It would be much easier to digest.

Thankfully she made it through the rest of lunch without thinking about Jim. Or Barbara's breasts.

She was wandering back to her desk when a very irate looking CMO almost ran her over.

'Sorry.' He did a double take when he realised who it was. 'Hey, Tessa, how are you doing?'

'Good, thanks, Frank.' She studied his harassed face. 'You, however, don't look too happy. Is there anything I can help with?'

'Not unless you're willing to inflict some serious injury on our president. I don't necessarily need him killed, just put out of action for a few months.'

'What did you have in mind? Shall I trip him up? Perhaps poison his coffee?'

Finally the man cracked a smile. 'That could work. If he's suffering agonising stomach cramps, he might forget all about this damn publication policy.'

Tess stilled. 'What's he got you doing?'

'Only revising the entire document in two weeks, making it even stricter than the industry standards actually require. I ask you. The man's a total freak.'

'Perhaps he's just trying to make this company different from other pharmaceutical companies,' she told Frank, overwhelmed by a desire to defend Jim.

'The flipping policy was all right by him when he used to work here though, wasn't it? I didn't hear him moaning about wanting to publish more when he was heading up the Zaplex clinical trial programme. But now he's come back as research president, he thinks he's flipping God Almighty ...'

Tess didn't hear the rest of Frank's rant. Her mind was stuck on the words *when he was heading up the Zaplex clinical trial programme*. Oh God, Jim *had* worked on the development of the product her mother had taken.

'Hey, Tessa, are you okay? You're looking a bit pale.'

She put a hand to her stomach, pretending a pain she didn't have, though the nausea she was feeling was real enough. 'Sorry, I think I must have eaten something dodgy at lunch. Bye, Frank.'

Hurriedly she made her way to the ladies' where she dashed into a cubicle and slumped down on the toilet seat, her body trembling uncontrollably. Why was she reacting so violently? Just because Jim had headed up the Zaplex clinical programme, it didn't mean he'd done anything wrong.

But it also didn't mean she could cross him off her potential suspect list.

She sucked in a breath. It was okay. She'd just have to search the database as quickly as possible. Before she became any more entangled.

Taking another steadying breath she straightened herself up and walked purposefully out of the ladies', towards the clinical trial department. And Barbara's office. Passing row upon row of modern desks, each with an obligatory computer monitor, Tess tried to put her personal feelings about the lady firmly out of her mind. This was simply one colleague talking to another. No need for the crazy butterflies buzzing around in her stomach. Absolutely no need.

'Excuse me. Do you have a minute?' she asked politely as Barbara looked up from her computer. Tess tried not to see her as a man would see her. As Jim had seen her. All luscious curves and deep, luminous eyes.

Barbara nodded. 'It's Tracey, isn't it?'

Tess gritted her teeth. 'Tess, actually.'

'Yes, that's right. You're the one who followed Jim around last week on his moral crusade.'

She should let that go, Tess told herself. 'I accompanied him, yes. Do I take it from your tone that you don't agree with what he's doing?'

'Oh, I'm sure it's very worthy,' she replied dismissively. 'And probably getting him one step further towards his cherished prize of CEO. However I'm more interested in his personal morals, than his business ones.' She narrowed her eyes and studied Tess in the same manner a lioness might eye up its rival. 'How did you find it, spending all that time with our handsome president?'

Tess froze, not knowing what to focus on first. The sharp reminder that Jim was probably only doing all this to get a promotion, or the fact that Barbara's innocent question was anything but innocent. At least if the glint in her eyes was anything to go by. She found herself squirming, about to blush and unable to do a single thing about it. 'We had a successful week,' she replied, hoping it sounded casual.

It didn't.

'Umm, I bet you did.' The corners of Barbara's mouth lifted in what could only be termed a sneer. 'It must be hard keeping secrets when you've got skin as pale as yours. I fear your pink cheeks are rather giving the game away. You slept with him, didn't you?'

If Tess's face had been pink with embarrassment before, it was rapidly turning red with anger now. 'Jim is single and so am I. What we get up to outside work is none of your business.'

Barbara laughed. 'Of course it isn't. But you and I should get together one evening and compare notes. It could be fun.' She leant back against her chair, clasping her hands casually together on the desk, a study of feline grace. 'Did you know he likes to make love in the shower? At least he did last time I was with him.' She frowned slightly. 'Now, let me think, when *was* the last time I went round to his apartment? Umm, yes, I know. It was Sunday.'

Tess stood rooted to the spot as a flash of pain tore through her heart. It didn't seem to matter that Jim's whole clean up campaign was apparently for the good of his career, not the patients. Nor that their night of passion had only ever been a one off. It bloody hurt to know he'd slept with someone else so soon after spending an intimate night with her. Especially as that woman was Barbara.

So much for his sodding rule. He'd broken it twice in one week.

'I'm really not interested in what you've been doing,' Tess replied coldly, using her anger and pain to work with her for a change. 'I'm working on a project for Jim, looking into the publications policy. In order to do that, I need access to the study database. I understand you're the person I need to request that from?'

Barbara smiled. At least on anyone else a curving of the lips would have constituted a smile. 'That's right. I can arrange that for you, though it would appear you're already a master at accessing all areas of our research and development organisation.'

Tess turned on her heel and walked out, grateful the high Jimmy Choo's she was wearing gave her a regal swagger as she did so. *Bitch*, she muttered under her breath. Jim flipping well deserved her.

Chapter Twenty-One

Jim tugged the bright purple T-shirt over his head and winced at his reflection in the E-type's rear-view mirror. Definitely not his colour. After climbing out of his car he made his way towards a mass of assembled runners. Somewhere in amongst that group he hoped he'd find a few other Helix employees. In particular, a long limbed redhead. As he neared them he craned his neck and screwed his eyes, all in a determined effort to see if Tess was there yet. He'd told Rick he was crazy about her, but at times he wondered if he was just plain crazy.

'Jim, over here.'

He shifted his gaze and found Georgina waving at him. The communications vice president was as dressed down as he'd ever seen her, which wasn't actually saying much. In beige cotton trousers, a navy blazer and colourful scarf, she still managed to look every inch the PR professional. Even on a Saturday.

'It doesn't look like you'll be doing much running,' he commented as he nodded at her jacket.

'What and have to wear one of those awful T-shirts?' She looked in mock horror at him. 'You must be kidding.'

He groaned. 'Please don't tell me I'm the only schmuck wearing one of these today.'

'No, of course not.' Pulling his race number out of her bag she swiftly pinned it to his shirt. 'You'll find a whole group of similarly dressed runners down at the starting line. I was just waiting here for you.'

'Right, I'll head down towards the gaudy shirts then. Whose idea was it to give Helix vivid purple branding anyway? What was wrong with blue?'

'Be grateful they didn't go for canary yellow.' She gave him a little push. 'Go on. Make the company proud. Win the race and we get a picture of our esteemed R&D president in the paper. Great publicity.'

'Even if I'm wearing this shirt?'

'Especially as you're wearing it. Now scoot.'

He inched his way through the growing number of runners towards the Helix group, smiling to himself as he spotted Tess's red locks. They were up in a ponytail today, making her look young and fresh faced. And sexy. Damn it.

A few of the Helix crowd caught his eye and smiled at him hesitantly. Jim nodded back, very much aware that making polite conversation with him was the last thing they wanted to do on their day off.

'Hi,' he greeted them, his eyes drifting over each employee in turn until they rested on Tess. 'Thanks for turning up today.'

Tess gave him only the briefest of glances before looking away.

'It looks like a good turn out.'

There was a muted murmur of agreement.

'Even the sun's turned up.'

One or two of them smiled, but not Tess. She was still looking everywhere but at him. He struggled with a few more attempts at conversation but it was blindingly clear they all wished he was standing somewhere else. Including Tess.

'Well, good luck.' Deliberately he turned his eyes towards Tess, staring at her until she was forced to look back. 'I'll see you at the finish line.' Hoping she'd read his silent message – he wasn't going to let her go until he found out what was wrong – he headed over to the 10K start line.

Tess found her eyes wouldn't do as she wanted them to. They refused to look away from Jim's powerfully masculine figure as he walked away from them.

'Wow. He certainly lives up to his sex symbol status. Look at those legs.'

Tess turned to find one of the girls from the clinical trial department practically salivating. 'I suppose it depends whether you're into the tall, dark, athletic type.'

'Show me a woman who isn't and I'll show you a liar.'

'Isn't it more important what the man is like inside the packaging?' Tess re-joined. 'Whether he's decent. Honourable.'

Her colleague blinked in surprise. 'Hey, relax, I'm not about to embarrass myself by swooning at his feet. I was just expressing a healthy appreciation for his very male form.' She looked at Tess quizzically. 'Don't you think our president is decent and honourable then?'

Tess groaned inwardly. Now she'd really fenced herself in. 'I didn't say that. I was just ...'

The sound of the loudspeaker, urging all the runners to get ready for the start, cut into her reply. For the first time in her life, Tess was happier to exercise than continue chatting.

By the time she staggered over the finish line half an hour later, she was more than ready to go home. Sadly Georgina wasn't having that. She shoved a purple fleece at them all and insisted they show solidarity by waiting for Jim to finish. Tess had no choice but to stand and wait with the others.

It wasn't long before she spotted Jim's dark head coming round the corner in second place, not too far behind the leader. Despite being only a charity fun run, testosterone was obviously riding high because the pair of them were actually racing. Tess watched Jim as he pushed himself harder, the muscles in his legs glistening as they pumped determinedly up and down. When he set his mind to something, he was immoveable, she thought. But how far would he go to get what he wanted? Would he cheat? Bend the rules? Cynically set up a clean up initiative just for the brownie points he might get from the board?

Though Jim edged closer and closer to his rival, at the finish he didn't manage to overtake him.

'Oh, bad luck,' Georgina commiserated when he made his way over to their group. Though his face was flushed and his purple T-shirt stained with sweat, he still drew the eyes of every female around him.

'Beaten by a twenty-four-year-old,' he replied disgustedly.

'God, I'm getting old. In hindsight it would have looked better if I hadn't tried to win. Just jogged happily behind him. But heck, my competitive spirit kicked in and before I knew it, I was chasing him like a madman.'

Tess edged away as the two of them talked, aware that this was her window of escape. If she left it any longer, he would turn those dark brown eyes on her and ...

'Tess, before you go, can I have a quick word?'

As if they'd been choreographed, the purple shirts vanished and she found herself alone with him. Even Georgina had sneaked off to her car.

'Are you going to tell me what's wrong?'

Stubbornly she refused to look at him. Call her ridiculous, but she was hurt, angry and totally unable to hide it.

'Tess?'

'Tell me, Jim.' She finally looked him in the eye. 'Do you stick to the company rules as well as you do your own personal rules?'

Surprise flashed across his face. 'What do you mean by that?'

'Forget it.' She made to walk away but his arm shot out, clamping down on hers.

'Now wait a minute. I've told you before, you can't throw an accusation at me and then expect to walk away with no explanation.'

'I didn't think one would be necessary. Rumour has it you're fiercely intelligent. I thought you'd work it out for yourself.' She could almost see the cogs of his brain shift.

Finally he thrust his free hand through his sweat dampened hair and sighed. 'Are you talking about the rule I have about not dating employees who work for me? I thought we'd moved past that. I know we shouldn't have ... hell, I shouldn't have ...' He let out an explosive breath. 'Tess, I've already apologised for that.'

'Well, maybe you should let Barbara know about the rule, too,' she shot back, sounding exactly like the jealous woman she didn't want to be.

'Barbara?' He looked totally baffled. If she hadn't been feeling so hurt, she might have found it funny. 'What on earth has she got to do with this?'

'About as much as I do, from what I can gather.' Tess looked away. She wanted to shower and change into clothes that made her confident. Put on her heels. She didn't want this conversation now, still in her sweaty running kit, knowing she looked a mess. But he'd started it. All she could do was get it over and done with. 'How did your thinking go? Having broken your rule with me, did you think, *oh shucks, I might as well break it again now*?'

'I think you'd better elaborate. I'm clearly not as bright as they say.'

'Did Barbara come round to your place last Sunday?' she asked him coldly.

He looked totally nonplussed. 'Yes. Why?'

His blunt reply wasn't a shock. She was used to his directness. However the pain it caused her, was. Twisting her body, she tried to move away but he held her tight.

'I don't take kindly to being cold-shouldered and then interrogated. Whatever you have to say to me, bloody well say it,' he ground out.

'Did you sleep with her?' she blurted, fighting to keep her voice from shaking.

He stared at her incredulously for a few short moments, until his guard came down. 'Does it matter if I did?'

'No,' she retorted sharply. 'I was just interested to see what sort of slimebag you really are.'

'Nice.' He wiped at the sweat still on his brow. 'Last Sunday I'd just arrived back from seeing my parents when I bumped into Barbara outside my building.' His voice was flat and emotionless. 'She'd come by to drop off some old clothes I'd left at her place during the time we were dating. I told her to keep them. Then she left.' He looked down at her. 'Where does that place me on this slimebag scale of yours?'

'So you didn't have sex?' she asked cautiously.

He let out a ripe oath. 'Absolutely not. Do you actually think I'm the type of man to come on to two different women at the same time?' Unflinchingly his dark eyes drilled into hers, forcing her to reassess what Barbara had told her.

Finally she shook her head. 'No, in my saner moments I don't think you're like that,' she admitted. 'I'm sorry. Going back over the conversation I realise she didn't actually say she'd slept with you that day. She just implied it. No doubt deliberately,' she finished bitterly, angry with herself for falling so easily into Barbara's trap.

He winced. 'Do I want to know what she did say?'

'No, you don't. Suffice it to say she guessed that we'd slept together. I think she was trying to make me jealous.'

A wry smile touched the edge of his mouth. 'Did it work?'

She wasn't answering that one. 'Look, it's time I headed for the shower. I must reek, and I know I look a state.'

'You look pretty good to me,' he told her softly. 'Though I have to say, I miss the shoes.' His handsome face, so harsh a few moments ago, relaxed as he looked pointedly down at her trainers. Then split into a grin as he gazed back up at her.

Her heart somersaulted. 'Please, Jim. I have to go.' Frightened of the way he made her feel, she pulled away from him and headed towards the car park.

'Tess. One more thing.'

With her heart flying into her mouth, she halted.

'You didn't tell me where I fitted on your slimebag scale.'

Slowly she let out a breath. 'I guess, since you didn't sleep with her, you're not on it.'

'Good.' He nodded. 'I hope to keep it that way.'

She hurried off to her car, hoping for the very same thing. Thinking he'd betrayed her with another woman had been almost unbearably painful. God alone knew what she'd do if she found out trial results on her mother's drug had been deliberately buried under his leadership.

Chapter Twenty-Two

Jim gazed out of his office window and watched the Helix employees making their way into work. His eyes drifted casually over them as he tried to figure out how to tackle the executive team meeting in half an hour. If only he'd had the sense to bring the publications issue up at the last meeting, when he'd gained their agreement on revising the educational goods policy – otherwise known, at least to him, as the tacky goods and fancy conferences policy. If he'd had half a brain he could have neatly wrapped them both up under the banner of honesty and transparency.

Instead he'd taken his eye off the ball, probably because it had been lingering on Tess, and now he was faced with another argument – sorry, healthy debate – on ethics with the same disgruntled leadership team. No wonder he was sneeringly called the moral crusader.

Involuntarily his eyes narrowed as a tall, slim female with shiny red hair came into view. He wasn't going to admit the sight was why he'd been staring out of the window for the last half an hour. She moved like a gazelle, all legs and grace. He hadn't been able to get her out of his mind all weekend. The way she'd blazed at him when she'd thought he'd slept with Barbara – he allowed himself a smug smile. *If* he chose not to take the prudent route, he might still have a chance with her. *If* he wasn't too scared to grab it.

But before he could begin to contemplate either, he had a meeting to get through.

'You are certifiably insane,' Webber thundered half an hour later, enunciating each word. 'First you hamstring our commercial team by not allowing gifts or entertainment. Now, by making sure we publish all the results of every damn study we've ever done, even before we're required to, you seem hell-bent on encouraging our competitors to stamp all over us.'

'That's one way of looking at it,' Jim agreed evenly. 'The other way would be to see that a declaration like this shows Helix to be an open, transparent pharmaceutical company that doctors and patients can trust.'

'Trust my arse,' Jack replied scathingly. 'It won't bring us any extra sales. Evidence brings that. As long as it's evidence in the right direction.'

'Then this new policy will ensure we're a lot more careful about the studies we design,' Jim continued, his voice admirably steady. 'If we undertake a study and it isn't in our favour, you can't possibly believe it's right for us not to publish those results? To carry on telling our customers one thing, when we're sitting on evidence that says something else entirely?'

Jack flinched and Jim knew he'd made his point. These people could disagree all they liked, but at the end of the day it was hard to argue against honesty. Even Jack Webber could see that.

'I like the idea of increased transparency with our trial results.' Georgina smiled over at him, clearly determined to let him know he had one friend in the room. 'From a communications angle, it fits perfectly with the "Leading with Science" initiative.'

Exactly, he thought with a flare of triumph.

'Do you really think we can improve our corporate reputation in this way?' Geoff asked Georgina pointedly.

'Yes,' she replied clearly, turning her head briefly towards Jim to give him a *you owe me one* smile.

'Okay.' Geoff swung his focus back to Jim. 'Providing you gain agreement, when are you proposing to implement these revisions?'

'Today was a heads up. We're still in the process of ironing out the details. Once we have them firmed up I'll bring the new policy and a full implementation plan to this meeting for final approval. But let me be clear. We can't afford to drag our heels over this. The company's reputation is at stake.'

Geoff nodded, but his face was as serious as Jim had ever seen it. 'So is its long-term viability, Jim. These are more big changes you're proposing. Whilst nobody here could say they're wrong, you're effectively asking Helix to compete with one arm tied behind its back.'

'With respect,' Jim countered, 'all I'm asking Helix to do is operate honestly, openly and ethically.'

Geoff grunted. 'Perhaps. But if that ends up adversely affecting our sales, the board won't need to look very hard for a scapegoat.'

Jim swallowed, hard. The underlying message from his CEO was very clear. If sales went down, he'd be out on his ear.

Tess settled at her desk, checked that the coast was clear, and tapped her new username and password into the study database she'd just been granted access to. At long last she was on the way to achieving what she had set out to do; finding out if Zaplex had caused her mother's death. As the screen proclaimed her entry accepted, her heart kicked up a gear and fingers that usually skimmed over the keyboard became clumsy and heavy. It was part excitement that she was actually getting somewhere. Part terror for what she might find.

An hour of fruitless searching later, she eased away from the computer screen and rubbed at her stiff neck. This wasn't going to be quite as easy as she'd thought. The database had clearly been designed by someone with no sense of order. She liked to count herself as intelligent, but trying to make head or tail of thousands of studies when even the names for the same drug varied between a number, a chemical name, generic name or brand name was going to be a herculean task. It would take weeks. Heck, maybe months.

'Tess?'

Her head snapped up. Jim. Thankfully looking at her, and not her computer. Hastily, guiltily, she minimised the screen.

'Mr President. We don't often see you mixing out here with the commoners.'

He flashed her that devastating smile, the one that lit up his face and made her heart perform a long, slow cartwheel in her chest.

'When I need a favour, I try to ask for it in person. I find I have a better success rate that way.'

Tess didn't doubt it for one moment. 'Should I worry?'

'Well, it doesn't involve jetting off round the world with me again.' He paused, eyes searching out hers. 'Sadly.'

'What does it involve then?' And why was her voice catching in her throat?

'We're in the process of revising the publication policy and I need you to think about how the changes should be communicated to the media. I've promised Geoff we'll get some good PR out of this and I like to keep my promises.' He bent to whisper in her ear, his warm breath fanning her neck. 'Although there are some promises, like keeping my trousers zipped, that I'm tempted to break.'

She flushed to the roots of her hair. 'That's, umm, yes. What are the changes to the policy?' she finally stammered.

He straightened. 'Your return to the safer topic is duly noted. I thought you'd want to know how the policy is changing, so I'm inviting you to the meeting this afternoon where we'll be discussing it. Can you make it?'

Her mind was still firmly fixed on his trouser topic – the ups, and particularly downs, of his zipper – so it took her a few moments to grasp that this was her opportunity to hear about the Helix publication policy. 'Sure. I'll see you there.'

He looked like he was about to leave, but then he paused. 'Bought any new shoes lately?'

'Umm, let me think. Yes. A turquoise strappy pair I absolutely couldn't manage without. How about you?'

He angled his head. 'Umm, let me think. A sparkly pink pair I thought would go well with my tie.'

With that he gave her another killer smile and headed back down the corridor. Turning back to her screen, she caught sight of her dreamy expression in the reflection and determinedly clicked the study database open again.

When Tess turned up to Jim's meeting later that day, she was astonished to find Jack Webber also there.

No doubt reading her surprise, Jim winked over at her and whispered. 'Keep your friends close and your enemies closer.'

He opened the meeting by telling them all he wanted Helix to have a public register of all their clinical trials. The register would list the studies and the results from those studies. Before they were published.

He'd barely finished his last sentence before Jack jumped down his throat. 'Jim, you know as well as I do the only people who'll bother to look at the results on this damn register will be our competitors. Imagine their delight when they realise they get to scrutinise our trial results only a few months after we do.'

'I'm inclined to agree,' Frank added. 'I understand the concept of what you're planning; that all results from our studies should be made public. As our policy stands at the moment, it's reasonable to assume that some studies might not get published. Hopefully that's purely because they aren't accepted by journals, but it could be argued there's enough wriggle room for us to not publish just because we don't like the way the results panned out.'

Tess sat, wide-eyed, staring at him.

'But whilst it's hard to argue against the policy being stricter,' Frank continued. 'I *can* argue that Helix needs time to fully digest and understand the results before putting them out there for the world to see. The only way this can be done is by publishing them in a proper, scientific journal. That way the data is put into the right context and we can ensure the results aren't misinterpreted.'

'That way Helix can also drag its heels on finding a

suitable journal to publish them in. Perhaps making sure unfavourable study results are kept away from the public eye for months, maybe even years,' Jim added dryly. 'I wasn't born yesterday. I know how this industry works.'

'Whose side are you *actually* on?' Jack asked Jim, his tone and his manner full of self-importance. 'Because it certainly doesn't seem to be Helix's.'

'I'm on the side of what is right,' Jim retorted with icy politeness. 'It's no longer acceptable for us to be doing what was done twenty, thirty years ago. Hell, dragging our heels over publishing studies wasn't even acceptable *then*, though I'm ashamed to admit it sometimes happened. Information we discover on our products can impact patients' lives. We shouldn't be holding any of it back.'

But you did. With painful clarity, the truth finally hit her. Study results *had* been *deliberately* hidden, which was surely what not publishing them actually amounted to. And Jim, by his own acknowledgement, was at the very least aware of this. Tess gripped the edge of her notepad and told herself to breathe slowly. In and out. In and out. Her body calmed, but her brain whirled. This was exactly what she'd expected to find. In fact all she had to do was get a copy of the current Helix publication policy and secretly tape the rest of this meeting. The story she could write would be dynamite.

So why wasn't she, inwardly at least, grinning with triumph? Getting ready to dance on tables? Imagining Hugh's delight when she told him she had his scoop? Why, instead, was she sitting here feeling so horribly sick?

The reason was standing in front of her, pressing home his point in his usual forthright manner.

Could she really betray Jim? Because if she did write that article, it was Jim who would be directly in the firing line. A man she had made love to and, God help her, despite everything, her heart was becoming dangerously entangled with. A man who, no matter what he might have done in the

197

past, was at least trying to atone for his actions. Unless this clean up act was all just a bid to further his career.

When she left the meeting an hour later, she was more confused than ever about what she should do.

'You're looking pensive. Is everything okay?'

She turned to find Georgina studying her.

'Fine, thanks.' And to prove it, she gave her a wide smile.

Her boss didn't look too convinced. 'Well, I hope you're still smiling when Jim catches you. He's really stirring things up now with this new publication initiative. And we've kind of promised Geoff that—'

'We'll get some excellent PR out of it all. Yes, I know, Jim's already found me.'

'Ah. Good.' She perched herself on the side of Tess's desk. 'Then maybe he also told you that he's got quite a lot, personally, riding on this.'

'He hasn't,' Tess replied flatly. 'But you've already told me he's in line for CEO when Geoff retires, so I guess he's hoping this will help that along.'

Georgina frowned at her. 'Tessa, do you really think Jim's sticking his neck out on all this to further his career?'

'Well, yes, that's what you meant, wasn't it?'

'Hardly.' She slipped off the desk and stood up. 'It was probably fair to say Jim had the CEO position in the bag if he didn't cock-up. If he simply chose to keep his head down and steer clear of trouble for the next few years. But now? At the meeting this morning Geoff pretty much threatened him with the boot if sales went down because of these new initiatives.' She straightened her jacket and looked at Tess. 'Jim's doing this because he believes in it. Far from furthering his career, he's in real danger of losing it, which will be a massive shame. Not just for Helix, but the industry in general. So we need to do all we can to help him make this a success.'

Too stunned to say or do anything, Tess remained transfixed in her chair as Georgina disappeared into her office.

Chapter Twenty-Three

It was the evening of the R&D ball. The ball Tess had dreamt up to celebrate the achievements of the group before many of them left to join other companies. Jim allowed himself a wry smile. *Left* hadn't been the word Tess had used, but rather *forced out*, which was sadly much closer to the truth.

He scanned the elegant hotel ballroom, astounded by the huge turn out. Had the boot been on the other foot he didn't think he'd have bothered to come. Unless it was to thump the person who'd been responsible for kicking him out. Maybe that's what they were here for.

He clenched his jaw, feeling his stomach starting to knot. He'd worked with some of these people. They were decent and hard-working. Generously accepting of him when he'd joined them as a naive doctor, determined to rid the world of cancer. Dealing with numbers on a spreadsheet had been tough enough, but now he was forced to look them in the eye. To acknowledge that those who'd helped him during his own career were now losing their jobs. Thanks to him.

Letting out a long, slow breath, he wished the damn evening was already over. If he escaped without being verbally or physically abused, it would be something of a triumph.

A vision in red caught his eye and moved towards him, her hips swaying provocatively. Barbara.

'You're a brave man coming here tonight.'

He glanced over at her, taking in the curvaceous body poured into a tight satin red dress. Remnants of the woman he'd once lusted after were still there, but now all he saw was her cold eyes. Her manipulative smile.

'You're a brave woman talking to me after the way you deliberately mislead Tess over us,' he countered.

Her eyes raked over him. 'Tell me, Jim. Were you and she just a one off? One of those drunken mistakes that happen when work colleagues are flung together for an intense period of time. Or is it more?'

Out of the corner of his eye he spotted what he was looking for. 'Whatever it is, or was, is our business.'

With Barbara's eyes burning a hole in his back, he strode off towards the very lady they'd been discussing. He was about to play with fire. Rumours would start to fly the moment he stopped and talked to her, but to hell with it. Let them gossip, speculate, wonder. After the way his relationship with Barbara ended, he should be used to that.

As he neared Tess, any words he might have said flew right out of his head. This was what being tongue-tied meant, he mused as his eyes drank her in. A crushed velvet dress in brilliant violet hugged her slender frame. Demurely high at the front, it dipped daringly low at the back, giving him a view of sexy shoulder blades. Her gorgeous hair was piled elegantly on her head, a few tendrils curling gently down to frame her face.

As if aware of him staring, she turned towards him.

'Stunning.' He managed to croak out the word as his eyes drowned in her beauty and his nostrils flooded with her scent.

Her soft pink lips curved up in a smile. 'I could repeat the same word back at you, but I'd hate to be accused of sucking up to the boss.'

'You can suck up ...' He stopped, shook his head and laughed. 'No, better I don't say that.'

She giggled and for a few glorious moments nothing else existed but him and her.

'How are you feeling?' she asked, breaking the spell. 'I can't imagine this is easy for you.'

'What, you mean facing the people I've *forced* out?'

'Oops, that wasn't very subtle of me, was it?'

'No,' he agreed. 'But you made your point.' He nodded over to the gathering crowd. 'And I don't expect anyone here would disagree with you.'

'You didn't have to come, you know. You could have pretended a prior engagement. Nobody would have known.'

'Take the coward's way out, you mean?' He shook his head. 'Not my style. I figured the least they deserved was the chance to take their anger out on me in person. Hopefully it won't involve the throwing of any hard, missile shaped objects.' Catching sight of a man by a microphone waving at him, Jim nodded.

'Time to face the music.' He put his hands in his pockets and drew in a deep breath.

Tess regarded him quizzically. 'Are you *nervous*?'

'Hell, no,' he replied swiftly, then gave her a wry grin. 'I might have to admit to being a bit rattled, though. I can't imagine they're going to be the most receptive audience I've ever spoken to. In fact I might not make it past the opening remark.'

'I think they understand why you had to do it,' she told him softly, her hand moving to give him a reassuring squeeze on the arm.

What with the kindness of her touch, and the gentle understanding in her eyes, his chest suddenly felt far too tight. He laid his hand over hers, a gesture intended to express his thanks, but as their skin touched, he experienced a jolt of pure, raw desire. Stunned, he simply stood there, clasping her hand, gazing into her eyes, totally unable, or unwilling, to break the contact. Her lips parted slightly and her pupils dilated, showing him he wasn't the only one experiencing it.

Tess was the first to look away. 'Jim, they're waiting for you.' Her voice was soft and husky.

Reluctantly he looked over to the waiting microphone. 'Right.' He cleared his throat. 'Wish me luck.'

She shook her head. 'You won't need it.'

He wasn't so sure about that. After flashing her a grateful smile he strode over to the microphone and turned to address the assembled partygoers.

'I'm not going to talk for long,' he began. 'Although I realise for many of you this will already be long enough.' There was a slight murmur. Tentative laughter or dogged agreement? He didn't know. 'Business can be tough,' he went on. 'And the pharmaceutical business tougher than most. We invest hundreds of millions on a hope and a handful of evidence. Sometimes it pays off. Many, many more times, it doesn't. But each and every one of you here can hold up your heads and know for a fact that through your skill, dedication and, at times, sheer genius, you did make a difference. Not just to Helix Pharmaceuticals, but to patients. That, at the end of the day, is what we're here for.' He paused. The room was ominously quiet. 'As your R&D president, I thank you sincerely for the work you've done. As a potential patient, I thank you for the work you will continue to do for the other organisations some of you will work for in the future.' He paused and swallowed back the lump lodged in his throat. 'That's all I wanted to say. Thank you for listening and enjoy the rest of your evening.'

He started to move away from the microphone, but then paused. 'Oh, and I almost forgot. For those who wanted to deck me the moment you heard the redundancy announcement, I will be hanging around tonight for a while longer.'

This time he heard laughter. Not only that, there was a sprinkling of applause. It wasn't exactly an ovation, but it was a damn sight more than he'd expected. A lot more than he deserved.

Tess was one of those clapping. The more she heard him talk, the more impressive she found him. Especially now she knew he meant what he said. He believed in the industry he was working for. And in the people who worked in it. He wasn't hard and unfeeling, as she'd once accused him of, but brave and determined. Sometimes that determination meant he had to make tough, unpopular decisions, but he didn't flinch from what he thought was right.

She sighed. And heaven help her, he looked unbelievably handsome in a tuxedo.

'At the very least, I expected a few boos.'

Tess turned to find Jack Webber standing next to her, a smile playing around his thin lips. There was something about the commercial president that made her skin creep. Perhaps it was his too dark tan, clearly gained from years on a sunbed rather than honest outdoor pursuits. Or maybe it was his slicked back hair. The combination made him almost a caricature of the office letch.

'Perhaps scientists are more forgiving than commercial guys,' she ventured, trying to move away from him.

'Whatever the reason, I'm disappointed not to see a drop of blood spilt. It's the only reason I blagged an invite.' He turned and gave her what he probably considered his winning smile. 'Dance with me, Tessa.'

It wasn't a question. Before she could find the diplomatic words to turn him down, she was propelled onto the thronging dance floor. At that moment, to add to her troubles, the music changed to a slow number.

'What do you think of Jim?' Jack asked as he put his arms around her, pulling her towards him.

'I hardly know him,' she returned stiffly, edging back. She didn't want to make an enemy of Jack, but he was holding her too close. And the smell of his aftershave was making her sick.

'You should have met the last research guy, Derek Stanley. He was great. Didn't have any crazy ideas about turning everything we did upside down.'

'You don't approve of what Jim's trying to do, then?' she

asked, knowing full well he didn't, but needing to keep him talking so she could extricate herself from his tight hold.

'Hardly.'

That was better. The only part of him touching her now was his hand. A too smooth, too soft, much too clammy hand that had settled on her bare back.

'The man's a menace,' Jack added scornfully.

'I don't think you should be discussing Jim with me.' The words were barely out of her mouth before the topic of their conversation loomed over them, his dark eyes looking dangerous, his face thunderous.

'You wouldn't be talking about me, by any chance?'

Totally unfazed, Jack shrugged his shoulders. 'As a matter of fact, I was.'

Testosterone filled the air as the men glared at each other.

Without warning, Jim took a step forwards and shouldered his counterpart out of the way. 'Then I suggest you go and talk about me somewhere else,' he told the commercial head bluntly, placing his more powerful frame between her and Jack. 'Somewhere I can't hear you.'

Jack's face flushed with anger and Tess held her breath, terrified he was going to create a scene. She'd been relieved to see Jim, but now he'd taken things too far.

After a moment's hesitation, and one long glower in Jim's direction, Jack stalked away.

Tess slowly exhaled. 'Well, thanks for the rescue, but the caveman approach was probably overkill.'

'You think?'

'Actually, yes, I do. Blimey, Jim, that was hardly the action of a colleague.'

'Your point is?'

He looked down at her from his impressive height and even though she saw herself as a strong, professional woman, her knees weakened at the force of his presence. 'You came across like a jealous lover,' she told him crossly.

'Funny, because that's exactly how I feel,' he answered, his voice low and deep. His eyes hot and possessive.

Air rushed out of her lungs and Tess found she couldn't breathe, could barely swallow.

'Tess, I know I said we should forget what happened in Singapore, but I can't.'

Even as her heart lifted, her brain froze. 'Please, let's not talk about this now,' she squawked. God, she couldn't have a relationship with this man. No matter how much she might want to, she couldn't.

He must have heard the desperation in her voice because he nodded once before holding out his hand. 'Then dance with me.'

For the second time that evening Tess was pulled into a dance. This time the hand on her back was dry and slightly rough. The heat from it burnt through her skin, sensitising every nerve fibre. And this time, when the man drew her closer, she didn't resist. She settled against his tall frame and let slip a sigh. This was exactly where she wanted to be.

Over Jim's left shoulder, she caught sight of Jack Webber staring at them. 'I do believe Jack's eyes are currently shooting daggers into your back.'

Jim grunted. 'The feeling is mutual. I can't abide the man. He's a dinosaur of the industry. When I saw him putting his grubby little paws all over you ...' His arms tightened around her, pulling her even more firmly against him. It felt sinfully good.

'I hope his hands weren't grubby. He had them on my bare back.'

'Yeah, I noticed.'

There was that note of possession again. She shouldn't want it, couldn't encourage it. But tell that to her heart, which fluttered alarmingly in response.

'I hope yours are clean,' she whispered.

He glanced down, eyes puzzled.

'Your hands. I hope they're clean.'

A quicksilver grin flashed across his face. 'My mother always taught me to wash my hands,' he replied, using one of the hands in question to gently caress her back. 'Christ, you've got a beautiful back,' he whispered hoarsely. 'So soft. Like silk.'

Tess swallowed. This was dangerous. He was impossibly gorgeous. Incredibly magnetic. How was she supposed to resist him?

'Hell, I can't believe you've got me waxing lyrical about your *back*,' he was muttering oblivious to her internal turmoil. 'Next I'll be saying what fabulous ears you have. Mind you, they are pretty cute.'

As he bent his head to examine them, his warm breath teasing her neck, she started to laugh. Just one more dance, she told herself. Five more minutes of heaven.

An hour later and Tess was home, changed into her pj's, and drinking a cup of hot chocolate on the sofa. Cinderella eat your heart out. With a wry smile she settled back against the cushions. In truth, this was definitely more her. Dressing up was okay now and again, especially as it gave her the opportunity to wear her party shoes – like the silver strappy Alexander McQueens she'd worn tonight – but in reality she was more a quiet night in type of girl. In her element with pizza, wine, a weepy film and chocolate.

Parties had their upsides though. Like dancing with a drop dead gorgeous man. It was just as well the music had changed and Jim's attention claimed by others. If the tempo had remained slow and Jim had continued to hold her in his arms ... she wouldn't be sitting here drinking hot chocolate.

What did that admission make her, knowing what she was doing behind his back?

The sound of the ringing phone jarred into her thoughts. Grateful for the distraction, she leapt up to answer it.

'Hey, Tess, it's Hugh. Remember me?'

Shutting her eyes, she slumped back against the sofa and told herself this was good timing. 'Of course I remember you. It's only been a couple of weeks since we last spoke. I didn't realise I was meant to check in.'

'Hey, touchy, touchy. What's the matter? All not well in the corporate world?'

She took in a deep breath and let it out very slowly. It wouldn't do to let Hugh know the mess she was getting herself into. He'd only harp on about her responsibilities as a journalist, a reminder she really didn't need. Her conscience was doing a good enough job on its own. 'Everything is fine, thank you. To what do I owe this honour?'

'I was just wondering how my story is unfolding. Have you got any further yet?'

She opened her mouth to speak then closed it again. What could she say? The truth? Yes, she already had enough evidence to write a pretty damning article on how Helix didn't automatically publish every study they conducted, but she couldn't write it. Because publishing it would not only expose the company, it would expose Jim. The same Jim who was currently risking his career to put things right.

But what about what happened to your mother?

'Tess?'

'Sorry, I, umm ...'

'Don't tell me you're getting cold feet.'

'No. Not exactly.'

'What does that mean? You're not falling for the bloody R&D head are you?'

How on earth? 'Don't be stupid. Why would you say that?'

'Because I understand he's a hit with the ladies. And because in our last conversation you told me he was broodingly handsome.'

'Just because I appreciate his looks doesn't mean I'm a pushover,' she retorted, as much to herself as to Hugh.

207

'Good, because if there's stuff going on there that shouldn't be, the public has a right to know. So do the patients who take their products.'

'You don't need to remind me of that.' Guilt made her voice sharper.

'Are you sure? Because it strikes me you're in danger of letting your feelings get in the way of an important investigation.' He paused. When he spoke again, his voice was calmer, softer. 'This issue isn't just about finding out what happened to your mum, Tess. It's bigger than that. You told me she wasn't the only one to die of a heart problem whilst taking the drug; that you've already spoken to relatives of other grieving families. So this is about seeking justice for them, too. In fact for everyone who may have lost a loved one through the manipulations of the pharmaceutical industry.'

They were the same words she'd spoken to herself. But that was before she'd joined the industry. Before she'd met the industrious, hard-working people employed there. And before Jim.

'I'm fully aware of my responsibilities,' she retorted stiffly. 'I'm still looking into this and I won't stop until I find out if data on the drug Mum took was deliberately buried.' Her eyes wandered to a framed photograph on the mantelpiece. One of her and her mother. They looked so happy. She missed her so much. Missed the happy family that had been her bedrock.

'That's good to hear,' Hugh replied. 'Keep me posted.'

Ending the call, Tess slumped back against the sofa. She could justify keeping quiet on what she already knew because, although not publishing studies wasn't right, it was going to be put right. Plus she had no proof that the studies that hadn't been published had caused any safety issues. But what if she found that proof?

Swallowing against the choking emotion, Tess stood and

picked up the photograph, tracing the familiar lines of her mother's face. As the tears flowed she clasped the frame to her, hugging it. Her mother deserved justice. She knew that. But in order to give her that justice, Tess would have to deeply betray Jim. The thought of doing that didn't just make her stomach churn. It made her heart ache.

If she couldn't find any proof of wrongdoing though …

Wiping away her tears, Tess walked purposefully to her briefcase, dragged out her computer and opened the study database. When she'd first hatched the idea of joining Helix it had been for the sole purpose of finding proof that Zaplex had killed her mother. It had given her an outlet for her anger. A target to blame.

Now she was hoping against hope that she wouldn't find anything.

Chapter Twenty-Four

Jim pushed himself to do another few kilometres on the rowing machine. He knew if he didn't, if he failed to absolutely exhaust himself to the core, then he'd spend the whole damn evening fantasising about making love to Tess again. Just like he had every night since he'd danced with her at the ball, and a whole bunch of nights before that, too. He'd gone beyond intrigued by and into full blown obsessed.

So when Rick had come to find him on the off chance he'd wanted to exercise early, Jim had shocked him by agreeing. It was that or stride over to the communications department, grab hold of Tess, and kiss her till her knees buckled. The latter option held far more appeal, but he didn't think it would do either of their careers much good.

'What are you up to tonight?' Rick asked as they crunched out repetitions on the rowing machine.

Jim scowled and notched the resistance up. 'The usual.'

When Rick started to grin in that knowing way of his, he scowled some more.

'Exercise and pizza then?'

'Exercise is good for you,' Jim grunted.

'Yes, but only when it's incorporated into a life that balances work and fun. Not when it replaces your social life.' Rick slowly came to a stop. 'It's Friday night, pal. You're young enough, just, to be hitting the bars and clubs. Picking up the hot looking chicks.' He grinned. 'Mind you, those streaks of grey in your hair aren't exactly running in your favour.'

'They're distinguished. A sign of maturity,' Jim retorted, then immaturely let go of the rowing handle with a loud clatter. He'd had enough.

'Well take that mature body of yours out of here and into

the real world.' Rick stood up and towelled off. 'Unless of course you're still pining after the communications lady.'

'Piss off.'

Rick laughed. 'You're sunk, mate. Might as well face up to it and do something about it. Anyway, I'm out of here. Unlike you, I've got a beautiful woman waiting at home for me.'

Watching his friend leave, Jim sighed. That was exactly what he wanted, too. To spend an evening at home with a woman he loved. Except that he'd tried that already, and trusting a woman with his love had turned out to be a real heart crusher. On the other hand, *not* trying again was pure cowardice, surely? And if he didn't try, he'd be left with the bleak prospect of spending the rest of his years alone.

Then, of course, there was the most terrifying thought of all – letting a woman as gorgeous, intriguing and vital as Tess slip through his fingers. That was bloody unthinkable.

When he saw the object of his thoughts walk into the gym, he told himself he was hallucinating. So he brushed the sweat from his eyes and took another look. His heart reacted before his brain had a chance to confirm, thumping away harder than it had when he'd been rowing.

It was definitely Tess, her slim frame encased in snug black lycra leggings and a vivid green work out vest. Swearing softly under his breath, Jim struggled to his feet. If this was some sort of bizarre test of his willpower then tonight he was going to fail. In fact with a bit of luck, he'd fail in spectacular fashion, going down with all guns blazing.

'Hey,' he called out as he walked towards her, hastily wiping the sweat from his face onto his shirt. Crude, but effective. 'I didn't realise you'd joined here.'

Tess's eyes widened in surprise when she turned to see him and his ego took a nosedive. So much for his hope that she'd chosen this gym because he was a member.

'That's because I've not been before,' she admitted. 'I

joined a couple of weeks ago, but I've only just got round to making it as far as getting changed.'

She looked as off balance as he felt. If only he knew whether that was because she was still attracted to him, or because she was standing in her gym kit in front of her sweaty boss.

'Well, congratulations. Getting changed is the hard part. It's downhill from now on.'

He mimicked pressing the decline button on the treadmill and was rewarded with a lovely smile. Far better than the pathetic joke deserved.

'Have you finished?' she asked.

He glanced down at his sweat soaked work out vest. 'A reasonable assumption, but no.' There was no way he was leaving now. Even if the extra exercise ended up killing him.

'Okay then.' She gazed warily at the array of equipment.

'They don't bite.'

'Ha, ha.'

'Which isn't to say they aren't capable of inflicting some sort of pain.'

'Exactly.'

Again she smiled at him and his breath caught in his throat. 'Well, I'll, umm ...' God, what was he now, a procrastinating fool? 'I'll leave you to get started,' he finished, cringing at his lameness.

Climbing on the nearest treadmill, he punched in a 10% incline as his punishment. He was hardly going to persuade her to take a chance on him with that sort of performance. Still, all was not lost. He'd enjoy watching her work out and *then* he'd talk her into having a drink with him.

Half an hour later, and Jim was still running. He was also beginning to doubt his sanity. If Tess's idea of an exercise regime was another two hours of hard grind, he was going to be dead on his feet and totally incapable of speech, never mind asking her out for a drink.

He almost sagged in relief as he spotted her moving off the

step machine and towards the exit. Quickly slowing down the treadmill he wiped himself down and strode after her.

'Had enough?'

She turned and nodded, her face aglow. 'I think I'd had enough before I started.'

He chuckled. 'I know what you mean. Still, it's a great way to set up the weekend.' At least it would be, if he had more in store than a takeout pizza.

'I'll take your word for it. I'll be happy just to make it home in one piece.'

She came to a halt outside the ladies' changing room and looked up at him questioningly. Probably wondering if he was going to follow her in there, too.

'How about you meet me in the bar for a drink when you've changed?' He smiled down at her. 'I'm buying. A reward for your hard effort.'

Before she had a chance to say anything, before he could even read her reaction, he headed off towards the men's locker room. It was a tactic he often used to good effect in the workplace. *Can you finish this by 4 p.m.?* Walk away. *I take that as a yes.* Walk away. Those who pegged him as diabolically stubborn were absolutely right. It hadn't taken him long in life to realise the easiest way to not take no for an answer, was to disappear before anyone had a chance to utter it.

When Tess arrived at the bar a little while later, he'd showered, changed into his cycling gear and was nursing a glass of beer. Her mouth gaped open when she saw him.

'I figured I deserve a beer.'

'I'm not disputing that. Just wondering why you've changed into more exercise gear.'

'Ahh.' He felt more than a little foolish now. 'I'm not driving back. I brought the bike.'

'What?' She looked at him as if he was bonkers. 'After that work out you've still got to cycle home?'

'Yeah.' He gave her a small smile. 'I hadn't planned on staying quite so long.'

'What made you change your mind?'

He stared straight at her, his eyes bold and direct. 'You.'

'Oh.' Her already slightly flushed face turned crimson. He loved that about her. That she was still innocent enough to blush.

'And before you start to wonder,' he interjected, suddenly realising how that sounded, 'it wasn't because I wanted to gawk at you in your tight lycra.' He grinned. 'Though I have to admit that certainly had a lot of merit. It was because I wanted to have a drink with you afterwards. Now, what can I get you?'

Having spent the last hour recovering from the shock of finding she'd joined the same gym as the man she knew she needed to keep away from, Tess would have killed for a large white wine. Especially as she'd also suffered the agony of exercising whilst trying not to watch that same man pound effortlessly up and down on the treadmill. But she had to drive home. 'Better make mine a sparkling water.'

He paid for the drinks and carried them over to a table by the window.

'How often do you come here?' And how cheesy was that question, she scolded as they settled into their chairs. It was only a whisper away from *do you come here often?*

Draping an arm over the back of his chair he took a mouthful of beer and considered her question. 'Are you asking because you're hoping to bump into me again, or because you're wondering whether to cancel your membership right now?'

There was that bluntness again. That willingness to face things head on. She wasn't so brave. 'Neither,' she lied. 'It was idle curiosity. I heard you run triathlons. Certainly you seem pretty fit.'

'I like to exercise.' He smiled over at her, a flash of white teeth in a crazily handsome face. 'I used to love doing triathlons, back in my younger days. Now they're starting to seem a little too much like hard work. In another few years I'll qualify for the veterans.' He shrugged. 'Still, it should give me a better chance of ending somewhere near the front, rather than the back.'

'So winning is everything eh?' She'd intended it as a joke, but he took her question seriously.

'No, not everything. I won't cheat to win, but winning is important to me.' He'd been toying with the beer mat in front of him, but now he directed his dark gaze towards her. 'What's important to you?'

Instantly Tess found she couldn't look at him. The single most important thing to her over the last eighteen months had been to find out why her mother had died. 'My family,' she answered slowly.

He nodded soberly. 'You told me back in the US that your mother died not that long ago. What other family do you have?'

The image of her father, fading away in a care home, swam before her eyes. 'A father and a brother,' she replied stiffly.

His eyes filled with sympathy. 'Sorry, is this too painful to talk about? I can't imagine how lost your father is without your mother. I know mine would be.'

'He is. We all are.' She couldn't carry on this conversation. She felt like a total traitor. Both to her family and to Jim. Gulping back the rest of her water, she rose to her feet. 'Thanks for the drink, but it's time I went.'

Jim watched as she stood up from the table, his expression confused. 'So soon? I was going to suggest we ditched the bike and car and headed somewhere for dinner.'

Vehemently she shook her head, too desperate to get away to worry about looking rude. 'No, thanks. I can't.'

He struck out a hand to stop her from leaving. 'Have I got this wrong, Tess?'

'I …' She couldn't think what to say, how to explain. *No, you haven't got it wrong, but this can't go anywhere because I'm a double-crossing bitch and you might have inadvertently killed my mum?*

As silence fell between them, his expression turned from one of frustration to one of hurt. 'If this blazing attraction I'm feeling is all one-sided, please, just tell me.' He gave her a small, wry smile. 'You're not usually afraid to speak your mind.'

This was it. Her chance to explain that she wasn't interested any more. That Singapore had been a drunken mistake. Her mouth dropped open, ready to tell him, but as she looked into his earnest brown eyes, the words just wouldn't come. 'You told me I should push you away,' she whispered.

He shook his head. 'I know.' He rose from his seat and placed a hand on her cheek, allowing his thumb to gently brush over her lips. 'I was wrong.'

His voice was low and husky, the slow movement of his thumb achingly seductive. Deep within her chest her heart began to swell and open, inviting him in. But how could it, knowing what she did? 'Sorry, I need to go,' she choked out.

With her eyes stinging, she grabbed her holdall and fled.

Jim spent his Friday night alone. This time the beer tasted flat and the pizza like cardboard. Only days ago, when they'd danced together at the ball, he'd been sure Tess had felt the same way he did. Now it seemed she couldn't even stand to have a drink with him. Was she trying to hide her feelings? Worried about having a relationship with a man she worked for? Or was he arrogantly assuming an attraction that simply wasn't there any more?

Abruptly he stood and shovelled the rest of the pizza into the bin. Whatever the hell it was, he was going to find out. He was falling for her, hard. Sure it scared the living daylights out of him, but so had bungee jumping from the bridge over Victoria Falls and throwing himself out of a plane on his first parachute jump. It hadn't stopped him doing either. Tess was about to find out he wasn't a man who ran away from a challenge. He ran headlong into it.

Chapter Twenty-Five

Tess cast her eyes around her dad's room and found him where they usually did, in his armchair. Today his head was tilted forward, resting on his chest, and his arms loosely crossed over his tall, thin frame.

'He's asleep.'

Mark crouched in front of him. 'Dad?' When there was no movement, he sighed and stood up. 'Well, I guess that leaves the conversation down to you and me. Maybe if he hears us talking he'll wake up.'

'Fair enough. But I'm having this chair.' Hastily she went to sit down. 'You can go and find yourself one.'

As he disappeared, muttering something rude about sisters under his breath, Tess let out a deep sigh and collapsed back against the small armchair. It isn't a bad place, she told herself for the umpteenth time as she stared out of the window at the impressive grounds. A former manor house, it had no doubt pulsed with life and energy many years ago. It was just that now, behind the well-preserved paintwork and the tidy front garden, life didn't pulse any more. It was ebbing away.

Her eyes moved sadly over the tall, frail man on the chair, and then over the room where he spent most of his days. It reminded her of a smart hotel room, bright and clean, and just as impersonal. In a bid to make it more homely she'd hung a few framed photographs on the walls. One glance at the laughing family staring back at her from the wall by his bed, and she had to bite her lip to stop from crying.

'I had to walk all the way to the dining room,' Mark complained as he came back in. He took one look at her and shook his head. 'Oh dear. You've got that *on the verge of tears* look. Want to talk about it?'

'It's nothing. Just being here. Dad.' But it was more than

that. It was a gamut of mixed-up feelings about a man who might have, no matter how unwittingly, been responsible for shattering the loving family in the photograph.

Mark wasn't easily put off. 'Don't lie to me, Tess. You come here every week. Why this time are you crying?' He bent to shake her gently by the shoulders, forcing her to look at him. 'It's that man, isn't it? The Helix research guy.'

She glared at him, nodding warningly over at their father. 'Please. We can't talk about that here.'

'Why not?' Mark set the chair down next to hers. 'Dad's fast asleep and even if he woke up, he wouldn't understand what we were talking about.'

'I know, but still.' She sucked in a deep breath. 'I feel disloyal enough discussing all this with you. Doing it in front of Dad too is like, I don't know, rubbing salt into a weeping wound.'

'Who do you feel disloyal too? Mum, Dad, me? Or him?'

'All of you,' she hissed, beginning to shake. 'You can't possibly understand how awful I feel. How torn.' Raising her eyes to his, she admitted what was in her heart. 'I'm falling for him, Mark. I don't want to, but I am.'

'Crap.' He hung his head, rubbing at his eyes. 'Please tell me you found out he wasn't responsible for the Zaplex clinical programme? At least then I can start to understand.'

'He was,' she blurted. 'But it doesn't mean he did anything wrong.'

Mark raised his eyes skywards. 'You fool. I thought you were more sensible than this. Heck, there's a possibility this man is partly responsible for our mother's death and you're *sleeping* with him?'

Her eyes darted guiltily over to her father. Thank God, he was still asleep. 'I'm not sleeping with Jim. At least not now. Not since that night in Singapore.'

'But you want to, don't you?'

'Yes,' she admitted, the truth hurting her as much as it was clearly hurting her brother.

Mark swore under his breath. 'You owe this to Dad, Tess. To me, to the other families you've contacted. Hell, to yourself. Finish what you set out to do. Don't be fooled by one man's good looks.'

'I'm not,' she countered sharply. 'But you don't know him like I do. Besides, I didn't say I was giving up. I've got access to the Helix study database now and I'm trawling through it. There are loads of Zaplex studies and for each one I have to wade through the study report because I can't tell from the title whether it's relevant or not, but I am making progress. I will find out if any results were hidden, Mark. Trust me.'

He exhaled slowly, threading a hand through his hair which then flopped back on his forehead. 'I do trust you. I also love you, which gives me the right to worry about you. If this man does turn out to be an unscrupulous bastard, he won't be the only one who's hurt by any fall out. You will be, too.'

'I know,' she whispered, looking down at her clenched hands. 'I know.' Then the blasted tears started to fall.

'Oh, God, don't go and bloody cry on me.' Swearing softly, he eased off his chair and gathered her into his arms. 'I'm sorry, I didn't mean to mouth off at you like that. It's just I hate to see you this screwed up.' He tilted her chin up so he could look at her. 'I guess this is where it would help to talk to Mum, huh?'

In between gulping in lungfuls of air, Tess nodded.

'I suspect a brother is a poor substitute when it comes to discussing matters of the heart.' He wiped away her tears with the sleeve of his shirt. 'But you could always try me out.'

She managed a weak laugh. 'There isn't much to say. Before I joined Helix, I believed, like you, that the company was a den of iniquity and the research head only one step removed from the devil incarnate. Well, guess what, there *are* things going on that shouldn't, and Jim isn't perfect, but ...' she fumbled for a tissue from her pocket and wiped her eyes.

'If results were kept back from studies he conducted, it won't have been deliberate, at least not on his part. He's a good man, Mark. Also smart, funny, dynamic, strong-minded—'

'Okay, I get the message. The guy is hot and you want to get back in his knickers ... sorry, pants.' He gave her the same grin he used to give her when he was twelve. 'See, I told you I could do this.'

This time Tess laughed properly.

And finally their father stirred. 'Margaret? Is that you?'

Tess gulped. 'Oh, Dad.' She shot off her chair and went to hug him, holding onto his hand. 'I'm not Margaret, I'm Tess. Her daughter.' Gently she kissed his cheek. '*Your* daughter.'

A brief flare of recognition flashed through his eyes. 'Tess?'

She clutched his hand tighter. 'Yes. I'm here with Mark.'

He turned his head to where Mark was standing, and Tess watched sadly as the clarity slowly faded from his eyes. 'Who are you?'

They stayed for another half an hour, the conversation awkward and disjointed. Finally one of the carers came in to take her father to tea.

With a heavy dose of relief – and an even heavier dose of guilt at the relief – Tess kissed him goodbye and walked with Mark out into the fresh air.

'Same time, same place, next Saturday?'

He nodded, giving her a hug. 'It's a date.' As he pulled back, he smiled. 'I forgot to say thank you.'

'You did?'

'Yes. Thank you for continuing to look into the drug Mum took. I know it can't be easy, going behind the back of the man you fancy.'

'You have no idea. But if I give up now, I'll be letting you, Dad and Mum down, so I don't really have a choice.'

He kissed her gently on the forehead. 'For your sake I hope you prove Mum's death was unavoidable. That it had nothing to do with the drug she took.'

Swallowing down the lump in her throat, Tess squeezed her brother's arm. 'So do I.'

About the same time Tess was arriving home after visiting her father, Jim was trying to take an interest in the live match on Sky Sports. A bottom of the table clash was never really going to capture his attention, but tonight it held about as much appeal as watching paint dry. Men in white shorts and blue tops ran themselves ragged on a muddy green pitch, trying to put the ball in the back of the net. All he could think about though was Tess, and what his next move should be.

When the match came to its inevitable, anti-climactic end, he zapped off the TV and grabbed the piece of paper lying on the glass coffee table. The piece with Tess's address scrawled over it, taken from the HR file he'd opened. It screamed misuse of power, but to hell with it. If the sales didn't continue as solidly as they had before he'd bulldozed through his changes, the company already had more than enough reasons to fire him.

Picking up his keys, he walked out of his apartment and down to his waiting E-type. As he turned on the engine she emitted such a pulsing, throaty roar he almost found himself stroking the damn thing. Modern cars, with their soulless exteriors, were far too quiet. Who wanted a machine that didn't talk to you?

On the other hand, he reflected ruefully twenty minutes later, the modern car did have some useful accessories his beloved Jaguar didn't have. Like a satellite navigation system. He pulled over and scrutinised the map again. Tess's was the second turn on the left, after the park. Yeah, he'd got that now. Putting the car into gear he drove down the street for the second time, finally ending up parking outside a smart old townhouse that looked like it had been converted into a block of flats.

He didn't immediately jump out of the car, cognisant of the fact that he was about to knock, uninvited, on a female employee's door. Even if he simply thought of her as a woman, it didn't make the situation any better. It was Saturday evening. She could be doing anything. Having a bath, sharing a meal with friends. She could be out, which actually, thinking about it now, might be a good thing. Or she could be inside right now, staring passionately into the eyes of another man.

He lunged out of the car, marched across the road and stabbed his finger on her doorbell.

'Hello?' Her soft voice came through the intercom.

Images of her smiling into a lover's eyes, wrapping those endless legs around him, crowded through his mind. 'Tess, it's Jim. Can I come up?' he barked.

'Jim?' She sounded confused, which didn't surprise him. His was probably the last voice she'd expected to hear over her intercom on a Saturday night. Or indeed any night.

'Yes. Can I come up?' He paused, finally remembering he was trying to woo this woman, not scare her to death. 'Please?'

The door clicked open and in a matter of seconds he'd leapt up the internal staircase and was standing outside her apartment. Magically, the door opened.

'Is everything okay?'

She stood in the doorway and his eyes immediately drifted behind her to the living room, looking for evidence of a visitor. He couldn't see anyone, though he could be hiding in the bedroom.

'Jim?'

Finally he looked at Tess. Her expression was so concerned, her eyes so worried, that he suddenly felt incredibly foolish. Clearly she was imagining all manner of problems to do with work, when the reality was much simpler. He'd barged in on her just because he'd had to see her. 'Everything is fine,' he told her succinctly.

'Then what are you doing here?'

Exactly. He dragged a hand through his hair and for half a second thought of lying and making up some lame excuse of a work issue that needed her help. 'I needed to see you,' he replied quietly. Honestly. 'Please, if you're on your own, can I come in?'

She opened the door more fully and he slipped inside, realising with a rush of relief that she *was* alone. Following a quick survey of the room, taking in the stylish mix of old architecture and very modern, bright furnishings, his eyes settled on her. She looked incredible, but also totally bemused, as if she couldn't quite believe he was here, in her apartment. She wasn't the only one.

'Would you like a drink?'

He relaxed slightly. If she was offering him a drink, at least she wasn't expecting to throw him out quickly. 'Please. A small beer, if you've got one?'

She nodded and disappeared off to the kitchen, returning moments later with a cold bottle for him and a glass of wine for herself.

He took a quick sip and cut to the chase. 'Why did you disappear in such a hurry yesterday?'

Her hands trembled slightly as she reached for her glass. 'It upsets me to talk about my parents,' she told him, her voice not quite steady, her eyes not quite meeting his. 'My mother's death is still very fresh and my dad—' She broke off for a moment, and he could see how painful this was for her. 'Dad has never recovered from losing her. He's in a care home now.'

Jim put down his beer and came to stand next to her, putting his hands on her shoulders. 'I'm sorry, Tess.'

Tess nodded, fully intending to move out of the way before she did something stupid like lean in towards him. That was when she found her feet wouldn't move. Before she knew it his arms were reaching behind her, drawing her closer against his broad chest, cradling her head with his hand. Instead of distancing herself, she found she was closing her eyes, shutting out everything but the feel of his embrace. The comfort. The sense of belonging.

His quiet groan brought her to her senses. Feeling torn and shaken, she moved hastily away. 'Is that really why you're here?' she asked on a shaky breath. 'To find out why I rushed off in case you'd upset me? A quick phone call would have saved you the hassle.'

'Perhaps, if that was the only reason I wanted to see you,' he agreed, picking up his beer again. 'But it wasn't.'

Tess's heart refused to settle, not helped by the slightly dangerous glint in his eye. 'What was the other reason?' She tried to sound calm, but the croak in her voice gave her away.

He regarded her steadily. 'I think you know.'

Her heart slammed into her chest. 'I thought we agreed we weren't going to pursue this ...' she groped for the right words, 'attraction between us.'

He smiled tightly. 'That was before I realised I couldn't keep away.'

She'd forgotten how dark his eyes were. Feeling too unsteady to stand, Tess lurched towards the sofa. 'Is this how it started with Barbara? One crazy night of sex, followed by you pursuing her until she couldn't say no?'

Sighing, he took another swig of his beer and went to sit on the armchair opposite her. 'This has nothing to do with Barbara,' he said heavily.

'I think it does. She's why you made your rule, isn't she?'

'Partly, yes,' he replied honestly. 'But partly because men in my position shouldn't proposition female employees who work for them.' He crooked her a wry smile. 'Yet here I am.'

'What happened with Barbara? How did it end?'

He let out a sharp, hard laugh. 'Don't tell me you haven't already heard that on the office grapevine. It was gossip of the month before I left.'

She shook her head. 'All I know is after it ended you went to join another company.'

'I came back early from a business trip and went to surprise Barbara in her office,' he recited flatly, draining back the last of his beer. 'The surprise was on me when I found her draped over her desk, being nailed by Derek. My predecessor. At the time, my boss.'

'Oh my God.' She knew she shouldn't, because clearly it had been agonising for Jim, but somehow the image made her want to giggle. 'Really, they did that at work, with the glass offices?'

'They weren't glass then.'

'Ah. Still, it takes some bravado to have sex in the office during work hours, with an unlocked door.' She couldn't help herself. Her eyes flickered questioningly towards him.

'No, I haven't. Not that the thought hasn't crossed my mind recently.'

There it was again. The searing heat in his eyes when he looked at her. 'So that's why you left,' she murmured, trying to get back onto safer ground.

He gave her a loaded glance. One that said her avoidance tactics wouldn't work for long. 'Yes. I couldn't get out of the place fast enough.'

'No wonder you made your rule.'

He leaned forward, bracing his arms on his powerful thighs. 'Being cheated on is hard enough, without having the whole office knowing your business. You could say it taught me an important lesson. Be careful who you trust.'

Her hand tightened on the wine glass she was holding. Terrified it might shatter she slid it onto the coffee table, but that left her with nothing to do with her now shaking hands. Hastily she clasped them in her lap.

'Tess?' Jim rose to his feet and crouched beside her, taking her hands in his. 'Are you okay?'

Swallowing tightly, she nodded. His hands felt so warm

and his handsome face was so close she could reach out and run her hands through his soft dark hair.

She shifted back on the sofa. 'Are you sure you're over her? Barbara, I mean.'

'I'm sure.' His tone, like his expression, was absolute. 'When she came round the other day, when you assumed we'd been together.'

'Yes, I remember.' She wasn't sure she'd ever forget feeling such raging jealousy.

'Well, she had more in mind than just dropping off my clothes. All I could think was it felt wrong. She felt wrong. My mind was full of you, Tess. It has been, ever since Singapore.' He raised her hands to his lips and started to kiss her knuckles, each one in turn. 'I was too hasty about what I said,' he told her huskily. 'At the time I didn't want another office affair, but now I think what we have could be far more than that.' Finally he leaned forward and gave her the gentlest of kisses. 'How about you? What do you think?'

His mouth began to explore further, nibbling gently, and a low moan of pleasure escaped her. 'I can't think at all while you're doing that,' she admitted breathlessly.

'Good. I don't want you thinking. I only want you feeling.'

Jim soon had his wish, because when his tongue unerringly found its way past her lips, Tess's mind stopped working altogether. She was sunk, lost in a world where nothing existed but the touch, the feel, the caress of this magnetic man.

Chapter Twenty-Six

Jim pressed home his advantage, easing Tess back against the sofa and plundering the delights of her mouth with his hungry tongue. Though he'd sensed a moment of hesitation in her, he wasn't about to stop. He was far too afraid that if he gave her the chance to think, she'd push him away. A decent man might have paused, making sure the lady really did want this to happen. He hoped he *was* a decent man, at least most of the time, but when it came to Tess he became someone else. A man with no control over his mind or body. A man convinced that if he hesitated, he would lose her.

His hand struggled to work its way under her blouse. Damn, her clothing was getting in the way of where he wanted to be. With ruthless efficiency, he rid her of the silky number, only to be forced to stop and stare at the lacy, dusty pink bra he'd just revealed. 'Have I told you how gorgeous you are?' he said hoarsely as his fingers danced over her skin, nipping under the lace. With a groan he opened the clasp, drawing it off so he could feast his eyes, and his mouth, on the dainty breasts beneath.

Tess fisted her hands in his hair, pushing his mouth harder against her. 'I'm not,' she told him in a voice that was as reassuringly unsteady as his own, 'but you make me feel like I am.'

'God, you are, you are. Your breasts are—'

'Still small.'

He lifted up his head from where it had been focussed and looked into her eyes. While she was smiling slightly, the vulnerability was still there. Whoever the bastard was who'd made her feel inadequate, he'd really done a number on her. 'Your breasts are one hundred per cent perfect, Tess. The most gorgeous breasts I've ever seen.'

To prove his point, he flicked at the pink nipples with his tongue, watching in awe as they tightened. Tess moaned, and he licked again, grinning as she started to writhe beneath him. 'See? If they weren't so perfect, neither of us would be getting such a buzz out of this.'

'Well, I am.'

He laughed and stood to take off his jeans so she could see exactly how much of a buzz he was getting. Her eyes widened and her tongue darted out to lick her lips. The action did wonders to his ego, and as for his desire, it went off the charts.

Breathing hard, he bent to tackle her trousers. 'If you'd prefer a bed, you need to say now.'

'Here is good. I don't think my legs work any more.'

Laughing softly he began to peel off the rest of her clothes with quick, sure movements. Within seconds he'd achieved one of his fantasies. Tess stretched out on the sofa before him. Naked. Her hair tumbling wildly around her face, her lips swollen, her face flushed.

Hastily he threw off his jeans and T-shirt, uncaring where they fell, and knelt before her so he could take her head between his hands and kiss the life out of her.

As he made love to her mouth, her fingers trailed down his chest and a deep groan escaped him. Heaven help him, this wasn't going to last long. Telling himself that foreplay was overrated, he yanked off his boxers and fumbled in his discarded jeans pocket for a condom, swearing under his breath when he couldn't locate it immediately. Finally he slipped it on and moved to lie on top of her. Capturing her mouth once more in a blistering kiss, he shifted his hips and thrust powerfully inside her.

The moan she emitted was loud enough to cause him to stop and start to withdraw.

'Did I hurt you? Too hard?'

Rigorously she shook her head. 'Too incredible.'

A slow smile lit his face. 'Too right,' he whispered, raining kisses all over her face as he started to move inside her, picking up a rhythm that soon rocked their worlds.

It was much later when they made it from the sofa to the bed, and even later still when Jim rolled onto his back, wrapped his arms around her and, with a satisfied smirk playing across his face, promptly fell asleep. Lying next to him, Tess watched the steady rise and fall of his chest. He looked peaceful, quite different from the dominant, commanding figure he was when awake. Carefully, so as not to disturb him, she reached out to touch the heated skin of his chest, to savour the coiled strength under her fingers.

But God, touching him, gazing at him, was both joy and torture. Heaven and hell.

Heaven because when she thought about Jim the man: the one she'd travelled the globe with, laughed with, cried with; the man who'd made love to her so passionately, so sweetly; then it gave her a deep-seated sense of happiness to have him here with her now, in her bed.

Hell because there was also another Jim. The one who headed up the Helix R&D department. The one she was betraying by going behind his back to look for unpublished study results.

With a deep sigh she lay back against the pillows. How could she have been foolish enough to sleep with him *again*?

'I hope that wasn't a sigh of regret?' Jim turned on his side, propping himself up on his elbow, gazing at her with sleepy brown eyes.

'No.' She tried to smile, moving onto her back before he could study her properly. 'I think it was hunger.'

'So no regrets?'

Swallowing down the lump in her throat, she shook her head. She couldn't regret something so magical, whatever the hurt she was bound to cause them both later.

Bending over her, he tenderly kissed her forehead. 'Then let me take you out to dinner.'

'Dinner?' She realised she didn't have a clue what time it was. The last few hours had been a blur of hot bodies and tangled sheets.

'It's only nine o'clock and I don't know about you but I've worked up quite an appetite.'

Tess hesitated. She knew exactly what she should do now, but God help her, she couldn't. Anyway, she *was* hungry, and the horse had already bolted, so to speak. So ignoring the part of her mind that rolled its eyes and vigorously shook its head, she went with her heart. 'Okay. I'll just grab a quick shower.'

His eyes lit up. 'Why don't I come in with you? Save time and water?'

For a split second Tess hesitated, her mind recalling the conversation she'd had with Barbara about how Jim enjoyed making love in the shower. But before she had a chance to fixate over it, he was scooping her up and marching her into the bathroom. After that, her mind was full only of him.

It was an hour later when they walked into the small bistro at the end of the road. A further two hours when Jim followed her back into her apartment, using his foot to slam the door behind him before he bent to devour her mouth. If she'd held the thought, even for a moment, of telling him to go home, he made sure it was soon forgotten as he carried her off to the bedroom.

Sunday morning. A time to laze in bed. To contemplate doing nothing but reading the papers. Or, in Tess's case, a time to fret, stew and call herself all kinds of names. She'd been weak and stupid, listening to her heart and her hormones and not her head. Her eyes wandered over the sleeping form sprawled across her bed, taking over even in his sleep.

With a heavy heart she went to shower, Jim's words from

yesterday echoing through her head. He'd been hurt by Barbara's betrayal. Now he was careful who he trusted.

Yet he'd chosen to trust her.

Quietly she began to sob, the water from the shower running over her face, washing away the fast flowing tears. She hadn't meant for any of this to happen. In the beginning it had been so simple. She'd had the moral high ground, hadn't she? All she'd wanted was an answer to a question. Why had her mother died? Yet here she was now, with the high ground blown from under her, blasted away by her duplicity. She had become a double-crossing Judas.

There was a way out. When she'd finished trawling through the studies and satisfied both herself and Mark there was nothing untoward, she'd hand in her resignation. Maybe, if she was really lucky, Jim would keep in touch and they could start something fresh, with no lies between them. Then she could meet him with joy in her heart, instead of this crushing guilt.

Of course if she did discover any malpractice – well then the way out wasn't just blocked, it was bricked up, with no escape route. It was either sell out her family, or sell out Jim.

Either way, at least the whole tortuous mess would soon be over.

After showering she padded over to the kitchen and put on the kettle, searching for her old coffee maker. She was a tea drinker, but Jim was more of a coffee man. She knew that from all the hours they'd spent together in meetings and airport lounges. Once she'd lined his stomach with caffeine and toast, she'd ease him out of the door, then boot up the computer and get to work. Time had run out. She could no longer kid herself that what had happened in Singapore was just about sex. Hearts were becoming involved.

'Umm, is that coffee I smell?'

Jim wandered into the kitchen wearing only his jeans. His dark hair was damp, his tanned chest bare. Solid planes of muscles glistened in the sun's rays as they bounced off his still moist skin. Desire swept through her and she had to force herself to look away. 'Yes,' she replied, her voice far too sharp. 'Help yourself.'

He raised an eyebrow at her curt tone, but didn't comment on it.

'Jim?'

'Umm.' He looked up from pouring himself a large mug of steaming coffee.

'Can we talk about work?'

'I'm with a sexy woman on a Sunday morning and you expect me to talk shop?'

'Please?'

He must have seen she was serious. 'If you must,' he replied with a groan. 'But you'll need to fill my stomach first.'

After serving him up a couple of slices of toast, she sat opposite him at the breakfast bar, twisting her hands nervously in her lap. 'When you worked for Helix previously, what was your role?'

'You already know that. I headed up a clinical research team developing our breast cancer treatment.'

'Zaplex?'

He nodded, munching his way through the toast like a starving man. Tess could only pick at hers.

'I know we've touched on this before, but how were the publications of the studies you performed handled?'

'I told you. The clinical team managed the studies. The medical writing team managed the publications.'

'But who was responsible for checking all the studies were published? That some weren't overlooked. Shouldn't that have been you?'

He paused in his chewing and looked over at her. 'Why do I suddenly feel as if I'm being interrogated?'

His body had stilled and though his voice was steady, Tess could detect an undercurrent of annoyance. It was enough to remind her that Jim wasn't an easy target. 'If we're going to do a big media splash on the new publications policy, I need to know if there are any skeletons in your cupboard,' she told him. 'This whole campaign could seriously backfire if someone finds out that the man leading this new initiative, the head of the R&D function no less, was responsible for hiding some study results.'

He rocked back on his chair, his face suddenly losing its warmth. 'Hiding is a very strong word, Tess, and this is old ground. I know publication of our studies hasn't always been conducted as rigorously as it should have been, that some of the smaller studies might well have been overlooked, and I take my fair share of the blame for that. But we're addressing this, so it won't happen again.'

'Why might their publication have been *overlooked*?'

The muscles of his jaw tightened. 'I'm not sure I like your tone.' He pushed away his plate. 'I suspect there may have been occasions when a study hasn't shown a benefit for our drug so the team have dragged their heels over publishing it. Perhaps buried it to the bottom of their to do list, in the hope it would be forgotten. And yes, perhaps deliberately chosen not to publish,' he admitted honestly, his eyes remaining on her. 'But remember industry scientists aren't alone in this. In academia too, they're far more interested in publishing positive studies. As are journals.' Sighing, he stood up from the table. 'Is this what you're talking about?'

She bit her lip, took in a deep breath. 'Partly.'

'Just so we're both absolutely clear, what *are* you referring to then?'

Steeling herself against the anger she could see bubbling inside him, she raised her eyes to his. 'What about studies that might have shown a harmful effect that you hadn't seen before?'

He let out a ripe curse. 'You think we, I, chose not to publish evidence on *safety*?' Dark eyes glittered ominously.

'What sort of company do you think this is, Tess? What sort of man do you think I am?'

With that, Tess knew she'd pushed too far. She'd wanted to get a reaction out of him and she had. He was livid. Hurt, too. Both of which were a good thing, she told herself. The previous night, waking up with him this morning – it had been too intimate. Too comfortable. Too much like a relationship she absolutely couldn't have with him. Not now. Perhaps not ever.

'I'm not here to judge you,' she told him, gathering up the dirty plates to avoid looking at him. 'I'm just doing my job.'

Jim watched Tess methodically load the dishwasher, anger and frustration boiling inside him in equal measure. Hell, he really couldn't work her out. Last night in his arms she'd been hot and passionate. This morning she was cold and distant. It was as if she was holding something of herself back, not willing, or not able, to totally open up to him. Maybe, he thought bitterly, because she thought he was callous enough to deliberately bury safety information.

'Okay,' he said when she'd finally stopped clattering the plates into the dishwasher. 'I understand why you asked your questions. And I won't push you to answer mine.'

She looked puzzled.

'The one about what sort of man you think I am.'

'Oh.' Her hesitation, and the cavernous silence that followed it, nearly cut him off at the knees. 'Well, I think you're—'

'No.' He quickly interrupted her. 'When you answer that question, I want the truth. Not what you think I want to hear.'

She nodded, but as he moved towards her she shrank away, leaning back against the sink, as if frightened he'd touch her. Anger bubbled over and he deliberately took a further three steps so he was standing right in front of her. 'Why do I get the feeling I've outstayed my welcome?'

'I'm sorry,' she whispered, her eyes darting towards his left ear. 'I'm not used to waking up and finding a man in my bed, or in my kitchen. I'm out of practice.'

'Well you'd better get used to it,' he told her in a voice loaded with frustration. 'Because I plan on invading both again very soon.'

Ignoring her desire to keep him at arm's length, he bent to give her a hot, searing kiss on the lips. Then he grabbed at the clothes still strewn over the living room floor and headed out of the door.

Chapter Twenty-Seven

Monday morning, and Jim should have been reading the revised publication policy he'd found waiting on his desk. God knows he'd started to, several times. But each time his gaze had drifted out of his window, waiting for Tess to come into view. With a snarl of annoyance he turned his back on the window and went to sit at his table instead. The woman was intruding on too many of his thoughts, taking up too much of his time.

He managed to bury himself in the policy for the next half-hour, scrawling his changes directly onto the document. It wasn't a bad job, especially considering the lawyers had swarmed all over it, using seven flouncy words when a single straight one would have done. Still, they were employed to protect the business so he had to let them have their way. Some of the time. When he'd made his final comment he stretched out his legs and figured he owed himself a break and a cup of coffee. In particular a cup from the machine in the communications department.

She was at her desk when he walked by, studying her screen, totally absorbed in whatever it was she was looking at.

'Hi.'

She looked up with a start. If he was reading her correctly, a *guilty* start. He smiled to himself. No doubt he'd caught her surfing the Internet for more outrageous shoes.

'Err, hi yourself.' He watched, amused, as she hastily minimised her screen. 'Can I help you with anything?'

'Well now, there's an offer.' He grinned, but she didn't smile back as he'd hoped. Instead she looked ... sad? 'Is everything okay?'

'Yes, of course.' Her smile surfaced, but it was strained.

'Did you sleep all right last night?' He ducked his head closer to her ear so nobody else could hear. 'Without some oaf in the bed next to you, taking up all the space?'

Her smile was slightly more genuine, but he could tell she didn't want him there, so he cut to the chase. 'How about dinner, tonight? I'll cook.'

She shook her head. 'Sorry, I can't.'

Okay. He'd been half expecting that, but the disappointment still felt like a punch to his gut. 'Name a night you can.'

Tess studied her screen, obviously finding it too difficult to make eye contact with the man she'd woken up next to only yesterday morning.

'I can make Friday,' she told him in a rush, as if she'd suddenly made a decision.

He opened his mouth to say something along the lines of *you're bloody kidding*. Friday? Five whole days away? Then, shaking his head, he stepped back. 'Okay, we'll go at your pace, for now.' He added the last two words in a slow, soft drawl. 'Friday night it is.'

He stalked back to his desk in an even more unsettled mood. The harder he was falling for Tess, the faster she was pulling away. He'd wanted to believe her hesitancy was because of their work situation, but now he was starting to think she simply wasn't that interested.

And didn't that thought hurt like a bugger. With a muted curse he rolled up his shirtsleeves, symbolic of how he was feeling. Whatever was going on in her mind, he'd drag it out of her on Friday. This half-baked, on off relationship was killing him.

Later that day his mood slumped further when he came back from a long-winded meeting to find Barbara sitting in his office.

'What do you want?' he asked irritably, shutting the door

237

behind him just in case she started talking about stuff other than work.

'Do you treat all your guests with such charm?' she enquired archly.

'Only the uninvited ones.'

'So let me guess, if I was a certain young redhead, how would you greet me then? With a smile? Perhaps a kiss?'

With a deep sigh Jim pulled out his chair and sat down. 'I don't have the time or energy for your games, Barbara. Just tell me what you came to discuss with me.'

She pouted a little and then raised her shoulders in a dainty gesture of annoyance. 'Do I have to have a reason for coming to see you these days?'

He scowled over at her. 'I'm not a fool. You never do anything without a reason.'

That seemed to amuse her. 'Okay, perhaps you're right. I did want to talk to you about something and actually, it is about your little redhead.'

Cursing strongly he pushed his chair back and stood up. 'Enough. I'm not talking to you about Tess. It's none of your damn business.'

'Oh, but it is my business. At least it is when she's asking for access to the study database.'

Jim knew she was looking for a reaction so he deliberately slowed his movements and sat casually on the edge of his desk. 'So?'

'So, I wondered if you knew why she needed it? I signed off on it last week, but I've been meaning to follow it up with you.'

'I've asked Tess to plan a campaign around our revised publication policy.' His voice was firm and sure, but the conversation he'd had with Tess Sunday morning niggled in his mind. 'I expect she's checking up on what we've being doing to date so she doesn't come across any surprises.' It was a perfectly logical explanation. Wasn't it?

Barbara scrutinised him with her intelligent eyes. 'Are you sure she can be trusted? As I understand it, she was a journalist before joining Helix.'

'What, exactly, are you implying?'

Slowly, like a snake ready to pounce, Barbara levered herself up from her chair. 'Just that there is a possibility she's here to do more than a communications role. Something you ought to bear in mind before you indulge in too much pillow talk.'

A swing of her hips and she was gone, leaving behind her a cloud of oppressive perfume that left a nasty taste in his mouth. Or was that down to the implications of what she'd said?

Wearily Jim sat at his desk and buried his head in his hands. A feeling of cold unease settled over him as he recalled Tess's aggressive questioning over what they did regarding publications. Her admitted dislike of the pharmaceutical industry. Was there a chance she wasn't just being thorough, as she'd claimed? A chance he was being *played*?

He rubbed at his eyes, feeling the start of a headache. This was crazy thinking. Tess wasn't anything like Barbara. Plus, wasn't it Barbara herself who'd thrown the accusations? Ergo, there was no way in hell he was going to give her thoughts the time of day. It made far more sense to believe that Barbara was the one trying to stir up trouble. She hadn't cared enough to remain faithful to him when they'd been dating, but now it seemed she couldn't stomach the thought of him with someone else.

'Jim, do you mind if I go early, because I've got a dental appointment and you know how bad the traffic gets, and I don't want to miss it because I forgot about the last one.' Pamela halted as she finally stopped speaking for long enough to look at him. 'Are you okay? You look kind of, well, pale I guess.'

'I'm fine.' Jesus, his head was beginning to really pound

now. First Tess's evasion, then Barbara's accusations, now his nice but clueless secretary. He needed to get out of here. The female of the species was driving him crazy.

'Well, if you're sure.' She hesitated in his doorway, probably debating whether to escape quickly or call 999.

'I'm sure. I've just got a headache. Nothing an evening away from here and a couple of paracetamol won't cure.' Or failing that a couple of beers with an uncomplicated male. He gave Pamela his best shot at a smile. 'Take yourself off to the dentist. I guess that's less painful than working for me, eh?'

She gave him a puzzled look before vanishing down the corridor.

Ruefully Jim reflected that he'd annoyed or confused three women today. He reckoned that must be some sort of record.

Tess screwed up her eyes and peered at the screen again. The screen Jim had been within a nanosecond of seeing her studying earlier. Even now, hours later, she broke out in a sweat at the memory. His visit had served a purpose though. Now she had a deadline – Friday. By then, for the sake of her sanity, she had to know, one way or another, if there was any incriminating evidence on Zaplex.

Her eyes scanned over the safety study she'd managed to find. It had been conducted in healthy volunteers which, if she remembered correctly, meant it was part of the phase one programme, undertaken to see whether the drug was safe enough to trial in patients. This study found no adverse effects of the drug on the basic tests like blood pressure and heart rate and had been published as part of a safety review. She was ready to dismiss it when a sentence in the introduction of the report caught her eye. It referred back to an earlier study that had assessed the heart – or cardiovascular, as she was now used to seeing – effects of Zaplex in an *in vitro* study, which was one conducted in a test tube or some other artificial environment, rather than in a whole person or animal.

Wearily Tess sat back in her chair. She hadn't considered pre-clinical studies. Heck, trawling through the clinical studies was bad enough, but maybe she should? Especially as this was the first study she'd seen that specifically mentioned the effect of Zaplex on the heart.

Quickly she dialled Roberta's number, willing her friend to be at her desk.

'I wonder if you can do me a favour,' she asked after the usual shoe purchase update. 'I'm following up on some work for Jim which involves looking at all the Helix trials on the study database, but it occurs to me that these are only the human studies. Is there a similar database for the work you guys do in the labs?' The weight of guilt bore down on her once more. Roberta was her *friend*, and here she was, using her. Her only consolation was that Roberta wasn't going to get hurt if there was any fall out.

'Yep, we've got a database for the pre-clinical work we do. Do you want me to send you the link? You'll need to set up a username and password.' Tess's heart sank. 'But, if you only want a quick peek, and if you promise on your shoe collection not to tell another living soul that I did this, you can use mine. I'm sending the details on an email as I speak.'

And now, not only was she using her friend, she was exploiting her kindness. Stammering out her thanks, Tess made a promise to herself that when this was all over she would confess everything to Roberta. Hopefully even if she couldn't forgive her, Roberta would understand what had driven her deception.

Fighting her shame, Tess opened the email, clicked into the pre-clinical database and found the search bar. After typing *cardiovascular* and the Zaplex chemical number, which she'd worked out as being HE 1278, into the search bar, she waited for the list of results.

Only a few came up. The first, according to the title, was an *in vitro* study undertaken to assess the effect of the study agent HE 1278a on the beat pattern, whatever that meant, of cardiac cells. Her biology wasn't great, but good enough for her to know that cardiac was something to do with the heart.

As she pored over the bare study results in the report, her pulse picked up speed. Odd, because despite reading it over and over again, cardiac appeared to be the only word she *did* understand. The rest might as well have been in Polish. Still, she had a twinge, a gut feel, that this was important. She scanned the other studies from the search but they all had a reference next to them, linking through to a publication. This one didn't.

After a quick check to make sure nobody was around, Tess printed off a copy of the *in vitro* report and slipped it into her handbag. That was when she noticed Jim's bold signature, as Zaplex programme head, scrawled across the front.

The sight of his handwriting ramped up her unease and she started to feel a little sick, not helped by the way her heart was hammering beneath her ribs. This was probably nothing, she reminded herself. A study conducted in a lab rather than in patients, with results she couldn't interpret. Big deal. It hadn't been published, but so what. From what she could see, a lot of pre-clinical studies weren't published.

But when she picked up the phone to Roberta again, her hands were trembling.

Walking down the sterile white corridor towards Roberta's lab, Tess didn't just feel sick, she was about to *be* sick. Nerves, fear, dread, guilt all conspired to churn her stomach. Spotting the ladies' she nipped inside and stood for a moment over the sink, staring at her pale, dazed reflection in the mirror. After quickly splashing cold water on her face, she squared her shoulders, slowly filled her lungs and walked back out towards Roberta's lab.

'Hey, corporate communications finally makes it onto research turf,' Roberta greeted her and gave her a quick hug. 'I knew the lure of the labs would be too great for you to ignore eventually. So, take a seat and tell me how I can help.'

Tess perched on the nearest chair and carefully took the report from her bag. Laying it out on the table in front of them, she gave her prepared story. 'Helix is in the process of updating its publication policy, with the aim of making sure the results of all the clinical studies it does are made public.'

'No hiding dodgy competitor studies, eh?' Roberta interrupted with a grin.

Tess winced. 'Exactly. I was wondering about the studies you do in the labs. From looking at the database, it doesn't appear all those studies get published, either. Would that be right?'

Roberta nodded. 'Yes. We simply don't have the resources to publish everything, because we do so many. Plus, to be honest, there isn't really any interest in most of the studies we do, because so many of the drugs we test don't even make it past the first hurdle.' She shrugged. 'It's a sad fact that for the thousands of drugs I work with, only a handful make it through into the clinical phase. Generally speaking, we publish our pre-clinical work if the drug makes it into patients, and particularly if the drug finally makes it to market. If the drug's a nonstarter, we don't bother publishing unless it has some interest to the scientific community.' She hesitated. 'Am I boring you yet? God, please tell me if I am, because I'm happy to talk about shoes instead, believe me.'

Tess laughed, finally starting to relax. 'We'll do shoes another time, I promise. For now, this is exactly what I need to know.'

'Okay then. I was just going to add that I think for us in the labs, publishing our work is more about building our profile as scientists and sharing that information with fellow eggheads. Our studies don't really become interesting to doctors until the drug goes into patients. Of course if it then makes it through all the hurdles, our research becomes an important part of the regulatory dossier.'

'I feel like a total jerk, but what is that?'

Roberta laughed. 'I wouldn't know how to put together a press release either, so no worries. About one in five thousand of all the drugs we test here make it through all the clinical phases with a profile that looks good enough to market. That's when the regulatory dossier comes in. It's basically a compilation of all the studies we do on that product, both the ones in the labs and the clinical ones in volunteers and patients. The dossier is sent to regulatory authorities like the FDA in America and the EMA in Europe. Those groups sift through all the evidence, weigh up the potential benefit to patients against the possible risk in terms of side effects, and then decide whether to grant the company a license to market that product.'

Tess looked down at the report she'd taken out of her bag. 'So studies like the one I have here would be used as part of that submission to show the effect of the product on the heart?'

Roberta picked up the study report. 'Umm, yes, this is looking at how cardiac cells respond to the drug. Basically seeing if it affects how the cells beat.' She peered closer at the report. 'But it doesn't look like this compound would have progressed to phase one, because whatever HE 1278a was, it caused the cells to beat really irregularly.'

Tess was hit by a sudden wave of dizziness and had to grip onto the arms of the chair to stop herself keeling over. 'Can you explain that a bit more?'

Her voice was unsteady enough to cause Roberta to glance at her quizzically, but thankfully she didn't comment. 'Sure. This study used highly purified cardiac cells from heart muscle to test if compound 1278a altered how they beat. It's not uncommon for drugs to do this, especially some of the old cancer drugs. This study found the test compound caused the cells to beat irregularly, even at low concentrations. If that were to be repeated in a whole heart, it could lead to a sudden cardiac arrest.' Tess gasped and Roberta smiled. 'Of course we don't know if it would happen in practice because this is only one study and you can't really take one piece of research in isolation. But for this compound it doesn't look good.' She pushed the report back towards Tess.

'Thanks, Roberta.' Tess tried to smile, though inside her stomach was pitching around like a rowing boat on a stormy sea.

'My pleasure.' Her friend paused and stared at her. 'Are you feeling okay? You're looking awfully pale. Even more so than usual. I hope you're not working too hard.'

'No, no, I'm fine.' If she didn't count the sudden need to throw up. 'One final thing. Where would I go if I wanted to see a regulatory submission?'

Roberta laughed. 'Trust me, you don't want to read one. Sometimes it needs a lorry to transport all the information. At least it used to, before electronic submissions. But if you want to see the various sections that make it up, and the studies that go into them, then it should all be in the study database you've been looking at. I think there's a tab you can click on that takes you to the contents of the dossier for that product. Providing the drug made it that far.'

Nodding her thanks, Tess dashed out of the room and made it to the toilets just in time.

One hour later, Tess was dashing up the stairs to her apartment. She looked so ill Georgina hadn't batted an eyelid when she'd pleaded the need to go home. Not even bothering to take off her coat, she sat straight down on the sofa, opened up her computer and navigated her way to the study database. And the contents of the Zaplex regulatory dossier.

It seemed the last eighteen months had somehow always

been leading to this moment. Both Tess and Mark had found it hard to believe their mum's death, only hours after taking a new breast cancer treatment, had simply been a coincidence. The odds were simply too long. Her mother had never *won* anything with such long odds, so it simply wasn't right that she'd lose the most important thing, her life, to similar odds. The conversation with Avril at her mother's funeral, and the subsequent conversations with people who'd lost a loved one in similar circumstances, had simply reinforced their thinking. Those families were consulting with lawyers, considering taking their cases through official channels, but Tess hadn't wanted the slow agony of waiting for others to research the case. Not when she knew she could do it herself.

All of which had led to this moment.

She was now in possession of a study report that confirmed Zaplex *did* have an effect on the heart, albeit in the laboratory. And, though she checked and re-checked the contents of the Zaplex regulatory dossier, she couldn't find that study listed anywhere.

Sinking back against the sofa, Tess felt strangely empty. It was as if she'd finally climbed to the top of the mountain, only to hate the view. This was exactly the evidence she'd joined Helix to find. Evidence that confirmed she'd been right to doubt, to suspect. Right to investigate.

But now she had it, what on earth was she going to do with it?

Her eyes fell on the report and drifted over Jim's bold signature. Burying her head in her hands, she sobbed her heart out.

When her tears had finally eased, she opened up her computer and emailed Hugh.

Chapter Twenty-Eight

At last, he'd made it to Friday evening. It had been one of the longest weeks in Jim's recent memory. As he shut down his computer, Rick popped his head round the office door.

'Are you exercising tonight?'

Jim tried not to look too smug. 'Not tonight, pal. I've got a date.'

Rick arranged his features into an imitation of astonishment. 'Well blow me, you sure kept that quiet.' He cocked his head to one side and studied him. 'The delightful Tessa, I take it?'

'Hopefully.'

Frowning, Rick moved into the office and closed the door behind him. '*Hopefully?*'

Damn, he shouldn't have used that word. Now he was going to get the third degree. 'I only say that because we made the arrangement on Monday and I haven't seen her since,' he replied casually, making a great play of shoving his computer into his briefcase.

'Is she avoiding you?'

Because that's exactly what Jim thought Tess was doing, he went on the offensive. 'Of course not. I've been tied up late in meetings. By the time I've wriggled out of the damn things, she's wisely gone home.' He didn't mention the times he'd then gone to the gym, hoping to catch her, only to find she'd given up on her plan to exercise there. Or she was, indeed, avoiding him.

'What, she's not waited for her sweetheart?' Rick replied teasingly.

'Why would she?' Even as he said the words, he knew if Tess were really keen, if she felt for him only half of what he felt for her, she would have hung around to see him. So no, keen wasn't the word he'd use to describe her. Nor was it how she'd sounded on the phone a few days ago when he'd called to discuss arrangements for tonight, and frankly just to hear her voice. He'd barely had the chance to confirm timings before she'd cut him off, claiming she was off to an exercise class. A class that was clearly more important than speaking to her occasional lover.

'Strikes me she's playing hard to get,' Rick mused as they walked out of the office together. 'Which, frankly, I applaud. It's about time you had to work for the attention of a gorgeous woman. Maybe now you'll know how the rest of us feel.'

'With a wit like that, you should be on the stage,' Jim muttered at a grinning Rick as they parted ways. Hell, he didn't mind working hard for this woman. As long as he won her in the end.

An hour and a half later he stood in his kitchen, chopping and dicing and wondering if he was going to end up eating the blasted green Thai chicken alone. Perhaps not a bad result because God knows, he couldn't cook. Quite why he'd said he would make her a meal was beyond him. It just went to prove how desperate he was to get her into his bed. And worm his way into her heart. Women liked a man to cook for them, didn't they?

With a grunt he slammed the knife onto the chopping board, slicing through the plump chicken breast. He'd never felt this uncertain over where he stood with a member of the opposite sex. Mind you, if his disaster of a relationship with Barbara was anything to go by, maybe he should have done.

The buzz of the intercom burst into his pity party, sending his pulse into overdrive. She'd come. Or had she? With nerves more aligned to those of a fourteen-year-old boy on his first date, Jim ran his hands under the tap, wiped them dry and walked to answer it.

'Knight's restaurant. Only open to gorgeous redheads.' There was a pause. One long enough to have him wondering if it really was Tess on the other end.

'It's Tess. Do I qualify?'

Did she ever. 'Oh, yes,' he replied strongly, his voice roughened by nerves and anticipation.

When he opened his door to her, Jim knew he was lost. Totally and utterly blown away. He ignored the hesitant look in her glittering blue eyes and focussed instead on the whole package. 'I'd forgotten how gorgeous you were,' he told her huskily, mesmerised by the sight of her. If he hadn't been so totally smitten, so hopelessly infatuated, he might have held back a little, giving her the space her wary expression told him she needed. Instead he cupped that uncertain, beautiful face in his hands and swooped down for a kiss. He was so hungry for her, so desperate to taste her, to feel her, that it took a few moments for him to realise she wasn't kissing him back.

Instantly he stopped. 'What is it? What's wrong?'

As Jim's smouldering dark eyes roamed over her face, searching for the answer, Tess felt trapped. She wanted to kiss him back so much it hurt, but the study report was burning a hole in her jacket pocket.

She should bring it up now – get it over and done with. *Jim, I'm aching to kiss you back, but before I do that, why don't you tell me why the regulatory authorities didn't get to see the damning results I have in my pocket?*

She bit at the underside of her lip. God, he'd just kissed her with such heat, such need. How could she possibly now question him without sounding aggressive and accusatory? Without hurting him? Whatever had gone on, she was sure it wasn't something Jim had known about.

'Tess?'

He was still looking at her, waiting for an answer. His eyes were hooded, watchful, but his mouth was tense.

She had to find another way of finding her answer. A more subtle, indirect way that wouldn't sound like she was attacking him. A way that wouldn't drive a wedge between them.

'Nothing's wrong,' she told him quickly. Then, to prove her point, both to him and to herself, she moved forward a step, lining her body tight against his, and kissed him right back. He responded enthusiastically, deepening the kiss, turning up the heat, and she fought away thoughts of the report and surrendered to him.

His hands crept under her blouse and nimble fingers trailed over her skin, leaving her impossibly sensitised to his touch. Tess pushed herself tighter against his powerful frame, willing him to dominate her. To fill her head so full of him she couldn't think about anything else.

To her intense disappointment he drew back, resting his forehead against hers.

'Why do I get the feeling you're trying to distract me with sex?' he asked eventually, his breathing coming out in quick, ragged bursts.

Embarrassed, she lowered her eyes.

'Hey.' He tilted her chin. 'I'm not complaining.' When she remained silent, he sighed. 'I missed you this week.'

'Did you?'

He gave her a wry smile, tinged with a sadness that made her want to cry. 'That was meant to be your opening to tell me you missed me, too.'

'Sorry.' God, this was so hard. How could she tell him what he wanted to hear when she'd spent the week snooping behind his back?

He let out a deep breath, betraying both his frustration and hurt. 'It's okay, you don't have to apologise for something you don't feel,' he told her tightly.

'No, it isn't that,' she countered quickly, her eyes pleading with him to believe her. Couldn't he tell, just by looking at her, it was far, far from that? 'I did miss you.'

'That's good to know, because I had the distinct impression you were avoiding me.'

She should have known he'd look out for her. He was that

type of man. One who charged, full throttle, after what he wanted. 'Sorry, I wasn't trying to evade you. I just … well, I had a busy week,' she finished lamely.

Jim nodded, though his expression told her he didn't believe her. Picking up her hand, he clasped it lightly in his, moving his thumb gently over her palm. 'Tess, I'm not sure what's troubling you, and I wasn't going to bring this up now, but let me get this off my chest and then we'll have a drink and talk of something else.' He paused, as if trying to find the right words. 'It's only fair you should know that I'm falling for you.' His eyes were dark and intense, his voice impossibly soft. 'Falling fast and hard. Very hard. Harder than I've ever fallen for a woman. Ever.'

Shocked by his declaration, she could do nothing but stare as her heart went into free fall.

A flash of intense disappointment registered in his eyes. Then he turned abruptly away and headed for the fridge.

'Wine?' he asked roughly, yanking open the fridge door with more force than was necessary.

She had to work hard to speak through the ball of emotion now clogging her throat. 'Yes, please.'

As Jim busied himself with pouring out the wine, Tess walked away, her head spinning, her heart doing somersaults. *He was falling for her.* She wanted to cry. God, and to laugh, with both joy and wonder. To fling her arms around his neck and never let go. What if she didn't mention the stupid report, ever? If she just forgot all about it. Then – her heart bounced in her chest – then she might have a chance of love with this incredible man.

She was so lost in her thoughts she almost jumped when he handed her a wine glass.

'Thanks.' Gratefully she took a sip. 'You have an incredible place here,' she remarked into the silence, buying herself time to think. Besides, it was true. A huge loft apartment, it was spacious and light with stunning original features, like the brick walls and steel girders, mixed intelligently with modern details such as the open spiral staircase leading to the mezzanine floor.

'Glad you like it.' He gave her a slight smile, but it was guarded now, nothing like the warm, frankly appreciative one he'd greeted her with. It made her heart ache. This strong, bold, larger than life man had opened up to her and she'd failed to respond. In keeping quiet, she'd hurt him. And if she quizzed him over the report, she'd hurt him even more.

'Feel free to have a look round while I tackle the dinner and try not to burn the place down.'

Tears welled in her eyes as he walked stiffly back towards the kitchen, his body language radiating disappointment. Why couldn't she have met him at a bar, or a gym? Anywhere where she could have struck up a relationship without the lies and dishonesty.

For a few minutes she watched him at work in the kitchen, noting with an ironic smile that he operated there in the same way he did at work. Dominating the space, taking control, forcing everything and everyone into submission. Even the vegetables, from the look of it.

In a bid to get her head into the right place she took him up on his offer and began to wander. Downstairs, besides the open plan kitchen and living area, there was a wet room, a small gym and a large office. Upstairs were three bedrooms and two further bathrooms. She lingered in what was clearly his room, unable to tear her eyes away from the giant mahogany bed. It was so easy to imagine herself sprawled across it, Jim running his hands over her. Telling her she was the most gorgeous woman he'd ever seen. And making her believe it.

The phone in her pocket vibrated and she pulled it out and glanced at the screen. A text message from Mark.

Good luck with Clooney 2night. Hope u get some answers x.

Her hands trembled as she pushed the phone back into her pocket. Hurt Jim, or let down her family? God, what a choice.

Letting out a deep breath, she blinked away the tears welling in her eyes and headed back downstairs.

Jim had barely tasted the meal he'd painstakingly spent the early part of the evening putting together. He was still too angry with himself for blurting out how he felt to Tess. When had he turned into such a blabbermouth? He'd known she was trying to put some space between them, yet *still* he'd gone and spewed out his feelings. What a jerk. That she'd not admitted to having any such feelings in return had been a further dose of humiliation. Not to mention a major heart breaker.

And if he really wanted to turn up the intensity on this pain fest, he only had to recall the look on her face afterwards. Delight was definitely not the word he'd use to describe her reaction. Terror, more like. So much so, he'd kept half an eye on her while he'd been cooking, certain that at any moment, she'd bolt.

Despite all that, he was still determined to win her over. Put simply, he was a stubborn git, totally incapable of admitting defeat on anything really important to him. And she was. His hopes of achieving his goal had risen slightly once they'd sat down to dinner. He'd kept his questions deliberately innocuous and thankfully she'd begun to relax, even asking a few of her own. What things did he like to cook – admittedly a short discussion – how long had he had his apartment? Casual, easy conversation, not the hesitant stuff he'd been dreading after he'd dumped his feelings on her. So easy in fact, that as he rested his head against the back of his chair and began to undress her slowly with his eyes, he was pretty confident he would no longer need to leap out and block the doorway to prevent her from leaving.

'... into the prescribing information?'

Oh crap. Her big blue eyes rested on his, waiting for an answer. 'What?' he blurted. 'Sorry, I kind of lost the thread of what you were saying there.' Too much focus on the undressing, not enough on the listening.

She looked slightly annoyed and yes, of course he should have been hanging onto her every word. But really, did she have any idea how distracting she was? A sexy woman, versus talk about *work*?

'I was wondering,' and her eyes added *Jim are you paying attention now*, 'how data from the clinical studies makes it into the prescribing information. You know, who decides what goes into the leaflet the doctors use to help them prescribe the medicine?'

'The drug datasheet, you mean. The SPC?' He tried to catch up.

'I think so, yes. When a patient takes a medicine, they get a leaflet telling them of the side effects they might experience, and whether to tell their doctor if they suffer from certain conditions. I know this all comes from the information the doctors have on the product, but where does that information come from? The studies?'

He rubbed a hand over his chin, trying to refocus his mind. It looked like jumping straight into bed with him wasn't high on her list of priorities right now, which was a damn shame, because it was the only thing on his.

'Yes, broadly speaking, the information in the document the doctors use, the summary of product characteristics, or SPC, comes from the studies. The company bundles up all the data from the clinical trial programme and submits it to the regulatory authorities. They determine if there is sufficient reason to give the drug a license, and they are the people who ultimately decide what goes into the SPC.' He tried not to sound as bored as he felt. It wasn't that he didn't want to talk to her. He did, about pretty much anything other than work. Of course he'd prefer the conversation after he'd dragged her up to his bed and made love to her while she was naked except for a pair of high stilettos. Though maybe he'd need a quick nap first.

'So what sort of information does an SPC contain?'

It didn't look like his fantasy was going to happen any time soon. With a heartfelt sigh he stood and started to pick up the dishes. 'It contains things like the dose, what the product is licensed to treat, the conditions it shouldn't be used in and the side effects that might occur. The company has plenty of opportunity to input, but ultimately it is the regulatory authorities who have the final say on the wording.'

'But what happens if the company doesn't submit all the information?'

In the process of picking up her plate, Jim stopped. 'What do you mean?'

She paused and seemed to stiffen her spine. Then she looked him in the eye. 'I mean, what if a company knows one of the studies it performed showed a side effect that might limit the product's use. What if they deliberately held that information back from the authorities?'

Jim froze, his blood turning cold. This was more than just idle after dinner conversation. This was Tess asking a very specific question, trying to hide it under a general query. 'That wouldn't happen,' he told her tightly. 'Why on earth would a company want to hide such information? Not publishing efficacy studies is one thing, but holding back safety data from authorities? Jesus, Tess. Can you imagine how damaging it would be to a company's reputation to bring a product to market, only to then find it harms patients? Not to mention the costs and hassle involved in then having to withdraw the product. No company wants that.'

Her chin tilted that little bit higher. 'But medicines have been withdrawn in the past.'

'Sure they have, because sometimes it isn't until a drug is used in millions of people that a rare side effect is seen, but believe me, it would never be deliberate. I've told you before, safety is absolutely paramount in any pharmaceutical company.' Slowly he carried the dishes to the kitchen. Then, with his chest feeling as if it were being slowly crushed by a vice, he turned and faced her. 'Why all the questions?'

Chapter Twenty-Nine

Tess's heart had been thumping loudly from the moment she'd started this topic of conversation. At Jim's quiet but deadly question, it threatened to explode. Looking hastily away from his piercing gaze, she clasped her hands together, as if in prayer, though she doubted divine intervention was going to save her. The evening had always been destined to arrive at this point, no matter how hard she'd tried to engineer a less confrontational approach. Jim was simply too smart to hoodwink. So fudging an answer to the question currently hanging between them like a grenade, ready to cause irreversible damage unless skilfully defused, was out of the question. With her mind scrambling, she rose from her chair and reached into her jacket pocket.

'Do you recognise this study?' Her hands shook as she held the report out to him.

He took it from her and flicked through the pages. 'Yes, I think so. Why?'

'Can you explain why it didn't make it into the Zaplex submission dossier?' Her voice came out as barely a whisper.

They stood only a few feet away from each other but Tess no longer felt like his lover – more his opponent. The tension swirling around them was so thick she could barely breathe.

'It wasn't in the dossier, because it wasn't a Zaplex study,' he replied flatly.

Her heart plummeted. Of all the things he could have said, that was the worst. This man who'd always been so upfront and honest up to now, was going to lie. 'Jim, I'm not stupid. I might be naive in the ways of the pharmaceutical industry, but I know this is the identifying number for Zaplex in the early studies, before it was given its proper name.'

'Just what are you accusing me of?' His dark eyes glinted dangerously and his body bristled with anger.

She shook her head. 'I'm not accusing you of anything. I'm ...' Her voice broke as she fumbled to find the right words.

'You actually believe I deliberately kept back a study from the Zaplex submission because it showed a potentially harmful effect?' His voice crackled ominously, a terrifying mixture of incredulity and white-hot fury.

'No,' she whispered. 'I don't think you did it deliberately. Perhaps there was a mistake.'

'There was no mistake,' he told her with biting bluntness. 'I repeat, this wasn't a Zaplex study. If you'd bothered to check the number properly, you'd see this was for chemical HE 1278a, an earlier discovery. When we found out it had this effect, we dropped it. However the isomer of it, HE 1278b, didn't cause the cardiac cells to beat irregularly. That was the one we pursued. Now known as Zaplex, and currently helping to prolong the lives of millions of breast cancer sufferers.'

Tess gaped at him. 'Isomer?'

'A product that has the same chemical formula, but the atoms that make it up are aligned in a different way, giving it a different structure. Sometimes that leads to different properties, as in this case.' His voice vibrated with tightly controlled anger. 'We let the relevant authorities know about this when we sought approval to trial Zaplex. Perhaps you should have done a bit more research before coming here and hurling accusations at me.'

Her legs buckled from under her and she lunged for a chair. God, could what he was saying really be true? She searched his stony face, trying to read his thoughts, but it was too implacable, too harsh. Then she looked into his eyes. Unblinkingly he stared back at her, and she saw everything. His horror at what she believed him capable of, mixed with his intense disappointment. And, oh God, his revulsion at what she'd done. She knew then, without a shadow of doubt, that he was telling her the truth.

'I'm sorry.' It was totally inadequate, but all she had to give.

'What were you doing looking into all this anyway?' he asked harshly. 'Have you been *trying* to ferret out some dirt on me? Hoping to ruin me?'

'No!' she cried, her voice breaking as tears started to spill. 'How could you possibly think that?'

'I don't know what to think any more,' he told her bitterly, thrusting his hands into his pockets and turning his back on her in a gesture of total disgust.

Tess watched Jim wearily sit down, the energy and vitality that was so much a part of him now shockingly absent, squeezed out by her hurtful allegations. What had she done to this beautiful, beautiful man? One who'd been nothing but open with her, even to the extent of sharing his feelings? *I'm falling for you, fast and hard.* Her heart ached as she recalled his words, and the burning look in his eyes as he'd said them. What had she given him in return? Dishonesty and pain.

She was left with two stark choices. Leave now, hand in her notice on Monday and spend the rest of her life trying, and failing, to forget all about Jim Knight. Or stay and fight for what she wanted.

Straightening up, she stood and walked over to him.

Jim sank his head into his hands, feeling like the biggest fool to ever have walked this planet. Would he *ever* learn from his mistakes? Once again he'd arrogantly assumed a woman was interested in him, when actually he'd only been a means to an end. This time, the end was, what? A blasted story? It was no bloody wonder she'd been blowing so hot and cold. She probably kept forgetting she was supposed to be finding him attractive.

Rubbing at his eyes with the heel of his hands, he tried to think. Who the hell was she working for? Her old paper? Was it a general pharma company slur piece, or was it more personal? Had she been employed to specifically target him?

'Jim, I repeat, I'm so sorry.' Slowly he looked up to find Tess kneeling in front of him, her blue eyes pleading. 'Not for doing my job, but for accusing you of doing something that, in my gut, I knew you hadn't done.'

She looked contrite, he'd give her that. Then again, at one time she'd also looked as if she liked him, *really* liked him, which just went to show how little he knew.

He kept quiet, deliberately schooling his expression into harsh lines. It wasn't hard to do. Not when he thought of how easily she'd played him.

'I came across the study when I was doing my research for the "Leading with Science" campaign,' she explained. 'Like I told you before, I wanted to make absolutely certain Helix had nothing to hide before I went full steam ahead with a PR campaign centred around increased transparency.' Her lips twitched a little. 'Journalists will be the first to tell you it's the people or companies who claim to be most honest, that have the dirtiest secrets. Secrets the press then can't wait to unearth, because it makes for such a great story. I didn't want this to happen to Helix, so I did a background check of my own, searching for any secrets that might, if they came to light, damage all the credibility you're trying to gain.'

'Are you really going to look me in the eye and tell me this was just you doing your job? That actually you weren't on the snoop for an attention grabbing headline, with me as the main fall guy?'

For the briefest of moments, he thought he saw her hesitate. Then she met his gaze head on. 'There was, or should I say is, no story.'

He continued to stare at her and she continued to meet his gaze unflinchingly. Finally, because he was losing himself in those beautiful blue eyes, in serious danger of saying to hell with it and just damn well kissing her, he broke the contact. 'Did you find any *dirty* secrets?'

She shook her head, her red hair tumbling over her

shoulders. 'No. I only checked Zaplex, as it was the biggest product for Helix. This report was all I found.'

He nodded but didn't say anything, just sat back against the sofa and levelled a long, long look at her. God help him, he wanted to believe her so much it was a physical ache. His body was straining with the effort of keeping his distance. Of not leaping off the sofa, clasping her in his arms and forgetting the last ten minutes had ever happened. 'You could have just asked me,' he replied at length. 'I thought there was at least some measure of trust between us.'

This time she visibly flinched. 'You're right. Again, I'm sorry. Old habits die hard. I'm a journalist. We don't tend to take what people say on trust. We investigate, dig out the truth.' Taking in a shaky breath, she raised her eyes to his. What he saw looked a lot like remorse, misery and ... was there more, or was it just his wishful thinking? 'I'm so sorry,' she repeated, her eyes filling with tears.

He'd never been able to stand by and watch a woman cry. He certainly couldn't do that to one he was falling for. Reaching out a hand he carefully wiped away her tears. 'Okay. Maybe I'm a gullible fool, but I'm willing to accept what you say as the truth.' His hand stilled as he searched out her eyes. 'But I've found it damn hard to trust again, since Barbara. Heck, I've gone out of my way to avoid getting into another relationship, one that meant having to open my heart again. Leave myself vulnerable. Because when it goes wrong ...' He shook his head, not wanting to go there. 'Then you came along. You got under my skin and I found I had no choice in the matter. I tried to duck out, to play safe, but I couldn't. Heaven help me though, if you do anything like this again. If you go behind my back, or mislead me in any way.' Jim shook his head. He couldn't say the final words ... *it will kill me*. They sounded too dramatic, but by God, it was exactly how he felt.

She swallowed hard, but nodded. 'I understand.'

He sighed and tugged at her hand, pulling her onto the sofa next to him. 'Well this is an end to the evening I hadn't imagined, and believe me, I'd imagined a few.'

'It doesn't have to end here,' she replied softly.

'Doesn't it?' He looked away, afraid to let her see how emotionally bruised he felt. 'Being accused of dishonesty tends to be a passion killer in my book.'

'That's not fair.' Her indignant tone almost had him smiling. It hadn't taken long for her spark to resurface. 'I didn't accuse you of doing anything knowingly, or deliberately.'

Then why did he still feel so crushed? 'You're playing with words. Whatever way you look at it, you came here thinking I'd been party to a potentially lethal deception. That I, or my colleagues, might actually have put profit before patient safety.' He swore under his breath. 'You really don't like the pharmaceutical industry much, do you?'

'No, I guess I don't.' She shifted away a little and he found he couldn't read what she was thinking. 'At least I didn't. When I joined Helix I felt as if I was joining the dark side,' she admitted.

'I know I've asked you this before, but I have to ask again. Why join?'

Tess's breath caught in her throat. Could she really carry on this lie? Wasn't it time to finally tell him the truth?

But she was so terrified he wouldn't understand. That he'd see the fact that she'd deliberately set out to deceive him, right from the start, as the ultimate betrayal.

They'd be over before they'd begun.

God knows she wanted to tell him the truth. To start again with no lies between them, but she wanted the chance to love him, even more. When he'd had more time to understand her, maybe even to love her back, then she'd tell him everything – and hope he'd forgive her.

Swallowing hard, feeling the burden of the lie lying heavily in her heart, Tess continued to stick to her original story. 'As I said, I joined for the challenge, and because I wanted to find out for myself if the pharmaceutical industry really is as bad as it's been painted.'

'And is it, in your opinion? Do you still think those who work in it are happy to put patients' lives at risk for the sake of profit?'

'A few, yes.' He looked surprised, but she carried on before he could argue. 'Maybe that's a bit harsh, but I still believe there are people in the industry who think of profit before the patient. I also believe they're part of a dying breed, thanks to leaders like you. People who are prepared to raise their neck above the parapet, admit things haven't always been done correctly, and put in measures to change that.'

'Good to see there's something you admire about me,' Jim muttered, then jumped up from the sofa, clearly annoyed at letting that slip.

She stood as well, placing a hand on his arm, stopping him from moving away. 'I can find lots to admire. You're brave and honest. Smart and determined. Strong and compassionate. A man I like and respect. So much so that I'm falling for you, too. Hard and fast,' she added, using his words.

'Yeah?' He stared at her for what seemed like a lifetime, his dark eyes searching hers, looking for the truth. 'It hasn't felt that way recently.'

'I know.' Her heart was in her mouth as she met his gaze. 'And now I want to make it up to you. If you'll let me.'

She watched with mounting relief as Jim's eyes darkened, seeming to liquefy. Circles of lava, burning with a heat that had nothing to do with anger. 'What did you have in mind?'

The rough edge to his voice had her pulse scattering. 'I thought we could have dessert upstairs, in that big bed of yours.'

'I'd planned on strawberries, ice cream and chocolate sauce,' he told her, his voice turning deeper, even rougher.

Her stomach went into free fall. 'Why don't you just bring the sauce?'

With a growl he reached for her and swept her into his arms. 'Sod the sauce, we'll have that later. Right now all I need is you.'

As Jim carried her towards the stairs, she felt a burst of pure joy. She didn't deserve it, she knew that, but somehow she'd been given another shot at happiness with this man. She was going to grab it with both hands, and fight for him with everything she had. Even if it meant more lies.

Draping her arms around his neck, she smothered him in a trail of hot kisses.

'And tonight,' he told her thickly, looking down at the scarlet shoes peeping out from underneath her trousers, 'I want you to keep your shoes on.'

Chapter Thirty

At some point during the night, between the second and third time he'd made love to her, Jim had thrown an arm around her and muttered, 'Stay the night.' Then he'd hugged her so tightly she hadn't had an option. Not that she'd wanted one.

As she slowly came round the following morning, her eyes adjusting to the sight of the giant mahogany bed she'd feared she'd never sleep in, Tess yawned and stretched. Her body still hummed with the satisfaction of a night well spent and a big, fat smile spread across her face. Idly she turned, expecting to find Jim sprawled out next to her, but there was only an indent in his pillow and the lingering fragrance of dark, sexy male.

Before she had a chance to wonder where he was, the bedroom door burst open. Jim strode in, already dressed in shorts and a bold turquoise athletics top, his hair sticking up at all angles. He flashed her a grin. A cheeky, boyish grin which, combined with the soft look in his eyes and the bed hair, instantly made him look more schoolboy than powerful businessman. Her heart lifted, swelled and threatened to burst.

'We need to go back to yours and get your running gear. I don't think these will do the job.' He held up his hand, her gorgeous scarlet Jimmy Choos dangling from the end of his fingers.

Bemused, she drew the duvet up around her shoulders. 'Whatever happened to good morning?'

'Damn, sorry, I'm out of practice.' He moved to sit on the bed, pulling her towards him to give her a long, deep, drugging kiss. 'Good morning, Tess.'

'That's ... umm. Wow.' She struggled to find her breath. 'That's a lot better. And now I haven't a clue what you were saying.'

Laughing, he waved her Jimmy Choo's at her.

'Ah yes, my shoes. What do you mean they're not up to the job?' It was Saturday morning. He wasn't seriously expecting her to …

'We're going for a run. Great way to start the weekend.' He frowned when she simply lay there, unmoving. 'You are planning on spending the weekend with me?'

'I'm not sure, because you haven't asked me yet.'

He gave her a sheepish grin. 'There's a reason for that. People who ask run the risk of getting an answer they don't want.'

'And what *do* you want?'

'That's a pretty loaded question, considering you're lying naked in my bed.'

Laughing, she shook her head. 'I mean, do you want me to stay for the weekend?'

'Yes. In fact I'm pretty certain I'm going to want you to stay for more than just this weekend.' Her face must have looked as dazed as she felt because he frowned. 'Sorry, I didn't mean to scare you.'

Her heart thumped happily against her ribs. 'You didn't scare me.'

'No?'

'No.' For further emphasis, she shook her head.

He studied her for a moment, seemingly uncertain. Then a wide grin split his face. 'In which case, we need to go and get your trainers.'

Laughing and shaking her head at the same time she gripped tightly to the sheet he was trying to remove. 'You go for your run, Mr Fitness Freak. I'm more than happy lying in your lovely big bed and going back to sleep for another hour.'

He stopped tugging for a moment to stare down at her. 'Is that what you usually do on a Saturday morning? Sleep?'

Giggling at his shocked expression, she settled back under the duvet. 'It's what most sane office workers do. Now go and run off some of that energy and leave me in peace.'

Moments later she heard the rustle of clothing. Then a large, naked male climbed on top of her. 'I've just thought of a better way to expend some energy,' he muttered thickly.

Tess gazed into his liquid brown eyes and smiled. 'I knew you'd give in to my way of thinking in the end.'

In a move that would have impressed a professional wrestler, he reversed their positions, lifting her so she straddled him. 'I don't give in, but I can compromise. We stay in bed *and* exercise. You can start first.'

She let out a squeal, something between a gasp of shock and a giggle. Then he put his hands on the side of her head and dragged her down to his hot urgent mouth. Leaving her gasping for a totally different reason.

Jim turned on the kettle and threw a couple of slices of bread in the toaster. Then he glanced at his clock and laughed to himself. One o'clock, and he was only now getting breakfast? Not that he was complaining. He'd take Tess's form of exercise any day.

He still had to pinch himself this was actually happening. That Tess had spent the night with him. That she was still here, now. Sure he'd allowed his hunger for her to ride roughshod over his pride, determinedly obliterating any lingering doubts about whether he could really trust her, but he didn't care. If she was using him, then so be it. Christ, if last night was anything to go by, she could keep on using him as long as she wanted.

The object of his thoughts chose that moment to wander into the kitchen. Her hair was tousled and she wore his black towelling robe. With, he'd like to bet, nothing underneath. Hallelujah. By rights he should be exhausted, but instead, he felt he could conquer mountains. Blindfolded. On one leg.

'Is toast okay for you?' He turned, pulling her towards him, running his hands over her slender body, kissing her softly on the lips. Just because he could. 'I can throw in an egg, but I'm not sure whether we're doing breakfast or lunch.'

Laughing she slipped out of his arms and pulled up a stool. 'I've upset your routine.'

'Yes. But you're welcome to do that anytime.' He kissed the top of her head before returning to the worktop to conjure a mug of tea from the boiling kettle.

Having handed her the cup, cringing slightly at the fact that it had Helix Pharmaceuticals splashed all over it, he made himself a coffee then set to work spreading butter on the toast. He considered adding jam, but decided his appetite couldn't wait long enough for him to find it. Then again, this morning wasn't all about him. 'Do you want something on that?' He gestured to the plate of buttered toast.

She looked at the stack and shook her head. 'Tea and toast. A perfect start to the day.'

Unable to resist, he leaned in for another kiss. 'Umm, tea, toast and Tess. An even better start, or should I say middle, to the day.'

Again she giggled, making him feel like a damn king.

'If I wasn't here, what would you do now?'

'Ahh.'

'Ahh?'

'Well, I'd have already been out of bed for ...' He glanced down at his watch. '... five hours.' Her eyes widened in horror. 'I'd have had a run, showered, changed and sifted through all my emails.'

'Oops.' She was biting her lip, trying not to laugh. 'I've done more than upset your routine. I've ruined your chances of winning your next triathlon and caused the potential downfall of Helix.'

'Exactly.' He found he didn't mind having the piss taken out of him. Not when it was done by a sexy redhead wearing nothing but a towelling robe. 'So you'd better make it a weekend to remember, or I'll have taken the double hit for nothing.'

She finished off her toast and licked her fingers, causing the part of him that should be worn out to twitch back into life. 'Well, if you like, we can go back to your routine for the rest of the day.'

'Service my bike, trawl the Internet for sports gadgets and watch a live game? Followed by pizza?'

Grimacing, she loaded her plate and mug into the dishwasher. 'On the other hand, we could come up with something different.' She leaned back against the worktop and he found himself willing the neck of the robe to separate just that little bit more. 'How about a walk in the fresh air, a trip to the supermarket to buy something I can make us for dinner, and then finding a film to watch on the TV?'

He considered carefully. For a nanosecond. 'Your proposal could work. As long as the film doesn't star a floppy haired wimp. And it features car chases, gun battles or gratuitous sex.'

She held out her hand. 'Deal.' But then her face crumpled. 'Oh God, I've forgotten Dad.'

Jim's hand tightened on hers and he pulled her towards him. 'Is today the day you usually visit him?'

'Yes. Me and my brother go every Saturday afternoon.' She turned to look at the clock on the kitchen wall and gulped. 'In half an hour.'

Gently he kissed the end of her nose. 'It's not a problem. Go and visit him. I'll spend a few hours doing my emails and keeping Helix afloat. We can do the supermarket, and other assorted activities, when you come back.'

'Thank you.' With a small sigh she stepped back. 'I guess I'd better get dressed.' When she reached the doorway, she paused, darting him a sexy look over her shoulder. 'I'll look forward to those *assorted activities*.'

Me too, he thought, grinning shamelessly. Me, too.

Making herself at home in his kitchen later that day, Tess couldn't stop smiling to herself. Yesterday she'd feared Jim would never talk to her again. Today she was in his kitchen, cooking him a meal. Would she have had that chance if she'd told him the real reason she'd joined Helix? She doubted it.

The thought stiffened her resolve. She'd fallen for the hard, stern research head. To find he was also gentle, amusing and affectionate made her want to perform cartwheels of joy.

The only sour note to the day had come when she'd been late meeting Mark at the care home. He'd asked about Helix and she'd snapped that they were already late and she'd talk to him about it next week. She knew he had a lot of questions but she hadn't wanted to answer them just before seeing her dad. Or before spending the evening with Jim. Of course Mark had been cross, but Tess was determined not to let that ruin her weekend. When he got to know Jim, he'd trust and believe in him, just as she did.

When Mark got to know Jim – could she really start to think like that? To imagine a future where Jim and her brother were friends? Introduce Jim to her father? Such thoughts hadn't seemed possible twenty-four hours ago, but now?

Now, she was still lying to Jim, so she had to stop getting carried away. Turning the sizzling chorizo and butternut squash over in the pan, Tess huffed out a breath. She'd take this one step at a time.

'There is nothing sexier than the sight of a woman in my kitchen.' Jim ran appreciative eyes over her as he joined her at the stove. 'Especially this woman.' He lifted her hair away from her neck and nuzzled, his mouth feeling soft and delicious against her skin.

She closed her eyes and simply enjoyed. 'Any burning issues on email that couldn't have waited until Monday?' she asked eventually, leaning into him.

'Hey, in case you've forgotten, I'm important.' His hand reached out and grabbed a piece of chorizo from the pan. 'Plus, sneaking off to my office got me out of cooking.'

'Umm.' Turning down the heat, she turned to face him.

'How many other women have you cleverly manoeuvred into cooking for you over the years, I wonder?'

His dark eyes turned serious. 'Not as many as you might think.'

She'd said it as a joke, but now she realised she wanted to know. Or did she? 'I'm thinking quite a number.'

'I told you. Over the last couple of years I've hardly dated,' he protested.

'And before that? I find it hard to believe there weren't legions of women willing to slave over a hot stove just for a chance to look into a pair of dark eyes that really resemble—'

'Don't you dare say Clooney.'

'I think I dare. You really do look an awful lot like him.'

He silenced her very effectively with a scorching kiss. When he finally let her go they were both breathing hard.

'You know most men would be flattered to be told they looked like a film star.'

'I disagree. Most men would rather be told they're liked for who they are. Not what they do, or who they look like.'

The vulnerability in his voice surprised her, coming as it did from a man who seemed so confident. She hooked her arms around his neck and dropped a soft kiss on his mouth. 'Well, I'm pretty hooked on the whole package.'

'I'm pretty hooked on your package, too.' He skimmed her body with his hands. 'And you should know,' he told her softly, his eyes darkening, 'I don't invite women into my home, or my life for that matter, casually.'

Her breath caught in her throat. God those eyes. They could melt her with just a look. 'Ditto for me with men.'

'Good to know.' After planting a gentle kiss on her forehead, he reached down to the wine rack and pulled out a bottle of red. 'Glass of wine for the cook?' When she nodded, he deftly poured out two glasses. 'The last woman in this kitchen was Barbara and, believe me, you outshine her in every conceivable way.'

'She hurt you.'

He considered her words as he drank from his glass. 'Yes, she did. I'd imagined myself in love with her, though looking back on it now, I think it was more a desire to settle down that coincided with her coming along, rather than a feeling that she really was THE ONE.'

'You made yourself fall in love.' It amused her that even when it came to matters of the heart, he thought he could get his own way.

'Exactly.' He leant back against the breakfast bar. 'It didn't lessen the feeling of being kicked in the balls and skewered through the heart when she betrayed me, though.'

Tess's hand jerked and wine spilt onto the floor.

'Shit, sorry.' Heart thumping, she dazedly looked around for a dishcloth.

'Don't worry.' He was there already, mopping at the spill with yards of kitchen roll. 'It's why I chose a slate grey floor. Hides all the accidents.'

He finished cleaning it up and threw the sodden paper towel into the bin. Then he peered down at her, concern in his eyes. 'Are you okay?'

'Yes, I'm fine.' Quickly she turned her attention to the frying pan, stirring the contents with a vigour that was totally unnecessary. 'Just clumsy.' Before he had a chance to quiz her further, she directed the attention back on him. 'Is it hard, working in the same company as Barbara again?'

He returned to his stance by the breakfast bar, though she was aware of his sharp eyes on her. 'No.' He paused, swishing the wine around in his glass. 'The bruise to my ego has healed and my heart's been captured by this fiery new communications manager.'

Her back to him, Tess shut her eyes. Oh God, what was she doing, continuing to mislead this man she was falling in love with? Her reasons might be more honest than those of Barbara's, but Jim wouldn't see it that way. He'd view it as, what did he call it? Another kick in the balls. Another skewer through his heart.

Feeling unsteady she reached for her wine and took a large swig. 'Have you forgiven Barbara?'

She turned to find him looking nonplussed. 'Forgiven her?'

'Yes. For cheating on you. Going behind your back. Maybe she had her reasons.'

He let out a harsh laugh. 'She had her reasons all right. She knew sleeping with Derek would give her a better chance of promotion. I never quite figured out why she didn't just dump me for him. Maybe she enjoyed the thrill of having two men at her beck and call.'

'Or maybe Derek was just a temporary diversion, one she had every intention of dropping. She knew telling you would hurt you, so she kept quiet to avoid that.'

'Are you defending her?' he interrupted, his expression incredulous. 'She lied to me, Tess. Deliberately went behind my back. There is no effing excuse and no, I can't ever forgive that.' Then he sighed. 'That blasted woman has taken up enough of our evening. Why don't I put on some music? We can smooch together while the dinner cooks.'

Jim went to turn on his music system and Tess stood where she was, her hands trembling violently. If he ever found out. Feeling sick to her stomach, she clutched the edge of the work surface. The desire to blurt out everything was almost overwhelming. Almost.

She turned to find him holding out his hand towards her, his lips curled in a crooked smile that shot straight to her heart.

No, she couldn't risk losing this man.

So instead of coming clean, she nestled into his arms and let the joy of being held by him drown out her fears.

Chapter Thirty-One

Jim didn't want to admit that when he walked into work the following Monday he had more of a spring in his step. It sounded plain daft. But over the last few days had his heart felt lighter? And his stride a bit ... well ... bouncier? Okay, yes, perhaps.

'Bloody hell, you actually look happy,' Rick remarked when they met in the car park.

'Maybe because I am,' he countered cheerfully. Rick halted, causing him to turn back and stare. 'What?'

'I don't believe it. Jim Knight has fallen in love.'

Jim's heart banged hard against his ribs. 'Let's not get too carried away here,' he murmured, but even as he set out to deny it, his mind played back his conversation with Tess last Friday evening when he'd admitted he was falling for her, hard and fast.

Had he already taken the fall? Was this feeling of inexplicable joy, where everything looked brighter and more colourful, actually love?

Rick gave him a slightly pitying look. 'You're walking around with a glazed look in your eyes and a smug grin on your face at seven-thirty in the morning. If it's not love, you've taken something illegal.'

'Shit.' But though his legs felt slightly unsteady, and his heart was racing like the clappers, his smile didn't budge. 'Looks like it's love then.'

He received a hard slap on the back. 'I bloody knew it. Feels amazing, doesn't it?'

'Yes.' If he'd been a man used to sharing his feelings, he'd have perhaps expanded further. Told Rick he'd never felt like this before. That even when Tess wasn't with him, like she hadn't been last night, he'd felt her presence. That just thinking about her, as he had been when Rick had caught him, made him come out in a goofy grin.

'Well, congratulations, mate. Welcome to a world where women rule the roost, but though we'll kick and scream and deny it till we're blue in the face, secretly we don't care because we worship the ground they walk on.'

Which just about summed it up, Jim thought with a laugh.

He was still smiling when he walked into the reception area and past the new photographs he'd had sourced depicting the various stages of drug development. Hopefully Tess would approve.

He was still smiling as he walked into the boardroom for the executive team meeting. In fact his smile remained right up until Jack Webber raised his hand when Geoff asked if there was any other business.

'I'd like to discuss my concerns around a recent hiring in the communications department, Tessa Johnson.'

Jim nearly shot out of his chair. It was only because he felt the weight of Jack's eyes on him that he steeled himself not to react. Not to look as shocked as he felt.

'Why are you bringing that to this meeting?' Geoff asked irritably. 'Surely it's a matter for you to discuss directly with Georgina.'

Jack acknowledged the rebuke with a slight nod. 'Of course, of course, and I apologise for not discussing this with her first.' He gave an irate looking Georgina one of his condescending smirks. 'But my worries aren't about her ability to do her job. Rather about her reasons for joining this company. A senior member of this organisation has expressed concerns about the fact that Tessa has been accessing the study database. As Tessa is a former journalist, this person is uneasy about the motives behind a communications manager looking into what is a clinical database.'

'Barbara's been talking to you,' Jim said flatly.

'She is the senior employee I mentioned, yes. And as the

head of the clinical trial department, she has a right to be concerned about access to what is effectively her database.'

'She's already discussed her issue with me,' Jim returned coldly. 'As her line-manager I told her what I'll now tell you. Tessa is running a PR campaign called "Leading with Science", designed to make the outside world aware of the measures we're putting in place in Helix. As improved transparency regarding publication of our clinical trial results is one of the lynchpins of the campaign, she wanted to make sure Helix had nothing to hide before announcing these measures to the world.'

'And you believe her?' Jack asked.

'Yes.'

'Tessa is an excellent new hire,' Georgina added. 'And I take exception to scurrilous accusations being brought to this meeting about one of my employees. It's because she's a journalist that she's able to bring a new dimension to the role. We should be congratulating her on the fantastic work she's done so far, not slandering her.'

Privately Jim applauded Georgina, though when she smiled over at him he found it hard to smile back. He was far too livid at the way his conniving ex had plotted with Jack Webber. A man she knew to be his nemesis.

When the meeting was over, Jim hunted Barbara down like a heat-seeking missile. He thundered into her office and slammed the door shut.

'You expressed your concerns to me about Tessa,' he barked, without preamble. 'I listened and refuted them all. Yet still you see fit to approach the commercial director, who has damn all to do with any of this, and get him to raise the issue at the executive meeting. Why?'

Totally unfazed by his outburst, she simply arched a dark eyebrow. 'Because I'm concerned the R&D president has been hoodwinked by a clever journalist into gaining access to confidential information.'

'Or maybe because you're temporarily man-free and have decided you want to get back into bed with the man you discarded, but need to remove the opposition first?'

That raised more of a reaction, her cheeks flushing red – he'd bet with anger rather than embarrassment. 'This isn't about my feelings for you. It's about my feelings for the company I work for. Besides, I don't count scrawny redheads as opposition.' She rose slowly to her feet and slunk around the desk, trailing her nails along the glass surface. 'Did you know she's been accessing that database at home as well as the office? That she's spent the equivalent of a working week trawling through it? That she asked Frank about where she could find all the Zaplex studies, including those not in the product monograph?'

'Yes.' Well, he knew about the database, anyway. 'I've told you, she's been looking to see if we have anything to hide, and using Zaplex as an example. She's doing her job, Barbara. Making sure we don't end up with egg on our face, or worse, when we launch the PR campaign.'

She stopped inches before him, her dark eyes staring into his. 'You really are sunk, aren't you?' With a small smile she straightened his perfectly straight tie. 'Never mind, I'm here to rescue you.'

'Capsize the lifeboat, more like,' he muttered, pushing her hands away. 'I'm warning you, Barbara, leave Tessa alone.'

He had one foot outside of her office before she replied. 'And I'm warning you, Jim. That woman is up to no good. If you don't listen to me, you'll end up looking a bigger fool than you did when you left here two years ago.'

Ignoring her words, and the hammering of his heart, Jim marched away from her office and straight down to the communications department. And to Tess.

When she looked up and saw him, her face lit up in the most beautiful smile. 'Jim. How lovely to see you. I saw the new photographs in the reception area this morning.

They look amazing.' She stood and, following a quick three hundred and sixty degree reconnaissance to make sure nobody was looking, reached out to squeeze his hand. 'Thank you.'

He found his lips wouldn't quite curve as he wanted them to. 'My pleasure. You were right. It looks a lot better than posh art.'

'Is everything all right? You look kind of serious.'

He stared into her wide blue eyes and saw concern. But more than that, he saw something that looked a lot like the choking emotion he was feeling. Instantly the angst that had coiled tightly round his heart slithered away. 'Everything is fine,' he reassured. 'Especially now I've seen you.' He tugged on her hand, leading her into one of the vacant meeting rooms before closing the door. 'Are you coming round tonight?'

Her face fell. 'I'd love to, but I promised to see my brother. Maybe after that, if it's not too late?'

He laughed softly. 'Trust me, it will never be too late. If I had my way, you wouldn't be going back to your apartment at all.'

Her eyes almost popped out on stalks and she darted a quick look outside which made him laugh. He didn't give a rat's arse who was watching. 'What, you mean like move in with you?'

'Yes.'

'Seriously?'

Her eyes shone like those of a child at Christmas. Jim realised Barbara had at least been partly right earlier. He was well and truly sunk. But he was damned if he ever wanted rescuing. 'Yes, of course seriously.'

A wide grin split her face. 'That sounds good to me. Living in your amazing loft. Oh, wow.'

He coughed. 'Umm, it is me you're excited about living with, isn't it? Not my place, but me?'

Her laughter filled the small glass meeting room. 'Why of course it's you, though your place does kind of make it a no-brainer.' After another surreptitious glance outside, she reached up and kissed his cheek. 'But if you lived in a hovel, I'd still want to be with you. I'd just make sure you moved in with me, instead.'

If he hadn't been in a glass meeting room at work, he'd have kissed the living daylights out of her. As it was, he settled for a long, dark look which he hoped conveyed exactly how he planned on celebrating with her later that evening.

Tess knocked on Mark's door feeling terribly guilty. Both about what she was going to tell him, and the fact that before she'd even entered his house, she was itching to leave so she could go to Jim's. Her heart rose and fluttered for a few beats. Soon to be *theirs*.

'So, are you finally going to tell me what on earth is going on?' he asked once they were sitting in his living room. 'Why you were in such a tearing hurry last Saturday?'

'Because I was going back to Jim's.'

His back stiffened. 'What happened to the study you told me you were going to interrogate him about on Friday evening then? Did that get forgotten in the heat of lust?'

'I did show it to him,' she retorted. 'And damn you, Mark, he nearly kicked me out, and quite rightly, too. He explained the study wasn't even in Zaplex – it was an … isomer, I think he said. Anyway, the point is it wasn't Zaplex, which was why it wasn't in the regulatory dossier.'

'So that's it?' He shook his head in disbelief. 'Despite what we saw happen to Mum, and despite what we know happened to the patients of the other families you've spoken to, you now suddenly believe Zaplex wasn't to blame?'

'Yes. I searched the whole database and there's nothing. No hidden studies.'

'Except for the one you tackled your lover about. And he

fobbed you off with some cock and bull scientific explanation he knew you wouldn't understand.'

'He told me the truth,' she countered, fighting her anger. 'And if you knew Jim like I do, you'd trust what he said, too. I can't find anything to connect Mum's death to Zaplex.'

'You mean apart from other patients who've also suffered heart problems?'

Tess hunched forward, cradling her head in her hands. 'Probably they were just coincidences, too. I've been so stupidly blinkered about Zaplex being the cause that I haven't really done my job properly at all. A proper journalist would have looked at all the angles. I saw Mum, then that lady at the funeral whose mother also died of a heart attack. After that, I was *looking* for cases of heart problems.' She regarded her brother sadly. 'I haven't investigated the whole picture here, Mark. Just what I wanted to see.'

He let out a deep breath and slumped back against the sofa. 'So I guess this leaves your lover conveniently in the clear then?'

Tess swallowed back the angry words she wanted to throw at him. Like her, he'd been burying some of his grief by focussing on revenge. Now there was no revenge to be had. No satisfaction in bringing anyone to account. All that was left was the tragic loss of someone they'd loved. 'We should gain comfort from the fact there was no malpractice involved,' she replied quietly. 'That in all likelihood she left us through a natural cause and not someone else's actions.'

A heavy silence stretched between them. 'I guess you're right,' he said finally, his voice resigned. 'But I wanted someone to blame. I thought knowing why she died might make it easier.'

Tess rose to her feet and went to sit next to him, putting her arms around him. 'So did I, but it isn't easy, whatever way.'

'No, it isn't.' He placed his hand over hers and sighed. 'So what are you going to do now? Stay with Helix?'

'I'm not sure,' she replied honestly. Funnily enough, it wasn't something she'd given any thought too. Since Friday she'd barely had a chance to breathe, never mind think. 'I have to admit, the longer I work there, the more I actually believe in what the company does. It's not all rosy, but then it isn't with any company. Newspapers aren't exactly whiter than white, either. Maybe I will stay. At least for a while.'

'And what about the research guy? Will you continue to see him?'

'Yes.' She hesitated. 'In fact I'm going to move in with him.'

His eyebrows shot up. 'Wow. You act fast.'

She smiled. 'It doesn't seem fast, not to me. When something feels right, like this does, I don't think time matters.'

'And you're absolutely certain he deserves your trust?'

'Yes.' Her reply was quick and firm and she pushed away thoughts of how she would have to answer if the question were posed the other way. *Did she deserve his trust?*

'Then I hope it works out for you, Tess. I really do.'

A lump the size of a walnut lodged in her throat. 'Thank you,' she told him, her voice cracking. 'That means a lot.'

'Hey, watch it. I don't want you blubbering on me again.'

Wiping her wet cheeks, she smiled and rose to her feet. 'Well, I'd better get on my way then.'

'You not staying for anything to eat?'

'Have you planned anything?'

He gave her a sheepish grin. 'Take out? Beans on toast?'

'I think I'll try my luck at Jim's instead.'

His eyes filled with understanding. 'Okay then.' He stood and walked with her to the door. 'I look forward to meeting this Jim guy soon.'

'You will.' She held out her arms and gave him a fierce hug. 'In the meantime, be good.'

'Yeah. No point telling you to do the same,' he muttered.

'From the sound of things good is the last thing you're being. I guess I should say, be careful.'

With a chuckle she let herself out. After months in darkness, she finally felt she was coming out into the light. Her heart was no longer full of anger and bitterness. Instead it was bursting with love; for her brother, her poor father. For Jim.

For the first time since her mother's death, she felt happy.

Chapter Thirty-Two

Wrestling with his bow tie, Jim eyed up the clock on his bedside table. He just about had time to call his parents. Since his father's heart attack he'd been in the habit of phoning nearly every day. Until he'd started dating Tess, that is. After that ... reaching for the phone, a self-satisfied grin crept across his face. Oh, yes, he knew exactly why thoughts of phoning home had escaped his mind these last few weeks. The time he hadn't spent at work, he'd spent with Tess. The only reason she wasn't with him now was because she'd told him it was easier for her to change into her posh frock at her own place.

But after this weekend, all her things would be at his place, he thought with a burst of pleasure. Boxes were packed, the van was hired and his own furniture rearranged to allow space for the pieces she'd wanted to bring. And for her shoes.

'Ahh, so I do still have a son then?'

Jim rolled his eyes as his mother's voice came on the line. 'It's not been that long.'

'It has,' she replied firmly, 'but if you tell me you've spent the time winning over that girl you're sweet on, I'll forgive you.'

'Well, actually ...' He laughed down the phone, amazed, as always, by her uncanny perceptiveness. 'I have.'

A shriek echoed down the line. 'About time too. So when do we get to meet her? You know it's your father's birthday in a few weeks. You could always bring her with you when you come up.'

'I could,' he agreed slowly. What would Tess say to a weekend away, visiting his parents? And why did the thought of introducing her to them not terrify the pants off him? He realised it was because he wanted to show her off. She was important. More than that, she was IT.

His heart scuttled into overdrive as the realisation of that hit him squarely in the face. As his mother continued to talk away in his ear, Jim's legs buckled and he lunged for a chair. Christ Almighty. He wanted to marry Tess. She was the woman he wanted to spend the rest of his life with.

He started to grin, but sobered up pretty quickly when he realised he didn't know whether Tess felt the same way. Since that memorable Friday evening they had only spent one night apart, but still he had a sense Tess was holding something of herself back. Occasionally her eyes looked worried, haunted even, and he wished he knew what was behind it. Maybe he'd find out tonight, though the Annual Pharmaceutical Industry Awards ceremony was hardly the place for a deep heart to heart. Hell, it was hardly the place for any type of interaction, meaningful or otherwise, which was why he normally avoided the event like the plague. But in her role as communications manager Tess had told him she needed to go. Jim had weighed up a night by himself against one with her, albeit with several hundred other pharma company employees, and here he was. Putting his damn tuxedo on. Tess hadn't just hooked him, she'd reeled him in and laid him out on a plate. He was totally hers, to do what she wanted with. He could only hope what she wanted was to keep him.

His mother's voice echoed down the phone at him, still chattering away ten to the dozen. Guiltily Jim brought his attention back to the other important woman in his life.

Across the banqueting hall an ocean of faces sat around elegantly dressed tables, finishing their meals and waiting for the awards to begin. Jim had been here for two hours; within two minutes he'd remembered why he didn't usually attend these functions. Tedious, dull, self-important. He could go on, but it would only make him grumpier. Any hope he'd harboured of being able to spend some time with Tess had been crushed once he'd taken a look at the seating plan. Now he found himself stuck on a different table, barely able to make out her flaming red hair through the throng of other diners. Worse was to come; the awards themselves were about to start. An hour of industry people engaging in an orgy of self-congratulation. Sure he understood the importance of the marketing campaigns. Without the sales from the products, there was no money to invest in finding new therapies. But really, did the commercial guys have to look and sound so smug? A clever campaign was worthless without a damn good medicine to base it round.

His internal rhetoric was interrupted by the announcement that the award ceremony would begin in half an hour. Taking the opportunity to excuse himself, Jim shot out of his seat and went to hunt down Tess.

'Jim, we don't often see you at this event.'

He bit down on his irritation and stopped to shake the offered hand; to engage in the expected small talk.

By the time he'd managed to extricate himself, Tess had disappeared. Letting out a regretful sigh, he thrust a hand in his trouser pocket and headed for the bar. If he had to listen to this pomposity, a large whiskey would probably help. Two might numb the pain. Three and he might even start to enjoy himself.

Then again … dressed in a flowing bright turquoise dress, Barbara came gliding towards him like a lizard looking for a sunny place to bask. Or maybe that should be a chameleon, as she could change her personality so easily. Tonight she wore the charming smile.

'Jim.' She reached to kiss his cheek. 'How unexpected. You don't often grace these occasions with your presence.'

'No.'

Her eyes flickered to the other end of the bar. Damn, that's where Tess was. 'I see what drew you here tonight,' she murmured. Suddenly she grabbed his arm and pulled him towards an empty table. 'Before you make an even further fool of yourself with that woman, do yourself a favour and listen to what I have to say.'

'I was rather hoping to get a drink.'

'Fine.' She waved over to a hovering waiter and ordered two whiskies. 'You're going to need it after you listen to what I've found out.'

'Listening to you would tempt any man to turn to drink.'

She didn't rise to his bait. Instead she leant forward and stared him straight in the eye as she spoke. 'I've done some further digging on Tessa.'

'Not this again.'

'Hear me out before you dismiss me,' she returned coolly. 'I have a good relationship with the breast cancer charities, both here and in the US. On a hunch I asked if they'd heard of Tessa Johnson and guess what? They had. It seems before she started work with Helix she was asking questions about Zaplex. Asking patients and families of patients whether they believe it causes heart problems.'

'No.' His chest constricted so sharply the word came out as a strangled cry.

'Yes, Jim. Tessa Johnson has been lying to you and to us. She came here to investigate Zaplex, not to work for Helix.'

The waiter chose that moment to serve up their whiskies, which was just as well. Jim had never needed the bite of one so much in his life. After draining his glass in one quick gulp, he shot to his feet. 'Thanks for the chat. I'll be seeing you.'

She reached out a hand to stop him, but he thrust her away. His brain felt numb, his heart like it was going to detonate on him. All he could think was there had to be a logical explanation for all this.

He had to find Tess.

She was sitting at one of the casual tables near the bar, her head bent low as she talked to the man opposite her. One of those preppy, smoothly handsome types. Preppy, handsome, *pushy* types, he thought with a burst of jealousy as he noticed how close the guy was sitting to her. How intently he was looking into her eyes.

'So, what happened to that headline grabbing scoop you promised me, Tess?'

Jim lurched to a stop, the breath rushing out of his lungs. He finally realised who she was talking to. A blasted newspaper editor.

'What scoop?' he rasped, pushing his way between them. Rudely interrupting their little powwow.

Both heads jerked round to look at him. Her companion looked merely bemused. Tess looked absolutely stricken. Worse, as she started to register what he'd overheard, the blood drained from her face and her hand flew to her mouth in horror.

The man stood up, holding out his hand towards Jim. 'Hugh Coleman, *Daily News*. We've met before.'

Jim pointedly ignored the outstretched hand. 'What scoop, Tess?' he asked again, his voice almost brutally calm.

'It was an item we discussed before she joined Helix,' Hugh interjected smoothly, shrugging his shoulders as if it was no big deal.

Jim wasn't listening. His eyes were focussed on Tess. The more he watched her, the more his heart began to slowly shrivel in his chest. The Tess he thought he knew, the one who was forthright and outspoken, would have told him quite clearly and concisely to mind his own damn business. By now she would have been stalking off, head held high.

This Tess looked like a startled deer. Guilt swum heavily in her clear blue eyes. Anguish lined her face.

'What scoop?' he asked again, his voice more shaky now as the shock began to wear off and the answer became blindingly obvious.

Over the tannoy, the host announced the start of the award ceremony.

'We should get back into the hall,' she said finally, standing up and avoiding his eyes like a condemned man avoids his executioner.

Jim was halfway towards grabbing her by the wrist and

dragging her out of the room when he considered where they were. Too many interested eyes, particularly those of the damn newspaper editor. And no doubt of Barbara, too, who would surely be lurking behind him, sensing victory. Shoving away his instincts, he clutched at his supposed control and nodded. 'I'll catch up with you afterwards.'

Tess walked dazedly back to the ballroom, the threat in Jim's softly spoken words reverberating inside her head, clashing with the feelings of dread and horror already there. Only hours ago she'd arrived in a happy bubble. It was now shattered beyond repair, replaced by a dark blanket of fear that was perilously close to suffocating her. Would she ever be able to think of him again without seeing his ravaged face as he'd stood, glaring at her? As if she'd ripped the heart right out of his chest.

'I've told Jim all about your little scheme.'

Tess stumbled, catching hold of the back of a chair to steady herself. She turned to find Barbara smirking at her. 'What scheme?'

'He might be blinded by lust, but I'm not. I know you were talking to cancer charities about Zaplex before you joined Helix. You thought you could make a name for yourself at our expense, didn't you?'

'No.' Oh God, it was all about to crash around her ears.

Barbara chuckled. 'Well, it looks like your game is up. Still, don't worry about Jim. I'll make sure he doesn't pine after you for long.'

Numbly Tess found her seat at the table. As the evening carried on she was totally unaware of the chatter going on around her. All she could think was how stupid she'd been not to tell Jim the truth when she'd had the chance. And how that stupidity, that fear of their relationship being over before it had properly begun, was going to result in the one thing she'd been terrified of happening. Losing him.

Chapter Thirty-Three

The cab ride home took place in stony silence. Jim had appeared at her side the moment the awards ceremony had finished. *Your place or mine* were the only words he'd uttered. There had been no hint of amusement at their irony. Only an expression of outrage, loaded with grim. She'd opted for home turf. At least then he couldn't have the satisfaction of throwing her out.

Frozen in terror for most of the ceremony, her mind was now racing, working out how best to approach their conversation. Briefly she wondered if she could bluff it out, as Hugh had already tried to do for her. But there wasn't just the overheard conversation to deal with. There was what Barbara had told him, too. Besides, barefaced lying wasn't part of her nature.

Unless she counted the fact that the whole reason she'd joined Helix had been based on a lie.

Tears welled in her eyes and she turned to stare bleakly out of the window. No matter how she might try to dress it up, spin the words, the facts were the facts. She had deliberately set out to deceive Jim and the rest of the Helix organisation. Her reasons for doing so, reasons she'd once believed to be just, now seemed hopelessly inadequate. Especially since she'd so willingly jumped into bed with him.

The cab pulled up outside her block and she quickly climbed out, wondering if Jim could hear the sound of her heart thundering in her chest. And if he could, whether he cared. She left him to pay the driver and scrambled up the stairs to the relative sanctuary of her flat. Part paid for out of her mother's inheritance, it had been a place she'd tried to find peace since her death.

She wouldn't find any today.

Her hands trembled as she fumbled with the key. Jim came up to stand alongside her, a towering, brooding presence. The lover had vanished, replaced by a cold stranger.

As they walked silently into her living room the pile of neatly stacked boxes mocked her. A harsh reminder of how excited she'd been earlier today as she'd finished her packing.

'At the risk of repeating myself,' Jim ground out slowly. 'What scoop was Hugh referring to?'

'An article exposing the pharmaceutical industry,' she admitted miserably. It was too late for anything but the truth.

Her words sliced through Jim's chest. There was no longer the lingering hope that all this was a simple misunderstanding, easily explained away. In six words, Tess had torn out his heart and pierced it with one of her pointed stilettos.

He'd been falling in love. She'd been trying to ferret out a story.

'Let me get this straight.' He tried to ignore the agony he was feeling and focus instead on the facts. 'Despite your previous denial, you did in fact join Helix in order to write an article on malpractice in the pharmaceutical industry?' When she didn't reply, just stared bleakly at him, he ploughed on, each word a further stab through his heart. 'My God, you must have thought you'd hit the jackpot when you found that *in vitro* study.' He laughed bitterly. 'A chance to really make a name for yourself with a headline grabbing article on how the evil pharmaceutical industry hid safety data.'

'It wasn't like that,' she tried to protest, but he just laughed.

'No? Then tell me, what was it like? Because it certainly wasn't as you claimed, was it? It wasn't just you doing your job, being a thorough, conscientious communications manager.'

'It is part of my job to—'

'Don't you bloody dare to continue to lie to me,' he

thundered, his control perilously close to shattering. 'You might have taken me for a fool once, but don't think you can do it again.'

'I'm sorry.'

Tess moved away and went to sit down on her sofa. She looked desolate, her eyes, when they finally found his, filled with shame.

She bloody well should be ashamed. 'Why?' he asked harshly. 'Why did you do it? To advance your career?'

'No,' she shot back sharply. 'I did it for personal reasons.'

He raised an eyebrow at that. 'Because you wanted to curry favour with the editor? Tell me, Tess, did it not occur to you how wrong it was to sleep with one man, just because you wanted to advance your cause of getting into bed with another?'

Within the blink of an eye, she'd stalked towards him and slapped him, hard, round the face. 'How dare you?'

He didn't flinch. Didn't even raise his hand to feel his reddened cheek, though it stung like hell. He simply glared at her. 'I dare, because from where I'm standing, that's exactly how it looks.'

'My mother died of a heart attack hours after taking Zaplex for the first time.' Tess flung the words at him, her eyes spitting with anger. 'That's why I joined Helix. To find out why she died. To find out if it could have been prevented.' Finally her voice broke and tears streamed down her face. 'Not so I could sleep with my flaming editor.'

Though his cheek was still smarting from her slap, his arms instinctively shot out to hold her. To comfort her. Until he remembered their relationship wasn't real. She didn't want such overtures from him. She'd probably never wanted them from him. All she'd actually wanted was dirt to help her story.

Sharply he turned and, for a few moments, he gazed unblinkingly out of the window. 'I'm sorry you lost your mother.' Slowly he moved to face her. 'But you have to know Zaplex didn't cause her death.'

'How could I have known that? She wasn't the only patient to have died from heart problems after taking it. I spoke to other families. Even the coroner said there wasn't enough evidence to rule it out.'

'Of course some patients taking Zaplex have experienced heart problems. Just as some have had strokes, stomach ulcers, other cancers. When you look at the number of patients taking it, and how ill those patients are anyway, none of that is a surprise.' His desire to shake her was so strong he had to clutch at the windowsill. 'In the two years it's been on the market there have been no safety signals to indicate a risk to the heart. The coroner wouldn't have had that information at the time, but we have it now.'

'What do you mean, safety signals?'

She was rubbing at her wet cheeks, her face so forlorn his chest tightened. Great, despite knowing their relationship was nothing more than a sham, his bloody heart still ached for her. 'You don't think a company gets a product onto the market and then simply sits back, job done, and reels in the profits?' he asked, deliberately keeping his voice harsh to remind him, remind them both, that he was the injured party. 'We have to keep up extensive safety surveillance, especially in the first few years. All reports of side effects are constantly monitored for trends, any signs to suggest a harmful effect that might not have been picked up in the clinical trials. We haven't seen anything with Zaplex.' With a rush of bitterness he thrust his hands into his pockets. 'Christ, Tess, I told you before, you only had to bloody ask. I'd have shown you the damn data. You didn't need to start snooping into the database.' He let out a grim laugh. 'But that would have meant trusting me, wouldn't it? And you didn't.'

Looking as drained and emotionally wrung out as he felt, Tess staggered back to the sofa. 'By the end, I did trust you,' she contradicted. 'But in the beginning? Can't you see, I thought the company was responsible for my mother's death. I wasn't prepared to trust anyone.'

'So what about the article you promised Hugh? I expect you've still got enough to write a pretty inflammatory piece.'

She sighed and shook her head. 'There won't be an article. I'd already decided that when I saw what you were trying to do.' Raising her eyes she forced him to look at her. 'I really admire everything you're doing to change things from the inside. To make Helix the ethical, responsible pharmaceutical company it should be.'

His pain was too raw, his heart too broken, to take any comfort from her words. 'It's a damn sight more ethical than the newspaper industry,' he shot back at her. 'I presume you'll be going back there? I'm sure Hugh will be pleased. The pair of you looked pretty cosy this evening.'

'He's a good friend,' she replied, looking down at her hands.

'How good, exactly?' he demanded. 'Good enough to have you scurrying from my bed straight into his?'

Tess's head shot up. 'You have every right to be angry, but not to be cruel,' she told him coldly. 'Hugh and I were lovers once, yes, but that was a long time ago.'

He felt himself tensing. 'Is he the one who called you—'

'A bag of bones?' She shook her head. 'No. Hugh's a good man. Kind.'

'I bet he is. Especially when there's something in it for him.'

Once more her eyes flashed angrily at him. 'It wasn't like that. He knew why I was leaving the paper and we agreed if I found any malpractice, I should write a report on it.' She jutted out her chin. 'I don't cheat on men. I never have. You're getting me confused with Barbara.'

Jim let rip a mirthless laugh. 'Well, you two certainly have a lot in common. You both took me for a ride.' He rested against the window ledge and let out a deep, exhausted sigh. 'Is that the reason you slept with me? To try and prise information out of me?'

'If you really think that, you don't know me very well,' she replied quietly. 'Can't you see that actually it was the other way round? I slept with you *despite* believing what I did about you. About the company. The very fact that I fell into your arms, even believing what I did, just goes to prove how crazily in love with you I am.'

Jim felt as if his head was going to explode. The emotion of everything he'd heard tonight was just too much. How could she lie to him one minute and then claim to be in love with him the next? It didn't make sense. Part of him wanted to ask her to look into his eyes and repeat what she'd just said, but he knew he couldn't put himself through any more torture. 'Nice words, sweetheart,' he told her coldly. 'But there's no point wasting them on me now. This farce has officially ended. Goodbye.' He strode out of the apartment without a backward glance.

The moment the door slammed behind him, Tess curled up on the sofa and wept. Painful, wracking sobs that just wouldn't stop coming.

It was over. Finished. She'd told Jim everything. The truth of why she'd joined Helix, of why she'd looked into the database. Even how she felt. Still, he'd walked away.

But how could she blame him? He'd admitted how hard he found it to trust, yet she'd lied to him. Worse, too scared of losing him to tell him the truth, she'd continued to lie to him.

Now she'd blown it. And it was entirely her fault.

Chapter Thirty-Four

With a sigh Tess sat back from her computer and glanced at the familiar surroundings of her *Daily News* office. It had been two weeks since her showdown with Jim, two weeks since she'd handed in her notice, with immediate effect, to a shocked but surprisingly understanding Georgina. It felt like a lifetime ago. Not that the heartache was any dimmer in her chest, or the images of Jim any fainter in her mind. No, some things remained all too vivid. The ease with which she'd slipped back into her old role had at least smoothed out some parts of her life though, even if emotionally she remained locked in the past.

Jim had been right about one thing. Hugh had been pleased to have her back. He'd even promised never to mention the pharmaceutical industry article ever again. Tess had other ideas. She was going to write it. Provide an insight into an industry that, up to now, had remained largely hidden.

She'd been working on it for the last couple of days, hoping that pouring her memories onto paper would prove in some way cathartic. It hadn't. All it had done was continue to remind her of what, or should she say who, she'd left behind.

With a deeply unhappy sigh, Tess focussed her thoughts back onto her computer screen. A few clicks of her mouse found her one of the breast cancer awareness websites.

She scanned a few pages and groaned out loud.

'That doesn't sound good. Are you okay?'

Hugh leant against the doorframe to her office, eyeing her warily. She half smiled. The poor man had slipped in to see her several times since she'd started back and each time he'd found her blubbing her eyes out.

'It's safe to come in,' she told him, beckoning him inside. 'No tears today.'

'You've switched to groaning instead?'

'Yes. At least for now.' She pointed to her screen. 'I'm reading some of the testimonials about Zaplex.'

'And you're groaning because?'

'When I was determined to believe Zaplex had killed my mother, I conveniently forgot how it was also saving lives. Listen to this. "Zaplex has given me several precious extra years with my grandchildren." That's from one seventy-five-year-old lady. Or how about this. "I've been able to live to see my daughter get married."' She hung her head in her hands. 'I was so blinkered. My obsession with the cause of Mum's death blinded me to the other side of Zaplex. The good it could do.'

'Hey, don't beat yourself up. The pharmaceutical industry has made its share of mistakes and some drugs do have dangerous side effects. It wasn't an unreasonable assumption that Zaplex was the cause of her death.' Hugh eased himself onto the chair opposite her. 'So, apart from wondering about your welfare, I also came in to find out if your article is going to be ready for Saturday's edition?'

'Yes.' She hesitated. 'You do know it isn't going to be the big exposé we first discussed, don't you?'

'More's the pity. Still, I'm wondering if it could be the start of a whole series. You know the type of thing. *Tessa Johnson's inside track on.* Today, the pharmaceutical industry. Tomorrow could be the oil industry. Perhaps the fish industry. We could have you doing a stint as an air stewardess. A police officer.' He paused, a gleam in his eye. 'What about the sex industry? A few months finding out about life as a lap dancer.'

She searched for something to throw at him. He was lucky her hands only connected with her pen and not the stapler that lay next to it. 'That'll do. I have no plans to lie my way into any more organisations, thanks very much. Once was definitely enough.'

Hugh considered her thoughtfully. 'I know you're hurting, and that you're feeling guilty about what you did, but in my book you haven't done anything wrong.' She started to argue, but he held up his hand. 'No, hear me out. While you were with Helix you did the job that was asked of you. You haven't spilt any secrets. Dished any dirt. You have nothing to be ashamed of.'

On one level she could acknowledge he was right. If she'd kept it at that, not strayed beyond the professional and into the personal, perhaps she could forgive herself. But she hadn't. 'Jim doesn't see it like that.'

'Then he's a fool who doesn't deserve you.'

His vehement reply made her smile. 'And you're a good friend for trying to make me feel better. Now, if you want this article for Saturday, you'd better make yourself scarce and let me get on with it.'

Once again Jim found himself driving to his parents' house to lick his wounds following the collapse of a relationship. Just as he'd done after discovering Barbara with her legs wrapped around Derek. Soon to be ex-Helix employee, Barbara. And not wholly his decision, though he hadn't argued when the HR director had stated that the clinical head role in the new-look R&D department was sufficiently different to the old one that it should be advertised. He also hadn't argued when they'd concluded that an outside candidate seemed a better fit for the role than Barbara.

As for Tess, as far as Helix was concerned, she didn't exist any more. The day she'd handed in her notice, her name had disappeared from the email system, her HR file marked as employment terminated and her personal possessions boxed up and posted. If only his mind was as ruthless. His bloody heart still felt like lead in his chest and everywhere he went, whether at work or at home, he was reminded of her.

He pulled into the gravel drive of his parents' cottage and took a few minutes to drag his weary, bone shaken body out of the car and up the path. Sometimes driving his E-type felt like riding in a horse and cart.

'Jim, darling.' Instantly he was enveloped in his mother's warm embrace. A few moments of blessed peace. 'Now, what happened to that girl of yours?'

Peace instantly shattered.

'I don't have a girl,' he told her tightly, pulling away to grab his overnight bag from the boot.

To her credit, his mother didn't say another word. She simply gripped hold of his hand and drew him inside.

He was greeted by a raucous, happy crowd in full party mode, all busily celebrating his father's birthday. And why shouldn't they? Seeing him back to full health again was indeed a fact worth celebrating. Pushing all thoughts of his crappy love life to the back of his mind, Jim pasted on a smile and went to join them.

It was many hours later before he found himself once again alone with his mother in the kitchen. She had that gleam in her eye. The one that said he wouldn't be going to bed until he told her everything. So he did.

She listened quietly, nodding her head from time to time. When he'd finally finished she sat next to him, put her arms around him and hugged him, just as she'd done when he was six. 'Oh, Jim, I'm so sorry. From the way you spoke about her, I really thought she was the one.'

'So did I, Mum. So did I.'

She gave his arm a gentle squeeze. 'You don't seem to be having much luck with women recently. Maybe it will be third time lucky.'

A mirthless laugh exploded out of him. 'You're joking, right? You really think I'm going to go through all this crap a *third* time?' Feeling restless, he stood and began to pace. 'I'm telling you, I'm never going through this again, ever. If that means living like a monk, then hell, I don't care. It'll be worth it.'

His mother frowned, the lines on her forehead becoming more pronounced. 'Have you considered that Tess might have been telling you the truth? That she really does love you?'

How like his mother to see the other point of view. 'If she loved me, why did she continue to lie to me? Even after she accused me over the study report she didn't tell me the truth. She carried on pretending she was looking into the studies for her job, when really she was trying to find out if I'd deliberately held back safety data. I mean, Christ.' He received a glare for the profanity, but figured it was worth it. 'How could she make love to me when she thought I was capable of that?'

'Perhaps because she really did fall in love with you,' his mother countered softly, taking his arm and pushing him, none too gently, back onto a chair. 'Think about it. Think about the woman you fell for. Do you really think she was so cold and calculating that she'd sleep with you just to glean information from you?'

He snorted. 'How the hell do I know? It's not like my track record with women is that bloody good.'

'The swearing is unnecessary,' his mother scolded. 'And so is the self-pity.'

Wincing at the dig, he sat back, ready to argue. Then he caught her dogged, unyielding gaze. 'Okay. You're right. On the second point, at least. It's time I hit the sack, before I do any more of either.'

With a gentle kiss to his forehead, she let him go.

The following morning Jim was woken with a cup of coffee and the newspaper. As room service went, it wasn't bad, though after spending most of the night staring at the ceiling, he could have done with it several hours later. Through bleary eyes he reached for the mug, casting a quick glance at the paper. The *Daily News*. No thanks.

He pushed it away but his mother put it firmly back on the bed in front of him. 'There's an article in there you might like to read,' she told him calmly before walking away.

He shuffled back against the headboard, all too aware of the sudden spike in his pulse. It told him this was Tess's article. The one she'd promised to Hugh all along. For a few moments he simply stared at the front cover, unable to look inside. It was only when he saw his hands start to shake that he berated himself for being a coward and thrust the damn thing open.

There, spread across two pages, was a report on changes in the pharmaceutical industry, written by Tessa Johnson. With a heavy heart he started to read.

He was so engrossed, reading it not once but three times, that he didn't notice his mother coming back into the room.

'Not bad, considering she only wanted you for the dirt she could find,' she remarked, a little too smugly for his liking.

'It covers a fair few mistakes,' he grumbled. 'The fact that Helix doesn't currently have policies in place to make sure we publish all our studies. That we give away too many incentives to doctors, in the form of expensive meals and travel to conferences.'

'And then she goes on to explain how the company is changing its ways. How Helix is determined to become more open and transparent in what they do. How impressed she was by the straightforward honesty of the R&D president. By his drive to clear the industry of its somewhat tarnished reputation. A reputation that deflects from all the good that it does.'

He had to concede all those points were in the article, too. In fact, if he was being really honest, he couldn't have written it better himself. Georgina was going to be beside herself. Suddenly his phone burst into life on the bedside table, vibrating away like a clockwork toy. He scanned the messages and almost laughed. Georgina was, indeed, cockahoop. And so were the board members. Whatever Tess had set out to do, he was forced to concede that in the end, Helix had been the one to gain.

'So?' His mother was still looking at him.

'So, what, exactly?'

'Don't you start being obtuse with me. You aren't too old to escape a tongue lashing.'

He raised his eyes to the ceiling. 'That's what I love about coming home. It keeps my feet well and truly on the ground.'

'It's also where you get some good, old-fashioned advice. I'm telling you, don't give up on that girl of yours just yet. Stop thinking about poor old you, and start to think about her and what she's been through. How she must still be grieving for the loss of her mother. Finding a scapegoat, a place to pin the blame, was part of that process. Yes, maybe she shouldn't have become involved with you while she was still investigating you, but people in love do foolish things. You shouldn't be too judgemental, not when you haven't been in her position.'

Carefully he folded the newspaper. 'Why are you defending her, Mum? You don't even know her. Why is she so important to you?'

'Because I know she's important to you.' She sat down on the side of the bed. 'When you spoke about her the last time you were here, your face positively lit up. Far more than it ever did when you talked about that floozy.' She patted his leg under the duvet. 'Just think about what I've said. That's all I ask.'

When she left the room Jim put his hands behind his head and stared up at the ceiling. His mother didn't have to worry – thinking about the whole sorry saga was all he seemed to do these days. A fact that thoroughly pissed him off. He was a doer, not a thinker. When he got back home, it was time for action. The details of that action he hadn't worked out yet, but the moping phase was over.

Chapter Thirty-Five

It was several days since he'd returned from his visit to his parents'. Nearly three weeks since he'd last seen Tess. That was about to change.

Or maybe not.

As he turned his car round for the second time, pointing it once again in the direction of Tess's apartment, Jim scowled. He prided himself on making a decision and sticking with it, so his current, pitiful, procrastination was seriously starting to jar. Why in God's name was he making such a big deal of this? All he had to do was drive to Tess's, drop off the latest Zaplex safety report – to prove there was still no evidence to suggest issues with the heart – and leave. Simple.

Liar. Because if it really was only about the safety report he could have posted the damn thing and been done with it. Instead he was, at the moment at least, heading towards her place. So, in fact it had nothing to do with the safety report and everything to do with his desire, or frankly his need, to see Tess again.

He turned down a side road, reflecting that he was probably about to make a total arse of himself, but he simply couldn't let things go without speaking to her again. There was unfinished business between them. He'd had time to consider and, yes, regret some of the words he'd spoken to her. He'd been angry, sure, but worse than that he'd been hurt, sliced apart, devastated by what he'd seen as her betrayal.

Thanks to his wise mother, though, he'd started to see things from Tess's point of view. He could understand why, after losing her much loved mother only hours after taking Zaplex, Tess had believed the drug was at fault. He thought he could understand, too, why she'd joined Helix. To prove her hunch, not further her career, as he'd cruelly suggested. That tenacity was part of what he loved about her.

Still loved about her, damn it. But what about her feelings? Could a woman who'd believed what she had about him, really love him? And could he bear to find out? Because if he went up there now he would undo any healing his heart might have done over the last few weeks. Admittedly it was pretty much zero, but still. Seeing Tess would rip those wounds wide open again.

He parked up round the corner from her flat and cut the engine. For once in his life he really, really didn't know what to do.

With a grunt of frustration, he thumped the steering wheel.

Tess was glued to watching another dowdy middle-aged woman have a startling TV makeover. Though the programmes irritated her, sometimes to the point where she found herself shouting at the television, she couldn't stop watching them. Every week they followed the same pattern. And every week all the ladies really needed was a new outfit and a bloody good cut haircut. It wasn't rocket science, and certainly shouldn't take up an hour of her evening just so she could be proved right. They didn't even focus on the shoes. Ever. Hugely shortsighted.

The buzz of her intercom surprised her. Rarely, if ever, did she get a midweek visitor. Cautiously she went to answer it.

'Tess, it's me. Jim.'

Thump went her heart, so ferociously it rattled her ribcage. Following in quick succession her mouth dried and her brain froze.

'Can I come up?' A pause. 'Please?'

With her brain still in meltdown, her fingers acted of their own volition. They pressed the button that opened the door before she could think to stop them.

A few seconds later and there he was, standing on her doorstep.

She tried not to stare, not to notice how utterly gorgeous he looked in his faded jeans and black polo shirt. It had only been a few weeks but already she'd forgotten, or tried to push out of her mind, the small details about him. The distinguished flecks of grey in his hair. How beautiful his eyes were. How they darkened when he was serious, so much so they were almost black. Like now.

His frown reminded her she was still standing in the doorway, blocking him from entering. Move back and let him in, or move forward and push him out?

She moved back.

'How are you?' His deep voice sent shivers of awareness through her.

What do you care? She wanted to yell back. *I told you I loved you, but you walked away.* Instead she bit her tongue, determined to appear as cool and collected as he obviously was. 'I'm fine, thanks. How are you?'

A wry smile slid across his face, temporarily lifting the bleakness. 'Very polite.'

She'd have given anything for a smidgen of his poise; his apparent indifference. Or maybe it wasn't just an act. Maybe he simply wasn't bothered any more. 'I'm trying to be polite,' she told him crossly, 'but I'm not sure how long it will last so you'd better say what you came to say. Before I start acting true to my hair colour.'

Again a small smile tugged at his lips. 'I came to give you this.' He handed her a slim report. 'It's the most recent safety review on Zaplex. I thought you might be interested. Perhaps you'll trust the facts, as you clearly have trouble trusting me.'

Probably she deserved it, but still, that hurt. She reached for the door, ready to shut it in his face, but he stuck his foot against it, stopping her.

'Sorry,' he interjected quickly, warily eyeing up the hand that had slapped his face last time they met. 'That was a low blow.'

And just like that, her anger deflated. It was impossible to keep it up when all she wanted to do was fling her arms around him and plead with him to forgive her. Beg him to love her. 'It's okay. After how I behaved, I owe you a couple of free hits. In fact, I owe you a lot more than that.'

'Anything you might have owed me was repaid by the newspaper article,' he cut in, moving his large frame into her apartment, though careful to keep his distance. 'Georgina was so ecstatic we had to peel her off the ceiling.'

'I meant every word of it,' she told him earnestly, needing him to believe her on this, if nothing else. 'I wouldn't have written it if I hadn't.'

He levelled his dark gaze on her and even from across the room, the intensity seared her soul. 'And what about us, Tess?' he asked in a voice that was so low she could hardly hear it. 'Did you mean any of that?'

'You know I did.'

'Do I?' His face was unreadable, his body still.

She nodded. 'You once asked me what sort of man I thought you were. Well, I can tell you. You're the sort of man I not only admire and respect, but I love with all my heart.' Her voice wavered uncontrollably and she was moments away from bursting into tears. 'I fell in love with you, Jim.'

Still he stood, eyes shuttered, his only movement a twitching muscle at the side of his jaw. Tess wanted to scream, to pummel his chest. Anything to get a reaction out of him.

'You have no idea how much I want to believe you,' he finally admitted. 'But I just don't think I can.'

Then, as if he could no longer keep up his act, he slumped down onto the sofa and rubbed at his eyes with the heel of his hands.

'Please?' It was a whisper, torn out of her at the sight of his despair. He was hurting just as much as she was, but the outcome was in his hands.

Slowly, as if his head felt suddenly too heavy, he shook his head. 'It turns out I'm not as brave as I thought I was. I'm scared to death of saying yes, and then finding myself kicked in the teeth all over again.'

She rushed to him, wrapping her arms around his rigid body. 'I'd never do that to you, because I love you, damn it. I. Love. You.'

He remained unmoving, his gaze focussed on the carpet and Tess began to cry. It was over. She'd failed to prove how much she loved him.

'If you loved me so much, why continue the lie?' he asked eventually, anguish etched across his handsome face and filling his deep brown eyes. 'I understand why you lied to me when you joined Helix, but not after that Friday. Not after I'd told you how I felt about you.'

'But you'd also just told me that if I ever misled you again, we would be over. How could I then admit that I hadn't only gone behind your back by searching the database, but actually I'd lied right from the start?' She swiped at her free flowing tears. 'Maybe it sounds stupid now, but at the time all I could think was that I'd lose you before I'd even had a chance to really get to know you.' She blew her nose and smiled miserably. 'But I lost you anyway.'

'Shit.' Letting out a deep, painful sigh, he hung his head. 'I can't see a way out of this. I'm sorry.'

He stood to leave but Tess grabbed at his arm. 'Wait. Would you believe me if you saw it in black and white?'

He lifted his head, his soulful dark eyes mirroring his confusion.

Not waiting for a reply, she ran over to fetch her laptop. After a few frantic seconds, she scrolled through her sent mail and found what she was looking for. Her email to

Hugh, the night before she'd gone to confront Jim with the *in vitro* study.

'Read this,' she told him softly, handing him the computer and pointing to the screen.

Cautiously he scanned the words. Tess read them over his shoulder, even though she knew exactly what she'd written.

Dear Hugh. Sorry for taking the coward's way out and doing this by email, but I wanted to let you know that I won't be giving you a story from my time with Helix, no matter what I might find out. I've fallen in love with the head of R&D. Pretty stupid, I know, but whatever he might have done, I forgive him. It's in the past and simply doesn't fit with the man I know now. Love, Tess.

Jim wiped a hand over his face and when he raised his eyes, she could see his shock. 'You were really going to forgive me, even if I had withheld that data?'

'Yes,' she replied simply. 'When you interrupted us at the awards ceremony, Hugh knew I wasn't writing a scoop for him. He was just trying to goad me into changing my mind.'

Jim swore softly, shaking his head, as if he couldn't believe any of this was happening.

'I knew there must be a logical explanation for the study not being in the submission. The man I'd come to love wouldn't have deliberately done anything unethical,' she continued, desperate for him to understand. 'Perhaps you'd missed it out by accident. Maybe someone else had put the dossier together and you'd simply overlooked the fact that the report wasn't there.'

'You had the excuses prepared for me, eh?' he asked, and this time his voice was gentle.

'Yes.'

He stood then and turned to face her, his heart in his eyes. Suddenly he was wrapping his arms around her and pulling her towards him.

'God, Tess, I love you. I love you so much.'

She noticed his hands tremble as they strayed into her hair, smoothing it down before holding her against his chest. Firmly, possessively. Like he was never going to let her go. All at once the tension drained from her body and she collapsed against him, sobbing quietly. She was home.

When he finally drew back, he planted a tender kiss on her forehead.

'I'm sorry about your mother.' He kissed her again, this time on the lips. 'And I'm sorry for the really shitty things I said the other week.'

She placed a hand against his cheek, feeling the roughness of his stubble. 'It's okay. You were hurting. I'm the one who's sorry ...'

He silenced her with a fierce kiss, full of hunger and fire. 'No more damned apologies,' he told her thickly when he finally let them up for air. 'We're putting all this behind us and moving on.'

She wanted to smile, but her lips wobbled. 'Moving on sounds good to me.'

'Yes, it does.' Then he was kissing her again. Her lips, her chin, her neck. 'And right now I want to move on to your bedroom.'

This time she managed to smile. 'I can go with that.'

As he reached underneath her and hauled her into his arms, a happy, joyous giggle escaped her.

A lot later, Jim hugged Tess, squeezing her against him. But when she turned to look at him, his face was serious.

'Are you okay?' A worry started to niggle at her. They'd just spent an incredible few hours reacquainting their bodies, but now his passion was spent, was he regretting falling back into bed with her? If so, why was he gripping her so tightly?

'I've been thinking.' He eased away slightly, moving to his side so he could look into her eyes. 'As I told you before, I'm done with casual affairs. I want to fall in love, settle down, raise a family.' With his elbow bent and his head propped up on his hand, he devoured her with his dark eyes. 'I've already done the first of those three things. Will you help me with the other two?'

'You mean—'

'Marry me, Tess.'

As joy bloomed in her heart, she took a moment to savour his words. And to draw out the moment. 'Shouldn't there be a will you, or a please in there somewhere?'

He shook his head. 'It wasn't a question.'

'Then it doesn't need an answer.'

Pushing her back against the bed, he grabbed her by the wrists. 'God knows why I fell for a woman who, I know, is going to give me nothing but trouble,' he growled.

'Because you love a challenge,' she replied sweetly.

He laughed, but then his eyes darkened and they searched out hers, this time with slightly less confidence. 'Will you marry me, please?'

Wriggling out of the grasp he had her in, Tess threw her arms around his neck. 'Since you asked so nicely, how can I say anything but yes?'

As Jim's heart filled his chest, his mind skipped to his mother and how she was going to be apoplectic with delight when he gave her the news. She was already a huge fan of Tess, and that was without even meeting her.

As Tess's eyes filled with tears of happiness, she also thought of her mum, and how she would have loved Jim. Tess was sure that somewhere out there she was looking down on them and smiling. Her death had been a tragedy. A life cut much too short. But it had also been the start of the journey towards Tess finding the love of her life.

Her mum would be delighted with that.

Thank you

Thank you so much for taking the time to read *Search for the Truth*. I love to spend my days writing of sexy heroes, and heroines smart enough to stand up to them. As enjoyable as this is though, the real pleasure comes from knowing their stories have been read.

So if you feel inclined to contact me (details are under my author profile) or leave a review to let me what you thought of this book on Amazon, Goodreads or any other book reviewing platform, it would truly be a pleasure to hear from you.

Kathryn x

About the Author

Kathryn was born in Wallingford, England but has spent most of her life living in a village near Windsor. After studying pharmacy in Brighton she began her working life as a retail pharmacist. She quickly realised that trying to decipher doctors' handwriting wasn't for her and left to join the pharmaceutical industry where she spent twenty happy years working in medical communications. In 2011, backed by her family, she left the world of pharmaceutical science to begin life as a self-employed writer, juggling the two disciplines of medical writing and romance. Some days a racing heart is a medical condition, others it's the reaction to a hunky hero …

With two teenage boys and a husband who asks every Valentine's Day whether he has to bother buying a card again this year (yes, he does) the romance in her life is all in her head. Then again, her husband's unstinting support of her career change goes to prove that love isn't always about hearts and flowers – and heroes can come in many disguises.

Kathryn's other novels are: *Too Charming*, *Do Opposites Attract?* and *Before You*.

www.twitter.com/KathrynFreeman1
www.facebook.com/kathrynfreeman
www.kathrynfreeman.co.uk

More Choc Lit

From Kathryn Freeman

Too Charming

**Does a girl ever really
learn from her mistakes?**

Detective Sergeant Megan
Taylor thinks so. She once lost
her heart to a man who was too
charming and she isn't about to
make the same mistake again –
especially not with sexy defence
lawyer, Scott Armstrong.
Aside from being far too sure
of himself for his own good,
Scott's major flaw is that he defends the very people that she
works so hard to imprison.

But when Scott wants something he goes for it. And he
wants Megan. One day she'll see him not as a lawyer, but as
a man … and that's when she'll fall for him.

Yet just as Scott seems to be making inroads, a case presents
itself that's far too close to home, throwing his life into
chaos.

As Megan helps him pick up the pieces, can he persuade her
that he isn't the careless charmer she thinks he is? Isn't a
man innocent until proven guilty?

Visit www.choc-lit.com for more
details, or simply scan barcode using
your mobile phone QR reader.

Do Opposites Attract?

Kathryn Freeman

There's no such thing as a class divide – until you're on separate sides

Brianna Worthington has beauty, privilege and a very healthy trust fund. The only hardship she's ever witnessed has been on the television. Yet when she's invited to see how her mother's charity, Medic SOS, is dealing with the aftermath of a tornado in South America, even Brianna is surprised when she accepts.

Mitch McBride, Chief Medical Officer, doesn't need the patron's daughter disrupting his work. He's from the wrong side of the tracks and has led life on the edge, but he's not about to risk losing his job for a pretty face.

Poles apart, dynamite together, but can Brianna and Mitch ever bridge the gap separating them?

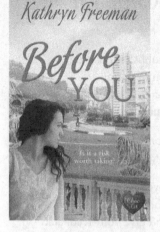

Before You

When life in the fast lane threatens to implode …

Melanie Taylor's job working for the Delta racing team means she is constantly rubbing shoulders with Formula One superstars in glamorous locations like Monte Carlo. But she has already learned that keeping a professional distance is crucial if she doesn't want to get hurt.

New Delta team driver Aiden Foster lives his life like he drives his cars – fast and hard. But, no matter how successful he is, it seems he always falls short of his championship-winning father's legacy. If he could just stay focused, he could finally make that win.

Resolve begins to slip as Melanie and Aiden find themselves drawn to each other – with nowhere to hide as racing season begins. But certain risks are worth taking and, sometimes, there are more important things than winning …

Visit www.choc-lit.com for more details, or simply scan barcode using your mobile phone QR reader.

Introducing Choc Lit

We're an independent publisher creating
a delicious selection of fiction.
Where heroes are like chocolate – irresistible!
Quality stories with a romance at the heart.

See our selection here:
www.choc-lit.com

We'd love to hear how you enjoyed *Search for the Truth*.
Please leave a review where you purchased the novel
or visit: **www.choc-lit.com** and give your feedback.

Choc Lit novels are selected by genuine readers like yourself.
We only publish stories our Choc Lit Tasting Panel want to
see in print. Our reviews and awards speak for themselves.

Could you be a Star Selector and join our Tasting Panel?
Would you like to play a role in choosing which novels we
decide to publish? Do you enjoy reading romance novels?
Then you could be perfect for our Choc Lit Tasting Panel.

Visit here for more details…
www.choc-lit.com/join-the-choc-lit-tasting-panel

Keep in touch:
Sign up for our monthly newsletter Choc Lit Spread for
all the latest news and offers: www.spread.choc-lit.com.
Follow us on Twitter: @ChocLituk and Facebook: Choc Lit.

Or simply scan barcode using your mobile phone QR reader:

Choc Lit   *Twitter*   *Facebook*
Spread